Toby Purser grew up in the Welsh border counties of Shropshire and Herefordshire. He read History at Oxford University (Mansfield College) where he was a scholar, and after a Master's degree at Oxford, completed a PhD from the University of Southampton. Toby is married to mezzo-soprano Cerys Jones. They have three young boys, to whom this novel is dedicated, and they live in the Cotswolds.

By Toby Purser

Fiction

The Devil's Inheritance

The Zaharoff Conspiracy (forthcoming)

Non-fiction

Medieval England

The First Crusade and the Crusader States

Raiders and Invaders: The British Isles 400-1100

Power and Control: Kingship in the Middle Ages

The Devil's Inheritance

Toby Purser

Copyright © Toby Purser (2013)

All rights reserved.

ISBN-13: 978-1490371542

Cover design: Diane Wheel
Cover photograph and original artwork : William John Jones

To my boys:

My very own shield-wall of Saxons

So! The Spear-Danes in days gone by
And the kings who ruled them had courage and greatness.
We have heard of those princes' heroic campaigns...

Beowulf

England and Northern France in the eleventh century

Cast of Characters in 1036

Royal House of England

Harold Harefoot, King of England, base-born son of King Canute
Queen Emma, widow of Kings Ethelred and Canute
Prince Edward, son of King Ethelred and Queen Emma
Prince Alfred, his brother

Ducal House of Normandy

William, base-born son of Duke Robert, great-nephew of Queen Emma
Mauger, his uncle
William of Arques, another uncle
Guy of Burgundy, his cousin
Herleve and Herluin, his mother and stepfather

House of Godwin

Godwin, earl of Wessex
Gytha, his Danish wife, sister-in-law to King Canute
Swegn, his eldest son
Harold, his second son
Edith, his daughter
Tostig, his third son

House of Mercia

Leofric, earl of Mercia
Aelfgar, his son and heir

House of Northumbria

Siward, earl of Northumbria, a Dane

Other European Houses

King Harthacanute of Denmark, legitimate son of Canute
King Henri of France
King Magnus of Norway
Count Baldwin of Flanders

The Church

Eadsige, archbishop of Canterbury
Stigand, a cleric from Norwich
Robert Champart, a Norman cleric from Jumièges

The Devil's Inheritance

Prologue:
Glastonbury, England, AD 1005

All the monks came to see the abbot die.

The service of Matins had been disrupted by a cry, and his subsequent collapse from a seizure had shaken the ancient community to the core.

For three weeks the abbot had lain motionless in the great chamber above the refectory. Two nights ago he had become delirious and it was plain to everyone, without the aid of the garrulous physician, that the end was near. The old man's face – and nobody knew for sure how old he was, not even the oldest monk in the abbey – was mottled and heavily veined, the silver hair damp with sweat.

One hour ago, soon after the service of Vespers, the last rites had been administered and the monks filed through the large room to pay their respects to the old man. A candle spluttered at the head of the bed, the only light in the room, casting flickering shadows over the anxious faces of the men crouched around the abbot.

At that moment, the abbot stirred in his bed and sat up slowly, waving back the crowding attendants. Since receiving the last rites, the dying man had become calmer, more receptive of his fate. The sweat had dried, leaving his face an almost healthy tinge.

'A vision,' said the abbot, quite clearly. The file of monks stopped and stared, taken aback by his sudden lucidity. 'I had a vision in the night.' The abbot sank back into the pillow, breathing heavily.

The watching monks paused for a moment, then all began to talk at once. This old man, who was perhaps so elderly that he could remember the glorious days of King Edgar, had a vision, and hovering on the verge of life and death his words would have more authority than anything on this earth. Words spoken *in extremis* were surely words from God.

'The Norsemen will come.'

He spoke again, his voice slightly tremulous. The excited chatter of the monks fell silent. 'The Norsemen will come and rule over all England.' There was a stifled cry in the darkness and a muttered prayer. The abbot went on, oblivious to the upset he was causing: 'They will come in their longboats, as in times of old, and they will kill and plunder this land. There will be a great battle and many Englishmen will perish. The kings of the ancient dynasty shall die, and their offspring shall flee across the sea into a long and uncertain exile.' Beads of sweat formed on the dying man's brow and his breath came in great gasps. 'But one son of the old blood shall come back. I saw in my dream the blessed Saint Peter consecrate a dignified man as king and then assign to him the life of a bachelor. He will reign over all England for three and twenty years.'

The abbot lay back, exhausted by his efforts to tell the dream. One of the monks, the cellarer, leant over and asked: 'Who is he, Lord Abbot, who is the king you saw?'

But the abbot did not hear the question and spoke in no more than a whisper, his eyes fixed on the ceiling. 'I saw the man ask Saint Peter, "Who then shall succeed me in the kingdom?" and the saint replied: "The kingdom of the English is the kingdom of God, and God has been pleased to make provision for its future."'

The abbot sighed deeply, as if emerging from a trance, and seemed glad that a weight had been lifted from his shoulders. His countenance was fresh, his eyes a clear blue and the lines on his face seemed to vanish as he smiled a little.

The cellarer leant over him again, insistent.

'Who is this king, Lord Abbot; tell us – who?' He shook the abbot gently, but the abbot was dead.

Part One

The Bachelor King

Chapter One
Guildford, England, January 1036

Harold stared at the fox.

It stood motionless in the snow, its long nose quivering slightly in the cold. Harold moved closer, dragging his feet in the ice and mud, and stretched out an arm. He could see that the fox was hungry, even starving, for his ribs stuck out sharply from his chest. Remembering suddenly, Harold dug into the pouch at his belt and pulled out a crust of manchet bread he'd saved for his puppy, Garth. Garth would eat plenty in the hall tonight, but the fox might never eat again. He chuckled with pleasure as he tossed the crust up into the air, watching it spin round and round in the dull glow of the afternoon sun. It landed with a quiet thud in the snow.

The fox had gone. Harold gasped. His breath formed a frozen cloud at the sight of two large deer-hide boots, two long legs and two hands reaching down to him, all enveloped in a dark cloak. Harold's face broke into a huge smile.

'Father!'

Godwin, Earl of Wessex, picked up his son and shook him with mock severity. 'How many times have you been told not to go out into the snow?'

'But father, the fox...'

'You'll catch a chill out here.' The earl led his protesting son into the snowbound courtyard and towards the hall, where a warm fire beckoned. Harold followed dutifully, clinging unhappily to his father's arm. He stopped suddenly, nearly pulling the arm out of its socket.

The fox had come back and was searching for the crust. It found it and chewed frantically, dripping saliva into the snow. It finished, and glanced up at the boy staring at it. The fox held the boy's gaze for a second, and was gone.

'Happy now, boy?'

Harold looked up at his father and nodded triumphantly. 'Piggy-back, father? Please, oh please!' He tugged again at Godwin's arm. Godwin winced, and before the boy could do it again, hoisted him up onto his shoulders and marched across the yard, whistling loudly. Without pausing, he kicked open the door to the hall and walked in.

It was a splendid hall and the earl of Wessex was justly proud of it. It was tall and gabled, of timber clamped with iron and some sixty feet long. Inside, the walls were covered with tapestries, an art the ladies were expert in, depicting scenes of battle from the great sagas, English and Norwegian alike. The floor was of variegated stone, covered each day with a fresh bedding of rushes, and benches lined the walls, each with embroidered coverings. The far end led to the earl's private rooms; his lady's bower and chambers for their growing family, and guest rooms. The earl was a central figure in the king's council and often entertained fellow earls and councillors to discuss important matters of the day. The nobleman's hall was at once home, fortress, farm, workshop, administrative centre and chapel. All men of every station dwelled within, on the floor of the hall, the threshing floor, or the prison; all lived by the grace of the same lord: Godwin, earl of Wessex.

'Harold!' A sharp cry pierced the empty hall, and a fat woman bustled towards them, squawking. Harold groaned and buried his head into Godwin's tunic. It was Agnes, the nurse. Clucking like an anxious hen, she took the boy from his father and led him protesting to a horrid broth made especially for small boys who stayed out in the cold.

Godwin winked at his son and walked to the fire in the centre of the hall where his reeve was in earnest discussion with one of the farmers of the estate. Both stood respectfully at the sight of their lord, but Godwin waved them down and took the flagon of mead from a servant.

'We were just arguing over the cure for dysentery, my lord,' said Penda, the reeve. 'Osric reckons he's found a new cure.' The reeve motioned to the farmer.

'Aye, my lord,' said Osric. 'I heard it from a farmer down at Godalming.' He took a draught of wine and went on, warming to his theme. 'You must take nine bramble chips, sing "miserere me deus" three times and say nine paternosters, and then you must boil the chips in milk with two other ingredients, which can be –' Osric leant forward and whispered, '– herbs from a white witch, or ale, wine, honey, your own sweat, spit or excrement. You then use the result as a potion and drink three doses a day.'

Godwin roared with laughter at this, and so did Penda. 'What rubbish,' he said after recovering his breath. 'I never did hear such nonsense in all my life. I'm sorry if I've offended you, Osric,' he said seeing the farmer's look of dismay. He took a swallow of mead and wiped his mouth. 'Now, if you will excuse us, Osric, I must talk matters of the estate with Penda.'

'Of course, my lord.' Osric bowed and took his leave.

'I hope I have not offended him,' said Godwin, grinning broadly.

'I don't think so, my lord,' said Penda. 'Osric always has some new cure every week.'

'Good. Now, to business.'

The conversation moved to matters of the land, which fields were ready for the winter crop, which needed to be left fallow. The winter months were normally occupied by ploughing, when the weather allowed, as it did not today. When the frosts came, the peasants worked on the lord's land, for vegetables and fruit, and set to work repairing and making cattle stalls, pens for the pigs, perches for the fowls and kilns for the baking. It was the task of the reeve to ensure that such chores were seen to, but Godwin had always made time to oversee his own estates.

'Is there any news from London, my lord?' Penda asked, when the earl had finished.

Godwin's face darkened. 'Not yet,' he said.

It was the day after Epiphany: a new year and a new beginning. The twelve days of Christmas had seen much feasting and jollity, and Godwin had managed to forget for a short while that King Canute was dead. He had forgotten for a time that effectively there was no king on the throne and that England was governed by the bastard son of Canute and controlled by his mother, Canute's mistress. Between them, Harold 'Harefoot' – as he was known because of his deformed right foot – and Aelfgifu of Northampton, Canute's whore, they ruled England. The rightful heir to the throne, Harthacanute, Canute's son by Queen Emma, was in Denmark, struggling to hold together the empire that his father had built up. For a short while Godwin had forgotten all of that, and had feasted the twelve days to the full, enjoying the sounds of laughter filling the large hall.

'No, there's no news yet,' Godwin said again, staring into the fire.

Penda nodded sympathetically, wishing he had never raised the subject. He knew, as many did, the precarious situation Godwin found himself in; the only earl to publicly support the absent Harthacanute while the rest of the council proclaimed Harold Harefoot regent while they waited for Harthacanute's return. It was, on the face of it, a compromise, but in fact Harold Harefoot was king in all but name. As a consequence, the earl of Wessex was dangerously isolated from court favour.

The door slammed. Godwin recognised Ulwin, one of his household troops. The soldier strode without preamble to the fire. His face was blue with cold, the long moustache fashionable amongst the soldiery tipped with ice. His short woollen cloak draped over a leather tunic and breeches afforded little protection against the winter weather.

Rubbing his hands over the fire, Ulwin announced: 'Ealdorman Wulfnoth has seized Alfred Ethelredsson, and it is said he intends to kill him and his men.'

Penda turned to Godwin, wondering who Alfred Ethelredsson was, but judging by the grim expression on his master's face, the earl knew.

'Saddle the horses, Penda.'

*

Gytha cursed under her breath as she pricked her finger on a needle. The blanket she was embroidering for her husband was a hunting scene, and with God's will it would be finished in time for his birthday. The bower was warm and cosy up above the hall, and for all the bother with the needlework, Gytha was content.

When she was fifteen, and a Danish heiress, an unknown thegn in the king's household had won her heart and brought her to England, where he had built all this for her; warmth, security, a family and a title: Lady of Wessex. And now there were four children. Of the boys Swegn was the eldest at thirteen, then came Harold – Harry, they called him – who was ten, and Tostig, who was seven. Edith was the sole daughter, and at four years of age was the apple of Godwin's eye, inheriting her mother's shock of blonde hair; all the boys had much of the dark brown colouring of their father. There was another one coming, too, for Gytha was with child and had been for several months. It had been an easy term so far, but she had cause to fear, two had been lost in miscarriages and little Gunnar had died at three years of age. Despite such a strong name for a small boy, his weak chest had defeated him. Gytha secretly hoped that this one would be a girl; she would call her Gunnhildr.

Gytha was Danish and Earl Godwin's fortunes had been made in a Danish court. Her father, Lord Thoril, had been a figure of power and authority in Denmark. By her brother Ulf's marriage to Canute's sister, Gytha had become a much sought-after marital prize. Godwin had taken her. Of all the well-born noblemen courting her, it had been the broad, handsome, but utterly unknown and poor son of a thegn from England who had won her hand. After Canute had been accepted king of all England, a young nobody arrived in the royal court with tales of glory and whispers of love. With his sweet words, and a little wine, he seduced her in a hayloft within earshot of the king's hall. The sharp pain of that first time remained vivid in her mind – his beard rough against her neck and his hands eager on her plump breasts. But he had not left her afterwards, some casual conquest now worthless as a virgin bride on the marriage-market, and their illicit union went on for several months. When Thoril discovered, as was inevitable as they became increasingly indiscreet, Godwin stole his thunder by asking Canute to give him Gytha.

Godwin had taken her to England, where she quickly settled amongst the fellow Danes in the court, matching her noble birth with his ruthless drive for power, and together they had risen far.

But Canute was dead. He had reigned over all England and Denmark for nearly twenty years. Under him, Godwin had become a belted earl in the king's great council and in recent years, second only to the king in matters of state.

With Canute's death in November, Gytha grieved not only for the past, but for what the future held. All they had striven for – the lands, the family, this hall – could fall prey to their enemies. Canute's indecision on his deathbed over the question of an heir had left the country leaderless and the nobles in dispute. Godwin had emerged isolated with the queen, Emma, outnumbered and out of favour. Emma had fled to her dower estates at Winchester and Godwin to Guildford, both to wait and see what the spring would bring.

The sound of shouting and scuffles dragged Gytha back to the present.

'You put a worm in my broth, didn't you, Swegn?'

Gytha sighed and set down her needle. Harold and Swegn were fighting again. She moved to the door, instinctively to take Harold's side, for Harold was her favourite. Quiet and sensitive, he had none of the loud, bullying nature of Swegn, who constantly teased the younger boy. She had seen Swegn once club a mole to death and chase after Harold with the body, nearly making the boy choke on his own vomit. Godwin had caught him, and beaten him, but Gytha shivered at the memory of the gleam of satisfaction in the older boy's eye.

'And what if I did, Harry; you deserved it,' Swegn was saying, squeezing Harold's arm and pushing him to the head of the stairwell as he spoke.

'I'm going to tell mother,' Harold choked.

'You wouldn't dare, you little...*turd*.'

Harold wriggled free from Swegn's grasp and stamped fiercely with his outdoor boots on Swegn's unprotected feet.

'I hate you!' he shouted and ran down the stairs.

Godwin saw the horses approaching before Penda did. There were three of them, the riders urging them on to a breakneck speed in the deep mud and slush that formed the road from the small town of Guildford.

'Wulfnoth,' said Penda briefly.

Godwin was about to tell Penda to call out the household guard when he saw the little figure of Harold running out of the hall, sloshing through the mud and out of the courtyard as fast as his legs would carry him. He ran without pausing down the road, into the path of the oncoming horsemen.

'No!-'

As he shouted, Godwin swung himself into the saddle and kicked the horse into a canter.

Harold was twenty yards along the road before he raised his head. He was crying so hard that he could not see for tears. He hated Swegn. Rubbing his eyes briskly, he thought he could hear hoofbeats. He blinked and looked ahead. The track was quite narrow, bordered on either side by high, snow-covered banks. The sky above was grey; the short winter day would soon draw to a close and it would be dark.

Harold stopped running, suddenly afraid. It was the sound of horses; he was sure of it.

Godwin could see them now. Harold was standing still, rooted to the ground at the sight of the horsemen rounding the bend galloping straight towards him. They must stop. Godwin willed them to stop. They did not. The gap closed. Twenty yards. Fifteen. Godwin spurred his horse again and thrashed into the mud, screaming at the boy to jump onto the bank. But the boy remained standing, mesmerised by the jangle of the harness, the frozen breath of the panting, snorting beasts and the flailing hooves...

Ten yards.

With a supreme effort Godwin leant from the saddle and swept Harold into his arms. At the last second, the riders opened ranks and Godwin passed through, sobbing aloud in his relief, scarcely able to hold the reins.

The horses stopped, sending a spray of mud onto the banks, staining the blanket of snow.

'Sweet Jesus,' whispered Godwin, 'thank God.' He hugged the boy close to his chest, whispering thanks over and over as the horse pawed the ground nervously.

The three horsemen trotted across to the man and boy. Godwin ignored them for a moment and when he looked up, his eyes blazed hatred.

'Wulfnoth!' he uttered.

The rider in a red cloak, much worn and mudsplattered, opened his mouth to speak, but thought better of it under Godwin's glare. A large nose dominated the weak chin, which was hidden by a drooping moustache.

'I should kill you for that.' Godwin's hand went to his sword.

In answer, the cold air filled with a screech as Wulfnoth ripped his own sword from its scabbard, and another, and another and it seemed that a forest of blades glinted in the 'tween light before them.

'I think that you're in no position to kill anyone, my lord of Wessex.' Wulfnoth spoke triumphantly, the weapons ranged against the earl proof of his advantage. 'You command no favour with the new king,' he added.

'He is not the king. He's nothing but a whoreson youth!' hissed Godwin.

'I could cut you open for that, Godwin...you may have been Canute's man, but he rots in the Minster at Winchester. Harold Harefoot and his mother are alive – that's the difference.'

Godwin lowered his sword, knowing he was beaten – for now. 'What is your purpose here, Wulfnoth, and who are these?' He motioned to the two other horsemen. One was scrofulous and unshaven, but the other fellow was truly hideous. Godwin held Harold tight as the horseman pulled off the hood that covered him, to reveal a face without a nose. Sometime ago, the nostrils and nasal flesh had been sliced off, signifying he had been caught and found guilty of horsethieving. The twisted scar of what was once a nose gleamed a dull purple against his white complexion. The man grinned evilly at Harold, who pressed his face into his father's shoulder.

'Alfred Ethelredsson's followers are dead,' said Wulfnoth curtly. 'He was captured whilst attempting to reach his mother and the treasury at Winchester after landing at Dover.'

'How do I know you're not lying?' Godwin demanded.

In a swift movement Wulfnoth held up a severed head from beneath the folds of his cloak.

Harold groaned and was sick into the snow.

Godwin shot Wulfnoth a look of loathing. 'Did you have to, in front of the boy?' He turned to Harold. 'All right, lad?' Only the slightest tremor in the earl's voice indicated his own fear. Harold nodded and tried to look away from the decapitated head. The hair, which had once been dark brown, was now smeared with black blood, and the eyes had rolled up into the skull. A thin line of blood trickled from the mouth down to the chin and below it, the neck had not been cut cleanly, but hacked at several times.

'Is that...Alfred?' Godwin asked.

'No,' said Wulfnoth, and tossed the head into the snow. 'One of his followers: a Norman.'

'What have you done with the English prince, then...is he harmed?'

'He's been sent to the king, who will no doubt deal with him as he pleases –'

'But he'll kill him. And you know that, damn you!' Godwin started forward, unable to contain himself.

Wulfnoth wrenched at the reins of his horse and began to move away.

'Be careful what you say and do, Earl Godwin,' he said over his shoulder. 'You who rose to good fortune under Canute. And you have a lovely son ... such a pretty boy. Take good care of him.' The man without a nose leered briefly, and they were gone, whipping their horses into the mire.

'Hellspawn bastards,' Godwin muttered, painfully aware of his inability to do anything.

They turned and rode back to the hall.

Later, in the privacy of the bedchamber, Gytha asked him what it meant for them. She was aware of Godwin prowling round the hall, listening to the conversations of the kitchen staff and the servants, or riding out with small groups of friends in conspiratorial huddles. She knew that the Christmas festivities had only hidden for short time the darkness that was the future and that something, sometime, would have to be done.

'I'll have to give my consent,' Godwin said, looking askance at her.

'Consent?' Gytha exploded. 'Consent to the murder of some thirty men and the captivity of Alfred? God knows what they'll do to him!' She was sitting on the bed, near to tears. 'I know we have had to look to our own in the past, but never this, never this...'

'Alfred is a threat, love, and he knows it. He did not come to visit his mother: he came for the throne.' Godwin moved from the fire and sat beside her. 'I'll do it for the boys...for our future,' he said gently, stroking her hair. She sighed and laid her head on his shoulder. The long tresses of her hair fell down almost to her waist and he felt a quickening between his legs as she ran a hand inside his tunic. Although he had been unfaithful more times than he had cared to remember, Godwin always came back to the Danish girl he'd fallen in love with as a humble thegn. And at two and thirty, she had not lost the alluring beauty of her youth and would yet bear him more children – as she was with child now. As he reached behind her to unfasten the thongs of her gown, he thought – not for the first time – what a lucky man he was. She kissed his neck, whispering into his ear, and pulled at his breeches, urgent to get to the physical evidence of his desire.

Then she stopped suddenly and pushed him away.

'What is it, my love?'

Godwin was confused by the sudden rejection.

Gytha sat up and looked her husband directly in the eye. 'What of Alfred...what will they do to Alfred Ethelredsson?'

Harold was crying. He heaved out uncontrollable great gasping sobs, punctuated by the occasional hiccup, so loud that he did not hear his father approach.

'Calm, now Harry. They've gone now. They cannot hurt us.'

But Harold shook his head, wiping his wet face on his sleeve.

'Put it out of your mind, lad.' Godwin stroked his favourite son's hair. 'Pray to God that He strikes them down in a bolt of lightning.' It was not the true teaching of the Lord, Godwin knew, but it was his kind of Christianity and what he believed God was for.

Harold swallowed hard and took a deep breath. 'It's not that, father...it's not even the head they showed us...they got the fox.'

As the boy broke into fresh tears, Godwin looked out of the window and thought longingly of the years of peace they had experienced under Canute.

Outside, it was snowing hard and a layer of pure white snow had already smothered the mud churned up by the day's events. A peasant dragged some dead wood across a distant field, and vanished, obscured by a gust of snowflakes.

Godwin sighed. It was going to be a harsh winter.

Chapter Two
Guildford, March 1040

It was said that the painted people had built the fort.

Many hundreds of years ago, before there was steel and iron, before Christ was known, tens of thousands of slaves had been forced to dig the vast ditches and form the great banks where their god-king would have his palace. It was whispered that pagan rites demanded a human sacrifice at the summer solstice, and that a boy and a girl were chosen to die on the stones...

A forest had grown up over the fort. The ancient oaks obscured the pattern of the banks of the old fort and the ditches had long been filled in. Some stones remained, scattered and moss-covered, but recognisable for the ceremonies that had once been. It was said that people of the old faith came back in the night, scorning the church, and performed rites on All Hallow's Eve and Midsummer.

Harold drew back the bow to his chin and sighted the stag. The animal stood stock-still, aware of danger but unable to locate it. Harold loosed the twine and watched the arrow hum across the glade. The stag leapt forward too late, the awful truth of its instincts clear, and crashed to the ground as the arrow pierced its chest.

'Good shot, Harry!'

Harold grinned at Tostig, who whooped with triumph and ran to the dead stag. The servants skilfully lashed it to a pole and began to drag it away.

'Let's go now, Harry,' said Tostig.

Harold looked at the darkening skies and nodded agreement. The light through the trees cast ugly shadows. The trees, still spindly from the ravages of winter, reared up around them in a grotesque embrace.

Harold was reminded of a dying man he had once seen in his father's household, clutching at the air in a last attempt to grasp life before the bloody flux claimed him.

'There's no need to fear the shadows,' he said as Tostig looked nervously around the clearing. 'You should fear the living, not the spirits that come in the night.' But even as he said it, the memory of Alfred flooded back.

Alfred Ethelredsson was dead. He had been taken through the snow to London, where Harold Harefoot had dispatched him to Ely to be blinded with hot irons. One week later, so terrible were his wounds, Alfred had died an agonising death at Ely cathedral. Within weeks people had flocked to his tomb, calling him martyr, and before long the first miracle was recorded in the church. His death had shocked many and was perceived as an ill omen for the ruler. Worst of all, the earl of Wessex had been implicated in the crime, and when the earl and his sons had ridden out of Southwark soon afterwards, an old crone at the gates of the town spat at them, screeching that one day the house of Godwin would pay a blood fee for the death of Alfred the Aethling...

Four years had passed since then. Godwin remained out of favour at court and they lived quietly in the earldom. Soon after Alfred's murder, Harold Harefoot had ridden to Winchester with the support of Leofric, earl of Mercia, and seized the treasury from Queen Emma, whose son, Harthacanute, never arrived to claim his throne. Emma had been hounded from the kingdom, to Bruges, where she awaited her son.

'Harry, Tostig!'

It was Swegn. Harold's face darkened at the sight of him, for the elder Godwin son had grown into an uncouth and foul-mouthed young man. It was a pity, said many, that Swegn, and not Harold the second-born, would one day inherit the vast estates stretching from Cornwall to Kent.

But Swegn was in no mood for wasting time. Something was wrong. His fine fur pelisse was ruined and his sweating horse appeared to have ridden non-stop from Guildford. He pulled the horse to a halt and paused for breath. 'It's father,' he gasped. 'He wants us back at the hall, now.'

'Why? Is something wrong?' Harold asked.

'It's the king. Harold Harefoot is dead.'

*

Godwin paced the length of the bower, ignoring Gytha's protests. The news was so sudden, so unexpected, that he had to think, and thinking meant pacing.

Now was the time. He would bring his sons to the new king and regain the position of power he had enjoyed under Canute. And the new king had to be Harthacanute. Unknown to many, Harthacanute had made peace with Magnus of Norway on the condition that if either of them died, the other would inherit his kingdom. That treaty had released Harthacanute from war and even now he was at Bruges with his mother.

Panic had seized London. Harold Harefoot's death had thrown the court into confusion. Aelfgifu of Northampton fled with some of the king's treasure. The London thegns were apprehensive of their fate, as they had been instrumental behind Harold Harefoot's election as king, and the earl of Mercia, the leader of opposition to Godwin, had fled home to Mercia, fearing reprisals for his part.

Godwin was delighted at the downfall of Aelfgifu. Who could have thought her son would die so young, and heirless? God, she was a beauty, though, and it was that beauty that had caused such division in the court during the last years of Canute's reign. Aelfgifu had enjoyed the tension and disturbance she caused with her good looks. The churchmen had urged Canute to give her up for the sake of his soul, but Canute had laughed at them. How could the church, with its practice of selling offices, possibly preach morality to him? Where bastards of the clergy were common and concubines abounded in the church, Canute had simply laughed, claiming that Scandinavian custom demanded at least one mistress. But he had gone to his grave laughing, leaving them a legacy of uncertainty and division.

'Harold Harefoot is dead,' Godwin said, when his sons arrived in the hall. 'He died two days ago. It's not known why. Some sort of seizure is the most likely explanation. Harthacanute is lying off Bruges with a fleet awaiting my message.'

The three boys showed surprise; they had not known this. Godwin could not suppress his smile of confidence. 'He will come to London and if necessary, take the throne by force, with my full and undivided support. The house of Godwin will be well rewarded for my services, I can assure you.'

*

Harthacanute came in the summer with a mighty fleet and the noblemen of England bowed down to the weight of his claim; he chose as his chief councillor Godwin, earl of Wessex, to guide him along the thorny path of kingship. He was Danish, and the years in Denmark had not endeared him to the people of England. At twenty-two years old, he was well versed in the art of war but didn't know how to handle men and win the popularity of the commoners.

One of Harthacanute's first edicts as king was to order the exhumation of Harold Harefoot from his grave in the Old Minster at Winchester and have the body thrown into a ditch. Godwin was aghast, but the young ruler was adamant and threatened to dismiss him if he did not hold his peace.

A large crowd gathered at the doors of the Minster as Harthacanute's housecarls, seasoned warriors from the Scandinavian wars, broke open the tomb.

'Sacrilege,' whispered the butchers and bakers, cobblers and fishermen grouped in Fleshmonger Street. The crowd watched in an awed silence as the group of soldiers carried the wooden coffin high above their heads. But someone must have frightened one of the horses, for it shied, knocking the coffin to the ground. It broke open on the hard cobbles and Harold Harefoot's cadaver spilled out.

The stench was appalling. The crowd fell back, gagging at the nauseous pollution. To make matters worse, it was a hot summer's day. The housecarls stared in shocked silence.

The crowd gradually dispersed, muttering prayers and throwing dark looks at the mounted men.

The soldiers dismounted and began to scoop the disgusting mess into the broken coffin. The sights of war were horrible enough but this was worse, far worse...

'Curse you!'

An old woman stepped from the departing crowd. She was bent low with extreme age, her face scored with wrinkles. 'This an ill omen for the new king! Harthacanute is cursed! Cursed for defiling the house of God and committing sacrilege!' She pointed a claw-like hand at the corpse: 'I curse King Harthacanute and proclaim that he shall not reign above two years.'

'Be gone, you old hag!'

Eadwulf One-Eye, leader of the troops, drew his sword and waved it at the woman. For five years he had been fighting for the king in Norway with the Jomsvikings, and while the sight of Harold Harefoot's corpse had shaken him more than he would admit, he could deal with garrulous old women. 'Get out of here, old witch! You'll frighten my men!'

But the old woman ignored Eadwulf and rambled on in a low monotone.

'We're cursed! The old bitch has cursed us!' A housecarl drew his sword and rammed it into the woman's stomach.

'Christ Jesus, what are you doing?' Eadwulf looked angrily at the shaking soldier and hit him in the face with the back of his mailed hand. The situation was fast growing out of control. Eadwulf raised his own sword and held it over the writhing, gasping woman. She was gibbering incoherently when he placed the point on her neck and pushed hard, holding the blade to the ground. The curses stopped abruptly; the woman wriggled like a worm caught on a needle, coughed blood and was still.

Eadwulf chuckled, glad to have eased the tension of the last few moments. 'She was a witch anyhow,' he said, withdrawing his sword and giving the body a kick.

*

The hanging of Ealdorman Wulfnoth was, by contrast, a popular event.

After Harold Harefoot's death, he had vanished, knowing that his part in the killing of Alfred Ethelredsson would make his life worthless. One day he was seen by a merchant at Winchester Fair, ragged and starving. They chased him for a day – but he was ill-fed and unfit. Without hesitation the king charged him with murder and sentenced him to hang at Guildford, where he had perpetrated the crimes.

Godwin took Swegn and Harold to the hanging. The gallows stood in the centre of the square of the town. A public hanging usually drew large crowds and today was no exception: the people of Guildford wanted revenge.

The law of the land decreed that if a murder was committed in the community and the murderer was not caught, then the community would have to pay a fine, which was usually substantial. King Harthacanute had charged the townspeople with the fine if Wulfnoth was not caught; he was, and the people were glad.

There was another reason why the people were pleased. The murders of thirty Normans in the area had badly affected trade. People stayed away, superstitious and afraid. Rumours spread that the Normans stalked the land seeking revenge, led by a tall man with flaxen hair and blue eyes: Alfred.

Now that Wulfnoth was caught, the town of Guildford hoped to return to a normal existence. The one regret was that hanging was too good for the likes of Wulfnoth. Many in the crowd were gratified to see the bruised and beaten state of him as he was led to the gallows. Godwin pushed to the front with his sons and explained that it would all be over in an instant if the victim did not struggle.

Wulfnoth struggled.

Four men held him down as his hands were lashed behind his back and he was hauled, kicking and wriggling and roaring, to the horse. The beast held still while he was pushed onto the saddle and the crowd fell silent as a priest mumbled a few words.

Wulfnoth surveyed the audience, his shouting ceasing. To Harold's eyes, he was unrecognisable; the gaunt cheeks, partially hidden by the straggling moustache, sat beneath long, wild hair. His eyes blazed red in the white face and bulged hatred when he saw Godwin.

The whip hit the flank of the horse and it jerked Wulfnoth into the air. Lashing out a foot, he caught the edge of the stirrup and hung suspended for a second, then dropped like a stone, jerking horribly. The crowd groaned as one as he struggled, some shouting obscenities, others praying, more than a few laughing and mocking him. After several long minutes of twitching and writhing, Wulfnoth's struggle finally ended, his feet gradually quivering to a stop, eyes bulging in a purple face, his protruding tongue like a puppet Harold had once seen at a

Christmas mummers play.

The hot reek of the excrement and urine Wulfnoth had passed in his death agonies wafted over the crowd. Harold turned away. His stomach had turned to water at the sight of Wulfnoth's naked terror. It was a punishment he would never willingly wish on any man. Even Swegn was silenced.

But Godwin did not move when Harold pulled at his arm. He was staring open-mouthed at the suspended corpse before him. It was as if he had seen his own nemesis.

*

In September King Harthacanute prosecuted the earl of Wessex for the murder of his half-brother, Alfred.

Gytha was hysterical. The hopes of returning to favour at court were dashed. Other nobles were somewhat bemused by this, for Harthacanute could not afford to lose the support of the most powerful man in the land - the very man who had put him on the throne and kept him there. Godwin was summoned to appear before the court on the first Wednesday of the month or suffer the extreme displeasure of the king.

Godwin remained calm. 'It seems that Alfred will haunt me for the rest of my days,' he said to Gytha.

'What are we going to do?' Gytha was more practical.

'Buy him off,' Godwin said bluntly.

'You mean...pay him?'

'Well, not exactly. The king had to raise great sums of money to pay for his invasion fleet – which he didn't need, thanks to me. He couldn't afford to pay for it and had paid off most of the crews. England cannot be without a fleet to guard her shores, so I shall present the king with a new, fully fitted-out warship with men and money. I will also publicly deny any involvement with the deaths of

Alfred and his followers and swear an oath to that effect. Pray God the king accepts that, and drops the charges.' His face darkened. 'Whatever happens, I shall be more wary of him in future; there is more of his mother in him than his father.'

Mercifully, Godwin was spared the ordeal of a public audience. He walked through the king's crowded hall, aware of the eyes following his back. Some were enemies, eager to benefit from the downfall of one so mighty, others were friends, remembering his past patronage and generosity. His mind wandered back to the acrimonious council held at Oxford after the death of Canute and how he had been so isolated. Leofric and Canute's bitch-whore Aelfgifu had defeated him then. It was different now. He had many friends, including Queen Emma; she would restrain her son.

The king was in the company of his mother when Godwin announced himself. Godwin bowed. 'My lord king,' he murmured, kissing the hand heavy with rings. 'Queen Emma.' He bent over the woman's hand and met her glance.

She was a remarkable woman. Born a daughter of Duke Richard I of Normandy, she had left her native land to be wife to the hapless King Ethelred II of England nigh on forty years ago. A bond had developed between England and Normandy, and it was hoped that a king with Norman blood in his veins would succeed Ethelred.

It was not to be. Ethelred, nicknamed 'the Unwise', was defeated time and time again by the invading Danes and ended his life in ignominious exile. But instead of retiring to a quiet nunnery, Emma astounded all sensibilities by returning to England and marrying Ethelred's victor, Canute. Furthermore, she had left her sons by Ethelred to lonely exile in Normandy and devoted the next twenty years to ensuring that her sons by Canute would succeed him. She had been thwarted in this when Harold Harefoot seized the throne, but his premature death turned the wheel of fortune full cycle. People said it was God's will; she believed it was justice.

'I accept your proposals,' said Harthacanute to Godwin.

Godwin broke away from Emma's gaze and smiled with relief at the king. Harthacanute rose from the heavy chair and gave Godwin a formal embrace. His tawny hair and long moustache reminded Godwin of the young Canute – even the slight trace of a lisp in his speech was Canute's.

'I would like you to meet someone,' he said, looking carefully at Godwin. At the click of his fingers a tall man stepped from the shadows. He bore the stoop of a man who feels self-conscious about being so tall. Godwin shook the proffered hand and studied the face, searching for signs of recognition, but saw none. The face was lined with worry and seemed to express perpetual weariness. Flaxen hair revealed a man younger than he looked, and the piercing blue eyes indicated that a shrewd and calculating man lay hidden behind the monkish garb and geriatric stoop.

'Earl Godwin, meet my brother.'

Godwin frowned. To his knowledge, Harthacanute had no living brother.

'Prince Edward, son of King Ethelred,' Harthacanute finished before Godwin could ask.

Godwin flinched as if struck hard. So this was Alfred's brother – and Harthacanute's half-brother. This was the last prince of the old blood. Stepping back a little to hide his shock, he glanced at Emma. The look on her face spoke volumes; there was little love lost between her and her English son. She had, after all, abandoned him to years of exile.

'Prince Edward will not be staying long,' Harthacanute was saying. 'He'll return to Normandy to prepare a household for when he comes to stay permanently.'

Godwin met Edward's gaze and found himself looking into a soul as icy as mid-winter. Neither spoke, but then there was no need. Each knew the measure of the other.

Later, Godwin was accosted on the way across the hall by a light touch on his arm. It was Queen Emma. He was anxious to get away, but his respect for the lady stalled him. They found a window seat away from the chatter of the courtiers and talked.

'Harthacanute intends to make Svein Estrithson his heir in Denmark,' Emma said. Svein was a good choice, and through his mother, Estrith, was Canute's nephew. 'He intends Prince Edward as his heir-designate to England,' Emma added. Godwin stirred with interest. Svein was a logical choice for Denmark, but Edward in England made less sense. Many of the nobles were of Anglo-Danish stock, and might look to Magnus of Norway to fill the place on the terms of the agreement between Magnus and Harthacanute a year ago, that if one should die childless, the other would inherit his kingdom. But did that treaty apply to England? It had been made before Harthacanute was king of England and therefore might refer only to Denmark. Godwin passed a hand across his forehead. It was a situation that could leave a legacy of division, as Canute's death had done.

'Who will you support?'

Godwin realised that Emma was reading his thoughts. He pulled at his moustache thoughtfully, not really wanting to commit himself either way just yet. In the yard below, a cartload of grain had become stuck in the mud and the ostlers were swearing at the stubborn mule to move.

'I don't truly know,' he said. His vote would be crucial, he knew, and many men would follow his lead. From his perspective, Edward would be a good choice. He'd be friendless in a court almost entirely populated by men established in the reign of Canute; he would need support and Godwin could supply it. The rewards would be great.

Godwin stood up. The ostlers had at last got the mule to move and he felt it was time he went too. 'I don't think we should dwell too much on the subject, my lady. The king is young and healthy and with God's grace he will produce many sons.' He bowed and kissed the queen's hand.

There was, at present, nothing else to be said.

Chapter Three
Lambeth, July 1042

The entire Godwin family was to attend the wedding. In her private chamber in the Godwin house at Southwark, the earl's daughter chose her clothes with the utmost care. Edith was most excited at the prospect of such a high society wedding and the fact that she was to be presented to the king. She would wear the very best. She would have the red under-tunic with the silk-embroidered sleeves, a present from Godwin on her last birthday, covered by the short-sleeved gown and a close-fitting headdress flowing into ornamental lappets at the back with a decorative headband.

At thirteen, Edith Godwinsson was old enough to enjoy the pleasures of the finest and most beautiful clothes Godwin could afford, but young enough to be at school. The wedding was a welcome break from her studies at Wilton Abbey, where she and other nobly born girls were taught the art of womanhood, chiefly how to be good wives and remain faithful to their husbands, who could do as they wished with other women. 'A woman's place is at her embroidery,' was the maxim of the stern Abbess Hild, who believed firmly that a good wife should be *'...cheerful, capable of keeping a secret, generous with horses and treasures.'* Edith pulled a face as she remembered these rules and for a moment felt a stab of rebellion. As the daughter of Earl Godwin, she wanted to be more than a husband's bed-mate; she wanted to advise him and counsel him on the running of the estates and any say he might have on the great council. It did not occur to Edith that she would marry anyone less than an earl, and she would not; she was the daughter of the greatest man in the kingdom – bar the king, of course. She looked in the mirror and sighed. Her hopes for being a woman of power would surely never be realised. She would have to resign herself to playing the dutiful wife and hostess for the rest of her life.

There was a soft tap on the door and Harold walked in.

'Harry!' she cried, throwing her arms around him. 'My favourite brother!' She stood back and surveyed the seventeen-year-old man before her. 'How are you? I did not think that you were coming – father said that...' The words came in a rush, spilling over one another. Edith blushed, feeling suddenly shy and foolish in his presence. Harold was as tall as a man, with long hair that was the fashion, and the beginnings of a moustache. With a slight shock, she realised he *was* a man now, capable of doing a man's deeds.

'I am well, thank you.' Harold smiled at her embarrassment. The girl's resemblance to her Danish mother was quite startling, and as Godwin's only daughter, she was spoilt outrageously. There were four sons now: Leofwine, another boy, had followed Tostig. Godwin was immensely proud of his growing brood and rarely ceased to boast of them in the company of courtiers.

'Will Swegn be there?'

'Yes, we all will.' Harold's smile slipped at the mention of Swegn. If there was one fault Godwin could find with his brood, it was with the behaviour of his first-born. Swegn had taken to hiring a band of brutal mercenaries and unleashing them in Denmark and Norway. Harold saw him as rarely as possible, but inevitably heard of his exploits in the king's service. He had spent the winter overseas with Harthacanute, terrorising people wherever he went. Rumours filtered back to England of the numerous killings he committed in the king's name. There was even a tale in circulation at court that they had broken into a convent and violated the nuns within, but Harold refused to believe that Swegn would go to those lengths. Godwin's greatest worry was what Swegn would do when he became earl of Wessex, and thus one of the most powerful men in the realm.

Harthacanute's rule had not been as beneficial as Godwin had hoped. Indeed, Harthacanute had not proved popular with many of the nobles. He used the kingdom of England as a source of money to fund his campaigns against Magnus of Norway. Denmark was the first kingdom, his patrimony; England was second, and sometimes a long way second. In addition to putting England second, Harthacanute had dismayed the nobility and outraged the populace by burning and looting the town of Worcester last year. Harthacanute had especially befriended Swegn, relishing the day when he would be able to reap the benefits when Godwin was dead. The king was regarded by many as untrustworthy and dishonourable, and had earned himself the reputation of being a pledge-breaker.

'Shall we go?' Edith was ready.

'Yes,' said Harold, looking her up and down. 'You look as ravishing as the bride.' The day would come, he thought, when Edith would make her own husband a happy fellow.

The little church of St Peter's was already packed with eager courtiers when they arrived. Godwin, ever quick to take advantage of such an assembly, mingled with the nobles and ealdormen, listening attentively with those eager to ingratiate themselves with the earl of Wessex, sharing a joke with old friends and showing due respect to the several bishops and abbots gathered to witness the day's events.

The Danish groom, Tofig, was making a good match today. Gytha, his bride, was the daughter of a powerful and influential member of Harthacanute's court, hence the glittering array of richly dressed nobles in the church. Tofig looked rightly proud as he stood at the altar awaiting his bride. A few yards away, the earl of Wessex watched him, remembering a similar wedding to another Gytha – his Gytha. Godwin's match with the sister-in-law of Canute had given him access to the court of the Danish king; he was a firm believer that if a man was not born to power and influence, he might yet marry it.

The blast of a horn silenced the congregation. They turned as one to watch Osgot escort his daughter to the altar. There was an audible gasp at the richly adorned wedding dress Osgot had bought for his daughter. He had spared no expense. The gown was stunningly embroidered in silk, pulled in at the waist by a red leather belt adorned with jewels; around her neck lay a pearl necklace. A coloured veil hung in luxuriant folds to her feet, held in place by embroidered headbands. She wore a gold bracelet on her left wrist and her tiny feet were just visible in red leather shoes.

As Gytha stood at the altar, Edith marvelled at how calm she was. She was only fifteen. Edith hoped that one day her wedding would be as fine as this; her father, she knew, would also spare no expense. The service was performed by no less a man than the archbishop of Canterbury, Eadsige, and when Tofig placed the ring on Gytha's finger and lifted the long veil to kiss her, the whole assembly in the church let out a great cheer, followed by several horns blasting a fanfare. The archbishop reddened at this unseemly noise drowning out the nervous choir beyond the altar, but shrugged as Tofig led his new wife out of the church into the waiting crowds who showered them with oak leaves to ward off evil spirits and bring joy to the marriage.

It was at the wedding feast afterwards that Harold saw the woman he would love for the rest of his life.

The feast was outside, as the weather was so fine. Osgot had ordered that trestle tables and benches be laid outside under the blue sky. Again, he had spared no expense; fresh chicken, beef, duck and swan were in abundance and from the great fire in the hall, sizzling chunks of roast ox were brought out. Barrels of mead and beer quickly emptied and the wine flowed freely. In the midst of it was the king, accompanied closely by Swegn, both enjoying themselves hugely. In the background two jugglers skilfully tossed long daggers into the air to the accompaniment of a sweet melody from the pipers.

'Who is she?' Harold had found his father in the crush, engaged in earnest conversation with an ealdorman from Wiltshire. The earl looked up, irritated by the interruption, but smiled as he saw it was Harold. Waving an apology to the ealdorman, he walked with his son through the crowd. 'Who is she?' Harold repeated, pointing to the woman at the far end of the table.

'Ah,' said Godwin with a knowing grin. 'That's Eadgyth Swan-neck. She is called such on account of her long, slender, and very pretty neck.' Harold looked again at the woman. She was indeed attractive, with golden-brown hair plaited in the fashion of noblewomen. 'She is nobly born,' said Godwin, 'but married.'

Harold screwed up his face in dismay. 'Married?'

'I'll introduce you, if you like,' said Godwin, and before Harold could protest, pulled him along the table.

'Mistress Eadgyth,' he said to the woman, 'may I present to you my son, Harold.' He bowed and signalled to Harold.

Harold kissed the proffered hand and blurted: 'Call me Harry, my lady; all my friends do.' He raised his eyes to hers and had to suppress a gasp of desire. Hazel-brown eyes stared back at him under the long lashes. Was it a haughty petulance or a hidden pain that was expressed in her beautiful face? Harold decided it must be haughty petulance and felt instantly as foolish and clumsy as a peasant. Her wide mouth flashed at him, revealing small, white teeth, and she vanished into the crowd. A glimpse of a delicate nose, a silver crucifix, a musky scent, was all Harold had and she was gone.

'Pity she's married.'

Harold spun round and faced Swegn. 'Yes, a pity,' he said slowly.

'Not that it could make any difference, of course,' said Swegn, with a wicked gleam in his eye. Harold regarded him with distaste. Swegn was drunk and made no pretence of sobriety. He hadn't bothered to shave for the wedding and an untidy growth covered his jaw. He wore rough riding clothes and stank like a pig. 'Don't look at me in that way, Harry.' Swegn swayed a little as he spoke. 'You're only my little brother and don't you forget it.'

No, I won't, thought Harold, and turned away, thinking better of what he was going to say. Swegn was a true Viking, a rakehell who did not care a damn about his father's good name at court. He would drink himself senseless with his outlaw companions, then satisfy his lust on a hapless whore.

Harold walked away, thinking about the woman he'd just met. She captivated him unlike any other woman had in his brief fumblings with the fairer sex. His knowledge of women ran to the kitchen maids and whores in the taverns, who were crude and wanton. He was quite bowled over by this woman's elegance and bearing, although she could not be much older than himself. A fresh wave of embarrassment came over him as he remembered the feeling of awkwardness and stupidity that had left him tongue-tied and dumb in her company. He was wearing his finest clothes too, and the gold dagger his father had given him, a gift from Byzantium, the gateway to the mysteries of the East. But she must think him coarse and idiotic; and in any case, she would have forgotten him by now. He could still see her, standing next to a short man with a clipped moustache and short hair. Harold swallowed. That man might be her husband. But he was old. She might have children by him. His imagination took him to a hall where two children played beside a bright fire, and later, her slender neck kissed by an ageing, balding man, his hand slipping inside that tight-fitting gown...

He turned abruptly, and all but walked into somebody. He muttered an apology, but stopped when he recognised who it was, forgetting the ache in his groin. The blue, piercing eyes, and straggly beard in the foreign fashion were instantly familiar.

'Lord Edward,' he murmured, bowing respectfully.

Prince Edward. Alfred's brother. They had not seen much of him at the court, but Harthacanute had openly declared him his heir in the event of his dying childless. The English exile who had returned after twenty-seven years in Normandy – Harold felt a surge of pity for this man, taken as a boy from his homeland and bred as a Norman. The English court was dominated by Danish nobles and men placed in power by the very man who had defeated Edward's father and brother.

Edward must have seen the pity in Harold's look, and maybe took it for contempt, for he turned away quickly. Harold watched the stiff back thoughtfully; Edward had returned to a land where his brother had met a horrific death that had been, if not condoned, then certainly acquiesced to by men in this court. Those same men could not afford to make an enemy of him now that he was the king's heir-designate.

Edward was followed closely by two men, clerics, to judge by their clothing. Both were clean-shaven, and wore their hair short in the continental fashion. Harold knew one to be Robert Champart, at one time the abbot of Jumièges, a secretive and tight-lipped little man. He nodded to them and watched them enter the hall.

The long summer day was drawing to a close. In the fading light the assembly was drifting inside, where the men would sit by the fire, drink more wine, and slump under the table. The more mischievous would remain sober and see that the bride was properly bedded, bearing witness to the consummation of the marriage.

The womenfolk played no part in this. Gytha had gone, with Edith and Tostig, back to the house in Southwark. Harold wondered whether Eadgyth Swan-neck had gone also, back to her children with her elderly husband. He shrugged off the thought and walked into the hall.

The benches and tables had been carried in, and the drunken nobles were fighting over the best seats by the fire. Harold made out the back of the king, leaning to hear a ribald tale from Swegn, probably an unsavoury tale of his exploits. Harold heard the king give a shout of laughter, and he made a conscious effort to avoid them.

Godwin had found him a seat. He was flushed with wine and enjoying himself hugely. 'Listen to the minstrel,' he said, pointing to a small man with a harp. With rare impatience, Godwin stood and shouted above the din: 'Quiet, you scum! Let us hear the minstrel!'

The minstrel bowed at Godwin's request. The crowd hushed and the minstrel began to sing from the 'Husband's Message', a popular song often sung at weddings:

The carver of this token entreats a lady
clad in clear stones to call to mind
and hold in her wit words pledged
often between the two in earlier days:
then he would hand to you through hall and yard
lord of his lands, and that you might live together,
forge your love.

He does not conceive, he said to me,
that a greater happiness could be his in this world,
than that all-wielding God should grant you both
days when together you may give out rings
among followers and fellows, free handed deal

*the nailed armbands of which he has enough
of inlaid gold.*

When he had finished, the crowd cheered and stamped their feet, looking at Tofig and his bride, who blushed furiously.

'A riddle!'

The king was on his feet, shouting above the hum of the crowd. He too was flushed purple from the wine and banged his goblet loudly on the table. 'Give us a riddle, minstrel. Make it bawdy and I'll give you a penny!' The men cheered with delight at this, but Archbishop Eadsige was preparing to leave, faintly embarrassed at the proceedings and aware that now the sober Christian rituals were over, and the civilising influence of women removed, the evening would deteriorate into a bawdy, pagan revel; one did not have to scratch far below the English sophistication of the court to discover the Viking beliefs and the old faith that characterised many in the Danish court.

The minstrel bowed at the king's wish, and began:

*I am the world's wonder, for I make women happy.
I am set well up, stand in a bed,
have a roughish root. Rarely – though it happens –
a churl's daughter more daring than the rest
– and lovelier! – lays hold of me,
rushes my red top, wrenches at my head,
and lays me in the larder. She learns soon enough,
the curly-haired creature who clamps me so,
of my meeting with her; moist is her eye!*

The minstrel sang this to the accompaniment of much roaring and cheering and when he sought the answer, he was greeted with a series of ribald replies.

It was, thought Harold, a good thing the archbishop had retired when he did.

'An onion!' The king's voice cut through the commotion. 'It's a onion!' he shouted again, raising his goblet to his mouth and taking a huge draught.

'You are quite correct, my lord king, I...'

The minstrel's congratulations trailed off as he stared at Harthacanute.

The king had collapsed to the ground and was writhing in the rushes. The crowd fell into a stunned silence. Godwin leant over the prostrate king but recoiled in horror as Harthacanute turned a puce colour and tiny bubbles of froth emerged from his nostrils and mouth.

'He's having some kind of seizure,' said Godwin in a panic-stricken tone. 'Call the archbishop, quickly!' At the desperate urgency in his voice, several men ran to the door in search of the churchman.

The king's gasping grew louder and louder, filling the hall with the choking, retching noise. His staring eyes swivelled to Godwin. With a trembling hand, he grasped the earl's tunic and tried to speak, but no words came out. With a sudden movement, his back arched and his breath expelled in one, long rattle. The eyes flickered once, and were still.

'Sweet blood of Christ,' said Godwin. 'He's dead.'

Archbishop Eadsige marched in and paused when he saw the king's body. He made the sign of the cross and closed the glazed eyes. He then knelt, and began the prayers for the dead. The awed courtiers stood back, shocked sober. Harold stood frozen, thinking how he would remember for years the white faces, the gaping mouths, the kneeling man intoning prayers by the corpse; and the tear-stained face of the young bride whose celebrations had been so cruelly ended. He uttered a quiet prayer and heard others do likewise.

'Mother of God!'

Eadwulf One-Eye pushed through the silent crowd. He stared at the body for a moment and looked up, his single eye bloodshot and blazing fear.

'Don't you see?' he demanded. 'The curse!'

Harold shook his head, doubtful, like the others, that Eadwulf was sober.

'I was sent by Harthacanute to dig up the body of King Harold,' Eadwulf explained. 'When we carried it from the Old Minster, it fell out of the coffin and into the street.' He paused, recalling the horror of that moment. 'A witch stepped forward and cursed us. She said that Harthacanute would reign for less than two years.' The crowd, listening intently now, shrank back with terror. Eadwulf went on: 'Don't you see? The king died unshriven, less than two years on the throne. He shall burn in hell and he is burning now!' Eadwulf was a big man, and had killed many men, but he felt the cold hand of fear on his heart now as he never had before.

The archbishop stood up. 'It is true,' he said, 'the king did not confess his sins before he died. We must all pray for him.'

A harsh voice with a foreign accent cut through the babble. It was Robert Champart. 'King Harthacanute designated his brother the Prince Edward as his heir in the event of his childless death,' he said. 'He has died and he was childless. Therefore I propose Prince Edward as the successor to the crown.'

Champart stepped back and the crowd looked at the tall, gaunt man as if seeing him for the first time.

Harold glanced at his father. It was for Godwin to take the lead and make a decision that could either unite or irrevocably divide the realm.

Godwin was aware that all eyes were on him. If he chose Edward, he would be following the dead king's wish, but that might invite invasion from rivals such as Magnus of Norway. But Edward was almost entirely without friends and would need help, and who better to aid him than the earl of Wessex and his sons?

He cleared his throat and pointed to Edward. 'The king is dead. Long live the king.'

There was a hush and every man knelt.

All eyes went to Edward, who bowed his head in silent dignity.

Chapter Four
Conteville, Normandy, July 1042

'William! William! Run, boy, do you hear me? Run like you've never run before! Run like the very hounds of hell were at your heels!'

William turned. He was standing in a field. In the distance his father was mounted on a grey palfrey, the same horse that had taken him to the Holy Land, shouting. 'Run!' his father called again. 'Don't look behind you!'

William ran. He lowered his head and ran through the long grass.

'William?' a soft voice called his name. He stopped running. It was his mother, Herleve. She was dressed in silk, and she was beautiful. She waved at him, disappeared, and was replaced by a gaunt figure in a black habit. William found himself walking towards the figure.

'No! William, you must run, now!' his father was calling.

The figure pulled off the cowl. It was his uncle, Mauger.

'Bastard! You bastard!'

Mauger opened his mouth and began to laugh and laugh, repeating one word: *bastard, bastard, bastard* –

And then William woke up.

The dull ache in his bladder told him that he'd had too much wine with dinner. There was a privy downstairs. Osbern could sleep on, but Turold would have to be woken. He would not mind.

The room was not quite pitch dark, as the grey light of dawn was beginning to creep through the crack in the shutters. The sleeping form of Osbern was just discernible for William to step gingerly past. The door creaked a little as it opened, but Turold, lying on a straw pallet in the hallway outside, did not move. William stepped past but paused – something was wrong. Turold's arm was twisted behind his neck. William bent over and a tide of fear enveloped him as he felt Turold's neck.

William's hand was sticky with blood. Turold's blood, from Turold's still-warm neck. Turold was dead.

A flint flared and a candle spluttered, and out of the dim light two strange faces emerged. William stared for a second and jumped over Turold, back into the room.

'Osbern!'

Osbern was up in a second, sword in hand. Somebody grunted and cursed in the dark. Grey shapes moved near the door. A hiss of indrawn breath escaped as one of the shapes launched itself in Osbern's direction. William found the wall and crouched beside it, cracking his knee on the stone.

The ring of steel upon steel filled the loft as Osbern's blade found the enemy weapon. Osbern grunted a familiar oath, and a figure crashed to the window, knocking the shutters open.

Light flooded in. William blinked. The dawn sunlight was dazzling in the confines of the room. Osbern was standing with his back to the window, panting with exertion, his sword red with blood. Another man faced him, staring at William. The would-be assassin by the window was lying in the corner, bleeding profusely.

Osbern stamped his foot; the noise was muffled in the straw. His opponent did not move. Then, as if by an agreed signal, both raised their weapons and swung at each other. Osbern halted in mid-swing and in one movement ducked the oncoming blade and thrust upwards, his entire body extended behind the outstretched arm. The point made a sickening crunch as it drove through bone, muscle and heart, before protruding from the man's back. Osbern shouted with triumph and began to pull the long blade from the slumped body.

'Osbern – to me!'

Osbern turned. The wounded man by the window had managed to get to his feet and began to limp towards William.

Osbern grunted and wrenched at his sword. It did not budge. He pulled again; it was jammed in the ribcage of the corpse.

William whimpered. The man had drawn a long dagger from his belt and raised it, ready to strike.

In that instant, William recognised him. Though the man was white with loss of blood and damp with sweat, William knew him to be one of Mauger's household.

Mauger.

'Die, you bastard!'

Bastard.

Osbern shouted a curse, released his grip from the useless sword and jumped in front of William.

The long blade took him in the neck.

Blood spurted in a red fountain and Osbern collapsed on top of his attacker. Then the door slammed open and Walter stood there, mouth working in disbelief, sword in hand, saying: 'Sweet Jesus.'

Bending swiftly, he cut the throat of Mauger's man, but he was already dead. Gently, he lifted Osbern and laid him down on the ground. Blood was running into the straw, turning the musty yellow stalks to a sodden mess.

'Oh God...if only I had woken earlier,' Walter sobbed into Osbern's shoulder, trying desperately to staunch the flow of blood. He turned to William. 'Are you harmed, boy?'

William shook his head, stunned.

'There is nothing we can do for him,' said Walter, cradling Osbern in his lap. Osbern's eyes flickered open and he looked at William. His face was whiter than snow. His voice was hoarse.

'William, take this ring.' Osbern handed the great steward's ring with the ducal seal to William. 'Give it to whom you see fit to be steward.'

William fell to his knees and took the ring.

'Avenge me, William. Kill them all.' Osbern was fading fast.

'I will,' said William, tears running down his cheeks. 'I swear it.' Osbern's eyes closed and as he died a faint smile appeared at the corner of his mouth.

'Come on, lad. It's over now.' Walter lifted William to his feet.

'Osbern and Turold died so that I might live,' said William when they reached the door. 'They died for me. I shall become duke and my vengeance shall be terrible.'

They buried Turold and Osbern as best they could in the early morning sun that dreadful day.

The dead men had not received the last rites, nor were they buried on consecrated ground, but Walter and the boy prayed fervently that such valiant and loyal men would be received into God's bosom; if not, they would find a resting place in Valhalla, the hall of warriors, for both had died with their swords in their hands.

William and Walter reached the fortress of Conteville in mid-afternoon, tired and hungry. Herleve held her son close and wept when they told her of Turold and Osbern; good men, simple and true, murdered in the sink of treachery that Normandy had become. They told her of the villages burned, the churches despoiled, the men slaughtered like cattle and the women debauched, and how terror and rapine stalked the land in the absence of the duke. 'If only Duke Robert had not left,' she whispered, 'if only he had not left us.'

William heard, and understood.

*

William was a bastard.

The base-born son of Duke Robert II, conceived in a night of passion with a mistress the duke had never wed, was, at thirteen years of age the only surviving son of the dead duke. Six years ago the duke had assembled the leading barons of the duchy and compelled them to swear an oath of allegiance to the boy. Such oaths were made to be broken, and when the duke died on a pilgrimage to the Holy Land, the lords of Normandy looked to their own. Of the many close relatives to the ducal line, some believed firmly that the right was theirs, not the base-born boy's. The rule of the archbishop, himself a member of the family descended from Rollo the Viking – he who had carved out the duchy from a war-torn Francia – had ensured that the other relatives had paid lip service to the oath and ensured a fragile peace of sorts. Everybody knew that the archbishop would die too soon to see the boy grow to manhood. Everybody, from the servants in the palace to the whores in the hovels, knew he was not long for this world. He was a good man, and fair, and most people agreed that he would find his way to the right-hand side of the Lord. It was not odd that the townspeople should discuss the likelihood of a churchman going to heaven; many churchmen should be damned to hell everlasting for their life of greed and violence in the name of God.

Mauger was one. The boy-duke's uncle was the greediest, most ruthless man that ever served the Norman church. Others were quick to take up arms and employ those trained in arms to do their killing for them at the expense of the peasantry. With these men waiting in the shadows, the people of Rouen mourned the approaching death of Archbishop Robert.

The people agreed on the consequences of the old churchman's death: disaster.

For two years after Duke Robert's departure, Archbishop Robert had ruled the duchy of Normandy with a steady hand in the name of his great-nephew, William, the boy-duke. In his capacity as count of Evreux, Robert had stayed the hand of all those who wished to remove the boy, and there were many.

The death of the archbishop had ended the peace that lay across the land. War came and engulfed the duchy; war that destroyed and shattered lives; a terror lay deep in men's nightmares, and they awoke only to find that it was real. So the townspeople of Rouen in the same breath prayed for the soul of the good archbishop and muttered curses at those who were preparing for war. Windows were boarded up, doors bolted and the streets gradually deserted as a single bell echoed through the walls of the town even as the March sun disappeared from the western horizon.

But William had escaped, with Turold, Osbern and Walter, and they had ridden fast from Rouen, to the west, to Conteville, where the boy's mother had protected him along with Herluin, her husband. On the way the little group of fugitives had seen sights of violence and misery that haunted them for days and nights. Montfort-sur-Risle had been devastated and at Thiberville a girl had been raped before them as they sought escape. Rough soldiers had dragged her from the house screaming and kicking past her stunned parents into the gutter. The glimpse of a tear-stained face, tangled hair, and white thighs forced apart and the drunken, jeering soldiers taking their turn, made the boy see her raped again and again in his dreams.

At nine years of age William was old enough to understand what they had done to her. He knew who had done it and who had started it all. Two men, both his uncles: William, count of Arques and Mauger.

Mauger. When William was a young boy, Mauger had sat him on his knee and called him a bastard. William had asked his father what a bastard was, and his father had become angry and sent Mauger away. But Osbern had him told what a bastard was and why so many men, so close to him in blood, should want to kill him. But Osbern had also told that him that a bastard was as good a man as any, and better. That knowledge gave William an unswerving confidence that someday he would strike back at evil.

And Osbern had died protecting the boy-duke, along with Turold, murdered at the command of Mauger who, with his brother William, count of Arques, had taken Rouen; Mauger seized the archbishop's throne, still warm from Robert, and William of Arques took the castle. Together, they ruled Upper Normandy with impunity, leaving the remainder of the duchy to the dogs. More women were raped, more fathers gutted in the streets, and more children sold into slavery. Everyone prayed for the return of peace and the rule of the rightful heir to the duchy.

Herleve slowly lowered the curtain to William's chamber and turned to Herluin. 'He is lying still now and will sleep.'

'He's safe here with us,' said Herluin. Herleve nodded, but remembered Herluin saying that four years ago, when William had first come, the horrors of the journey fresh, and still vivid enough to make him wake screaming even now. Herluin led his wife down the stair and to the hall, where Walter was sipping mead. He came often to see his sister and the boy, and would be leaving on the morrow.

The fire in the stone hall crackled and sent a thin stream of smoke through the hole in the roof. Conteville castle consisted of a stone tower built on a great mound and encircled by a wooden palisade and a series of ditches. The tower included several floors, with a guardroom, a hall, private chambers and a cellar. Given time to prepare, it could withstand a short siege.

They talked well into the night of the continual war in the duchy of Normandy. It seemed that almost all those who had sworn the oath of allegiance to Robert's son had reneged on that oath. The result was government at the point of the sword.

'Alan of Brittany has pledged his support to us,' said Herluin. 'He will send us troops and money. Count Gilbert will come as soon as he can.' Walter nodded. Gilbert was count of Eu and bastard son of Duke Richard I; he was William's cousin and would remain loyal.

Herluin stood suddenly and kicked the fire into a blaze. His movement startled the hounds that lay in a cosy slumber amongst the rushes. 'If only Robert had not left for the Holy Land,' he said in a rare burst of irritation. 'God, but he was only twenty-four. It wouldn't have come to this if he had stayed.'

Walter was more pragmatic. 'Aye, but he did go, and it has come to this. We shall see the boy right. One day he shall rule over this godless province, I swear it.'

*

The sun blinded William for a second. A spur jingled, a foot stamped in the dust, and the sword hit him full on the head. William collapsed to the ground and rolled instinctively to the right. The sword banged on the cobbles and he was up, hefting the great sword in his right hand. He licked the sweat from his upper lip. Christ, the heat was unbearable in this mail tunic and coif; he would faint if this wasn't finished soon. He raised his sword and swung it to the right. At the last second he changed his line and lashed out his foot, catching his opponent in the midriff. With a roar of triumph William kicked the sword into the air and raised his own above the prostrate figure beneath him.

'*No, William...no!*'

The cry stopped him.

'Jesu, did you forget who I was?' His opponent crawled out from under him and shook his arm. William remembered with a shock who he was.

'You nearly killed me, William,' said Will FitzOsbern, picking up his battered shield and brushing the dust from his breeches.

'It's the heat,' said William slowly.

He shook his head, still dazed from the blow, though the helmet had taken the brunt of it. He took it off and peeled off the mail coif underneath. His close-cropped hair was matted with sweat. 'Let's have some wine.'

Herleve watched the two boys proudly. The tower offered a splendid view and on a day such as this, she could see the fields stretching far into the haze under the blue sky. Down below, the boys compared bruises and she heard William's bellow of laughter as he clapped Will on the back.

Will FitzOsbern was the only son of Osbern the steward; the man who had leapt in front of the dagger meant for William on that fateful journey four years ago. Will had quickly formed a firm friendship with William after his arrival from Breteuil. Both were of an age, although William was the taller of the two. At thirteen, William was as tall as any man and had the strength to go with it.

Down in the courtyard, the boys turned and headed towards the guardroom. No doubt to play dice and drink rough wine with the men-at-arms, thought Herleve with a stab of jealousy. William had the gift of getting on with anyone in any place. His quick wit and skill with arms had made him popular with the soldiery, who treated him with respect, seeing in him a natural leader of men.

Herleve was about to return to her needlework when she heard an angry shout.

'Cousin Guy!'

The object of William's attention was a boy of his age, Guy. A son of Renauld of Burgundy and Alice, Duke Robert's sister, he was visiting for a short while. Although he and William were cousins, there was little love lost between the two. William was tall and strong for his age, interested only in martial feats; Guy was bookish and easily led. The contrast was graphic: William and Will FitzOsbern, hot and exhilarated from their bout, towered over Guy, who was clad in a fine linen tunic and carried a roll of parchment under his arm. He ignored William's hearty greeting and walked on. William said something – Herleve did not hear, but it seemed insulting, for Guy stopped and turned. He shouted one word, loud enough for Herleve to hear from the top of the tower:

'Bastard!'

William raised his sword. Guy dropped the parchment and ran. He got as far as the kitchen and the chicken coop before sprawling face first into the mud. Will and some of the guards collapsed with laughter, but Herleve put her needlework down and hurried down the stairs, knowing that it was no joke to William. The use of that word was enough to send him into a blind fury – as Guy well knew.

When she reached the door of the tower William was already upon Guy. She could only stand and watch him punch the smaller boy in the face, rubbing his fine clothes into the mud.

'Name of God!' Herluin had arrived unseen and pulled them apart, cursing. William stood back, panting, the rage gone from him as soon as it had come.

'Get inside, both of you.' Herluin was deadly serious. 'I've got news.'

William looked up, and for the first time noticed the dust on Herluin's cloak and boots and saw that his face, usually so calm, was red with exertion.

They assembled in the main hall of the tower. Herluin swallowed some wine and threw his cloak onto a chair. He walked to William, put his hands on his shoulders and said gently: 'Uncle Gilbert is dead, William.' William did not move. Count Gilbert of Brionne had shared the guardianship of William. 'He was murdered when he was out riding.'

'Who, Herluin? Who did it?' William asked huskily.

'Richard of Gacé, boy. Richard...' Herluin could not speak. The treachery was difficult to believe. Richard was Robert of Rouen's son...another of William's cousins. Thank God the old man was not alive to see the betrayals, the murders – and the one by his own son.

'Richard of Gacé...?' William had turned deathly pale.

'Gilbert knew this might happen,' said Will.

'Yes...yes, he did; he must have known,' replied Herluin. He turned to William. 'I – I do not think you are safe here now, William.'

'No.' William's eye met Herluin's. Herluin felt that he had failed to honour Duke Robert's promise to guard the boy until he reached manhood. It hurt to admit it, how it hurt... The murder of Alan of Brittany in his bed soon after Epiphany was the beginning of the end; his valuable supply of men and money had dried up and the comté of Brittany was torn by strife. Now, Gilbert's death was the end of all hope.

William did not blame Herluin. He did not blame anyone except himself. He hated men, yes; he had learnt to hate a long time ago, but he still blamed himself. Turold. Osbern. Alan. Gilbert. How many more? Where would it end? How could he avenge them when Mauger was firmly ensconced in power at Rouen and the duchy was still locked in civil war? Last month Prior Richard of Saint Vanne had tried to proclaim the Peace of God, a papal edict prohibiting private warfare on certain days of the week, but to no avail. Local lords continued to inflict grievous harm on their neighbours, and it was always the common people who suffered the most.

'I have a message from Walter,' Herluin went on. 'He is on his way here now and will take you into hiding.'

'Where?' asked William.

'I do not know.' Herluin shrugged, defeated. 'Probably a village where you will live with the ordinary folk.'

'But what of my training in arms, my education – the scriptures and my letters?' William was aghast.

'Hush, William.' Herleve recognised the quick obstinacy that had made his father Robert so many enemies.

'We'll have to wait for Walter. Pray God he gets here safe and fast.' Herluin took charge again. 'Will – you are welcome to stay as long as you wish. Guy, you also, although you might like to return to your mother in Rouen.'

Guy nodded, and cast a shifty glance at William, who stared back with renewed hatred. Both boys were aware that Guy's mother was in Rouen with her brothers William of Arques and Mauger. Guy's bruised face held William's gaze for a moment and dropped to the floor.

'Of course I shall go with Uncle Walter,' said William, smiling. 'Enough lives have been lost.'

Only after he had left the hall and walked slowly to his chamber and only after he had softly closed the door did the tears begin to flow down his cheeks.

*

In the palace of the archbishop of Rouen, Richard of Gacé fell to his knees before the richly dressed cleric.

'It is done, my lord archbishop,' he said, pressing his lips to the fat, bejewelled fingers of the archbishop. Mauger regarded Richard's sweat-stained tunic with distaste and quickly withdrew his hand. Taking a sweetmeat from a bowl offered by a cringing servant, he said quietly: 'Is the bastard still at Conteville?'

'Yes, my lord, he is.'

'Does he really believe he is safe there?'

Richard did not answer. He watched the quivering jowls as the sweetmeat was devoured and noted with fascination a bead of sweat appear from under the lank hair. With a start he noted the piggy eyes watching him with a revulsion that he knew to be mutual and said hastily: 'Will he stay at Conteville, my lord?'

'He has nowhere to go, has he?' Mauger spat out a stone onto the floor.

Richard nodded. With Alan of Brittany and Gilbert of Brionne dead, the boy had run out of places to hide. Richard prepared to leave.

'I did not give you leave to go, Richard.'

Richard reddened and muttered an apology. Mauger leaned from the chair and fiddled with the small gold chain around his neck. 'I want him, Richard,' he rasped. 'I want him here, where I can control him.'

'William?'

'Who do you think, you fool?' Mauger beckoned Richard forward and grasped his cloak. 'Take thirty men and bring the bastard to me. Do it now and don't let anyone stop you.'

*

June gave way to July and Walter had not yet appeared. From the tower, Herleve watched anxiously across the golden fields and cider orchards until her eyes hurt from the glare of the sun and the horizon became dimmed by the haze. She could not believe that her brother would fail them now, unless something had happened to him. Could Mauger's long arm of death extend to Walter? She pushed the thought hurriedly from her mind. Walter was from peasant stock, like herself, and surely Mauger would not bother a man of low station. But the fear lingered in the back of her mind, as Walter's standing had greatly improved under Robert - and he was known to be a guardian of the young duke...

For William, life went on much as before. Sickly Guy had returned to his mother, probably to seek favour with Mauger. The shadow of Mauger hung over them, but Will FitzOsbern remained, and together they took their lessons with Brother John. The fourth son of a landowner from Thury-Harcourt, John had been given to the church at the age of ten, but had always harboured a desire to acquire martial skills rather than embrace the spiritual peace of the church. He livened up the lessons in the chapel by concentrating on the classics and often skipped the more tedious passages from the scriptures, while in return William gave him lessons with his sword.

Once free of the chapel, they practised the art of war. William lived for the hours of riding and swordplay under the eye of Roger, a grizzled veteran of Duke Robert's time, who drew castles in the dust and described how best to take them by storm, or how to lay siege. Most castles, he explained, consisted of a timber fort on top of a high mound; the defendants could be starved or smoked out. To avoid a lengthy siege - which was dangerous, for the delay allowed other enemy forces to come to the aid of the besieged -taking it by trickery or treachery was the best course of action. He taught them to ride at the quintain, a gallows-like structure with a sack of sand hanging from the cross-beam. A good horseman could hit it with his lance and dodge the flying sack; if he mistimed it, the sack would swing back and deposit him in to the dust. It was a hard lesson to learn, but William got up again and again and eventually mastered it: anything his men could do, he was determined to better.

Still Walter did not come.

The peace was broken some four weeks after the news of Gilbert's death. The silent heat of the courtyard echoed to the shrieking of Herleve's maid running up from the village.

'What is it Julia...is it Walter?' said Herleve, meeting the girl in the hall.

'No, my lady,' Julia gasped. 'A large party of horsemen are riding here...it is said that they are Mauger's men.'

Cold dread flooded through Herleve.

'Who told you this?' Herluin demanded when he entered the hall with the boys.

'Joan, the smith's wife. She heard it in Lisieux market.' Julia sat abruptly on a stool, worn out.

'Did she know who was in command of the group, Julia?' asked Herleve gently.

Julia raised her tear-stained face to her mistress and said: 'Yes...Richard of Gacé.'

Herluin was thunderstruck. 'William, warn the guard and call out all those off duty –'

'Herluin of Conteville, bring out the bastard!'

'Body of Christ.'

Herluin cursed as he strode to the door. Richard of Gacé was in the yard, accompanied by some twenty horsemen. The castle guards were kneeling in the dust at swordpoint. Herluin crossed to the other side of the hall and peered through the narrow window. There was a mounted soldier armed to the teeth. He did not recognise him. 'We are taken,' he said simply.

'God have mercy.' Herleve hugged William. 'Why didn't we send you away before, why...?'

Herluin moved to his wife. 'Go and talk to him. Keep them busy, offer them wine, and water for the horses – they look as if they need it.'

'But –'

'Don't argue, woman, just do it!'

Cut short by the uncharacteristic anger in Herluin's voice, Herleve walked quickly to the door.

'Listen, William.' Herluin turned to the boy. 'When my father built this castle, he had a passage dug from the cellars to the outer bailey. Normandy then was no more peaceful than today.' He walked to the oak table and heaved. The two boys helped him clear the space and on the floor beneath it, an iron ring came into view. Herluin seized it and pulled the trap-door upwards, tipping rushes and dust onto the floor. William peered down. Stone steps disappeared into the gloom.

'He isn't here, I tell you!'

Herleve's voice carried loudly across the hall. Her tone was desperate; Richard would be upon them at any moment.

'Down the steps, now.' Herluin hissed. 'You'll find a passage behind the wine barrels. Take these.' He grabbed a candle and flint from the table, uttering a silent prayer of thanks to the forgetful servant who had left them there.

William took the candle and took a faltering step into the darkness.

'I'm going, too,' said Will FitzOsbern.

Before William could protest, Herluin lowered the door and they were left in the darkness.

When Richard of Gacé pushed past Herleve and walked into the hall, he saw Herluin leaning on a table and his lip curled in a sneer.

'Where is he, Herluin?'

Herluin shook his head.

'Like that, is it?' Richard's face creased into ugly anger at Herluin's cool response. 'These are dangerous times for such as you. Bedding Duke Robert's whore does not give you the right to talk to me like that...' Richard put out a dirty hand and caressed Herleve's jaw. 'You know how to please a man, I don't wonder.' Herleve recoiled from his wine-sodden breath and unwashed odour. Richard looked up and down the length of her body. 'In good shape, still.' He placed an arm around her waist. 'Come to think of it,' he said conversationally, 'I wouldn't say no to a roll in the hay. Isn't that what the peasants do?'

'Leave off the Lady Herleve,' said Herluin quietly, advancing from the table.

'Ah, Lady Herleve, is it now? Not bad for the daughter of a tanner.' Richard's voice was thick with jealousy that was plain to them all. As a younger son, he would be lucky to inherit anything but a few acres at Gacé, and he would never be a master of such a castle as this. If he could bring back the bastard boy to the fat churchman, the reward might be great, but if not...

Richard pushed Herleve away. He couldn't touch her, however much he wanted to – there would be no estates if he did, for even the churchman would frown upon that. He turned to Julia. He would have her instead; a servant wench was no loss to anyone. He detected the fear in her eyes and grinned. This was easier game. He took hold of her neck and squeezed.

'Tell me, Herluin.'

Herluin shook his head.

'I'm warning you, lord of Conteville.' Richard's hand found Julia's skirts and slid up her thigh. She whimpered. Richard licked his lips; she was pretty and full-bodied. He liked them that way. 'What do you know, Herluin?'

At Herluin's silent refusal, Richard tore savagely at Julia's gown. The thongs broke, baring her large, white breasts. She struggled; Richard slapped her savagely across the cheek and she was still.

'I'll cut her, Herluin.' Richard had drawn a dagger and held it to a breast cupped in his sweaty hand. Julia let out a sob.

'They left two days ago,' Herluin blurted out before Richard's knife could cut Julia.

'You do know something, then.' Richard grinned wickedly. He put the dagger back in the sheath, but kept his hand on Julia. 'I do believe our wench is becoming quite excited.' Julia shook her head frantically, dumb with terror. Richard bent and licked her neck, his unshaven chin rasping her shoulder. Then he let go of her abruptly and turned to Herluin, standing powerlessly by.

'Last chance, lord of Conteville: where have you got the bastard?'

Herluin looked at Julia, who shook her head fractionally, urging him not to speak, not give William away. Still looking at Julia, Herluin spoke loudly and clearly: 'Rot in hell, you whoreson whelp.'

Richard stared back for a moment, frozen with rage. He grunted, seized Julia's arm and hauled her to the table. 'Hold her down, lads.' Three of his men came from the door and pinned the girl's arms and legs to the table. At Julia's scream, Herluin moved forward, but Herleve checked him. 'You can't do this, Richard!' he shouted.

'Can't I?' Richard knelt above the girl and dropped his breeches, Julia struggled, lashing out with her feet. Richard made a fist and punched her face repeatedly. He looked at his men, and leered. 'You can have her afterwards, lads.'

*

William lit the candle and by its dim light the contents of the cellar emerged. But for the sweet smell of wine pervading the air, it might have been a tomb. Will tugged at his arm. 'I can't see the passage Herluin spoke of,' he whispered. William did not answer. He was thinking hard; time was short. There was only one candle and when that ran out they would never find the passage, and besides, Richard's men would be down before long. 'That door leads to the courtyard,' he said, pointing to the main door. 'I think it's on this side.' He turned to the opposite wall. It was lined from top to bottom with rows of barrels.

'God's truth,' said Will.

There was nothing for it but to shift the barrels. It was a race against time. The candle was burning perilously low when Will noticed a draught blowing the flame. William got down on his hands and knees and groped along the wall. 'Got it,' he gasped. It was another ring, covered with grime. He pulled. A little door creaked open. 'Watch the candle!' he hissed, as a great draught swept up from the hole. The candle flickered and continued to burn brightly. William took it and peered into the hole. 'There are some steps leading below, like those into here,' he muttered. He was interrupted by a shout followed by a prolonged scream.

'Jesus, if they do anything to my mother –'

'She wants us to go, William.' Will was resolute. 'We've got to go.'

Walter knew something was wrong as soon as he entered Conteville.

Five days ago he had left the village of Pontorson on the Normandy–Brittany border. The brief stop at Mortain for a fresh horse and food had been the only break in an otherwise non-stop journey. The killing of Gilbert of Brionne had come as a shock to him. The death of Alan of Brittany had put them all on their guard, but this...Gilbert was a man of peace, a good man, and had no place in the lawless world he had fallen prey to.

Gilbert's murder would mean a new start for William. Pontorson was the furthest place from the grasping hands of Mauger, so far to the west of the duchy that the natives considered themselves Breton. Indeed, many of them were; they scorned the Norman laws and way of life. He would be safe there. He had to be; there was nowhere else to go.

It was only a stroke of good fortune which prevented Walter from entering the castle.

The horse he had hired from Mortain had worked a shoe loose after crossing the Orne; the morning's ride had consequently become increasingly uneven and painful on the tracks baked stone-hard by the July sun. He left the horse with the smith and set out to walk to the castle. But a chance remark from the smith about his wife's panic put Walter on his guard. The absence of the soldiery at the wooden gates of the palisade confirmed his worst suspicions. He walked back to the village, wondering what to do. The people in the street had seen a large party of horsemen ride into the castle bailey not an hour since; they knew no more. Walter was about to leave when he saw William and Will running down across the market, barging past a stall in their haste.

'William!'

William stopped dead, recognising the voice. Walter waved and he saw him through the crowd.

'The castle is taken,' William said when they met, heaving for breath.

'How did you escape?'

Will explained about the passage under the hall. 'It is Richard of Gacé,' he added.

Walter cursed. 'Are they after you now?'

'No. But they will come soon enough,' said William.

'Then there's no time to be lost. The smith's wife works in the castle; he will be loyal and lend us some horses.'

'Where will we go?'

'A place far from here. Somewhere safe...Pontorson. On the Breton border.'

William nodded and they left Conteville.

They arrived at Pontorson six days later. The small village was three leagues from the coastline, which was dominated by the famous abbey of Mont Saint-Michel. Walter had prepared for them a hovel on the outskirts of the village. Will was aghast at the sight of the two-roomed mud-and-thatch structure that so many of the ordinary folk lived in.

'My mother grew up in a house like this,' said William when Will protested. Walter nodded. 'Aye, there were seven of us.' He gave them a handful of coins and told them to report for work with Peter the Woodman in the morning.

'Work?' Will exploded. 'Jesu, you can't expect me to sully my hands!'

He turned to William, but William was already hefting an axe he'd found in the sty at the back. He gave Will a broad grin and said: 'If I'm expecting to govern these good people, I want to know how they live. Now I can find out. We'll stay.'

Chapter Five
Winchester, England, August 1042

The air in Queen Emma's bower was warm and sweet in the midsummer heat. Stigand opened the shutters and breathed in the fresh air. The scent of the honeysuckle on the walls below floated into his nostrils and he smiled with contentment. Winchester was so agreeable in the summer, unlike London, which stank of the rank waters of the Thames.

'Close them,' said an imperious voice behind him.

The queen's cleric obediently closed the shutters he had just opened and the room grew dark again, muffling the sound of the buzzing bees and the rattle of the carts on the Roman cobbles below. Stigand sighed; the old queen had taken the death of her young son hard – very hard. At first, she had refused to credit the news, insisting that he was only twenty-five and had been in perfect health when she last saw him. But then, none of Canute's sons had reached a great age: Harold Harefoot had been a mere twenty years of age on his death, and Svein eighteen. As the news sank in, the old queen had started to beat the walls in her anger, screaming that her son had been poisoned by someone – anyone, even Godwin, perhaps. Stigand had patiently explained that this was out of the question, as the flagon of wine from which the king had been drinking when he fell down and died, had been shared by most other men in the hall.

'He will not be king.'

Stigand turned and faced the queen. This was the most irrational statement of all. He knew who 'he' was, although she refused to acknowledge him. Prince Edward, her son by King Ethelred, the last prince of the old blood. She simply would not countenance her own son's claim. Stigand crossed his arms and studied the woman sitting on the bed. Her face was blotched from weeping, her hair loose in strands, her wimple on the floor. He felt a twinge of pity, but tempered it with wariness. She was a tenacious, ruthless woman and not easily defeated.

'Magnus can be king of England,' she said, proving his point.

Stigand drew breath. What was this mad scheme? 'Magnus is Norwegian, my lady, and has no claim to the throne –'

'– no more claim than my husband Canute did, except by right of conquest,' said the woman on the bed. Stigand reminded himself to be patient. In her old age, Emma was beginning to lose her grasp of events. She would soon be fifty-six, though she was still beautiful, the delicate cheek-bones growing even more prominent with age. It was easy to see how she'd captured the hearts of two kings, but at this moment, she looked a lot older.

'Madam...' Stigand began wearily.

'You can write.' She was standing up now, warming to her theme. 'Find ink and parchment and tell Magnus to come and take what is his.'

Stigand hesitated, his mind working furiously. He did not understand. What treachery was this?

'Do you not see?'

The queen confronted his bewilderment. 'Magnus and Harthacanute had an agreement three years ago, to the effect that should either die childless, the other would inherit his kingdom.'

'But surely, madam, with all respect, that treaty was made before Harthacanute was king of England, and therefore it refers only to Denmark...'

Emma looked at Stigand in silence for a moment before saying: 'You are more stupid than I thought. Who cares? Who is to know?' She sat on the bed again. 'The story goes that Magnus is half English anyway.'

'Oh? How so?'

'His mother was Aefilda, a thegn's daughter from York. She was captured on a raid by Norwegian Vikings and raped by a jarl. But they found her so comely and desirable that they took her back to Norway, where King Olaf took a fancy to her and bedded her as well. The result was Magnus. Not a great pedigree to be proud of, but there's English blood somewhere!'

Stigand frowned, shocked more by the queen's obvious enjoyment of the girl's plight rather than the content of the story. The old woman really was raving, he thought. 'But –'

'Write the letter, cleric.'

Stigand saw the hard eyes and knew how set the queen was on this course. If it should go wrong, his fortunes were staked to hers...so why should he be the one? 'Should not a clerk pen the letter, my lady?'

'Do it yourself. I have not forgotten that you are an ambitious man of humble birth with a Norwegian name.'

Stigand blanched at that. Emma's threat was a naked one. He might invite disaster by writing such a note of treachery to Magnus, but if he didn't write the letter, then his career would come to an abrupt end.

Stigand bowed, admitting defeat, and moved to the door but the queen hadn't finished yet.

'Do not let Edward discover my letter, Stigand.'

The imperious voice stopped Stigand at the door. 'It will be the end of us if he does.'

Stigand noted the emphasis on 'us' and sensed the malice implicit in the instruction. He nodded frantically and stumbled from the chamber. Outside, the summer sun was now obscured by a thick mass of cloud, as dark as his own prospects had just become.

The day had gone sour.

*

It was not until ten months after the death of Harthacanute that Prince Edward was crowned king. His accession to the throne of England was in little doubt after the earl of Wessex and the people of

London proclaimed the English exile king. All the chief men in the realm were somewhat puzzled by Earl Godwin's immediate backing for the friendless Edward. Godwin himself was a product of Canute's reign, and had always considered himself to be an Anglo-Dane, alienated from the Norman tradition the English prince had grown up with. But those who knew the earl were aware that Godwin would not back an unknown prince entirely from the goodness of his heart.

As the winter closed in after the worst harvest in years, the councillors huddled round hall fires and reflected quietly on the earl of Wessex's choice. By Christmas it was clear that Svein of Denmark, King Canute's nephew, was not going to claim the throne, so busy was he fighting Magnus of Norway in a desperate war to hold on to Denmark.

So it was Edward, whose father was Ethelred, whose father was Edgar, whose father was Edmund, whose father was Edward the Elder, whose father was Alfred the Great, who would be crowned on that blustery spring day, 3rd April 1043.

*

On the morning of Edward's coronation, Godwin summoned his two eldest sons to speak with him on a matter of importance. The Godwin house in Winchester was crowded with Godwin relations and friends, all standing around, interrupting the preparations and obstructing the busy servants. Above it all, Gytha's strident voice could be heard issuing orders. Intrigued by his father's summons, Harold pushed through the commotion to find his father and Swegn already waiting by the fireside in the earl's private quarters. Godwin began, his face alight with excitement: 'One of the reasons I gave Edward my full support was this; in return for my pledge of aid to Edward and my influence upon Leofric and

Siward, it was agreed that you, my first two sons, shall be made earls.'

Harold suppressed a gasp of delight but Swegn grinned with naked greed. 'He shall make you earls in a couple of days from now,' Godwin went on, rubbing his hands together in triumph. 'What lands, father?' asked Swegn quickly.

'You shall have Herefordshire, Gloucestershire, Oxfordshire and Somerset,' said Godwin. He turned to Harold. 'And you shall have East Anglia.'

Harold's head swam in dizzy euphoria. So this was the price Edward paid for Godwin's support – his two sons were to be given powerful earldoms in their own right. The power of the house of Godwin almost doubled overnight. The wily fox! Leofric and Siward wouldn't like this, for sure.

'The ceremony will take place soon after the coronation. Naturally your lands are richer, Swegn, as you are the elder son.' Godwin was saying. 'But you shall both be able to establish your own households and manage your estates, and if you need help and advice, then come to me.' Godwin hadn't mentioned the rest of his bargain with Edward, the part that meant more than the rest put together: Edward, the bachelor king, had consented to take a wife, and that wife would be Edith, Godwin's daughter. Godwin's grandson would be king.

Godwin clapped his arms around his sons and led them into the main hall. 'Let's go, my boys. There's a kingdom to rule. England needs us, now.'

The waiting family members followed the earl and his sons out into the yard. Godwin shouted for his horse and threw the groom an unexpected coin for his services. *It moves*, he thought as he mounted the horse. *It moves.*

*

Harold was overawed by the coronation ceremony. He'd arrived early, his head still spinning from the news that he would be an earl. Beside him, Swegn stood silently, and for a short time, the two brothers were united in their excitement. Gradually, Harold pushed his excitement to the back of his mind and began to take stock of his immediate surroundings. The Minster was filled with people of the court, with the Godwin family at the fore. Their chatter ended abruptly at the blast of a trumpet. All heads turned to the great west doors that had been opened especially for the occasion. The procession into the church had begun, and in the awed silence Eadsige, archbishop of Canterbury and Aelfric Puttoc, archbishop of York, led Edward through the door. Both prelates were splendidly attired, but Edward's costume drew gasps of admiration from the court. He wore a purple silk gown from his shoulders to the ground, clasped around his neck by a gold brooch; his white tunic was embroidered with gold trimmings and studded with jewels. Behind him, the bishop of London held the crown above Edward's head. It was a simple gold coronet with a single large jewel at its centre, said to be the same jewel that Alfred the Great had worn in his crown.

The choir then began to sing: 'Let thy hand be strengthened and thy right hand be exalted. Let justice and judgement be the preparation of thy seat and mercy and truth go before thy face.' The procession moved past the congregation to the high altar, where Edward took his seat on the throne. His face, slightly flushed, was calm and set with a confident expression. The two archbishops knelt at his feet. After a moment of silence, Eadsige turned to the waiting crowd and shouted: 'Do you, the people and the clergy accept this man Edward as your king?' To which the crowd roared the affirmative in unison, thus electing and acclaiming the king in the time-honoured fashion. Harold, caught up in the emotion, shouted as loudly as the rest of them. Edward, a direct descendant of Alfred, was the seventeenth in line from Cerdic, who had come over in the dark days soon after the Romans had left Britain. And Cerdic in turn was the ninth from Woden. The royal house of England was without doubt the most distinguished in Europe.

As the choir sang the hymn 'Te Deum Laudamus', Harold sensed the emotion running through the people present. He swallowed nervously, the enormity of the event leaving him breathless. At that moment he swore silently that he would serve this tall and sloping man to the best of his abilities. He would pledge his lifelong loyalty to him.

The archbishops were now asking Edward to take the triple oath. Edward turned to the congregation and spoke in a firm voice: 'I promise that the church of God and the whole Christian people within His dominion will keep true peace. I will forbid rapine and wrongful acts to men of every degree. I promise to ordain justice and that mercy will be observed in all legal judgements so that merciful God should have mercy on me and on us all.'

The new king had been acclaimed by the laity. He had sworn a coronation oath. Now, at the heart of the ceremony, Edward would be anointed king. This was the part that would make Edward different from any other mortal in that church. He would be God's vicar on earth. Staring at the man now seated on the great carved oak throne by the high altar, Harold held his breath, aware that everyone was equally transfixed by the ceremony. The choir began to sing 'They anointed Solomon' and Eadsige poured chrism, the holiest oil known to the church, onto the top of Edward's head.

Next came the investiture with the regalia. As the choir sang quiet hymns centred on Christian kingship with its duties of defending and instructing the church, defending and bringing peace to the people and terrifying the infidel, the ring, the sword, the crown and the sceptre were bestowed on Edward. The ring was the seal of holy faith and with its help, the king was to drive back his foes, destroy heresies, unite his subjects and bind them firmly in the Catholic faith. The sword was for the protection of the kingdom and the camp of God; with it, the king would smash his enemies. The crown was the crown of glory and justice, the sceptre the rod of the kingdom and of virtue. Eadsige handed the sceptre to Edward, and the choir prayed that God would honour Edward before all kings, establish him on the throne of his realm, visit him with an increase of children, allow justice to spring up in his days, and receive him with joy and gladness to reign in the everlasting kingdom. At this, the watching congregation knelt in silence while the prayer was said. But alongside Harold, only Gytha saw how tightly Godwin clenched his fist as the choir prayed that God would visit Edward with an increase of children.

The benediction followed. Eadsige turned and called out: 'May God make you victorious and a conqueror over your enemies, both visible and invisible; may He grant you peace in your days, and with the palm of victory lead you to His eternal kingdom. May He grant that you be happy in the present world and share the eternal joys of the world to come. May God bless this our chosen king that he may rule like David, govern with the mildness of Solomon, and enjoy a peaceable kingdom.' As Eadsige finished, the choir broke out with the anthem: 'Vivat Rex! Vivat Rex! Vivat Rex in eternum!' and the congregation, seeing the archbishop beckon them to rise, stood and replied, 'Amen!'

It was over. Edward was now truly king of all England, acclaimed by the people and anointed by God to do God's duty on this earth. Harold, realising he'd been holding his breath these past minutes, expelled the air slowly and savoured the moment. Edward, the prince of the blood and exile, was the true king of England and he, Harold Godwinsson, would soon be belted an earl in the service of King Edward.

'Move along, Harry!' Harold turned, startled out of his reverie. Swegn's ugly grin leered down at him, and he said again, 'Move, can't you? There is someone I want to talk to at the feast.'

Harold nodded absently and shuffled obediently to one side. The king and his prelates had processed to the royal palace for the coronation banquet. There he would sit in state on the dais, displaying the regalia and flanked by the two archbishops.

'I'll never forget that to my dying day,' said Tostig, as Swegn pushed past. Harold grinned and turned to Edith. 'Edith...?' She wore a sombre dress that day, with a dark blue wimple framing the delicate white skin of her face. She appeared not to have heard Harold as she watched the procession leave the church. Instead she said quietly, almost to herself: 'He is like a saint. Such a man could never sin. He is truly a man of God.' Harold followed her gaze and nodded in silent agreement; if ever there was a king who exemplified the demands of saintliness, it seemed to be Edward. He glanced round and saw Godwin looking not at Edward, but at his daughter. Something in Edith's admiration of Edward - which amounted almost to adoration - had given Godwin pause for thought.

The great hall was packed when they arrived, with Edward seated at the high table. Godwin led his family to seats nearby with other nobles, and prepared to swear homage to the new king. For although they had placed Edward on the throne, the nobles were expecting to receive the new king's recognition of their lands and titles. Seated near Edward were ambassadors from Europe, there to acknowledge his position and for him to make his peace with them. Henry, king of France, Henry, emperor of the Germans, Svein of Denmark and other continental nobles had sent representatives. Following his international acceptance, Edward duly accepted the homage of the great lords of England. This done, the feasting could begin.

Godwin's grin of relief was plain to see as he returned to his place at the table. Around them, the silence following the oath-taking was ended in a series of cheers and laughter, and the wine began to flow freely. 'Where is Swegn?' Godwin noticed the absence of his elder son before the others.

'Over there,' said Tostig, pointing to the far end of the hall. Harold looked up from his cup. The king had supplied them with good wine from Bordeaux, and it tasted all the better for his paying for it, in the tradition of the king feasting his servants at his expense. But on following Tostig's arm, Harold's mouth went dry, and he nearly choked on the wine. Amongst the throng of people by the entrance of the hall Eadgyth Swan-neck stood, unmoving in the crowd milling all around her. And there too was Swegn, talking in earnest to her.

Harold rose from the table so abruptly that a plate crashed into the rushes. Slowly he picked up the plate that had fallen unnoticed by those nearest him, and looked again at Swegn. He had his arm against the wall and his hand on her arm. Ignoring Godwin's query, Harold stumbled from the table and pushed past the servants. Drink had begun to take its toll on the jubilant guests in the hall and the wine-thick voices carried far, some slurred and insensible, others still vibrant with wit. Harold pushed aside a drunken thegn, ignored the half-drawn sword waved at him and pushed forward, his eyes fixed only on Swegn and Eadgyth. She cast quick, furtive glances about her like a trapped animal. Harold could still not hear what was being said. Then, as he was about to push forward and interrupt, Swegn gave an abrupt wave of dismissal, turned on his heel and walked away, only a few paces from Harold. Eadgyth remained still for some minutes, unaware of Harold gazing at her, and then took a step forwards. Harold shrank back and prayed that she would not see him.

She did.

Holding his gaze, she walked up to him and for a second Harold thought she would walk on past him with a glance of disdain. But she paused, leaned over to him and whispered: 'Meet me in the Minster at midnight if you want to help me.' So stunned was Harold by her proximity, the sweet smell of her scent, and the glimpse of her white bosom beneath the low-cut gown, that by the time he opened his mouth to respond, she had vanished. A whisper in the crowd, a breath of scent, and she was gone, as before, when he had first met her at the wedding feast of Tofig the Proud, the day Harthacanute died... But what would she want with him, a crude boy lusting after her haunting beauty? Was it connected with her conversation with Swegn? In a fever of excitement, Harold returned to his seat, hoping that Swegn would not be there. He could not dare face any enquiring glances now; he would give it all away instantly. He would play the hero in the saga; he would be Beowulf and slay the monster Grendel. His heart beat faster as he realised that he had made his decision. He would go and see her.

Godwin finished his meal with a quiet belch. Ignoring Gytha's look of disapproval, he wiped his mouth and poured wine for the family. Godwin stood up and raised his goblet. 'To my daughter, Edith,' he said, and everyone took a drink. When he had finished, Godwin bent and kissed his daughter on the cheek.

Edith was delighted at such unexpected attention. It was unusual for noble ladies to attend the great feasts of the menfolk, and seeing the swaying, noisy courtiers, Edith could understand why. But today, the king had made an exception for his coronation, and well-born ladies were invited to feast with the new king. And she was pleased she had come. The ceremony had left her wondrous with awe, breathless at the solemnity of the proceedings and the sanctity that shrouded the whole event. And at its centre was Edward. He had played the part to perfection, with his sombre, saintly air. He had about him an aura of a man of destiny. Indeed, had not today's ceremony restored the ancient line of Alfred and Cerdic after the Danish invasions and so many years of exile and danger?

Above them all, Edward surveyed his subjects in silence. His eyes caught Edith's for a moment and she shivered, conscious that he was staring straight through her.

'You'll know him soon enough.'

Edith felt a grip on her arm and instinctively drew back as she realised that it was Swegn. He was drunk again, but as yet, still coherent. 'What do you mean by that?' Edith was annoyed by his affrontery.

'You, my pretty sister, are part of the deal.' Swegn tapped his nose with his forefinger and nodded secretively.

'What deal?'

Edith looked for her parents, but they had gone, lost in the crowd of happy, wine-sated people of the court.

'The deal between our beloved father and the new king, sainted bachelor that he is,' Swegn sneered at the figure on the dais. He leant forward and breathed wine and onions into Edith's face. She recoiled in disgust but he gripped her arm and said thickly: 'You, my sweet, virgin sister, are to be wife to King Edward. The king's bride: Queen Edith. That was the other part of the bargain and that is why he is up there in all his crowning glory.'

*

Harold wondered whether she would come. He remained unsure that he had heard her words correctly; the hall had been packed and noisy. He could have mistaken her words for a murmur snatched between the sound of clinking cups – it was past midnight and there was no sign of her. He was, after all, mistaken. Or maybe she was in danger and could not come, spirited away by her husband, trapped and helpless.

He dismissed the last thought from his mind. The stone church was an empty shell now, a carcass after the day's tremendous events.

Harold shivered, and walked from the west door, where the new king had processed in and out, the light from his candle throwing a low, flickering light onto the tombs that lined the walls. The candle hissed and he quickened his step, his best leather boots clicking on the paved floor.

Ahead, the throne loomed large. Empty and desolate in the darkness, it was little more than an oak chair now. But in the daylight, in all the pomp and glory of the ceremony, the gold cloths and the occupant, it had had power – great power. Godwin had once told Harold that the throne was to men what a candle was to a moth; it attracted and lured them to its mystical glory, and then destroyed them on contact. Harold saw that his father was right. In the shadows the throne, once an empty chair, now seemed to put forth its own light.

The light grew, illuminating the carvings on the back of the chair. Devils with forked tails leered in grotesque greeting, angels hovered precariously around them in silent admonition, and Jesus sat above them all, on the right-hand side of God, his carved halo bright and shining. Harold stretched out his hand to touch the carved wood.

'Harold!'

The voice hissed from the shadows like a spirit.

Harold stepped back so quickly he nearly fell over. The light moved, away from the throne, and he realised that it was not coming from the throne at all. It was a candle. He drew a ragged breath and glanced up at the throne again. It was shrouded in darkness again, nothing but a chair. But still, a moth to the flame...

'Harold Godwinsson; is it you?'

Harold raised his candle and saw Eadgyth. Her audible sigh of relief and shaking hand made it clear to Harold that she was as chilled and frightened as he was. And in the candlelight she appeared small and pale, her hair no longer tied back severely, but loose and untidy. In the moment when Harold realised that she looked more beautiful than ever, he also knew that she was in need of help.

'Come on,' he whispered, and led her to the small north door before their candles finally spluttered into darkness.

Outside, it was colder than in the Minster. The night sky was clear and dotted with stars; the lights from the hall were visible in the distance and the drunken shouts from those revellers still standing echoed across to them.

Harold removed his cloak and wrapped it carefully around Eadgyth's shoulders. She smiled her thanks and Harold shivered with pleasure this time, a warm glow rising inside him that made him suddenly light-headed. They remained still for some moments, neither speaking.

Harold thought that she would begin, but as she did not, he cleared his throat and said:

'What is it, then, that I must help you with, my lady?'

He sensed Eadgyth turn to him in the darkness. 'You may call me Eadgyth, Harold Godwinsson.'

Harold felt her hand on his and swallowed nervously. 'And you shall know me as Harry from now on,' he said as firmly as he could. 'Now tell me. How must I help?'

The smile died from Eadgyth's lips as she spoke. 'You know that I am married. He is Thorgils of Midhurst, a brutal man, much older than me, who married me for my noble birth. But I have not supplied him with a healthy son, or indeed, any children.' Eadgyth leaned forward in the dark, close enough for Harold to breathe her scent. He took her hand and held it tightly. 'He wishes me dead, Harry. There are no grounds for divorce and as he holds his manor from the Abbey of Steyning for three lifetimes; it must revert to the church in the case of a lapse in the male line. He wants a son and I cannot give him one. He wants me dead, and he wants a new wife to breed with, or he will lose his lands.'

Harold did not know what to say, he could only hear her words spinning around in his head. *He wants me dead. Dead.* He noticed her bruised eye.

'Did he do that to your eye?'

Eadgyth took his hand and guided it along her cheek. 'Yes,' she whispered. 'For talking to Swegn, your brother.'

'Were you asking for help from Swegn in the hall?'

'Yes.' Eadgyth nodded and caught her breath in a sob. 'But he said that he would only help if – if I should offer myself to him in return.' At this, she began to weep, burying her head on Harold's shoulder. Harold clenched his hands in silent rage. Curse Swegn. It was typical of him to make such a suggestion. In all likelihood he had no intention of helping her, but wanted her body for his pleasures and would afterwards deny having ever made such a promise. But she had refused him and Swegn had dismissed her plea for aid.

'I will help you,' Harold said. 'As from tomorrow I will be earl of East Anglia and as such will act as your protector.' Her sobs ceased and Harold found himself kissing the tears from her cheeks, his lips seeking hers, and meeting them. She responded with a passion that surprised him, pulling his head closer and parting his lips with her tongue. Harold's hands grasped her hips and she uttered a moan as his hands slid between her thighs under the folds of her dress. She broke away and stepped back. In the silence that ensued, Harold's mind raced, still dizzy from the kiss and her passion, the speed with which it had happened, and now it was as if they had never touched.

'I must go,' she said hurriedly. 'Thorgils will miss me soon, when he emerges from his drunken stupor.' With another light touch on his hand, she turned and ran into the night, leaving only her scent in the cold air.

Harold let her go, waiting a moment in the darkness, but when he stepped forward, a footfall in the darkness halted him, and the voice that came from the shadows of the doorway was dreadfully familiar, and filled with a choking menace.

'A true man of honour and a damsel in distress to be rescued indeed.' A flint flared and Swegn emerged in the light of the candle in the doorway. Harold was too shocked to speak. How much had Swegn heard? He made to go past his brother but Swegn's arm shot out and hauled him up against the wall, slamming the air from Harold's lungs. Harold gasped and uttered:

'How much did you hear?'

Swegn grinned. 'Everything. And what would Thorgils think if he knew his woman was whoring her body to any noble at court in return for protection, I wonder?' Swegn licked his lips.

Having recovered his breath, Harold said slowly: 'You wouldn't...you won't say anything, will you Swegn?'

Swegn squeezed Harold's arm until he could see Harold grimace in pain. 'No. Not yet.' He twisted harder. 'But I might if the time is right, little brother.' He gave another twist and then let go, blew out the candle and strode off into the night.

Harold rubbed his arm. Curse Swegn. God alone knew why he had been blessed with such a brother. The threat from Swegn was a real one, but he had to help Eadgyth. And remembering her soft skin on his, her pleading voice in the darkness, he knew that to be true. Whatever the risks, she came before Swegn. And Harold knew why: he loved her, and would have her one day.

Chapter Six
Gloucester, November 1043

'Harry! The king will see us now!'

Harold turned at Godwin's command. The large hall of the royal palace at Gloucester was packed with courtiers here for the king's court. They stood back respectfully as the earl of Wessex and his son, the newly made earl of East Anglia, marched to the king's chamber. Godwin stopped at the door with a clink of spurs and knocked once. The door was opened by the priest Robert Champart from Normandy, one of those who'd followed Edward from exile and had been rewarded with a place in the king's private council. Godwin frowned at the simpering cleric and pushed past.

'It seems that conspiracies are afoot to oust me from the throne before I have become comfortable on it,' said the king without preamble. He was seated on his great chair, two large wolfhounds at his feet.

Godwin straightened his cloak and looked around the room. Earl Leofric of Mercia was present and he noted with surprise Earl Siward of Northumbria leaning on the window-sill. He must have arrived only yesterday. Godwin turned to the king and asked, 'Do you have evidence, sire, of such a plot?' He noticed that Robert Champart had rejoined the king's side. The little man must have scuttled from the door to reach the king.

'This, my lord of Wessex – this.' Edward handed Godwin a letter. Godwin unrolled the parchment and read aloud: 'I beseech you to raise a fleet and come to England and take what is rightfully yours. By the treaty made with my son Harthacanute you are the heir to the throne of England: if either of you died childless the other should inherit his lands. I urge you to stand by that treaty and invade England, to which end I have secured part of the treasury here at Winchester.'

At the foot of the letter was scrawled the name EMMA in large writing.

'Sweet blood of Christ,' Godwin breathed. 'The old queen.'

'But why?' said Harold from over Godwin's shoulder. 'She is your mother, sire; I do not understand.'

Godwin looked up and caught Edward's eye. He knew. He understood. There was once a young, beautiful woman of determination and not least, ruthlessness, who'd jumped from one king's bed to another with somewhat indecent haste. And she had found more happiness in Canute's bed than ever with Ethelred. With Canute, Emma had been content and most of all, she had devoted herself to the advancement of her sons by him. The sons in exile in Normandy had been forgotten.

Godwin read the letter again and groaned inwardly. Harthacanute's death had shattered her. After the interlude of Harold Harefoot and his scheming bitch of a mother, the restoration of Harthacanute had heralded a new beginning for Emma. But instead, her last son had choked to death at a wedding feast without an heir. And of all the ironies, Edward Ethelredsson had returned, seemingly from the grave, to be king. All the while, Godwin had been too absorbed with securing his future and that of his sons to pay attention to the woman, twice widowed and so many hopes dashed.

'What would you counsel, my lord of Wessex?'

Godwin looked at the king and saw a grim hatred that made him flinch. A shadow of fear crossed his heart and he wondered if he had misjudged Edward dreadfully. Supporting Edward had allowed him to take the throne and bring his Norman lickspittles along, and the grant of an earldom to Swegn and Harold had been little more than an acknowledgement of the power that Godwin already wielded within England.

But what Godwin had wanted most from Edward's coronation had not yet been fulfilled: Edward's marriage to his daughter, Edith. It had been put off, Edward suggesting that they allow the girl to grow a little older before facing marriage, despite the fact that most girls were married off at fourteen. Godwin said: 'I would urge caution, sire, and restraint.'

'Restraint?' Edward's normally patient features darkened with rage. 'After what she has done, you ... you urge *restraint?*'

Godwin stepped back from the king's fury and heard Robert Champart snigger. He reddened, but Edward had not finished. 'She is my mother by Christ's cross and she urges – no, beseeches – Magnus of Norway to invade my kingdom in the name of some forgotten treaty made before Harthacanute was king of England.'

Godwin attempted to placate the king: 'Sire, I should think that the queen is upset over the death of her son and perhaps out of her wits – or was when the letter was written.'

'Just as she was when her beloved Canute died, eight years ago?' sneered Edward, rising from his chair. 'When she deserted me. Only when Harthacanute could not leave Denmark did she write to me and my brother. And we all know what the consequences of that were.'

A needle from the ladies' embroidery chamber could have dropped to the floor then, and all the men in the room would have heard it.

'Yes, we know what the consequences were. We remember Alfred,' Godwin tempered the anger in his voice, aware that he was on very dangerous ground. 'Are you suggesting the queen deliberately lured Alfred to his death?'

Edward hesitated, and in that moment Godwin wondered whether he would accuse Emma, maybe even Godwin, of complicity in Alfred's horrible death. 'No,' Edward said eventually, his anger abating at the sight of Godwin's tense white face and staring black eyes. He waved a casual hand and sat down again. 'No, of course not. But I cannot accept your counsel for restraint. She shall be deprived of all her lands, chattels and any treasure she might have secreted away from the royal coffers in Winchester. She shall be moved to honourable retirement, but her powers will be severely curtailed. My lords of Northumbria and Mercia, you shall accompany me to Winchester to arrest the queen. And you also, Godwin,' he added with a smile of triumph.

The tone was final and Godwin knew that it was the end for Emma. Never again would she advise, meddle or strive to hold sway in the court she had once dominated. And Godwin, if he were to remain in favour at court, would have to acquiesce in her downfall. But he needed to know one last thing. 'Sire, could you say how you came about this information?'

Edward said briefly: 'A cleric of hers wrote it – against his wishes, so he says. It was Stigand, bishop of Elmham.'

A hiss of indrawn breath followed this calm announcement that a bishop had been involved in the conspiracy. Harold knew Stigand, and had met him, as Elmham was near Norwich, in his earldom. Fat Stigand, with the narrow eyes; a clever man, clever enough to gain his reward from the queen – for he had been promoted at her insistence – before betraying his erstwhile mistress.

'He will be punished, naturally,' Edward was saying. 'Despite his honesty in handing over the information to me, a move which I suspect was done more in hope of self-advancement than fear of hellfire and damnation.' He chuckled softly, then clicked his fingers, serious again. 'My lords; prepare for the journey. We leave in the morning.'

*

Harold returned to the hall in a despondent mood. As a king's earl he had the right to counsel the king, and in doing so spent much of his time travelling with the king's court on its itinerary between London, Winchester, Oxford and Gloucester. On his estates in East Anglia, Harold had been blessed with honest reeves, in whose hands he was happy to leave the management of his lands while he followed the court and thought of Eadgyth.

Eadgyth. It was a rare day that passed without him thinking of her. They met every week, in secret, to talk and whisper of love, to kiss, but no more; she would not go to his bed. She feared God's wrath too much to commit adultery, and if she should conceive a child after years of a barren marriage to Thorgils, what then? Harold had listened, and agreed, frustrated beyond all belief. He wanted Eadgyth, but all he could do was profess his love, kiss her moist lips and leave with an ache in his groin. But at least the beatings and threats from Thorgils had ceased after the earl of Wessex had made it known that Eadgyth was under his and his son's protection. Thorgils had cursed and fumed and thrashed his servants, but surrendered to the Godwin family will.

It was in such a melancholy mood that Tostig found Harold, staring into the dead ashes of the previous night's fire whilst the servants cleared the tables around him. Slapping him on the back cheerfully, Tostig said: 'Who said that Judgement Day is nigh?' Tostig pealed with laughter and Harold had to smile at his infectious good-humour. 'Dear Harry, now that you are an earl, and wealthy with it, could you not see your way to lending me some money?'

Harold sighed and cast Tostig a look of exasperated affection. 'How much do you need now?'

Tostig jumped with delight, and said quickly:

'Five pounds?'

'Five pounds!' Harold exploded with exaggerated wrath. 'Sweet Jesus, a peasant could live on that for two lifetimes! I'll give you two pounds.'

'Three,' countered Tostig.

'Two,' Harold said again. 'And that's my final offer: take it or leave it.'

Tostig hesitated, then grinned sheepishly. 'I'll take it, thanks.'

Harold dug into his purse with much huffing and puffing and pulled out the coins. Two pounds was a fortune for a peasant, who would be lucky to earn as much in a lifetime of toil. Still, Harold could afford it; the money from the home farms on his estates provided him with plenty.

Tostig took the coins and grinned. 'I know that earls of the king don't normally play at knuckle bones or nine men's morris, but I'm sure you'll make an exception for me?' Harold bit back a curse at the boy's cheek, but his reply tailed off as he caught sight of a stocky fellow with greying hair approaching them. His appearance was familiar, but as yet, Harold could not place him.

'Are you Harold Godwinsson, earl of East Anglia?' asked the stranger.

'I am.'

At that, the man drew his sword in one swift movement.

Tostig reached for his own sword, shouting, 'How dare you draw your sword in the king's hall and before one of his earls?'

The older man didn't flinch.

'Stand aside, boy,' he said in a voice of crushed stone. 'I am Thorgils, thegn of Midhurst.' Too late, recognition flashed through Harold's mind. Too late, he stared white-faced at the tip of the blade held unwaveringly to his chest. The tip moved upwards and touched his neck. None of the nearby courtiers moved, shocked at what was happening.

Thorgils pressed the point of his sword onto Harold's neck, and smiled at the sight of Harold's obvious fear. He twisted the blade and broke the skin, so that a trickle of blood ran down onto Harold's shirt. Then he said: 'I have come to charge you, Harold Godwinsson, with the crime and sin of adultery with my wife. I demand a trial by battle before the king.'

*

Godwin approached the meeting with Queen Emma with mounting dread. The journey from Gloucester to Winchester had taken five days. Five days of ceaseless rain and mud. Mud was everywhere; in boots, in gloves, in the lining of breeches and in the backs of throats. Godwin was thankful to be dressed simply in rough hunting wear.

The hectic ride had begun smoothly enough. The straight Roman road took them to Cirencester, but after a short rest to change horses, Edward urged them on with a fierce energy Godwin had not seen in him before. But Godwin had fast begun to accept change in Edward, and knew that the king could be capable of anything in his current mood. The interminable rain left a grey mist hanging over them like a shroud wherever they went, occasionally bursting into a shower to bring steam off the sweating horses, and churning the roads into yet more mud. But the king seemed possessed by the devil and drove them relentlessly on, and his earls cursed the day Queen Emma ever thought to betray her son as the rain dripped mercilessly into their faces.

On the eve of the sixteenth, a fortnight before Saint Andrew's day, they drew the exhausted horses to a halt outside the hall in Winchester, shouting orders for a fire. Servants scurried, panic stricken at the presence of their king, to bring fresh rushes, dry wood, and to rouse the butchers from Fleshmonger Street to bring meat for the king.

Seated by a roaring fire after a meal of roasted beef, Edward was in no mood to relax. Even now, in this warmth and comfort, Godwin saw again the hatred in Edward's eyes and recalled his screaming, hectoring curses in the rain and mud on the road from Gloucester. Had Emma lured Alfred to his death that January day? She couldn't have known that the visit would end with his death, even if she had planned his capture. Or could she? And Edward had narrowly escaped with his life, otherwise both of them would be dead.

'We'll go now.' Edward's voice cut through the gentle hissing of the wet wood and broke into Godwin's thoughts.

'Surely, sire, it would be best to wait until the morning?' Leofric of Mercia was quicker than Godwin.

'We are tired, sire, and would like to rest.' Siward of Northumbria voiced his agreement with Leofric. 'Perhaps we should allow the queen time to prepare...'

'I do not think the queen should have time to prepare,' said Edward coldly. 'After all, she gave me no time to prepare – did she, my lords?'

Siward had no answer for that. Godwin stretched his legs and yawned. It was a long time since he was accustomed to making such journeys – not since the days of Canute. His mind wandered back to those days. There was a man born to lead, and a man for whom many would lay down their lives – and had done so.

One thing was for certain: Canute wouldn't have wasted his time chasing an old woman on a dark November night.

Edward waved his hand and a servant rushed forward with a finger-bowl. 'My lords,' he said, standing and drying his hands on the proffered towel. 'Come with me.' The earls stood with him, any question of disobedience stifled by the king's mood. Outwardly, they did not dare to disobey, but each cast weary glances at the other as, ignoring the aches and pains of the ride, they followed the king through the door.

The walk to Emma's house took five minutes, maybe less; Godwin was not sure, so swift was the king's anger. The queen's large, stone house was in the shadow of the Old Minster, and the church loomed large above them, casting a great shadow across their path in the pale moonlight. The street echoed to the tramp of their riding boots.

'Open the door!' Leofric hammered on the great oak door of the house with the pommel of his sword, the heavy blade glinting in the dark. The racket set off neighbouring dogs barking.

A small window in the door creaked open and a thin-faced servant peered out. 'Who are you to disturb the Queen Emma's residence at this hour?' he asked imperiously.

Edward stepped forward and pushed his face next to the door.

'I am your king.' The face behind the door turned white. 'Open this door now, or face the consequences.' The window closed and they heard bolts drawn and a shout within. Then the heavy door swung open and Edward pushed his way through into the hallway. 'Call my mother,' he said to the fellow, who was clad only in a nightshift, holding a candle.

'But she is abed, sire. I dare not wake her,' said the servant. The candle shook in the stand and Godwin thought that it would fall and plunge them into darkness.

Then Edward took two strides and seized the man by the scruff of the neck. 'You will do as I command,' he said, his voice cold with anger. He stepped back and drew his sword. The blade ripped from the scabbard with a piercing shriek in the room.

'Put down your weapon, Edward,' said a voice from the shadows. 'I will not have drawn swords in this house.'

Edward lowered the blade slowly as a figure emerged from the stairwell. 'Mother...?'

'What is it you want at this hour, Edward?' said Emma.

Edward slipped his sword back into its scabbard. 'You betrayed me,' he said simply. He held up the letter addressed to Magnus of Norway. 'This missive came into my hands recently.' He waved it at his mother, whose pale face registered growing horror in the light of the candle. 'You conspired to overthrow me from my rightful place on the throne in favour of a base-born Norwegian. You wanted to get rid of me. Your own son.'

Emma slumped to the ground with a short cry. Godwin stepped forward to assist her, but Edward's hand on his arm stopped him. The king did not go to her. Godwin stood with Leofric and Siward, silently cursing the king's intransigence. Godwin clenched his hands and felt the sweat run freely down his back. Jesus, had it come to this? Emma raised her eyes and met his stare. He held it fractionally, then looked away. Beautiful and clever, she had captivated hearts – not least his – but she had made enemies also and couldn't count on Siward or Leofric.

'Godwin...?' Emma's plea was but a distant echo of all that they had shared in twenty years.

But Godwin didn't answer. He was a survivor of that shared past, and to continue to survive, he must now choose the winning side.

Edward snorted derisively, knowing that he had won. 'You are guilty of conspiring to remove me from the throne and replace me with a usurper,' he said to his mother. 'I confiscate all lands and movables from you. They are to be given over to my keeping, along with all the treasure and money that you might have appropriated from the treasury here in Winchester. However,' he paused, glancing at Godwin, 'I shall not outlaw or exile you. You shall remain here on whatever small maintenance I shall see fit to provide, and you shall no longer participate in public life. Madame, you are no longer welcome at my court.'

Emma bowed her head and gave out a low groan. She would no longer be known as the king's mother, she would not witness his charters and would have no influence in court. It was the end. Now she had noone to turn to. She was totally alone. 'How did you know?' she asked in a whisper.

Edward, turning to go, paused and shot his mother a contemptuous glare. 'Your cleric,' he said. 'Your chosen confidant: Stigand.' At Emma's sob of despair, Godwin felt another wrench of pity at this cruellest blow and the dismissive manner of its telling. 'He shall be deposed from his post as soon as the court ratifies the confiscation of your property,' said the king, turning to his waiting earls. 'Come,' he said. 'We have finished here.' And with that, he walked through the door without a backward glance.

Daring to cast Emma a quick look of heart-felt sympathy before he followed Edward into the dark night, Godwin thought, 'Please God I don't fall foul of him.' *Please God.'*

Chapter Seven
London, February 1044

The king approved Thorgils' claim for a trial by combat.

The law stated that any man with an accusation of murder, robbery, rape or adultery, and who could produce witnesses, could present his case to the king in one of several ways. He could demand a payment of a fine, equal to the defendant's rank, or he could demand a trial. There were three different trials: trial by water, where the defendant had to seize a stone from a cauldron of boiling water and walk three yards with it. If, after three days, there was still blistering on his hand, he was deemed guilty in the eyes of God. Trial by fire involved the defendant crossing a path of burning coals bare-footed; if his feet remained blistered after three days, he was guilty. Trial by combat was the third and ultimate trial, whereby the accuser would fight the defendant to the death; if the defendant was innocent, then God would protect him and strike down the accuser.

Godwin couldn't believe that Edward would consent to Thorgils' claim to a trial by combat. It was an ancient custom, but one that extended back into a more barbarous age, before the days of King Alfred. Most disputes were now settled by the oaths of witnesses. Failing that, heavy fines were imposed, or even exile. A fight to the death these days was almost unheard of. Canute had preferred to take large fines and enrich the royal treasury rather than encourage bloodshed – legal or otherwise – amongst his subjects.

Harold was unperturbed by the danger. 'If the king wishes us to fight, then we shall,' he said. 'I am not guilty; I have done no more than kiss Eadgyth. I know that God will support me and that I shall defeat Thorgils.'

Godwin was taken aback by his son's calm confidence. 'But you're a boy, a lad of only seventeen summers. Thorgils is a grown man, and has been in battle against the Welsh, and fought in Canute's service –'

'He is old and will not survive such a pace that I shall set.' Harold flashed his father a grin, but the earl was not convinced. 'Why couldn't you leave the girl alone? Why did you become involved? If it had been Swegn, I'd have expected it, but you...'

Harold's grin faded as he saw the look in Godwin's eye. It was a look of disappointment; he'd let his father and the family down. 'But why has the king supported Thorgils' claim for a trial by battle against me?' he asked. 'You said he needed our support when he became king.'

'Because, boy,' said Godwin wearily, 'I have misjudged him. I saw him bring down his mother – he did it himself, and I believe he enjoyed it. I swear I've not seen so much hate in a man for years. He's not the man I thought he was. He's unpredictable – dangerous, even – and driven to harshness by the years of exile.' Godwin laid a hand on Harold's shoulder. 'I fear that he is using this as a means of getting to me – to us. Thorgils is a man of no standing in the court and Edward knows that he cannot be accused of taking sides because Thorgils is not *his* man, in the way that Robert Champart is. But he can use Thorgils to attack us. I'll see the king and ask him to change his mind. A fine will do.'

'But I am innocent,' Harold protested hotly.

'Aye, lad, perhaps you are, but there are other men on this earth who are not so trusting.'

'Men such as...?'

Godwin looked grim. 'Robert Champart. I'll wager he's the man behind all this.'

Godwin saw the king again, but Edward refused to change his ruling. By the ancient law of the land, Thorgils was within his rights to make a claim, and supported by witnesses who had seen Harold with Eadgyth. Edward could not deny such a right. Godwin offered money, much money, but the king was not to be moved. It would be a trial by battle and God would favour the innocent man.

'But the boy's a stripling; an untried youth. You cannot put him against a hardened warrior like Thorgils!' Godwin exploded on realising the full extent of the king's stubbornness. 'Let me fight for the boy – I'll champion him.'

But Edward shook his head. 'Thorgils has put forward no man to champion himself, so the law does not allow the defendant to nominate a champion, either.'

'He'll kill my boy!'

Edward pursed his lips. 'That is for God to decide.'

The interview was over, and Godwin bowed and left the room shaking with anger. There was still a chance that Thorgils' witnesses wouldn't come forward, or if they did, then their evidence would be discredited. The court was alive with rumour, the courtiers unable to digest the speed of events. First the destruction of Queen Emma, and now this. Godwin was aware of the many eyes on him as he strode through the outer chamber from the king's private rooms.

Were they watching and waiting for the king to bring down Earl Godwin himself?

Godwin was certain that Edward wanted him to defy the royal demand by favouring Harold. He could not allow himself to be provoked. And besides, if he defied the king now, he would put the wedding with Edith in jeopardy. Harold would have to take his chance. He was a man now, and the time had come to prove it.

'I did all that I could,' he said firmly to Gytha. 'But Edward was set on it. It's his opportunity to tempt me into defiance and allow him the chance to attack my position at court. He has got rid of his mother, and he means to put me down, either by inviting rebellion or...by the death of one of my sons.'

As he spoke, Godwin saw real fear fill Gytha's eyes. 'You cannot allow this,' she said fiercely. 'You must put a stop to it –'

'How? By rebellion....?'

'If needs be – yes.'

Godwin shook his head. Taking Gytha's hand in his, he said gently, 'Do you think I have not considered that? If I defied the king and called out my army, then nobody – nobody – would stand by me. Most people of the court see this as a private quarrel; they are only intrigued that it is to be trial by combat, but do not have the wit to realise that it runs deeper than that. The king is testing me.'

'So Harry will fight?'

'Yes.'

Gytha shook her head, refusing to accept Godwin's logic. 'Can we not persuade him to plead guilty and pay a fine? It does not matter how large.'

'He will not plead guilty. He says adamantly that he is innocent. And the king will do more than fine him; he will exile him and he'll not stop at that.' Godwin pulled Gytha close to him. 'There is still a chance that Thorgils' witnesses will back down and that his case will collapse. We must hope for that.'

*

The trial was set for 18th March. The king remained resolutely opposed to changing his mind, and the atmosphere at court quickly reached hysteria pitch as the rumours flew about in contradictory circles.

Harold remained calm. He prepared in his own way for the coming fight, ordering the armourer to fashion a new coat of mail – a byrnie – and a helmet fitted with a nasal-guard with a leather breastplate made to measure to wear beneath the byrnie. With Tostig, he practised swordplay by day, and at night prayed to God as he had never done before.

The day of the trial dawned bright and cold; there was a frost underfoot which showed little sign of thawing. Harold dressed carefully, attended by Tostig and Leofgar, and went down into the hall after breakfasting on cold sucking pig and ale. Godwin and Gytha were waiting for him; his father was grim and businesslike, his mother pale and silent.

'You'll know what to do, boy?'

Harold nodded. Godwin, famed for his skill with the sword and axe in his youth, had trained all his sons, and taught them all he knew. Harold was a quick learner, dextrous and strong with it.

'Get him on the ground and finish him,' Godwin went on. 'It's brute strength that wins a fight such as this. Strike his sword from his hand and kick him to the ground.' The earl leant forward and rasped: 'Have no mercy, my boy. Finish him when the time comes, else he'll be up and he'll kill you first.'

Harold nodded, and accepted the cup of wine Godwin thrust into his hand. The liquid was warm and spicy and spread like a fire through his body. He drained the cup and felt a surge of confidence. 'I am innocent,' he grinned, 'I cannot lose.'

Harold glanced at his mother, and the smile died on his lips. She seemed grey and worn, and he belatedly realised a little of what she had suffered these past weeks. 'God is on my side, so I shall return.' He stooped and kissed Gytha on the cheek, and followed his father into the yard, where the horses were waiting.

The trial was due to take place in the king's courtyard by the palace, but before that, there were the oaths to be sworn. The royal hall was already packed when the Godwin party arrived. Thorgils was standing in the corner, well-armed and grimly professional. There were no women present in the hall. Harold's chest tightened at the sight of the councillors and courtiers, who fell silent at their entrance, reducing their loud speculation to whispered comments in huddled groups. They were looking at him, Harold realised, with sympathy and pity, and it struck him then that most of them did not believe that he would defeat Thorgils. A sudden anger rose within him, and he set his jaw: with God's grace, he would not die today, as they thought he would.

The king called them to order and commanded the claimants to step forward. He asked in ringing tones whether they still held true to their original oaths of accusation and denial. Thorgils swore loudly that he did, and when Edward turned to Harold, Harold said in a steady voice:

'I swear by Almighty God on the True Cross that I am innocent of the crime I am accused of.'

A murmur like a breath of wind passed through the hall. Tense and expectant, the courtiers knew that Harold had forfeited one of his last chances to avoid the fight. By admitting his guilt, he could have paid a heavy fine, or even lost his estates and faced exile, but at least he would have avoided the death most people felt was coming to him. The only hope left now in the Godwin camp was that Thorgils' witnesses might prove weak and unconvincing enough to force the king to drop the case.

'Bring in the first witness,' said Edward from the dais, unmoved by Harold's bold statement.

The first witness was an old retainer of Thorgils', who swore that he had seen Harold and Eadgyth making love in Thorgils' own bed. The crowd groaned with horror, and there were some sniggers. Then a neighbouring thegn of Midhurst stepped forward and denounced the witness as half-blind and said that he had, in fact, left Thorgils' service two years ago. General laughter followed this, and Thorgils seized the old man and pulled him away, indignant and embarrassed.

The next two witnesses were both maids who also swore that they had seen Harold with Eadgyth in an intimate embrace. But, following the old man's discredited evidence, the council were not inclined to believe the word of two girls in Thorgils' pay.

'Call the last witness,' said Edward, visibly annoyed by the reception Thorgils' witnesses were having.

'You'll not fight,' said Godwin to Harold, brimming with confidence. 'The king can't possibly pronounce a trial on the basis of these witnesses. The council simply won't have it.'

But Harold didn't share his father's confidence. 'Wait a moment. Let's see what the last witness has to say before we can be sure of that.'

The doors at the far end opened, everyone craned their necks to see who it was, and when it became apparent, a shout of horror passed through the crowd; all pretence of disinterest was abandoned, for suddenly the trial had assumed a far greater importance than before.

The last witness was Swegn.

Harold thought that it was a mistake. The last witness couldn't be Swegn; he'd just walked in late, in his usual fashion, pushing to the front to see what was happening. But then the king was saying: 'Do you stand witness for Thorgils in this case?' and Swegn was nodding, and swearing the oath, and Harold knew that it was no mistake. Swegn had lusted after Eadgyth all along, and as he couldn't have her, because she wanted his younger brother instead, he was siding with Thorgils.

'Sire, I protest!' Godwin started forward to the dais. 'Swegn cannot possibly stand as a witness.'

'Whyever not?' asked Edward coldly.

'Sire...it is obvious that Swegn is jealous and driven by self-interest to antagonise his brother.' Godwin's voice was tight, and barely contained his anger. 'Let me deal with him outside this court. It is a family matter and cannot be part of this trial.'

There were no cheers following Godwin's plea, only a doubtful silence. The courtiers, Harold realised, wanted to hear what Swegn had to say and the king, enjoying Godwin's discomfort, was going to let them.

'It makes no difference to me or the court what goes on behind closed doors in the Godwin household,' said Edward. 'But this is my court and I see no reason why Earl Swegn should not give his testimony with the other witnesses Thorgils has called.' He nodded to Swegn, who cleared his throat and held his head up high, announcing, 'It is my regrettable duty to report, in all honesty, that I have indeed seen Harold with the wife of Thorgils, who is called Eadgyth, I believe –'

'As you damned well know!' shouted Godwin.

'– and Harold has told me himself that he has made a cuckold of Thorgils more than once,' Swegn continued as if Godwin had not interrupted.

'You swear that is the truth?' said Edward.

'It is,' said Swegn. 'I swear it on the True Cross.'

'You liar!' Godwin, unable to contain himself any longer, thrust forward and seized his son by the scruff of the neck and shook him violently. 'Curse you, Swegn. You're lying. Harry, tell him he's lying!'

The court, shocked to silence by Swegn's damning evidence, looked at Harold with bated breath.

'He's lying,' said Harold. Contempt welled up inside him and pushed aside the fear, and he drew himself up and looked down at Swegn, but Swegn avoided his gaze. 'My brother lies; I insist on my innocence in this accusation.'

Edward turned to Swegn and said: 'Do you stand by your testimony?' Swegn nodded, flinching at Godwin's hiss of rage. 'Then I have no choice but to commit this case to trial,' continued Edward.

A flutter of satisfaction passed through the watching crowd; they would, after all, have their fight today.

Godwin shot Swegn a withering look of contempt and pushed him aside. 'Well, boy,' he said to Harold. 'Your brother has decreed that you shall fight today, God rot him.'

The hall was fast emptying now, as the councillors and courtiers made their way to the yard, where a timber platform had been erected for the king and his councillors to sit upon. Godwin propelled Harold along with the jostling crowd. 'Thorgils is an old man, and is governed by his anger. You stay calm and wait for him to come to you; he'll make a mistake and then you'll have him.'

Outside the air was cold and clear, and seemed unsuited to a killing. Harold breathed in deeply, and stretched his arms, flexing the weight of the sword in his right hand. 'I must go to the king. Remember: wait for him to come to you.' He grasped Harold's arm briefly and marched off through the crowd.

'Watch the ground, Harry.' Tostig was beside Harold. 'It's somewhat slippery now the frost has thawed a little.'

'Let him come to you and kick his sword from his grip,' added Leofgar. 'Give him no mercy; he won't give you any.'

While they were talking, the crowd had formed a rough circle in the yard, with the king at one end. At the base of the platform, Thorgils was adjusting the thongs to his boots, attended by his men. The king, Godwin alongside him, sat silently above the hubbub. Of Swegn, there was no sign.

Then Edward rose, and a hush fell upon the excited crowd.

'The right of trial by single combat is an ancient one and today, in the sight of God, we shall see justice done. He who dies today is guilty in God's eyes; guilty either of of bringing slanderous, false accusations, or of committing the sin of adultery with another man's wife, which, as we know, was forbidden by the Church Fathers and is condemned by the scriptures. Let the trial commence.'

Harold swallowed the bile rising in his throat; his heart thudded thunderously beneath the byrnie. He was grateful when Tostig squeezed his arm, saying, 'Fight for Eadgyth. Give her freedom after this day.'

It was the right thing to say. Harold, fired by the memory of Eadgyth's plea for help, stepped into the ring full of fighting fury. The man who called himself her husband would be punished for the pain he had caused her. Thorgils, seeing Harold was ready and waiting, also stepped into the ring, his face twisted with an ugly menace. But he was not holding a sword, as Harold expected. Instead, he wielded a great double-headed axe, and raised it defiantly at Harold.

Harold didn't falter. Behind him, Tostig shouted that it would not be a fair fight, but someone – Harold thought it was Robert Champart – replied that it was within the rules. Tostig cursed, and retreated into the crowd.

Thorgils had taken up his stance, two yards from Harold, but Harold waited for him to come forward, as Godwin had suggested, and he did, hefting the axe from hand to hand. He moved round, and the two circled one another, watching like wary dogs eyeing each other for the first bite. The ground beneath them crunched, and Harold remembered Tostig's warning. The yard was paved with cobblestones, but the passage of many horses in and out of the king's palace had loosened them over the years, leaving treacherous pools of icy water where the stones had gone.

The axe came down before Harold could sidestep, and missed his ear by an inch. It hit the cobbles with a clang and was up again in a flash, ready for the next strike. Any thoughts of a fair trial were quickly forgotten as the crowd bayed for blood, their initial suspicions confirmed: the Godwin boy stood no chance.

Harold almost agreed with them. Thorgils had moved so fast that he'd not seen the axe until it was too late, and then the older man was on guard before he could counter-attack. Harold stepped back a little, suddenly claustrophobic in this enclosure of men, mouths agape, eyes staring, all of them screaming and baying like hounds in on the kill. Harold took another step, saw Thorgils raise his arm, and then

Harold slipped on a patch of frost and crashed to the ground.

Harold heard the roar of the crowd and rolled to the right. The axe-blade, fractionally slower this time, banged again on the cobbles, and Harold was up, breathing hard, facing Thorgils.

Thorgils was in a killing-mood now, and sensed victory, angry that he had not already despatched Harold. He came forward again, swinging the axe impatiently. Harold dodged it, but sensed the crowd pressing forward somewhere behind him, and knew that he could go no further. Thorgils swung again, but Harold was ready this time and ducked the blade, thrusting out his sword at the same time. Thorgils, taken aback by the sudden counter-attack, jumped back, and Harold pushed forward again, gaining the lost ground, and they were back where they had begun, panting with effort.

With Godwin's voice in his head – *stay calm and wait for him* – Harold stood his ground and caught his breath. But Thorgils could stand no more. With a loud cry, he raised the axe again and thundered forward. Glimpsing the spittle on his chin, and the vein throbbing on his forehead, Harold knew that this was his moment. The axe came down, but Harold's long sword flickered forward and met Thorgils' chest. It stopped him dead, crunching through mail, leather, skin and bone, such was the impetus of Thorgils' charge. Harold wrenched the point of the blade clear and Thorgils held the axe above his head for several seconds before releasing it.

'*Finish him, boy!*'

Godwin was standing on the dais, screaming above the roar of the crowd. Thorgils, one hand searching for the long dagger at his belt, the other pressed to his chest in an attempt to stop the blood spurting through, staggered back, stumbling on the treacherous ground.

Harold needed no second bidding. Raising his sword, he thrust it towards Thorgils' neck, seeking out the unprotected flesh, found it, and rammed the blade home. With a scream that became a gurgle, Thorgils flailed at the blade with helpless hands before crashing to the ground, twitched once, and lay still.

It was over.

Harold sank to his knees and sobbed with exhaustion. Hands seized him and hauled him to his feet, cheering, and Tostig was beside him, shouting his relief. The crowd parted at the sight of Godwin descending from the dais.

'Well done, boy,' he rasped.

Harold was surprised to see tears pouring down his father's face.

'I thought I'd lost you there, boy.' Godwin embraced him tightly. It did not have to be this way; Thorgils could have changed his claim, or the king could have refused it. The king should have refused it. God damn Edward.

The courtiers fell silent as the king rose from his chair and waved for silence.

'God has given Harold Godwinsson the victory today. I pronounce him innocent of the charges against him.'

Seeing the king's face a mask of tight fury as he slumped back into his seat, Harold knew that Godwin had been right all along: Edward had hoped for his death today, but Harold's unexpected victory had ruined all his plans.

Godwin noted Harold's look, and gave his son a wary nod. 'Come on, lad. We must go to your mother; she'll be frantic with worry now.'

They pushed through the cheering crowd, who only minutes before had bayed for Harold's death, and went to their horses, not seeing in the crush, the black look of hatred set on Robert Champart's face.

Gytha knew by the way Godwin walked through the door. With his nod of confirmation, she rushed out to the yard to where Harold was dismounting.

'Mother!' He took her in his arms and held her shaking frame close. 'I am alive, mother – Thorgils is dead.'

Gytha steadied herself and allowed Harold to walk her to the hall. 'Swegn stood witness against me, mother,' he said when they were by the fire. 'He lied, and said that he knew I had committed adultery with Eadgyth.'

'Swegn....?' Gytha was shocked out of her tears of relief. 'Swegn betrayed you at the court?'

'Yes, mother. I am so sorry.'

Gytha looked to Godwin, who saw by the look of disbelief on her face that she expected him to deny it.

'It is true, my love,' he said gently. 'Swegn did stand testimony against Harry, God strike him dead for it.'

'Mary, mother of God,' said Gytha, shaking her head. 'My own son. Brother against brother. How could he, knowing that Harry faced mortal combat?'

Godwin shrugged. 'He wanted the girl for himself, lusts after her, but she has eyes only for Harry –'

'If he touches a hair on her head,' said Harold. 'I'll kill him.'

'No!' said Gytha fiercely, not doubting the sincerity of Harold's threat. 'I'll not have my sons take up arms against one another. Promise me that, Harry.'

But Godwin spoke first. 'It is an unfair promise for the boy to make, given Swegn's treachery today.

However –' he held up a hand before Gytha could protest, '– I must say this, Harry. I forbid you to see the girl for a year – in public, at least. The king will be furious that you won today, and we cannot allow him another opportunity to bring us down.'

Harold gaped in dismay. He'd won today, killed Thorgils in fair fight with the aid of God. Hadn't he earned the right to take Eadgyth for himself?

'It would look bad if you took Eadgyth immediately after killing her husband,' said Godwin. 'You must wait.' Then he added, gently, 'I'll ensure Swegn goes nowhere near the lass.'

Harold could see the awful logic of it. Curse Swegn. And curse the king, too.

'One thing is certain from today's events,' continued Godwin. 'Swegn is no longer welcome here. At least in that respect Edward has succeeded in dividing us, God damn his soul.'

Chapter Eight
London, January 1045

Gytha entered her bower with a sense of foreboding. Godwin lay on her bed, half-dressed and half-asleep, murmuring into the pillow. He gave a start when he saw her and smiled a lazy smile as she climbed onto the bed and knelt at his side.

'He does nothing, curse him.' Godwin spoke into the pillow. Gytha poured some oil into the palm of her hand and began to rub the back of Godwin's neck vigorously.

'Who, my love? Who does nothing?' she asked between rubs.

'The king. The king pursues a policy of no policy.'

Gytha understood the scattered line of her husband's reasoning. It was well known that the king opposed Godwin's view that Svein of Denmark should be supported with ships and men from England to fight Magnus and prevent him from invading England. 'He has no love of England's Danish heritage,' she said whilst continuing to massage the muscles in Godwin's neck.

'He cares not for my nephew Svein, and does not believe that Magnus is trying to emulate Canute and rebuild the mighty Scandinavian empire. All he cares for is his Norman friends.' Godwin snorted into the pillow. 'Have you finished, woman?' Gytha gave up her attempts on Godwin's back as he rolled over and began to lambast Edward's favourite courtiers. Robert Champart had been promoted to the bishopric of London last year; Herman, a cleric from Lotharingia, was soon to become bishop of Wiltshire, and Stigand had been forgiven and reinstated for his part in Queen Emma's treachery. 'I did not even like Stigand,' Godwin was saying. 'To betray the queen in the way he did...such a man could be capable of anything.' Godwin ignored Gytha's hand stroking his hair. 'As for Champart, that man's odious and the king heeds his words too much.'

'We should be happy, love,' Gytha spoke into his ear. 'Our daughter is wife to the king and she will wield some influence over him.'

Godwin grunted. At last, Edith had been married to the king, and would get with child soon enough. She was a forceful girl, too, and would not be content to be a mere ornament in the king's court. She would have her say, and she would stand by her father. Any son of hers would be king, and that meant Godwin's grandson would be king of England one day. 'There is much to be happy about,' Gytha bent and kissed his brow. 'Swegn and Harry are earls of the king; Edith is his wife and your nephew Beorn will be made earl this year – the king has promised.'

Godwin sighed. 'You are right as ever.'

'Make love to me,' she whispered in his ear, her breathing uneven and rapid. 'Now. I want you now.' Her hand moved along his chest and down to his legs. With a slight shock she noticed for the first time how grey the hair was at his temples. But there was still plenty of time. Plenty of time.

When Swegn told Edith of Godwin's plans to marry her to the king, the whole world as she knew it changed in one moment. At first, she was unsure whether Swegn was telling the truth, as he was drunk, and may well have been lying, as he usually did, whether drunk or sober. She had sat in total silence after he'd gone, oblivious to the singing and dancing all around her. It was not such an impossibility to think that Swegn was right. Indeed, a plan like this bore the indelible stamp of her father's mind. It was just like Godwin to dream up such a plan, so that his grandson would be a king. She had looked at Edward on the dais, and remembered how dignified and saintly he had been in the church before the feast. But he was old – forty, at least. But then, he *was* the king. And to be queen of England and mother to the future king...

Now, though, lying in pampered luxury, Edith thought back to that day with bitter regret at ever having entertained such high hopes. Eighteen months after Swegn had told her the news, and just over a week after the wedding, the truth about Edward was all too apparent to her. He might be a king, and king of England, of the line that bore Alfred and Egbert, but he was a cold and distant man, set in his ways – which were more Norman-French than English – and worst of all, he had shunned her bed.

Get with child, Godwin had said, the morning of the wedding. *Get his seed inside you and you shall bear the heir to the throne of England.* It would not only be Godwin's salvation and England's too – for the people would wholeheartedly welcome an heir – but it would be hers. A baby would be hers; her flesh and blood. It would be a release from this cold and empty household, where the king sat in the shadows and whispered French out of Godwin's sight.

'My child, you have been weeping.'

Edith quickly dried her eyes and straightened her wimple. 'I – I did not hear you come in, Edward.' He always moved as stealthily as a cat, as if he suspected her, creeping into her bower in his soft leather shoes. So different from the boisterous heartiness of her brothers.

'You should rest, my dear. It has been an eventful few days.' Edward bent and brushed his lips against her forehead in a paternal gesture. Edith fought the desire to recoil, and let him do it; it was the only physical contact they had.

'I do feel a little unwell.'

She settled against the pillows and hoped he would go. Strange that he could be so calm and yet exhibit such a rage against his mother. The events of the November night in Winchester were familiar to the court, and only served to make Edith more uncomfortable at his quiet calm. Such a man was unpredictable.

Edward flashed an awkward smile at her and clenched his hands behind his back. She looked out of the window and took a sweetmeat from the bowl at her bedside.

'My Lord.'

They both turned to see who was at the door, each glad of a diversion. Robert Champart stood there, head bowed, awaiting the king's pleasure.

'So, Robert, what is it?' Edward slipped into Norman-French quite naturally. Indeed, he spoke it better than English after twenty-eight years in Normandy. His English remained hesitant, and often he would exaggerate that hesitancy to confound his English councillors, particularly Godwin, who spoke only Danish after his native English.

'My Lord, I am sorry...but there are some letters. They are very important, I think.'

'Thank you, Robert. Wait one moment.' The relief was plain to see in Edward's face as Champart bowed and left the room. He turned to Edith, speaking in English: 'I'm so sorry, my dear, but I must go.'

'Must you?' Edith had a good grasp of French and knew exactly what Champart had said. She took another sweetmeat.

Edward shrugged. 'Business of state. I am sorry.'

'Are you? Perhaps some other time.'

Edward kissed her cold hand and left as silently as he had came.

Edith wiped her hand and swallowed the sweetmeat. Marchpane – her favourite. At least it had been once in happier days than these. Hers had been a rich and privileged upbringing and the best had been expected for her. She had the best now, and she hated it. She hated Edward, who was old and indifferent and schemed against her father. She hated Robert Champart, now the bishop of London, and she feared him. She did not fear Edward, but Robert Champart was evil and looked at her with an unashamed lust that did not befit a man of the church – or indeed any man, whatever his station. Edith knew that his hatred of Godwin was even greater than Edward's. She knew because she heard them whispering their plans in French which they thought she did not understand. Like every educated noblewoman, Edith had been taught classic French, Latin and, at Gytha's insistence, a little Danish. She had no trouble adapting to the Norman-French that Robert Champart spoke, and thus she learnt of his naked ambition; to destroy the power of the house of Godwin and then to become archbishop of Canterbury, a position of enormous power and influence from where he would even aspire to rule the kingdom. For Champart used the king, flattered him with sweet words about Normandy, foisted Norman clerics into the king's chapel and swayed Edward against the advisors in the great council. The man was evil and very clever with it.

Just then, Harold swept into the room and all her dark thoughts were banished.

'Harry!'

Edith jumped off the bed and ran to her brother.

'How are you, sweet sister?' Then Edith felt Harold's strong arms circle her waist and she burst into tears.

*

To Harold, Edith's marriage to the king was ironic. It was the culmination of Godwin's plans, part of the bargain that had put Edward on the throne and in return had sealed the power of the house of Godwin as the highest in the land. But Harold, watching Edith at the altar with Edward, felt a heart-wrench of jealousy. He would give all he possessed to stand at the altar with another Eadgyth, his Eadgyth. It was ironic that Edward was marrying an Edith that he did not know or love, while Harold could not marry the Eadgyth he did love.

Since the trial by battle with Thorgils, he had seen her only once. Harold, sent off on errand after errand to keep him occupied, could only communicate to Eadgyth through a faithful servant who carried their letters from Southwark to Midhurst. Any protests from Harold to his father fell on deaf ears. Godwin would not jeopardise his position at court merely because his son refused to satisfy his lust elsewhere.

At the sight of his sister, all Harold's jealousy dissolved. 'Jesus - has he been beating you?' He stroked her hair.

'I wish he would,' Edith sobbed into his tunic. Harold, perplexed by this show of abject misery, offered a kerchief. 'He does not touch me at all. He does not love me; he is cold,' she said between blowing her nose and drying her eyes.

'You mean...you mean the marriage is not yet consummated?' Harold asked incredulously.

'Yes.'

'Did you refuse him? You are not –'

'I am not cold to him, Harry, if that is what you are trying to say.' Edith had regained some of her composure and considered her brother's disbelief. 'I know that father told me in his crude, inimitable way, to get with child, to get Edward's seed inside me. But on our wedding night, he did not come to my chamber, so I went to his.' Edith's mouth twisted into a bitter smile. 'Do you know what he was doing, Harry?' Harold shook his head. 'He was playing dice, Harry; dice, for God's sake. On his wedding night!'

Harold frowned. What kind of a wedding night was that?

'And do you know what he said when I came in, Harry?' Edith continued, tears welling up in her eyes. 'He said he would not lie with the slut who was the fruit of Godwin's loins. He said he would rather...' Edith stifled a sob and struggled to speak.

'Go on,' said Harold gently. The tears had washed away the last of her face cream and lip-rouge ran across her cheek like a blood-smear.

'He said he would rather...rut with a whore than with Godwin's offspring.'

'My God.'

Harold held the girl tight as she broke into fresh tears. What kind of a man was Edward? He was no man at all to turn on his mother and dispossess her of all her worldly goods – they all knew of that – and now to wreak his revenge on Godwin by shunning his daughter's marital bed; a bitter and cunning revenge on the man who'd thought to have a grandson as king of England. He was no man, this. A returned exile, more French than English, a man without honour. A man without a soul.

'You must bear up, sister.' Harold spoke into her neck. 'You are the queen and Edward's wife. Nothing can change that, now.'

Edith drew back and nodded slowly. 'It is what I have concluded these past few days. I must make the best of it.'

Harold held her close again, marvelling at her resolve and quiet determination. Truly, Edward did not appreciate what a wife he had.

'All he does is talk in whispers to his foreign friends,' she said. 'You know that Robert Champart aims to be no less than the next archbishop of Canterbury?'

Harold nodded. 'Aye; he wears his ambition like a diadem, that one. He is Edward's evil genius.'

'But archbishop Eadsige will live a while yet?'

'He might have a few years left,' said Harold, 'but not many.'

'You won't tell father that Edward has not lain with me?'

Harold looked at Edith's pleading face and saw her fears. He shook his head. 'I won't tell father, but the truth will come out eventually. When he knows...'

'Will he blame me?'

'Not if I tell him what you have just told me. You're his dearest child and he'll always love you. On that score you have nothing to fear. But you will have to suffer Edward as your husband. Nothing can change that.'

Edith gave a wan smile. 'I know that. I will bear it as best I can.'

Harold kissed her cheek. 'Send for me or Tostig if you need us – we will do what we can.' *Which is very little*, he thought privately. And as he left the royal palace a thought struck him with a sudden force. Edward wasn't really a changed man; it was just that they hadn't known him before. And now they knew what he was, they wished they did not.

*

That summer saw the threat of invasion from Norway grow ever more apparent. The king took personal command of the fleet at Sandwich in June and held court at Winchester. Harold, when not required in the king's presence, often stayed at Godwin's hall at Guildford. Godwin had made his home the centre of the various activities of his sons, where he encouraged them to learn the rules of court and the machinations of government rather than waste time in the shires passing judgement on a poor peasant who'd stolen a neighbour's chicken. Find a good reeve, he said, and delegate the business of the lands to him. As long as he was not too corrupt – and they were all corrupt in some way – all would be well. Harold had done this and consequently spent much time at Godwin's side. He had few qualms about his absence from East Anglia; it was a dull, flat country, and the people were surly and indifferent. Cold winds blew across the sea from Russia beyond Norway, and on a winter's evening, Harold could well believe it. Longing for the warm, rolling countryside of his native Sussex, he left as often as possible for Guildford. Eadgyth was another reason why he came to Guildford: it was only a day's ride from Midhurst on the South Downs.

As for Swegn, he had few qualms about anything. He used his lands to fill his own coffers and then spent freely on his retinue, which consisted almost entirely of dissolute sons of noblemen and hired mercenaries.

The weeks leading to the end of July had been tense, with the king daily expecting an invasion from Magnus. The five ports of Sandwich, Rye, Hastings, Winchelsea and Romney were on constant watch and the king grew more and more irritable and irrational. The atmosphere in court frequently turned nasty as the invasion threat fuelled the hatred between Godwin and the bishop of London. Godwin continued to urge active support for his nephew, Svein, in Denmark, but the king would not hear of it, even though it might force Magnus to pull back.

Most worrying of all was that Robert Champart, who was now openly flouting his Norman lineage, backed the king and usually had the final word.

*

'Harry! Harry! A letter for you!'

It was a day when Harold had escaped the intense politics of the royal court at Winchester for the solitude of the fields around Guildford and Tostig found him in the shade of the great tree they had always sought during their childhood years.

It was not so much a letter as a short note, and Harold gave a grunt of alarm as he read it.

Come to Midhurst, for I have word that your brother Swegn is in the area and may come visiting. Eadgyth.

'What will you do?'

Harold regarded Tostig's eager face. He'd caught the sun, and there were freckles on his nose. 'It doesn't seem urgent,' he said slowly, 'but I'll go all the same.'

'And the king?'

Harold sighed. If the king summoned him now and he was away, and if Magnus should invade, then he could face exile for his disobedience. And Godwin would lose all sympathy with him, for he had forbidden his son to see Eadgyth again. 'Is Cousin Beorn on his way here?' he asked.

'He's expected in a few days' time,' said Tostig. 'He's still at Bedford, attending his new lands.' Beorn's earldom consisted of Bedfordshire and Hertfordshire, and his promotion had done much to restore the balance at court in Godwin's favour, much to the annoyance of Robert Champart.

'Do one thing for me, could you, Tostig?'

Tostig smiled.

'Anything for you, dear brother.'

'Could you ride ahead to meet Beorn and tell him to cover my duties? If the king should require my presence, say I am sick.'

'You are going to Midhurst, then?' Tostig's freckled face was serious. Harold nodded. 'Be careful. These are dangerous times.'

Harold grasped his brother's shoulder. 'I shall be careful.'

He was careful enough to take with him ten housecarls. Trained soldiers, loyal and tough, natives of Sussex, they gave him comfort, and he knew them all; their wives and children, their mistresses and their problems. But it was strange to ride through the countryside with an armed escort. He did not usually do so; England was a peaceful land, not like Denmark, where there was constant war with

Norway, or like the duchy of Normandy, where neighbour killed neighbour in the horror of civil war in the absence of a grown duke to govern them.

Tostig was right, though: these were dangerous times. In the fever of fear that swept the countryside, rumours of invasion were rife, and it was said that armed bandits terrorised the land while the earl of Wessex was away guarding the seaways with the king. Not least, Harold thought grimly when a smith recounted this latest tale, Swegn and his hired killers.

They arrived at noon the day after they'd left Guildford. The journey had been hot and dusty and the housecarls, like all good soldiers, saw that the horses received water before they did. Leaving them by the duckpond in the centre of the village, Harold walked alone to Eadgyth's house, set back behind the little church. Aside from the buzzing of the bees, the still air carried no sound. The house seemed all but deserted and fear gripped him. Was it a trap? But a trap set by whom? Thorgils was dead, long dead, and killed by him, Harold Godwinsson, in fair fight before the king and God. He had killed no man before and no man since. Murder was a sin and he had committed murder, even though God had willed it. Harold pulled at the leather body armour that chafed at his neck. He should not have come.

The door opened slowly. Segild, Eadgyth's toothless old maid, peered into the porch. Recognition dawned and her wrinkled face broke into a smile. 'Why, my lord Harold.' She bowed her already stooped back. 'My lady is expecting you.' Harold felt relief wash over him and followed the old woman's beckoning finger into the gloom.

'Harry? Harold, is it you?' Eadgyth's voice was low, tremulous.

'Yes.' Harold took her hand in his, unsure of himself, as they had not met for some months. She stepped from the shadows and he saw that she was wearing a long gown belted at the waist, which fitted her form like a glove.

'Swegn was here...' she began.

'When...what happened?' Harold tightened his grip. 'Tell me – did he harm you?'

'They didn't find me. We heard that he was coming with his men, and we hid in the woods. The villagers told him that I had gone away.'

Harold breathed a great sigh of relief. 'Thank God. He has grown more wild in recent months – the power has gone to his head. Father does not know how to control him, and the king allows him free rein, while his Norman advisors look on in glee in the hope that Swegn will be the end of the Godwin family...'

'Hush.' Eadgyth placed a finger on Harold's lips. 'Don't talk. We are safe and unharmed.' She replaced the finger with her lips. Harold bent and she slipped her arms around his neck, her hair, honey-gold in the sunlight suddenly flooding through the door, tickling his nose, and the taste of her overwhelming his senses. 'Come outside,' she broke free, and led him by the hand into the garden. The August sun was still high in the sky above them, and danced around gaps in the heavily leafed trees like a will-o'-the-wisp. They walked in silence to the woods and paused on reaching a clearing, where the long grass was lush and cool, and there they sat in the shade.

'The beech leaves are like a silken maiden's gown,' Harold murmured.

'You always loved poetry and reading.' Eadgyth lay in the deep grass, contented.

'It is a way of bettering ourselves,' said Harold, 'of rising above slaughter and squalor. Perhaps one day everyone shall have the chance to read poetry. Do you remember "The Wife's Plaint"?'

Eadgyth nodded. It was a favourite of his, about two lovers forced to live apart, waiting for one another.

'And do you remember the ending –'

'Alas for those who must wait for the beloved with aching heart so long!' Eadgyth laughed.

Harold smiled. 'It's us, isn't it?'

Eadgyth said: 'Yes, it is.' She sat up, her eyes flickering with sudden shock. 'But what of the king, Harry...does he know you are here? And your father; he will have you horsewhipped if he discovers...'

'To hell with the king.' Harold pushed her into the grass, 'and damnation to my father!' He found her lips and kissed her long and hard, like a man thirsty after so many days in a desert. His hand slipped beneath her gown and found her soft breasts. Her moan told him she was willing, and ready, and her hand in his breeches told him she wanted him now.

'Here,' she said, when he disentangled himself as the need for air grew desperate. 'Take me here.'

'Outside?' Harold's eyes widened as he understood her command. 'Like animals?'

'Why not?' Eadgyth pouted. 'It's clean and cool.' She lowered herself onto the grassy bank and raised her gown to her waist. Her legs were long and white.

'Christ. Why not?' Harold took his eyes from her thighs and, laughing like an idiot and drunk on lust, ripped his shirt from his back. 'You're not wearing much for a lady.' He ran a hand along her leg. Eadgyth giggled as she remembered she wore no underclothes: in this weather it was too hot to bother.

'Do you think me lewd and rough?' She said, running her hands around his broad back. 'Do you think me a whore, a Jezebel, a wanton hot for your body?'

'I truly think you have bewitched me!'

Harold pulled at his belt and then unbuttoned her gown. She raised her arms and he pulled the gown over her head. She lay naked in the long grass, her breasts like upturned fruit, the nipples pink and stiff as he had always imagined them to be. Slowly he kissed them, moving his hot hand along her stomach to her legs. The hair between them was as silky and golden as the hair on her head. Involuntarily she opened her legs and lifted her thighs in the grass. Harold moved on top of her and kissed her again, feeling her guide him into her. Harold placed his hands either side of her shoulders. He thrust slowly, not wanting to be too quick.

'It's so good,' she whispered, wrapping her legs around the small of his back.

'It is,' Harold gasped. 'Jesus, I love you.' He thrust harder, unable to fight the pleasure building up inside him, hearing Eadgyth groaning into his neck, small animal cries of delight and ecstasy, her body moving to meet his in an attempt to join the two of them together for all time.

'Not yet,' she murmured, ceasing her moans. Harold paused, realising she must have sensed his climax coming as his breathing slowed, and he bent and kissed her nipples, rubbing them with a vigour that must have pained as well as pleasured, but in her passion she did not care, writhing with the joy and ecstasy of it. 'Now!' she cried, and he thrust himself over the brink; he gave a great shout and spurted into her, aware of her twisting, gasping form beneath him, trying to make it last and last, crying, *'Oh God, oh God, oh God,'* into his ear.

They lay still, the breeze cooling their heated, sated bodies.

'Have we done wrong?' Eadgyth said after a long silence.

Harold rolled off her and sank back into the cool, long grass. 'You must never think that - '

'But fornication is a mortal sin!'

'Aye, but the Bible was written by old men who did not know what love is.'

'Harold, how could you say such a thing!' Eadgyth sat up in the long grass, shocked by his words.

Harold eyed her bare breasts, still flushed from the love-making, and grinned at her prim stare. 'I never had much time for the church and its teachings. Most men of the church are too busy seeking self-advancement in the world rather than attending to the word of God.'

'I know there are such men as Stigand and the Norman, Robert Champart who would sell their souls for worldly gain,' Eadgyth protested, 'But there are good men, like Ealdred, and Wulfstan.'

'Yes, I suppose there are.'

'But you're a pagan at heart - I'm sure of it.'

Harold gave a low laugh. 'More than you think, my sweet. Mother and father brought us up as English noblemen in all ways, but underneath the Danish influence was still strong, and beneath that, the Viking beliefs. Mother is Danish, though it is many years since she saw her homeland, and father came to power and holds all he does now because of his allegiance to a Danish king. And we have Danish names, Swegn, Tostig and I, although Swegn is the wildest. He is like a Norseman unleashed on a raid, so much so that sometimes I think...' He broke off.

'What?' Eadgyth stroked his arm. 'What do you think?'

'I am saying too much, but I'll say it anyhow. You've probably heard it whispered around court. The rumour that Swegn is Canute's son.'

'I never did hear such a thing!'

'Oh, yes.' Harold smiled at her surprise. 'My mother and King Canute were close at one time before she met father. And there may have been a price for the truly rapid rise to power of my father, from a humble thegn's son to the greatest earl in the land.'

'Are you suggesting that she...?'

Harold put his lips on hers and stifled what she might have said, and later regretted, then he jumped up and reached for his clothes. Chastened, Eadgyth said: 'It would explain so much. Swegn is so unpredictable. He frightens me.'

'It is only a rumour, mind.' Harold was pulling on his breeches. 'Put about by our enemies jealous of my father's power – men such as the Normans – and I doubt it is true. But Swegn will do for us if we do not keep him in check.' Harold's face hardened. 'We must away. The men will be fretting.' He helped her to her feet, then, as she bent to pull on her gown, he drank in the sight of her naked body, and said: 'God, but I could take you again.'

Eadgyth grasped his hand and shot him a wicked smile, aware of the effect she was having on him, and wanting more. 'Stay the night.'

'The king...'

'To hell with the king, you said!'

Harold struggled briefly with his conscience and gave up. It was a losing battle anyway. He grinned and said: 'To hell with the king, then. There must be more of Swegn in me than I thought. I'll stay the night.' Eadgyth clapped her hands with joy, but he added: 'Only the one night, and we must go back and stable the horses first.'

'I know of several girls who'll be happy to stable some of the men for the night,' said Eadgyth.

Harold roared with laughter, and led her through the woods to the village, where some of the soldiers had already made the acquaintance of the village girls. 'There, what did I tell you?' Eadgyth asked, to the accompaniment of lewd jeers from the lounging troops at the appearance of their lord and his lady from the woods, his lady all the more dishevelled for the experience.

'They're good lads,' Harold beamed, unaware of Eadgyth's scorching blushes at the jeers. Then, gripped by a sobering determination, he swore to himself that if he could not see Eadgyth in public, then he would stay true to her and look at no other woman, and perhaps one day make her his mistress and keep her in style.

'I'll stay the night and brave the wrath of the king tomorrow. You'll have to make the most of me while you can.'

And she did.

Chapter Nine
Rhuddlan, October 1045

Wales. Where the rain clung to the fading green leaves in great clumps and where the mists of autumn smothered the valleys, the warmth of the air cloying and claustrophobic. Where it rained incessantly. Wales, land of mountains so tall that the peaks vanished into the mist, unclimbed by man; of unending rivers gouging paths through hidden crevices; of little people with forked tails, it was whispered across the border in England.

Swegn wasn't impressed. They must be devils, these Welsh, with forked tails, to live in a such a godforsaken place as this. But Swegn was in an angry mood before leaving England. It had been a long, hard decision to come to north Wales in the perpetual rain and beg for aid against the king of southern Wales. It was all the fault of the king, calling his earls out to the fleet at the first sign of invasion. Swegn, under pain of exile, had gone south to Winchester, and awaited the pleasure of the king with all the other earls. But in his absence the king of south Wales had wrough thavoc in Swegn's lands in Herefordshire. On his return, their were countless reports of pillage, destruction, murder and rape.

Not that Swegn cared for the menfolk slaughtered in front of their children, or of the women forced and then carried off into the mountains - he was not averse to such activities himself - but that it should happen on his land, to his people! It had become a personal affront, so much so that whispers at court suggested that he was not fit for office. There was also the financial impact; a burnt farmstead could not pay its rent or yield its taxes. So when the doddering fool of a king sent the fleet back to Sandwich and the summer drew to a close, Swegn went north, or else he would lose his earldom. He decided that he would exploit the age-old rivalry that existed between the different Welsh kings; they were savages and it would do no harm to set them against one another.

Thus it was that, on a warm October evening when the leaves shone gold in the rain and the days were becoming noticeably shorter, Swegn Godwinsson arrived at the court of King Griffith ap Llewelyn, king of Gwynedd and Powys.

Griffith ap Llewelyn stroked his moustache thoughtfully and studied the English earl before him. The man was outrageous but had nerves of steel, riding into the heart of Wales - where no sane Englishman dared to go - and demanding an alliance with him against the king of the south. Griffith was tempted, but he would not make that apparent just yet. He surveyed Swegn Godwinsson with interest. He was more Dane than English; taller by a head than most men in the hall, like the Vikings Griffith had met in Ireland. He searched the earl's face for a sign of weakness. There was none. It was a brutal face, set with animal cunning. And he was brave, or stupid, enough to come into this lion's den of Welsh swords and spears with only twenty men. Griffith had heard much of the Godwin brood and he could see why the sire of this man had risen from a humble thegn to become the greatest power in the land.

Griffith knew of the expected invasion from Norway and how the king of England fretted over his throne. It was good for Wales and gave Welshmen asorely needed opportunity to attack the vulnerable border country. Old allegiances were broken and new ones made in the shifting sands of Marcher politics: Griffith himself had harassed Shropshire, the earldom of Leofric, who was absent at the court of the king, while in the south Griffith ap Rhyderch,the so-called king of Glamorgan, raided Herefordshire with impunity, and now here was the earl of that land asking him for an alliance. Griffith knew very well that the English hoped to set one Welshman against the other. It would benefit Griffith enormously, but not now. After Griffith's victory over Hywel of Deheubarth, the north had become peaceful. He had sworn over the dead body of Hywel that the killing of Welshman by Welshman had gone on long enough; he could never start another war with his countrymen while peace was so firm. There would be a day when the king in the south would be defeated and he, Griffith ap Llewelyn, would be king of all Wales, but not right now.

Griffith looked round the hall, amused at the quiet tension as the men awaited his reply. Swegn Godwinsson stood near the fire, an empty goblet in his hand, his eyes unblinking as he assessed the Welsh prince's mood. Griffith glanced at his wife,

Morgannwy, feeding his second son, Dafydd. He looked again at Swegn, and the men waiting in the hall knew that the decision had been made.

'No.'

The relief was audible, as many in that hall had young children and wives to care for, and jubilant, for there would be no war. Swegn Godwinsson turned on his heel and left without a word. But watching him go, Griffith knew that he would be back one day, and that he would have to agree to an alliance eventually.

*

Swegn Godwinsson came again, early in the new year, and this time, Griffith agreed to a treaty. In the great hall at Rhuddlan, oaths were sworn and hostages exchanged. It was a devil's union, Welshman and Englishman both knew, and hated it and each other for needing it at all.

Swegn left Griffith's hall feeling far happier than he had after his first and inglorious visit in October, but there was as yet an insurmountable problem: the king. News of Swegn's first visit had spread and Edward had demanded to know what his earl was doing at the court of the king of north Wales, a sworn enemy of the king of England. To the discomfort of Godwin, and to the delight of the Norman favourites, Swegn had stammered a feeble reply, but Godwin had stepped in and protested to the king about the raids on his son's lands. Edward had balked and retired to pass judgement, and in the meantime Swegn had gone off to Wales again, but this time ignoring Godwin's advice not to do so.

They headed for Hereford, the shire-town of Swegn's earldom, where Swegn would call out the fyrd and use Griffith's promise of safe-conduct to cross Powys and raid and pillage along the Wye valley to Brecon, where Griffith ap Rhyderch would never expect to find an English army. They crossed the Welsh-English border at Knighton, skirting the great ridge and ditch where Offa's Dyke was most prominent. From there, they followed the river Lugg to the small town of Leominster, arriving at nightfall as the first fall of snow began to cover the hard ground in a white sheet.

'We'll sleep here.'

Swegn indicated a large house in the middle of the main street. It belonged to Oswy, a reeve on the home farm, who would give his lord shelter and food. 'The men can find bedding in the stables along the road near the abbey, or in any other warm bed they pay for. See to it, Eadwulf.'

Eadwulf One-Eye, that same retainer of Harthacanute who had witnessed the corpse of Harold Harefoot spill onto the street at Winchester, did as he was bidden. Within minutes, the reeve Oswy had been woken, and put his bed at his lord's disposal, but nothing had prepared him for his lord's next demand.

'I want your wife in my bed when I go to it,' Swegn said after swallowing a tankard of mead offered by Oswy. It was a while since he'd had a woman, and on entering the house he had noticed the pretty face and shapely bosom of Oswy's wife. She would do, as Swegn couldn't be bothered to send Eadwulf out on the streets to find him a whore.

'My lord, I...' Oswy's protest died before it left his lips. Swegn's look was enough: he would lose his position, if not his life, if he did not comply.

'I'll take your wife either with or without your consent,' confirmed Swegn. 'Either way, it matters not to me.'

Oswy nodded and went below to fetch his wife. Swegn retreated to his chamber and began to undress. When a knock at the door followed shortly afterwards, he was disappointed to see not the reeve's comely wife but Eadwulf, who filled the room with his ugly, damp presence.

'Curse you, Eadwulf, what is it?' Swegn looked past the soldier at the open door, hoping that Oswy's wife would appear.

Eadwulf showed no reaction to his lord's anger.

'It's the men, my lord. There's trouble at the stables. They belong to the abbey, it seems, and the men are not allowed to stay.'

'What?' Swegn was incredulous. 'Can you not put them elsewhere?'

Eadwulf hesitated. 'It is snowing, sire, and...'

'And...?'

'The people of the town say they do not want to harbour the man who seeks treaties with the Welsh.'

'Jesus wept!' Swegn's eyes bulged out of his face with rage. 'Would they play me for a fool? I'll put the town to the sword!'

'It is true, my lord, I –'

'Get out and let me dress!' Fury gripped Swegn; fury born of frustration. Damn the abbey to hell for disturbing his bed. He took the candle Eadwulf had left and clambered down the narrow stairs. At the bottom, Oswy waited with an anxious, white face, and beside him, his voluptuous wife.

'You!' Swegn shouted, poking his finger at Oswy. 'Come with me. You are known in these parts. And you,' he pointed at Oswy's wife. 'Stay here. I mean to have you later.' Swegn pushed Oswy outside into the street and shouted for Eadwulf.

Outside, Swegn's men stood in the street, tired and angry. There were swords drawn and the steel glinted in the torchlight. Oswy stood in the shadow of the door, nervous at the sight of the men, no more than hired killers who slept with their boots on and worshipped no god known to honest Christians. The grumble of dissent rose to a roar as Swegn appeared at the doorway, fastening his cloak around his shoulders. Eadwulf shouted for silence, and Oswy recoiled at the sight of his cheeks that were raw with cold and the patch on his eye that looked hideous in the shadows. A hand grasped his neck and Swegn said: 'Take me to the abbey church.' Oswy walked ahead obediently, hearing the laughter of the men behind, and the crunch of many boots on the frozen snow.

'The earl of Hereford to see the abbess,' he said when they reached the lodge by the main gate.

'Abbess?' asked Swegn.

Oswy swallowed. 'Yes. It is a nunnery, my lord.'

'Christ Jesus. Are you saying that my men have been ordered out by some bloody women?' Swegn spat his anger into his reeve's face. Oswy held his lord's gaze, not daring to wipe the spittle from his cheeks. 'I thought you knew that, my lord.'

'No, I did not.' Swegn turned to his men. 'Wait here, lads. I'll get you a bed for the night.'

The door opened, and a nun led Swegn, Eadwulf and Oswy along a stone passage and into the silent cloisters. The nun approached a large door and rapped on the oak. At the soft command from within, she opened the door and the men walked in.

The abbess, a slight figure heavily cowled in black, motioned to the nun to leave and waited for the door to close before speaking. She spoke in a soft voice and the men guessed that beneath the cowl there was a young woman.

'What business have you calling at my abbey at this hour, Swegn Godwinsson?'

Swegn, already incensed at missing the comforts of Oswy's wife, was further enraged by the truculent tone adopted by this nun. 'I have every right to enquire why my men have been turned out into the street at this hour, abbess.' He moved closer to the nun and placed his hands on his hips.

'That much is straightforward enough, Earl Swegn.' The abbess was not intimidated by Swegn's manner. 'The stables belong to the abbey, and your men – if that is the correct word for such a following as you employ – were stealing our hay for their horses.'

Swegn was silent, his mouth working unspoken curses.

'You are a godless man,' said the abbess.

'What do you know of men?' Swegn sneered, moving closer to her.

'What little I know is enough to tell me that you are animals...'

Swegn lunged and caught the nun a ringing blow on the cheek. Hair tumbled from the dislodged headpiece and blood sprang from the woman's mouth.

'Lord Swegn, I beg you, think of what you do!' Oswy stepped towards the abbess. 'She is of the church, my lord: a holy woman.'

'To hell with the church,' said Swegn, aroused by the distress and weakness of the woman before him. He grasped her wrist and jerked his head to Eadwulf. The big soldier moved to the door and slid the bolts across.

'What do you mean to do, lord?' Oswy, seeing the door barred, and the look in Swegn's eye, knew the answer but could not believe it could be so.

Ignoring him, Swegn forced the abbess to the ground. 'I'll show you what a real man is,' he said, unbuckling his breeches.

'No,' said the abbess quietly. 'You will go to hell for this.'

'Silence!' Swegn shouted, breathing hard and hearing his pulse racing in his head at the daring and the stupidity of what he was doing. 'Get down, woman!'

Swegn knelt above the abbess, who started to protest, but Swegn thrust his fingers in her mouth and pinned her to the floor with his knees.

'My lord, I beg you...' Oswy stepped forward, but Eadwulf's muscled forearm barred the way.

'One word, Oswy, one word, and Eadwulf will cut off your ears,' said Swegn, lifting the nun's long gown. Eadwulf's grip tightened and Oswy stepped back.

'That's it,' the one-eyed warrior murmured into his neck. 'You stay there.'

Swegn looked at Oswy and sneered. 'But at least I won't touch your precious wife now.' Oswy nodded dumbly, thanking God that his wife was safe, but the abbess...Jesus, what kind of man was this?

The news reached Guildford just as Harold was preparing to leave for Cambridge, his neglected earldom. The family had assembled to celebrate Christmas and Harold had taken the opportunity to go to Midhurst, to see Eadgyth. Still he didn't dare to tell Godwin, though he suspected Gytha knew; but if she did, she said nothing. His secret was safe from his father and the court – at least for now. So when the messenger arrived, red-faced and half-dead from the cold, Harold's first thought was that his meetings with Eadgyth had been reported to the king, and that he had put the family into dire trouble. Leaving the saddle-bags in the yard, he ran inside fearing the worst.

'He will be the end of us!' Godwin was shouting. 'All I've worked for and he would destroy me!'

'Who?' Harold asked in the pause that followed while Godwin drew breath. Godwin looked at Harold and for a heart-stopping second, Harold thought that it was indeed him, that the news of his love-trysts with Eadgyth was out.

'Swegn,' said Godwin. Harold's face showed relief, not shock, but Godwin was too incensed with rage to notice as he told Harold the details.

'Good God,' Harold breathed, all thoughts of Eadgyth out of his mind. He looked at the various members of the family – cousin Beorn's normally untroubled face creased with worry, Gytha tearful, and Tostig shaking his head with the wonder of it all.

'A woman of the church,' Godwin shouted, 'a nun, a virgin bride of Christ...!'

'He always was the wild one,' Tostig whispered.

'Does he not realise that this could destroy us?' Godwin took Gytha's hand and gripped it tightly. 'The king...the king will use it against us. His Norman scum will have us now.'

'They say Swegn might even have abducted the abbess,' said Beorn, 'and fled the country.'

'I hope to God he has fled the country.' Godwin walked to the fire and took a draught of mead. 'He's no son of mine, God rot his soul.'

The great council met four days later at Westminster. Godwin, Harold, Beorn and Tostig rode through the snow virtually non-stop and took up residence in the family house at Southwark, arriving the day before the council convened.

The earls Leofric and Siward, and the churchmen Wulfstan, Eadsige and Ealdred were all present, having attended the king's Christmas court only weeks before; Leofric and Siward nodded sympathy, but the bishops were grave and tight-lipped. Standing alongside the king were Bishop Robert and several other foreign clerics. Robert's eyes blazed triumph as Edward read the sentence, which not even Godwin's persuasive charm could alter; that Swegn Godwinsson be exiled from the kingdom for an indefinite period and that his lands be sequestered by the crown.

The silence that followed was broken by a snort of triumph from Bishop Robert as Godwin stood there, white-faced and speechless, helpless to do anything about it.

Chapter Ten
Pontorson, Normandy, August 1046

William sized up the block of wood through narrowed eyes and lifted the heavy two-handed axe. With a grunt he lifted it above his head and dropped it onto the wood. There was a resounding crack, the log split and William smiled with satisfaction. In the years he'd been at Pontorson the one thing he had mastered was the use of the axe.

'I dare say you would defeat Roland himself if you met in battle.'

William wiped the sweat from his eyes and grinned up at Will FitzOsbern. 'God forbid I meet Roland in the field of battle.'

Will slid from his horse and sized up the duke before him, much as William had sized up the log minutes earlier. Will stood six feet tall, as broad as he was muscular, but William was a head taller, his chest barrel-like, and the long arms sweeping from wide shoulders had ended many a fight in an ale-house before it had properly begun. His hair was close-cropped and the wide nose looked as though it had been broken, a sit had – by a horse a year ago. The deep-set eyes were a mild grey, but could turn black if he was angry. Today though, they were bright, and the thick lips beneath the wide nose split into a good-humoured grin at the sight of his oldest friend, and the only person he could trust after the years of hiding.

Will was pleased with what he saw. William, bastard duke of Normandy, had grown into a man. Surviving infancy and a long and dangerous minority, eluding his enemies, many of them close relatives, he was now of the age and bearing to seek what was his by right.

William asked: 'Have you heard from Adela?'

Will frowned. Adela was a lusty girl in the village whom William had got with child; she had begun her confinement last week. He recalled her wide, sensual mouth and high cheekbones and smiled briefly. 'Forget her.' William's eyes flickered annoyance. 'There is news from Herluin.' William's eyebrows shot up, the annoyance replaced by curiosity. 'News is that FitzThurstan has the castle of Falaise.'

'He stands by me and holds my birthplace?'

Will nodded. 'It is true. Falaise holds for you.' He held William's gaze, knowing what it meant.

The exile was over.

The castle at Falaise had been built on an escarpment of rock overhanging the river Fal over a century before. The stone keep where Duke Robert had lain with Herleve eighteen summers ago formed the central tower of the fortress which dominated the small town. Since the deaths of the duke on his pilgrimage to the Holy Land and the Archbishop Robert, the castle had passed into different hands, each lord eager to hold the fort which was the key to control over Lower Normandy. But in recent months, Richard FitzThurstan, lord of Creully, had seized the fort and claimed it for the boy-duke. Peace of a sort had fallen over the area while the barons waited for the boy to claim his inheritance, if indeed he was still living.

'Welcome.' Richard FitzThurstan took William's horse and handed him a stirrup-cup of cider. 'The lord of Falaise comes home.' William drank from the cup and surveyed the deserted castleyard. Few signs of habitation were manifest; there were no squawking hens, no hurrying servants preparing dinner in the hall, but weeds smothered the walls and there were cracks in the cobbles, and the wooden bridge – that same bridge where his father had first glimpsed the lovely Herleve washing her clothes – was badly in need of repair. FitzThurstan followed his gaze and said: 'It is not much of a home, I'm afraid. Few men have bothered to keep the castle in a state of repair and it has passed through many hands since you last saw it.'

William nodded, saying nothing, but Will saw his look, and knew that another debt had been accrued.

The lord of Creully led them to a chamber by the hall which had been made habitable with a warm fire and hangings on the walls, and there he told William what his duchy had become. War had reigned supreme since the death of the archbishop nine years ago; neighbours rivalled one another for the land and all Normandy saw a great proliferation of castles, like mushrooms in a field, that dominated the countryside and people. Mostly built of timber defended by earth ditches and ramparts, these forts dotted the landscape. War raged around them and centred on the sieges and counter-sieges of the forts. To gain control of Normandy, William must first take these castles.

William appreciated this. He had seen with his own eyes the ravages of war in the duchy without a duke and the establishment of castles across the land. He knew also that in those castles a new class of rulers had grown up with new ideas. Richard FitzThurstan was one of those new men and he was saying that those others were weary of the devastation of the duchy. The barons of Lower Normandy wanted independence from Rouen and from the clutches of Mauger, who ruled Eastern Normandy like a prince. Richard judged that the time was ripe for a new leader – bastard or not, it didn't matter.

As he spoke, FitzThurstan assessed the young man in front of him. He had taken a risk in leaving the shelter of Pontorson where he'd lived these last years as a peasant woodsman, leaving only to make brief excursions to Conteville. Treachery and hate were not new to the lad, and it showed in his eyes – wise, embittered eyes in a young face. Physical prowess and bravery won the hearts of warriors, and his exceptional height and strong chest and arms would make him a great leader of men in battle. But though his strength might win men over to his side, he would need cunning and intelligence to keep them there. Was the lad up to the task? He was in no way educated to assume the government of the duchy; his training in arms had been sporadic and he was barely literate: FitzThurstan doubted if the youth could even sign his own name.

'You will be well rewarded for your support, Richard,' said William once FitzThurstan had finished his gloomy summary of the situation in the duchy.

'Time enough for that when you have the duchy,' said FitzThurstan, well aware that the boy could not keep his promises yet. 'Lord Herluin asked me to give you this,' he reached into a chest tucked away in a corner of the chamber. Struggling with the latch for a moment before lifting out a long object wrapped in cloth, he stepped back to the fire and in the light of the flames unwrapped the object. It was a sword. Double-edged and two-handed, it shone brilliantly in the light. 'I polished it only yesterday,' he said, passing it to William. William hefted the weight from side to side and swung it down. It was no axe, no crude chopping implement for wood. It had a certain grace, and in the light of the fire, a deadly beauty. 'It was your father's,' said FitzThurstan.

'My father's...?'

'He left it behind when he embarked on his journey to the Holy Land. It is yours to claim, as he wished you to do.'

William could see very well that it was truly a duke's weapon and a warrior's weapon, fit for a Roland. 'A man can fight battles to equal those of Roland with this,' he murmured, marvelling at the sheer edge of the blade.

'You know the *chansons,* then?' FitzThurstan was reaching into the chest again.

'I do. I cannot read, but I can tell all the tales,' William said proudly.

'And this was your father's pendant.' The lord of Creully held up a silver chain. 'And his brother's before him and your grandfather's before that. It is the chain worn only by the dukes of Normandy.' William set down the great sword on the hearth and examined the pendant. 'See the three lions,' FitzThurstan pointed. 'The emblem of the ducal house.' William touched the cold silver and shivered. 'Your mother kept these safe all along.'

'She didn't tell me,' William protested. He had visited Conteville frequently but Herleve had not once mentioned this.

'She didn't judge you were ready,' Richard smiled. 'But now you are.' He leant forward and William stooped a little as the baron fastened the chain around his neck. 'You're the son of Duke Robert come to claim his own.' FitzThurstan grasped William's hand and nodded in satisfaction as he felt the strength in the tall frame and saw the determination in the grey eyes.

*

William surveyed the curious faces filling the hall and judged that the time had come for him to speak. Of those in the hall, some he knew, many he did not. They were local lords, petty barons and knights who devoted their time to defending their families in these leaderless years. None had actively opposed him, but few had supported him by openly defying Mauger. All were heartily sick of the internecine wars and had rallied on hearing of the arrival of Duke Robert's bastard appearing from hiding at Falaise, seeing at last a potential leader who could hammer peace on the anvil of Normandy. William had seen them studying him and knew that they were sizing him up. He did not know it, but most of them looked at him with approval, seeing in his build and quiet confidence sure signs that here was a leader of soldiers.

When William stood up to speak, there was instant silence. Having studied him, the barons wanted to hear him speak and judge him on his words as well as his looks. William, feeling a rush of doubts assail him, was glad of the encouraging smiles from Herleve, Herluin and Will at his side, and he began confidently: 'When my father left for his pilgrimage to Jerusalem, he made the lords of the duchy swear an oath of allegiance to me, his heir. That oath was broken by almost all, led by the example of my own uncles. We all know the consequences of that treachery, but at the oath-swearing here in this very hall my father said of me: "He is small, but he will grow." I have grown, and I have come to claim the duchy that was held by my father, my grandfather and Count Rollo, he who sailed from the north and settled here.' William paused and held up the silver pendant. 'You see that

I am wearing the silver chain that is worn only by the dukes of Normandy.' The eager faces of the barons crowded forward. 'And by my side, I have my father's sword, the great sword of Duke Robert. The time has come for me to wield it in the governance of the duchy. And here, I have a letter from the king of France, Henri Capet.' The audience stirred, for this was a new and unexpected development. Henri of France, although grandly titled, in fact ruled only over the tiny strip of land from Paris to Orléans; the rest of France was ruled by independent princes in Brittany, Burgundy, Flanders, Maine, Aquitaine and Touraine. And Normandy. In name, however, Henri was the overlord of all those provinces, and though most paid only lip-service to that claim, it was a claim based on the ancient rights of the far-off days of the glorious Charlemagne, when France had been united under one king, and the present king was constantly seeking to reassert that claim. Though powerless outside their domain of the Île de France, the kings of France were not to be ignored.

'The letter contains a further pledge of support from the king of France to his vassal, the duke of Normandy: me.' William paused to allow the words to sink in. 'As you are aware, Henri supported my father's decision to appoint me as his heir when I was but a boy, and continued to do so after the departure and death of my father. Before Archbishop Robert died, I went to Paris, where I swore loyalty and took the oath of homage to the king. In return, he pledged his support for his youngest and most vulnerable vassal. As you also know, King Henri was in no position at that time to enforce his position as my overlord and protector, but today, two things have happened since that small boy journeyed to Paris to swear an oath that in fact meant very little. Lords of lower Normandy, the king of France has more power available to him now than he did ten years ago. And secondly, this –'

William drew from its scabbard the great sword that hung at his waist. The rasp as the steel scraped from the leather filled the silent hall. William placed the tip of the weapon on the rush-strewn floor of the hall and knelt before the assemblage of barons, saying:

'I do solemnly swear on this sword of my forefathers who ruled Normandy and in the sight of God, that I shall not rest until I have recovered what is rightfully mine and the duchy is under my governance after so many years of war and bloodshed. I swear that all those unlawfully murdered shall be avenged and that all perjurers shall be sent to hell at the end of this sword. So God help me, or I shall die in the attempt.'

William stumbled to his feet, suddenly exhausted and aware of the tremor in his voice as he spoke. Please God nobody would notice the nerve twitching in his left cheek, else they would think him possessed.

The crowd of barons remained absolutely silent.

It was Will FitzOsbern who stepped forward and shouted: 'Long live Duke William! Long live the duke!' And in reply, the lords shouted 'Long live the duke!' and Will was shaking his hand, and his mother kissing him, and Herluin shouting above the din: 'That was well said, lad.' And the barons in the hall were kneeling to swear allegiance, knowing that at last they had found a leader.

*

The heat of August merged unmercifully into a hotter September as William established himself at Falaise. The loyal barons to whom he had sworn his oath had returned to their castles. Hope began to replace despair, and messengers on fast horses sped from manor to manor spreading the news of the young duke's return. But the dust-covered peasants on the road-side were most concerned with the cider harvest – and afraid that a violent death would visit them in the hot, still, orchards.

It did not. As the word spread like wildfire to Upper Normandy where Mauger and Robert held court like joint-princes, William prepared the castle and small garrison for the mighty army that would bring bloodshed before the last throes of summer gave way to autumnal rains. But silence followed the news of the young duke's reappearance and investiture at Falaise. Herluin warned William that in the event of any confrontation it was unlikely that those lords who had so enthusiastically cheered him in the hall that first night would actually fight for him. They would stay safely at home and look after their own, neither opposing nor helping either side.

As the heat of the sun relented, and the apples were harvested and the days grew shorter, it seemed that all Lower Normandy was waiting for the blow to fall.

Then, towards the end of October, William received a message from Grimoald, lord of Plessis, inviting William to Valognes in the Cotentin and proposing an alliance.'

'Grimoald was here at your investiture, was he not?' said Will.

'He was,' said William. 'He is one of the lords in the west who have remained neutral these last years, neither opposing nor supporting me. If we can win him over now, it could bring the remainder of Normandy to me.'

'It may be a trap,' said Herleve quietly.

William glanced at his mother. The thought had occurred to him – how could it not, after all the betrayals of the past? 'But we can't wait much longer for the enemy to come to us, whoever he is – Mauger, anyone. We must act.'

Will nodded. 'I agree. It's a chance we should take. We shan't succeed in anything if we sit and wait for our enemies to surround us. Something must be done.'

'Not we, Will, but me.' William raised a hand to forestall Will's inevitable protest. 'I'll go with a small escort, so as not to attract attention. You shall stay here and guard the castle. If it is a trap, they shall come here to take the fort, not come after me.'

Will said nothing, but when Herleve left the chamber, he rounded on his friend. 'You fool. You damned fool. They will kill you. Let me go, and bring more men.'

'No.' William grasped Will's arm and said between clenched teeth: 'Turold. Osbern. Alan. How many more must die? Not you, Will – not you. It is for me to go, and for me alone. I am the duke now, and I must now prove myself worthy of those men who died for me.'

Will held his friend's gaze for a long moment before saying: 'It is for you to do what you think is right, William. I understand. Pray God will keep you safe.'

William smiled a rare smile, glad that at last he could act without fearing for someone else. 'Stay and guard the fort with mother. I'll send news.'

*

The road to Valognes took the ducal party north west of Falaise, where they crossed the river Orne at Thury Harcourt. William insisted on taking only five mounted men for an escort; too many would attract unwanted attention, and to this end he carried no banner. The three lions of Normandy were left flying above the castle at Falaise, where it would be believed that the young duke of Normandy sat waiting until his enemies came for him.

After Thury Harcourt, the small party headed through Aunay-sur-Odon and onto Caumont l'Éventé, where they rested. The road divided here, west to the village of St-Lô, and north east towards Bayeux. At La Molay-Littry they turned towards Isigny, by the estuary of the Vire, and after a night's rest they would cross at low tide to Sainte-Marie and thence to Valognes.

William woke with a start, sweating in the cold. Heaving with relief at the familiar darkness of the still room, he leant back. Christ, it was that dream again. The same dream, where a man – it might be his father – appeared and someone was shouting at the boy by his side. *Bastard! Bastard!*

The girl in his bed stirred, but didn't wake. She murmured and reached out for his warmth. William grunted and rolled off the straw mattress, placing the blanket over her bare rump. It had been Ralf's idea to get the girls, and he grinned at the memory. He had chosen the best, the one with hair to her waist and creamy skin, unpitted like the others. She had a low laugh, a husky voice, and had jumped on him with a wild passion that only exhausted itself several hours later.

William went to the window. Drawing back the cloth, he saw the first grey light of dawn hover uncertainly over the horizon. He wondered what Will was doing at Falaise. He'd be asleep now, but within the hour he would be up and about, supervising the repair of the walls which were still in need of restoration after the years of neglect.

The sound of a nervous whinny from one of the horses in the stables at the back of the house floated up to the room as William turned to climb back into the bed. Maybe the girl would wake soon and they would make love again before the journey resumed. The horse cried again, and William returned to the window, annoyed, but uneasy. He drew back the cloth in time to see a shadow, unmistakably that of a man, flit across the yard, illuminated briefly by the streak of light to the east. Someone who was attempting to conceal his presence. Not allowing the import of this to sink in, William seized his heavy leather riding tunic and pulled it over his head. The leather was old, and reeked of sweat and horsedung, but it would turn a blow. The girl, smelling sweetly of apples and hay, had turned her nose up at the stink; but William had laughed and pushed her down on the bed.

The door creaked open. The faint light of a candle beyond revealed the silhouette of a man.

'Is that you, Roger?'

William reached for his sword as he spoke, and raised it in the darkness, thankful that the girl in the bed was fast asleep.

'Yes...it's Roger,' came the reply. 'There is some trouble downstairs, my lord; can you come?'

'Yes, I'll come.' William stepped forward and brought the sword down into the shadows. It made a dull chopping sound, not unlike an axe penetrating wood, and the intruder slumped to the ground, pushing the door further ajar. William put his foot on the man's neck and wrenched the blade from the skull. He leant against the doorframe and wiped his brow. There was no Roger, of course; the five men with him included a Robert, Urse, Ralf, Rannulf and Simon, but no Roger.

A woman's high-pitched scream of terror shattered the warm silence. William hurried to the stair, breathing quickly now, gripping the great sword in hands damp with sweat. Light flickered ahead and giant shadows leapt at him as he stumbled down the steps. Another scream, this time close by, and one of the girls Ralf had procured ran sobbing up the stairs towards him, her gown torn to shreds and her hair wild. Somewhere below him, a sword rasped against another.

'Ralf? Urse?'

There was no answer. Then the light changed, and as it illuminated the large room of the ground floor, William saw the naked body of Ralf under the table, a bloody gash searing his stomach, and Urse and Rannulf locked in combat with three other men. It was an unequal struggle, for the intruders wore mail and helmets while William's men were clad only in undershirts and breeches.

'My lord, you're alive, thank God!'

William wheeled round, blinded for an instant by the candlelight in his face from above. 'Jesu, Simon; you might have killed me...'

'We did fear for you, my lord, when the first man got through, but you live.'

'Yes.' William's voice was grim. 'I despatched him to hell. He used a name to trick me, but he chose wrongly. It was a mistake; his last.' He gestured down the steps. 'We must go to their aid.'

'No, my lord.' Simon's mouth closed tightly.

'No?'

'No.' Simon did not flinch at William's stare. 'Orders from Lord Herluin, my lord; I am to protect you at all costs. We must go back to Falaise. These men will cover our retreat. They are sworn to die for you.'

God's truth that men would readily lay down their lives for him! William studied the older man's face and saw a wealth of experience and confidence. This man would sooner knock him on the back of the head and carry him back to Falaise than allow him to enter the desperate struggle in the room below. 'We must go now, my lord,' said Simon gently, seeing the tears of rage well up in the young man's eyes. 'There is a back window we can escape from. You will fight one day.'

William jerked his head in silent capitulation. They would go. Once again he would run away, and leave better men to their fate. 'Who are they, Simon?' he asked hoarsely, blinking back the tears. 'Who are they?'

*

Two days later, Herluin answered his question.

'Grimoald of Plessis, Ralph Tesson of Thury, Haimo of Creully, Nigel, the vicomte of the Cotentin and Rannulf, vicomte of the Bessin.'

Continuous riding had taken them from Isigny through Ryes, north-east of Bayeux, where Simon assured William that the local lord would be loyal. Herbert of Ryes remained true to Simon's word and stood guard the night they stopped, reprovisioning them with food and fresh horses.

'Grimoald of Plessis,' said Will slowly.

'He supported me before,' said William to Herluin. 'He was at my investiture. I thought that if he came over to me, I would win the support of all the lords of the west.' William spoke rapidly, his cheeks still burning from the memory of the humiliation when Herluin had said: *You would not have gone if I had been here to stop you.*

But Herluin said gently: 'There is more yet.' He looked at each of them in turn. 'The man who masterminded this was not Nigel of the Cotentin or Grimoald of Plessis. It was a well conceived plan and reveals a greater unity against you; what we have feared all summer, in fact. William, it was your cousin Guy. As Mauger's creature, Guy planned this murder attempt.'

An audible hiss of shock went through the chamber. William paled: cousin Guy, who'd jeered at him six years ago in a dusty courtyard at Conteville, and whose face he'd battered. Childhood hatred had followed him, and now that he was wise to the ways of the world he marked his entry into manhood with betrayal.

'Splendour of God!' said Will FitzOsbern. 'We should have known; a creature of Mauger. We ought to have suspected...'

'As the son of Alice, sister of Duke Robert, and Renaud, sometime count in Burgundy, Guy claims the duchy of Normandy,' said Herluin, when the initial shock had subsided. 'It is of course a deliberate move to oppose William's claim to the duchy he made in August.'

'Guy's castles on the Seine at Vernon and Brionne on the Risle are well fortified and hold key strategic positions in Upper Normandy', added Will. 'We're in no position to take them.'

William leant against the cold stone wall and took a deep breath. Apart from his mother, none of those in the room were blood relatives, and yet all displayed a intense loyalty to him, as had all those who had died, from Turold in the very beginning to Ralf at Isigny; laughing Ralf, who'd found them the girls, and had died in his bed, gutted like a fish. Why could some men be so treacherous and yet others so loyal? Was what he had worth it? It was only a flight of steps above them, in the small chamber overlooking the river, that Duke Robert had taken Herleve and begun all this. Perhaps it would be better if...

'William, are you ill?'

Herleve was at his side. She seemed to bear the shock better than the men. He took her hand thankfully and smiled. 'There is only one course of action left open to me now,' he said, addressing everyone but looking at Herluin. 'With the lords of the Cotentin after my life and my cousin Guy defying me in the east, I must go to my overlord, King Henri of France.'

Chapter Eleven
Paris, Île de France, October 1046

Henri Capet was a man of astute political acumen and, more unusual among political rulers of the time, he was an accurate judge of character. Descended directly from the Hugh Capet who had displaced the last Carolingian king, Henri had only one ambition: to restore the full meaning of his empty title. As king of France he was overlord of Flanders, Normandy, Brittany, Burgundy, Aquitaine and Maine, but in reality he was merely a landowner of the royal demesne estates; a territorial prince. Powerless to use force against the lords of the principalities, he emphasised his position as titular head of the kingdom. For much of the past decade Henri had been struggling to contain the growing ambition of Odo II of Blois, who claimed the kingdom of Burgundy. This caused dissent amongst the nobles of the Île de France, who seized the opportunity to make trouble for the overlord. After this threat had been stifled, another, more dangerous rival to the king had emerged: Geoffrey the Hammer, count of Anjou. Geoffrey was ruler of Maine as well as Anjou, and by his marriage to Agnes, mother of the duke of Aquitaine, he had gained the support of the duke, William the Sour. So it was that, with this new threat emerging, Henri would welcome the plea from his vassal in Normandy, and use him to bolster the power of the Hammer in Anjou.

To William, Paris - the ancient Roman town of Lutetia - seemed a vast citadel as he rode through the Porte Gibard, across the Seine and onto the Île de la Cité. He had not seen a town comparable to this since the day Archbishop Robert had died and as a small, frightened boy he had been bundled into hiding down the streets of Rouen. He was impressed by the large town walls, the gates, the churches of Notre-Dame, Saint-Séverin and Saint-Germain-l'Auxerrois, whose tolling bells gave the city a sense of authority and power. And as he, Will and Herluin approached the royal palace, the feeling that Henri would help them grew; he had supported him when he was a boy and he had marched into the Hiemois and the valley of the Orne several times to quell the unrest and war after the death of Archbishop Robert, and he would help now. Henri would help them, and the hope that replaced despair would now, God willing, be channelled into positive action.

The king saw them after high mass. Short, stout and with a neatly trimmed glossy beard, he regarded the tall, clean-shaven Normans hesitantly at first. Then he stepped off the dais and walked the length of the huge hall, greater than anything the Normans had seen before, and more ornate and intricate than the crude, rough halls in the duchy.

'William, my boy,' he said, embracing him and kissing both cheeks with great elaboration. William stood back, surprised by the forwardness of such a greeting.

'But how you've grown,' Henri was saying. William forced a smile, aware that, however much this man appeared to be an ageing and doddering relative, he held his future in the palm of his hand.

Besides, though the king of France was now middle-aged, he'd been well respected for his military skill as a younger man. 'You are a man, now. And so like your father...' Henri's voice trailed off as his eye met Herluin's. 'Aye, the years go so fast. So fast...' With an impatient gesture, he led them across the hall and into a smaller, but luxuriously furnished chamber alongside. 'I trust that you have been supplied with refreshments for yourselves and your men?'

'Yes, sire, we have.' William was conscious of respect.

'And you have to come to renew your vows of homage to me as your overlord?' The king gave William a quizzical look. 'I have heard of your claim at Falaise and have been waiting.'

'Yes, sire, but there is another matter for your attention, sire.' William glanced quickly at Herluin: the king did not know the latest. 'Rebellion, sire.' Henri stopped in his tracks. 'The lords of the Cotentin and Guy of Burgundy are in open revolt against me.'

The French king turned to the Normans, his plump face purple with rage. 'If they revolt against you, William of Normandy, then they revolt against me.'

'I know, sire. That is why I came to you.'

'You did well to do so, William. Who are they?'

'Grimoald of Plessis, Nigel of the Cotentin, Rannulf of the Bessin and...my cousin, Guy of Burgundy.'

'Guy of Burgundy? Then he is Mauger's creature. By the mass, does Mauger think he can play me for a fool?' The answer was clearly 'yes', but William remained silent at the Frenchman's outburst and hoped that a more practical response would be forthcoming. It was. 'I will summon all my levies between here and Orléans. That will account for some two thousand men.'

'Will they come?' said Herluin.

The French king shot the Norman lord a look of rage through narrowed eyes. This impertinence from the Norman was tantamount to insult, but Henri chose to consider the question as a matter of serious military importance. 'The men from Corbeil, Melun and Rochefort will come,' he said. 'I am quite confident of the men from Orléans and Saint-Benoît-sur-Loire, but none will come from Compiègne and Soissons. Of that, we can be sure.' The latter towns were north of Paris, to the borders of Beauvais and Valois. There, the castellans of the border castles exploited the nebulous jurisdiction of the king's frontiers to the full; Henri had wasted many years exerting his rights of overlordship in the area to no avail. Henri turned to William. 'How many men can *you* raise?'

William took a deep breath. This was to be the fist time that his position as duke of Normandy would be evaluated in terms of men on the field, rather than the platitudes of false loyalty he'd heard so far. It was clear that Nigel, Rannulf, Guy, Ralph Tesson and Haimo of Creully were not for him; the men they commanded as their vassals wouldn't come either. That accounted for most of Lower Normandy; the whole of Upper Normandy was under Mauger's sway. 'Richard FitzThurstan is loyal, and Robert Montgomery - I think Ralph of Briouze.'

'And Hugh of Grandmesnil,' added Will.

'I can supply about fifty men from Conteville,' said Herluin.

'In all about five or six hundred men,' said William, realising the utter helplessness of his situation.

'If they come,' said Henri, with a grin of pure malice at Herluin. 'Which they might not when word gets round of this latest rebellion.'

William glanced dejectedly at Herluin, knowing that it was all in the hands of this Frenchman – and that afterwards they would be in his debt.

'I will help you,' said Henri and, as if reading William's mind, he added: 'But first, you must swear your oath of homage to me. Come, kneel and place your hands between mine.'

William knelt. He had no choice but to subordinate the duchy to the king of France for the first time. He well knew the story of the legendary meeting between his ancestor Rollo, the first duke of Normandy and King Charles of France. Rollo had refused to kiss the king's feet and his manservant had tripped the king backwards when asked to do the deed. Charles had been deposed by Hugh Capet and here was William, swearing liege loyalty to *his* ancestor.

'Here, my lord king, I become liege man of yours for life and limb and earthly regard, and I will keep faith and loyalty as duke of Normandy to you for life and death; God helping me.' William stood and accepted Henri's kiss of peace and in turn leant and brushed his own lips against the Frenchman's cheek.

'As your liege lord, I am bound to help you,' said the king. *For better or worse*, thought William. Henri was pleased and William suspected why; with the fledgling duke firmly employed as his vassal and protégé, Henri could give weight at last to his rights as overlord of all the other duchies, and assert his position as king of all France. But better still, he would use Normandy and the young duke as pawns to block or balance the power of Geoffrey the Hammer, the overmighty count of Anjou. It was a complete reversal of fortunes for the king of France. 'You did right in coming to me,' Henri went on. 'There is no one else you can turn to.' He studied the Normans in turn, resting his eyes on the tall duke. 'We are allies and our cause is blessed by God, is it not?' They nodded, each aware that the alliance was an uneven one, and that they were as a stallion and a mule under the same harness; they knew it and Henri knew it, but there was no other way.

'Good,' said Henri, taking their silence for consent. 'Then I suggest that you return to Falaise, call out your men and await my word. As soon as I am ready, I shall bring my army into Normandy and deal with those who dare to defy the law of their king.'

*

It was a shock to see the hundreds of horsemen lined up against them at the edge of the woods. It had been raining heavily for several days and showed no sign of easing; mist shrouded the tree-tops and would soon descend to cover the line of French and Normans huddled at the field-edge, awaiting the attack.

This day was long overdue. William had known from his youngest years that he would not gain acceptance as duke without fighting for it. But it was ugly, all the same, to see the banners of Nigel, Rannulf, Ralph and numerous others lined up against him. Dismay followed shock; from what he could make out through the rain, it was clear to William that the rebel forces numbered at least a thousand, and most were mounted. Sitting in the saddle frozen with fear and cold, William knew what that meant: Henri's bold boast that he would bring two thousand or more men had fallen flat; he had just over a thousand, mostly horsemen. Three hundred men from central Normandy had come in answer to William's call, but most had stayed in their castles and halls, anxiously awaiting the result. Only after the battle would they come out and proclaim lifelong support for the victor.

A set-piece battle was a rare event in the pattern of sieges, counter-sieges, betrayals and murders that had characterised the governance of the duchy over these ten years. The result today would be decisive. It was almost exactly ten years since Archbishop Robert had died and anarchy had gripped the land. But now Duke Robert's bastard was a grown man come to claim his own, backed by his sovereign lord's army.

The reckoning was upon them.

'How are you, boy?'

The king was in a jovial mood and flashed William a grin. He didn't look like a man who had spent Christmas urging his rain-sodden troops across Normandy. By-passing Rouen, the royal army entered Upper Normandy through the town of Evreux. Marching undisturbed across the heart of the duchy through Mézidan, Henri had met William and his levies at Caen, near the north coast. Wheeling south, the joint forces crossed the marshy plains of the Val d'Auge and thence to Argentan. There, they heard of the oncoming rebel forces moving eastwards. Henri insisted that there would be no evasion; the royal army had decamped and struck north again to meet the rebels who had crossed the Orne.

William glanced at the French king and envied the older man's easy confidence. The army had rested the night at Valmeray, but William had not slept well. Up at first light to hear the scouts' reports and mass on an empty stomach; breakfast followed, but while the king and Herluin had cheerfully partaken of salted beef and cold ale, William's stomach remained a knot of fear.

'Don't be afraid, William.' Herluin was beside him. 'We all of us know fear, and those who pretend not to are either fools or liars.' William gave a wan smile, grateful for Herluin's presence. 'Remember, keep your knees in tight, stay close to the king and keep your shield strapped firm to your arm. When the battle begins, you'll feel the rage run through you, and with God's grace the day shall be ours.' He leant towards William and adjusted his shield. It was a body-length shield, and consisted of several strips of oak bound by leather and tapering to a point. The shape was such that the wider part at the end would shield the vulnerable left shoulder, whilst the length would protect the torso and left leg. The right side would be defended by the swinging sword William held in his hand: Duke Robert's great two-handed weapon. William swung it down, noting with satisfaction the swish it made as it travelled through the air, trying to ignore the trembling hand that was damp with sweat under the leather glove.

'I mind my first battle,' said Herluin, as Will FitzOsbern rode up alongside them. He gave William a quick, nervous grin. 'It was with your father against his brother, the duke as he was. After Robert's victory I was rewarded with the lordship of Conteville. It was a bloody business, though.' Herluin's face darkened with the memory of a battle fought between two brothers over twenty years ago. He looked up, saw the two young men looking glumly at the wet ground. 'Is this a time to be reminding you young bloods of a distant time of grim death when today we meet to destroy the enemies of the rightful duke? Will, son of Osbern the Steward, tell us how the armies are arrayed, and tell me that today you will avenge the death of your father.'

'There will be vengeance today.' Will's eyes flickered bleakly. 'Blood will be shed – much blood.'

Herluin saw the same look on William's face. He turned abruptly, glimpsing movement in the mist. 'What's this?'

William followed the line of his stepfather's outstretched arm. 'There's a line of horsemen coming from the woods. It's an attack!'

Others thought so, too, and for an instant, panic seized the ranks of waiting horsemen; swords were wrenched from scabbards, horses shied, shouts and cries rippled through the rain and mist. William's own horse sensed the danger and danced excitedly in the mud, sending up great sprays around it.

'Wait!' King Henri was standing in his spurs waving his sword. 'Hold! There are only ten men – it is no attack, but a parley!'

As the small party of horsemen emerged from the rain, it became evident that it the king was right.

'By the mass; there's Ralph Tesson's banner,' said Herluin.

'Are you sure, man?' Henri manoeuvred his horse alongside Herluin's and peered through the rain.

'It is,' confirmed William. 'I recognise his face.'

'I'll not treat with him,' growled Henri.

The small party halted, close enough for the French to see the embroidery on the damp banner and the horses' breath. Ralph dismounted and signalled to his men to remain where they were. Seizing the banner, he sloshed through the mud to where William was.

'I come to surrender my services to my duke and my lord king!' he bellowed through the rain. He walked up to William and grasped the horse's bridle. 'I have realised the error of my ways, Duke William.' The lord of Tesson smiled and William glimpsed broken, black teeth beneath the wiry, rain-flecked moustache.

'Accept this, my duke.'

William took the banner Ralph passed him and held it tightly; he was about to speak when Ralph ripped his sword from the scabbard and pointed it at William.

Several things happened at once. Someone shouted 'Murder!' and Herluin kicked his horse alongside Ralph and seized him by the throat. Henri simply swore and drew his sword, but William had no time to move and fought to control his horse from shying at the sight of the long blade directed unwaveringly at its rider.

'Easy!' Ralph removed Herluin's hand from his neck and reversed the sword so that the point faced his own chest. 'This is no clumsy assassination attempt – God knows we've had enough of those. Here is my sword; I put myself and my men at your disposal. Do with me what you will, my duke.' Ralph threw the weapon with a flourish into the mud.

The decision was simple, and William did not hesitate to make it. Aware that Herluin's eyes were on him and that Henri was keeping a judicious silence, he said: 'It is my will that you fight with me today, Ralph of Tesson. Pick up your sword and join me in defeating the rebels. You shall be rewarded for your services.'

King Henri clasped William's arm. 'You did right, boy.' He turned to Ralph. 'But first, messire of Tesson, as you have shown us in the past that your loyalty is somewhat dubious, you shall take the oath of homage to your lord duke; the assembled lords here will bear witness to the fact.'

Ralph hesitated and saw the hard, unrelenting faces. The king, his glossy, well-trimmed beard sodden in the rain; Herluin of Conteville, grey stubble ill-concealing an ancient scar across the left cheek; and the duke, no longer a boy to be trifled with, but a man, whose grey eyes above a tight mouth stared down at him – old enough now to seek what was his. Ralph saw them and knew he was beaten. He bowed his head and took William's hand.

'Kneel, Tesson,' rasped the king. 'Kneel before your king and swear allegiance to his duke.'

Ralph knelt reluctantly in the mud and struggled to remain upright. Grasping William's hand, he uttered the oath of homage.

'Sworn before God, his king, duke and lords,' said Henri as William pulled Ralph from the mud. 'And if you renege on that oath, Tesson, I'll have your guts torn out.' Satisfied that all was in order, Henri rode away to see to his men. Ralph turned to go, but William grabbed his arm.

'I'll not forget what you did today,' he said.

Ralph looked up and when he realised the sincerity in William's voice, he grinned, forgetting the humiliation of the previous moment. 'I sense that you're a good lad,' he said. 'I see your father in you. I'll bring my men up from the woods.'

Ralph's men numbered over a hundred, mostly mounted, and as they swelled the ranks of the royal army, William felt his spirits soar. Ralph's defection was a sign, a good omen for the duke. Will thought so too, and when the king informed them that the battle was about to begin, both men were glad, because they knew that today they would win.

The enemy cavalry were formed in small groups, each with a leader carrying a pennant to signal the commands. Henri's army would meet them in similar formation; there were no archers in either army and the infantry would be held in reserve. It would be a day for the cavalry, no slogging match between foot-soldiers in the mud. Henri's household and baggage were gathered on a small hill at the rear and at the front of his army his household troops gathered around the Oriflamme, the legendary banner of the kings of France since time immemorial. It was even said to be the same Oriflamme under which Roland had fought and died in the Pass of Roncevalles. Beside it, the three ducal lions of Normandy hung limply in the rain. The sight of the banners side by side could not fail to raise the hopes of the royalists.

When Henri's army was ready, the king said: 'If the rebels charge first, we will meet them in the middle of the field.'

Guy charged first.

'They're coming,' murmured Will as the distant blare of horns sounded through the mist. Swords were drawn and shield fastenings were tightened; the Norman cavalry closed up and waited. As yet, they could see very little, then another blast on the horn, urgent this time, announced the rain-sodden movement of horses coming at them through the low cloud. William calmed his sweating horse and heard his heart thudding beneath his mail hauberk. Why didn't Henri give the order? The king's hornblower beside him wet his lips, holding the horn with shaking hands. He was unarmed; it was his job to stay by the king and sound the battle-orders. A sword would encourage him to fight and leave the king at a crucial moment.

'Steady,' said Henri, and checked his horse. The Frenchman's cheeks glowed pink above his beard; and William, to his discomfort, realised that Henri was enjoying this.

The charging horsemen were clearly visible now, the long straggling line battling on through the mud towards them.

Still Henri did not give the order.

Guy's banner in the van was well ahead of the others, his household soldiers screaming dimly along the line which was ragged now; only fear drove them on. William swallowed. If Henri did not sound now, the line, ragged though it was, would smash the stationary troops of the royal forces and the day would be lost before it had properly begun.

Then: '*Now!*' snapped Henri; and battle was joined.

*

William's first battle remained a dim memory of mud, rain and mist, and of hundreds of horses pushing, screaming and kicking through it all. At the trumpet call, he kicked his spurs into his horse and as a result was nearly unseated in the mud. Almost from the start, he was separated from the king, Herluin and Will. It took most of his energies to stay on the horse as they surged forward to meet the enemy. The rain seemed heavier than ever as it drove down into his eyes, making it difficult to see, especially as his helmet slipped down and blinded him momentarily.

It was a nightmare, worse than all his fears could have led him to expect. Herluin was beside him, exercising all his skills as a horseman to guide his own horse and William's through the mire. Both armies were now in the centre of the field and as the impetus of the charges was killed off by the mud, separate groups of soldiers formed into contingents and chose their targets. Two rebel horsemen were coming at William and Herluin.

'Meet them side on,' Herluin shouted, kicking his horse forward.

William picked his man. Instinct told him that in this field of horror, all the niceties of his training would go for nothing. Brute strength and luck were all that mattered. He yanked at the reins as his opponent raised his sword and his tired horse turned to the right, as Herluin had shouted, and the blow took him full on the shield, splintering it into firewood. Grappling with the sword, William brought the blade to bear. His opponent, caught off balance by William's move, was struggling with the mud, but leered up at William.

William raised the blade. 'I am your duke!' he shouted. The rebel made no reply. William was seized by a sudden violence that left him taut with rage. 'I am your duke! How dare you defy me!' The rebel grinned and brought his own blade up. The weapons met with an ear-bursting clang and sprang apart again. But William moved forward, feinted to the left and straightened his arm. His sword pushed past the other and drove into the rebel's throat.

For a moment, the man sat there, then he slumped back, his eyes still registering surprise, and William wrenched the blade free. The rebel's hands went to his throat, and with a choking cry he fell into the mud.

William didn't see him fall. A red mist was all he could see, though the sky above him was white. Red anger and rage; the battle-rage that Herluin had spoken of before the start. He was, for the moment, mad; his mind was filled with unspeakable thoughts and his sword, already wet with blood, would strike home again and again until it was soaked to the hilt. He spurred his horse on, into the mud; vengeance would be his.

*

'So this is war.'

Will FitzOsbern was alive. Pale and shaking, the great smear of blood on his sword indicated that he shook from rage as well as fear. He averted his eyes from the grey brains splashed on the tip of William's sword. They had found one another somehow, in a lull, aside from the main body of troops. The rain was now torrential.

'The king?'

'The king lives.' William spoke in a deadpan voice. 'Haimo of Creully unhorsed him, but the household troops surrounded Haimo and trampled him to death.'

'We should rejoin the king,' said Will, wiping his face.

William nodded, and they moved towards the Oriflamme, still high above the mass of soldiery. A new horn blast drifted across to them, and out of the mist a group of knights crashed into the beleaguered flank of the French household guard. Seeing this, William rode into the kicking, screaming mass. The Oriflamme was down, but the king was still alive, and was cutting a swathe around him.

But Herluin was down. William saw him first. He tried to move forward, but his exhausted horse could go no further. Screaming with rage and frustration, William kicked his feet free of the stirrups and jumped to the ground. But he could not run far, as the mud was deep, and his heavy body sank into it. In what seemed like an eternity, he made progress, but it was too late; Herluin was gone, surrounded by a forest of horses' legs and great hooves.

Then William became aware of the danger he was in. There were men a great height above him, and it was only by the grace of God that a blade did not strike him down. Will was shouting at him from behind as a huge black stallion reared from nowhere. At the same moment, William saw Herluin struggling to his feet, blood pouring from his mouth. As the older man bent to retrieve his sword from the mire, the rider of the stallion noticed him and raised an axe above his head.

'Herluin!'

At the cry, the rebel rider turned and saw William standing alone and on foot. He turned the horse, still fresh and eager, and bore down on William. William raised his sword and waited.

'Bastard!' The rebel was shouting. 'Bastard! Base-born whelp, unfit to be duke!'

William waited. Oddly calm, he felt no fear; he was for the moment. At the last second, even as the axe descended to crush his skull, William thrust his sword out with both hands and impaled the great stallion as it galloped into him. The animal reared, taking the sword with it, and William fell into the mud and rolled. The hooves missed him, and he was up, sobbing at the weight of the mud on the hauberk pulling him down. The unseated rebel was just rising when William reached him and kicked him back to the ground. William crashed onto him and pulled off his helmet, ripping away the mail coif at his throat. A scarred, bearded face stared back at him, eyes wide with fear.

'Who are you?' William demanded.

'I am Hardez of Bayeux,' stammered the rebel.

'Do you know who I am?'

'Yes...my lord duke. I beg you – have mercy on me. I – I will be loyal to you from now. Spare me!'

'Mercy?' William's eyes were cold. 'Mercy? You know aught of mercy, or of loyalty, or of sparing people.' He placed his face next to Hardez's and hissed: 'You shall die, you whoreson scum.'

'Please God, no –'

Hardez struggled, but was met with an iron strength that bound him to the ground; William whipped his dagger out from his belt and slashed once, twice into the unprotected neck of the man beneath him. Grunting with the effort, he struck again and again, heedless of the blood pumping into his face, and would have continued long after the bleeding had stopped had it not been for an insistent voice shouting in his ear.

It was Herluin.

He took the dagger from William and helped him to his feet. 'We have won,' Herluin was saying. 'The day is ours!'

'You are unharmed?' William spoke hesitantly, as if Herluin was not there at all. He took his sword from Herluin.

'I am unhurt,' said his stepfather. 'It would take more than that to finish me.'

William turned, dazed, hardly aware of the scores of soldiers streaming away from the battlefield and into the woods and to the swollen banks of the river Orne.

The day was indeed his.

'William.' The king of France, also on foot, walked up to him. 'William, you are alive.' It was a simple fact. He lived; others did not. 'It is said you fought like three men today, my boy.' Henri paled at the remains of Hardez of Bayeux's pulped neck and face, seeing the spurts of blood drying on William's face and hands. 'Come,' he said, quickly recovering his poise. 'We are chasing the rebels; Guy is among them. Will FitzOsbern is asking for you.'

Will. Will was alive, too. He needed him.

'There shall be more killing today –'

'Yes.'

Henri flinched at the searing hatred in the boy's eyes. He was young to hate like this – too young.

William raised his sword. The killing-rage had not left him. It was still there, and would be unleashed again. 'Vengeance is mine,' he said. 'And by God, I'm going to have it.'

*

In the event, Guy of Burgundy escaped and fled to his great fortress of Brionne on the Risle. William failed to take it by storm, and the stage was set for a lengthy siege. The retreat on the marshes became a rout and so many fleeing rebels drowned in the Orne that the mills of Barbillon were jammed with the dead. For months afterwards, swollen, putrefying corpses continued to surface on the river bank.

In October of that year a great council met outside Caen and solemnly proclaimed the Truce of God. Private war was banned from Wednesday evening to Monday morning of each week, and during the whole of Advent, Lent, Easter and Pentecost. Only the king of France and the duke of Normandy were allowed to wage war during these prohibited times. King Henri returned soon afterwards to France, leaving William to deal with the rebel leaders, many of whom he could not afford to punish too severely. With Mauger still firmly in control in Rouen and Upper Normandy, and with Guy secure beyond the walls of Brionne, William's situation was far from safe. But the man who had struck down the mighty warrior Hardez of Bayeux and who had routed his enemies on the field of Val-ès-Dunes, would now begin to command a greater respect from his vassals.

William's minority was over.

Chapter Twelve
Guildford, England, June 1048

The death of Magnus of Norway came as a great relief to the English court.

Since the start of Edward's reign the threat of invasion had hung over the realm like a funeral pall. Even without the treacherous correspondence of Queen Emma, Magnus' treaty with Harthacanute had given him a claim to England; only the war with Svein of Denmark had kept him from England's shores.

'I still can't understand the king's refusal to aid Svein.' Gytha announced as she finished a section of her embroidery. It was a scene depicting her husband riding with his sons.

Godwin grunted and shifted nearer the fire. It was a high summer's evening but he felt the cold so much more these days and he often needed help mounting his horse.

'Edward has no interest in Danish affairs,' he said. I've said it before. The days of Canute are long gone.'

'But surely Edward realises that if Harald Hardrada defeats Svein, he'll be free to invade us?'

'I've told Edward that time and time again. You're right, though; Harald Hardrada is a far greater threat than Magnus ever was. He is Christendom's most feared warrior.'

Harald Hardrada; Harald the Ruthless. The very name sent shivers of fear down the spines of his enemies. At fifteen, he'd escaped the massacre at Stiklestad with only a wound, leaving his dead brother in the field. Forced into exile, he fled to Russia, then fought against Poland before joining the famous Varangian Guard in Constantinople, and saw action in the Greek islands, Asia Minor and Sicily. Along the way he had amassed a fortune in booty, conquered more women than cities and killed more men than he cared to remember. If a man sat and wrote a saga ascribing a series of fantastic deeds to one man, he could feel no shame in naming that man as Harald Hardrada.

'He is a living legend,' said Godwin, thinking of Edward and how different the two kings were, though they were of an age.

'Will he invade England?'

Gytha's question was on the lips of all the courtiers. Trepidation had followed relief over Magnus' death for this very reason.

'I don't think so,' said Godwin slowly. 'I think that because Hardrada is determined to defeat Svein and bring him to his knees, he will not concern himself with us – yet.' Godwin coughed and moved nearer the fire, his face twisted with another anger. 'But God knows we have troubles enough at court here.'

Robert Champart, the Norman bishop of London, had gleefully capitalised on Edward's antipathy towards the house of Godwin, and several more foreign clerics, many of them Norman, had filled the official posts in the royal household. One Norman, a knight, was Ralf of Mantes, Edward's nephew by his sister Godiva, and he had been granted some of the lands once held by Swegn.

But worst of all for Godwin, the king's estrangement from his wife had deepened. It was now common knowledge in the royal court that the marriage had never been consummated. Edward had proceeded to exclude Edith from all court business, discontinuing her privilege of witnessing royal charters – this at Bishop Robert's insistence. The marriage was a farce, and the court knew it. Edith was yet a virgin, Edward lived the life of a bachelor, and Godwin would never have a grandson who would grace the throne of England.

And last but not least of the troubles was Swegn. He'd left England after the rape of the abbess in Leominster, and gone to Bruges for the winter, and then to Denmark where he had perpetrated another crime so heinous that he was forced to leave immediately. And after that, his whereabouts had become a mystery. Some said he was in Ireland with the Vikings. Merchants reported sighting him in Byzantium, with the emperor.

Godwin didn't know where his eldest son was and, if truth be told, he did not care. He had cut him off, declaring publicly that he was no son of his. But Swegn's crime and exile had severely damaged the earl's standing in court, and for that, Godwin was most bitter towards his son.

'Harry will have Wessex,' Godwin spat into the fire. There was that one certainty in all the doubts and confusion: Harold would be earl of Wessex.

*

It had been a glorious summer for Harold. Swegn's departure had enabled him to see Eadgyth without constraint, such was Godwin's fury with his elder son; and, as long as his liaison was not too public, he was free to establish Eadgyth as his mistress. They would never marry. Godwin would soon announce an ambitious alliance for his son with a foreign noblewoman, and Harold, much as he loved Eadgyth, would not break his father's heart by marrying in secret. But it mattered not in the slightest; she was happy to be his mistress, and he loved no other. Already, they had a son, conceived in that first time in the glade, and they called him Godwin.

In this way, Harold divided his time between his earldom in East Anglia, and Midhurst. He had also taken over some of Swegn's lands in Gloucestershire. Life was good, and the king and his French advisors could go hang for all he cared.

Harold set down his book and yawned. It was not without considerable irony that he noted the similarities between the problems of the ruler in Pope Gregory's 'Pastoral Care' and those in Edward's court. Godwin had sent him the book, and told him to read chapter four carefully. Harold chuckled as he remembered this – his father had known he would appreciate the text. Gregory might have been describing Edward; refusing to aid cousin Svein in Denmark, openly supporting the Norman clerics under Bishop Robert and now becoming embroiled in the increasingly dangerous disputes between the kingdom of Germany and the pope. Was Edward casting his net too wide and allowing events to slide out of control? If he was, and if events did slide out of control, then he would surely blame one man: Godwin.

Edward was fast becoming a man who had lost his way. His leadership was vague, his advice dissipated and the result was confusion. Pope Gregory might well have written his book for Edward.

Eadgyth entered the bedchamber with the baby. She had about her the happy glow of motherhood, denied her during the years with Thorgils, and didn't notice Harold's glum expression. Harold had taken to bringing estate business with him to Midhurst and the chamber was littered with scrolls: letters, charters, court proceedings and one or two books, lent by churchmen.

'We shouldn't be involved in the dispute with the Germans,' said Harold. 'Normandy, France, the papacy and Germany don't concern us.'

'Your father says we should be helping Denmark,' said Eadgyth.

'He's right. The king has begun all these diplomacies, and then cuts us adrift before we're finished. He can't concentrate long enough on one task to complete it. In the council last week he broke off the talks to discuss his new church. Can you credit it? A new church is more important than arranging peace for the realm.'

'Is that the church at Westminster?' The baby in Eadgyth's arms gave a cry and Eadgyth unbuttoned her gown and lifted her breast to its mouth. It had the same blond hair and blue eyes of Harold.

'Yes. It will be a copy of the abbey at Jumièges in Normandy. It's not difficult to detect the influence of the odious Norman Champart in this again. Edward means to be buried there.'

'He has lost your respect,' said Eadgyth simply. It was a fact, not a question.

'Yes,' said Harold heavily. 'He has lost my respect and he his own awe and constancy.' Harold fingered the book on the table and remembered Edward's coronation. That day had heralded a new beginning, a day of wonder and splendour, the return of the old blood: it had come to nothing. Jealousies, suspicion, past hatreds and secrets were too much, too powerful to allow for a fresh start. The bachelor king had shunned his wife, remained closeted with his foreign favourites and thought only of his new church. Harold stood up and put his arms around Eadgyth. Despite all, it had been a good summer and he had Eadgyth.

She tilted her head and met his lips. But although she sensed his growing passion in his caress, there was an unease in his eyes she couldn't easily dismiss.

*

Matters came to a head the following summer, when Edward formed a tentative alliance with the emperor of Germany, the pope, and Geoffrey the Hammer of Anjou. The opposing side consisted of Baldwin, count of Flanders – whose naval bases formed a base from where the Viking mercenaries raided and plundered the south coast of England – and Henri of France along with his young vassal William of Normandy, who also joined the league.

Events quickened when Emperor Henry III called on Edward to make good his alliance and asked him to give him naval assistance when he made another determined effort to put down the rebellion in Flanders. Edward agreed, and the entire fleet was summoned to Sandwich to prepare for a naval blockade.

*

Godwin was in good spirits when he entered the king's quarters.

The blockade was going well – so far. But most importantly, Edward was supporting Svein of Denmark, Godwin's nephew. For the time being, England and Denmark were allies.

Harold, Tostig, Gyrth and Beorn were already with the king, and Godwin swelled with pride when he saw them: Harold, tall and confident, was settled now that he had a son and responsibilities; Tostig and Gyrth joked with their cousin Beorn. His kin; his men. Edward was powerless to uproot him, despite his evil councillors. But the Normans, Bishop Robert and Ralf of Mantes, were also present. They needed watching closely.

Godwin bent over the king's hand. 'My lord king, what is it you require my presence for?'

When Godwin straightened he saw for the first time the look of satisfaction on the Frenchmen's faces and knew that something was wrong. Edward seemed tense, but not nervously so, rather like a cat eyeing a cornered mouse.

'We waited until you came, my lord of Wessex,' Edward said. 'There is news.'

'Good news, sire – or bad?' Godwin thought of the blockade and the Viking pirates. Or had the alliance with Denmark collapsed?

The king stroked his beard. 'That rather depends on you, Lord Godwin. Your son has returned to us.'

'My son?' Godwin echoed disbelievingly.

'Yes.' There was no doubting the satisfaction in Edward's voice now. 'Swegn is here.'

Apparently, he had returned from Denmark in disgrace, and had slipped through the blockade into the small family harbour of Bosham. Then, without hesitation, he had ridden to the king at Sandwich, alone and humbled, to plead mercy and to beg for the reversal of the exile laid upon him. Edward said this was a matter for the house of Godwin to decide for itself.

*

They met later, in the evening.

Harold was impassive, arms folded in controlled anger; though Godwin had raged after the king's calm announcement. Swegn's return came as no great surprise. It had been a question of when, not if, he would come back. What would he be like? Sneering and arrogant, or humbled, throwing himself upon their mercy, begging them to put his case to the king? And later, if they were successful, he wouldn't thank them, wouldn't show any gratitude, but would carry on in his destructive ways as before. Perhaps the king hoped for this, so that he wouldn't have to lift a finger to defeat the Godwin family.

But there was no question of that. Harold had decided long ago that Swegn would get no help from him, and Tostig was of like mind; Gyrth would simply do as he was told. Father, though, would have the hardest decision to make. He'd have to close his mind to his first-born, a hard choice and one that Edward was playing upon by putting the decision in the hands of the family. Beorn was the weakest link. Pleasant, friendly Beorn, whose brother was fighting for survival against the Hardrada; Beorn was weak and easily led. Too friendly, and very popular at court, he was malleable and Swegn knew it. Beorn had agreed to refuse Swegn when he came, but it could be a different matter when Swegn actually approached him, so Harold watched him carefully.

Swegn came humbly. He was clean-shaven, well-dressed, presentable and repentant. He entered the room with a look of seriousness that was uncharacteristic. He did not grin, or toss his head; he did not even smile at them.

'Well?' Godwin was stony-faced.

'I came to beg forgiveness, father.' Swegn bent on one knee and kissed Godwin's heavy ring. The earl trembled slightly, then squared his shoulders.

'Get up, boy,' he said harshly.

Swegn stood, and looked his father in the eye with true sincerity. 'I am sorry, father. I – I beg forgiveness for the trouble I have caused, I...'

Swegn's voice trailed off miserably into nothing, his brothers and cousin keeping quiet. The silence dragged on. Swegn shuffled his feet, wishing it would end.

'What of the abbess, Swegn?' Godwin's voice remained steadily hard.

Swegn said falteringly: 'A...a moment of weakness, father.'

'Weakness?' Godwin exploded. 'Weakness?' He pushed Swegn back with a prodding forefinger. 'We are all weak betimes, Swegn, but we do not become animals, like the rutting stag!'

Swegn looked into the bleak eyes of his father and saw no sign of mercy. He noted the grey hair around Godwin's temples , the crow's feet and the heavy bags under his eyes. He saw an old man, not far from his grave, and smiled.

Godwin saw the smile flicker across Swegn's lips and took it for contempt. 'I'll tell you what a moment of weakness was, Swegn,' he said slowly, deliberately. 'It was the moment I begat you.'

Swegn blanched. He took a step back and stumbled. 'Maybe it wasn't,' he whispered. 'Maybe it was when you let Canute lie with my mother.'

The blow landed on his cheek.

Swegn rolled to the ground and lay there, panting, his cheek stinging. Nobody went to him. So the old man thought it was true, then. It must be, for him to react like that. Swegn rubbed the sore flesh that was already welling into a bruise, and got to his feet, unsteady and for once, uncertain what to do next.

Godwin stood with his hands tightly clenched behind his back. A nerve twitched furiously above his right eye.

Swegn turned soundlessly to Harold, who shook his head before the question even left his lips. 'Tostig...?' Tostig stared at the ground. 'Gyrth?' Gyrth cast a quick glance at Harold and met a cold stare; he shook his head. 'Beorn?' Beorn shook his head quickly, but Swegn did not give in; he knew Beorn to be the weak one. 'I helped Svein in Denmark,' he said, looking intently at his cousin. 'He needed me and I helped him. Will you not return the favour for him? Your brother?'

Beorn paused, and met Swegn's glance. Swegn detected the hesitation and grinned: the old, cocksure grin. Beorn saw it and opened his mouth to speak, but Harold cut in first – 'Get out, Swegn. Get out before I shove my sword in your guts!'

Swegn took a deep breath and walked to the door. He stopped and made as if to speak, but thought better of it, and left, closing the door quietly behind him.

The king saw them all the following day.

'What is your case, Swegn Godwinsson?'

'I have no case, lord king.'

Swegn looked at Godwin, his brothers and cousin; it was clear to all of them that the king was gaining mischievous pleasure from the dispute between the Godwin kin. Edward's Norman acolytes looked on eagerly.

'Your kin will not intercede on your behalf?' Edward's blue eyes glittered coldly.

'No, sire. I throw myself upon your mercy.'

'You do not have it.'

'Sire, I beg you – '

'You have four days to leave the country.'

Someone gasped. Bishop Robert stifled a snigger and turned away from Godwin's glare.

The tone in Edward's voice was final and Swegn recognised it for what it was. He bowed and left the hall without a backward glance.

'Now, to other business,' said Edward when Swegn had gone. 'News only this morning has reached me of a disastrous defeat of Mercian forces.'

The atmosphere changed abruptly. 'Griffith ap Rhydderch, so-called king of Glamorgan, has raided up the river Severn in alliance with the Irish Viking fleet. In the Forest of Dean he met Bishop Ealdred of Worcester and defeated the Herefordshire and Gloucestershire levies in the battle.'

Godwin broke the shocked silence. 'Was Ealdred killed in the fighting?'

'No, he was not, God be thanked. Godwin, take the Mercian squadron and close off the Severn estuary. Go with Tostig.' Edward glanced at Harold. 'The earl of East Anglia remains here. Beorn, you go to Pevensey with the Wessex squadron and wait until I send further commands.'

*

Beorn waited a week and heard no news from the king. He made his headquarters the Roman fortress at Pevensey and encamped within the ancient walls. On the morning of the eighth day after departing from Sandwich, he climbed the flint walls of the ruin and sat in the sun, watching the bobbing sails beneath the clouds scudding across an otherwise clear horizon. He bit into an apple and wondered if there were orders, and whether there would be enough wind to move.

'Lord Beorn!'

A messenger was running across the grass. Beorn took a final bite and threw the core into the ditch. 'What is it?' he asked, carefully negotiating the stonework.

'Swegn Godwinsson would speak with you, my lord.'

Beorn nearly lost his grip and fell off the wall. Cursing softly, he negotiated the last few feet and jumped onto the grass. 'Swegn – here?'

'Yes, my lord; at the gates.'

Beorn thought quickly. It was clear why Swegn had come to him; he was the weakest one of them all – Harold had told him that. Too friendly for his own good, he had said, and he was right. So now what would he say to Swegn? God knows this last week he had wrestled with his conscience enough. Swegn said he'd helped Svein, fighting for survival in Denmark, and Svein would expect his brother to return that help.

'He would speak with you, my lord – urgently.'

It would be urgent, Beorn thought as he hurried across the grass. Swegn's time had run out; the four days were up and he was outlaw: wolf's head. Any man could strike him dead and not stand trial for it.

So what did he want with Beorn?

At Swegn's familiar grin, Beorn's stomach turned to water. He was hopelessly lost without Godwin or Harold, and Swegn knew it.

'Beorn.' Swegn laid a hand on his cousin's shoulder. 'You must help me. I know that you wanted to do so last week, but the pressure of my father and brothers on you was too great. Don't worry – I forgive you. What do you say?' Swegn spoke in a soothing voice, hands clasped together.

Beorn didn't know what to do, and was furious with himself. Why could he not tell Swegn to get out, as Harold had? Instead, he stammered: 'Surely the king's judgement cannot be reversed?'

'The king's wish is his own. He makes – and breaks – laws,' said Swegn. Beorn had no answer for that. 'We cannot discuss it here,' Swegn said quickly, before Beorn could reply. 'We'll go to my ship.'

That made good sense, anyhow: the king's men could come upon them at any moment, and Beorn could be arrested for harbouring an outlaw.

Harold was annoyed at being left behind with the king at Sandwich while all the others set off to deal with the Welsh uprising. There was a reason, Godwin had told him before he left for Bristol: the king wanted them separated so they could not conspire against him. *There is no trust,* said Godwin, *be on your guard. Watch the Frenchmen, especially the oily bishop of London.* Harold obeyed, although there was nothing outwardly circumspect in the king's dealings. His hands were full with the foreign alliances and now the Welsh raids, and the quarrels in court were temporarily suspended for the greater good of the realm.

Swegn worried Harold, though. The way he'd backed down without a fight was uncharacteristic; how swiftly he had accepted the king's judgement and departed, without strong words or threats of violence. And although the crisis in Wales had united the court, the immense satisfaction shared between the king and his Normans over Godwin's discomfiture was undisguised. Harold had plenty of time to think about this, and he concluded that they had not seen the last of Swegn. He had so many enemies that there was nowhere he could go but England: he would be back.

*

The sea was calm and warm. Swegn lay back on the boards of the little rowing boat and stared at the coast. 'I missed this,' he said. 'I missed the warmth, the sunshine. God, but it's cold in Denmark.'

Beorn felt relaxed and accepted the flagon of wine Swegn passed him.

'What did you do out there, that was so grievous?'

'Not much,' said Swegn briefly, taking the flagon back.

'You must have done something to incur my brother's wrath.'

'I do not wish to discuss it any further.' Swegn's mouth shut like a trap, his eyes black with fury. Then he burst into a peal of laughter. 'Come on,' he said, 'We're there, now.'

Beorn stood unsteadily in the small boat, glad that Swegn's mood remained good. But it was puzzling how the man could be so friendly one minute, and the next...

'Catch!'

Beorn looked about wildly for the rope, but too late it splashed into the water. Swegn laughed and clapped him on the back. 'I thought that the Danes were all expert seamen,' he said.

Beorn grinned sheepishly, 'Not this one.' Swegn smiled back and passed the rope.

The deck of Swegn's ship was steady; only the mast creaked gently far above them.

'I usually get seasick,' said Beorn, leaning against the side.

'The wind's getting up.' Swegn pointed to the grey clouds on the horizon of the blue sky. 'What do you say to sailing to Bexhill?'

Beorn nodded agreement. It seemed a reasonable plan of action.

'You'll be caught out, sitting here. How many ships do you have under your command?'

'Eight, all told. The others lie around the point.'

Swegn gave the orders to set sail and while they waited for the wind to get up, fetched some wine and food and placed it on a bench. 'To business,' he said, filling two cups. 'Will you plead my case to the king?'

The question was put simply, and Beorn knew Swegn required a simple answer.

'Yes,' he said after a long pause. 'I will do so.'

Swegn sighed with relief. 'I knew you would.' He held out his hand and Beorn grasped it tightly, wondering what he had said. Swegn was staring at him, his blue eyes glittering oddly, as if he was fevered. Was he drunk? Euphoria, perhaps?

Swegn laughed and drank deeply from the tankard. The ship was beginning to move quickly under the fresh wind. 'Don't get sea-sick, cousin. This is good wine and I don't want it wasted!' Suddenly serious, he added: 'You are positive that you will help?'

Beorn avoided the intense stare again. 'Yes, of course...as far as I can be.'

'*No!*'

Swegn banged the bench with his fist. Beorn flinched at the sound, and a group of seagulls screamed past them. 'You must be sure. I cannot have my father and Harold making you back off at a shake of the head – like last time!'

As he spoke, Swegn waved his dagger in the air. Swegn was so unstable and unpredictable. Beorn was suddenly afraid – what was he doing here? He should be at Pevensey, in command of the king's ships, not on Swegn's ship communing with an exile, wolf's head.

'Take me back to Pevensey,' he said sharply, with a confidence he did not feel. He stood on the rolling deck and moved away from the table.

'You're not leaving me...are you, Beorn?' Swegn's voice had dipped to a hoarse whisper.

'I have to think.' Beorn folded his arms and shivered, not with cold, but with fear, though he tried to contain it within him.

'You can't leave me now!' Swegn held the dagger to Beorn's face. 'You want my land, don't you? That's what it is – you want to keep my land. So does Harold; you've divided my earldom between you and my return ruined your careful plans!'

It was true that they had shared out Swegn's lands, but only to prevent the Frenchmen from gaining them and thus weakening the power of the house of Godwin. 'It isn't true, Swegn, we didn't – I...'

Swegn's dagger took him in the stomach. Beorn's mouth fell open, his eyes wide with shock. He tried to speak, but Swegn twisted the blade deeper. 'I am your kinsman,' he gasped eventually, holding his hands to the wound. Blood spurted out between his fingers.

'You betrayed me,' Swegn spat through clenched teeth.

Swegn's face was a mask of hatred as he raised the dagger and struck again and again, ignoring Beorn's cries as he stabbed his neck and stomach.

Eventually, Swegn stopped, heaving with exertion, and looked at the bloody corpse on the deck. His own hands, arms and face were covered with blood: Beorn's blood. He dropped the dagger.

'Put ashore at Bexhill,' he said to the speechless crew. He felt no emotion, no compunction. The ship rolled slightly and the dagger clattered across the boards. 'Bury him deep.'

*

Swegn's crime was enormous.

It was Harold, sick with grief and guilt, who recovered the body and buried Beorn alongside Canute in the Old Minster at Winchester, in the presence of friends and sailors from London. Two days after the funeral, the king convened a council and declared Swegn nithing. This meant that he was a non-person, beyond the pale - even worse than an outlaw.

After the murder, six of Swegn's eight ships deserted. Two were captured by the men of Hastings, who unceremoniously hanged the crews and took the ships to Sandwich.

Swegn fled again to Bruges, where he was given asylum by Count Baldwin.

One man was considerably pleased by these events: the bishop of London. Robert Champart believed that with God's grace, he would have to do nothing but simply watch the house of Godwin tear itself apart.

Chapter Thirteen
Falaise, Normandy, September 1049

'Marry her, William; it will be a good alliance.'

William turned from the window and considered Will FitzOsbern's advice. It had been Will's idea and he was full of enthusiasm for it.

'It'll seal Normandy's security with Flanders. Baldwin is rich and powerful – with him as your father-in-law, we shall be safe.' Will spread his hands in a gesture that meant there was no argument against this.

William knew that Will's logic was irrefutable. 'But is she comely?' he asked.

Will sighed with exasperation. 'Yes, she is.'

Matilda of Flanders was Count Baldwin's daughter; through her mother, Adèle, she was a niece of the king of France and she was Will's choice for Duke William's bride. It would be a good match in more than one way: Baldwin was powerful and it would seal William's precarious position in the alliance against England, Denmark and the pope. And a union with the French royal blood would rectify the stain of bastardy in the young duke.

'But we're cousins,' said William, still hesitant. It was true; William and Matilda were cousins in the fifth degree, as they were both descendants of Rollo the Viking.

'*Distant* cousins,' said Will. 'Others closer in blood have married. Think of this: she is the niece of the king of France.'

William couldn't deny the sense of it. His position in the duchy depended upon a few trusted magnates, as Mauger still reigned supreme in Rouen and Guy was defiantly holding the walls of Brionne. He needed all the outside support he could get.

'And she will bear you sons.'

'I'll marry her, then.'

Will grinned with relief. 'At last you see sense.'

'But I want to go and see her for myself and ask her father for her hand.'

Will's grin vanished. 'That isn't wise, as you well know. You need not go in person; you needn't meet her until the wedding. It's a risk, as you'll have to cut through Mauger's territory to the north.'

'I must see her for myself.' William set his jaw.

Will gave in. 'Very well, but take an escort –'

'Not too many; it will attract attention.'

'Whatever you think best.'

Will may have won the battle for the bride; but William could dictate the details.

'You'll stay here,' William went on, 'and attend to my business. I want to see this girl by myself.'

Matilda was in the stables when the stranger arrived. Her morning ride had left her flushed and exhilarated. On her return, she found the courtyard of her father's great palace deserted.

The count of Flanders had two sons and two daughters: Baldwin and Robert, Matilda and Judith. Matilda was nineteen, Judith a year younger. The sisters were close and there were no secrets between them, so when Judith overheard their parents discussing a marriage proposal from Normandy, she immediately told Matilda, and they guessed rightly that the young duke was proposing marriage to one of them. Which one, they did not know, but Judith was sure it would be Matilda, as she was the eldest.

'Take this,' the stranger said when Matilda emerged from the stables. He assumed that she was a servant, but she knew instantly who he was, though she took the bridle dumbly from him. The close-cropped hair, the simple cut of his clothes – almost that of the peasantry – and the grim, businesslike look about the ten men in his train, armed to the teeth. All this marked him out as a Norman, and his accent confirmed it.

And there could be only one Norman come to visit the court of Baldwin at such a time: William, the duke of Normandy.

Duke William was tall, but he dwarfed her. He was broad and carried himself proudly; he wasn't handsome – not even really very good-looking – but he wasn't unattractive. It was an interesting face, dominated by the wide nose, the thick lips, and grey eyes. Matilda watched him joke with his men unaware of her true identity, and was in an agony of suspense. Had he come to marry her or Judith? She heard stifled laughter, and then her own smile vanished, for she quite distinctly heard William utter in a voice hardly lowered – *I wouldn't say no to a tumble in the hay with that one* - and she turned crimson with embarrassment as the men glanced at her, sniggering openly.

Then Count Baldwin marched from the hall and shouted a greeting. Handing William a cup of wine, he said with a wide smile: 'And I see you have already become acquainted with my daughter, Matilda.' He gestured to Matilda, standing silently by William's horse.

But all Matilda's indignation vanished at William's complete humiliation, and she found it difficult not to laugh. Instead, she maintained a prim smile as he stuttered over her hand. 'I am sorry...I mistook you for a servant.' Behind him, the men waited in mortified suspense.

Matilda met the grey eyes of the Norman with a steady glance, her own green eyes dancing with amusement at his discomfort. She was momentarily tempted to slap his face, but as he stared at her, she knew that she had the answer to her question. She realised now why he was so embarrassed and why his men stood rooted to the spot.

Matilda knew that it was her he had come to marry.

*

When Judith managed to control her fit of hysterics on learning how her sister had become acquainted with the duke of Normandy, she said that it could have been worse. 'He could be fat, ugly and old. He is none of those.' Matilda agreed; she was lucky, and it could be worse. 'He is virile,' Judith went on. She ran her tongue along her upper lip and Matilda giggled.

'But he is still base-born,' she protested.

'No matter,' said Judith leaning from the window of their bower. 'He is strong and he will look after you. Look, he's leaving.' They moved to the window and saw the small party of horsemen canter from the yard. 'I wonder what he is like in battle,' said Matilda dreamily. 'They say that he slew Hardez of Bayeux at the field of Val-ès-Dunes.'

'More importantly,' said Judith, 'What's he like in bed?'

Matilda burst into a fresh fit of giggles at this, struggling to control herself even as Marie, the maid, entered the room and announced that her parents requested her presence.

Matilda left Judith still giggling and went into the hall where her parents were waiting. Her mother rushed forward to meet her, her face alight with pleasure. 'The duke of Normandy has asked for your hand in marriage, my darling.'

Some inner stubbornness made Matilda look past her excited mother and say to her father: 'He is base-born, father...a bastard.'

Baldwin replied honestly, 'We know, Matilda, and we have always said that you shall marry one of standing comparable to your own...'

'But then –'

'He is the son of Duke Robert. He is the duke of Normandy.'

'Only part of it – and he might lose that.'

'Not with my help. And it is vital to the alliance. Normandy, France and Flanders must stand together.'

Matilda nodded. She was aware that her parents wouldn't force her to accept. Unlike some, she had the choice. She thought of the man she had seen in the yard: young, strong – brutal, perhaps – but not to her, not to women. Her instinct told her that. And his eyes that hid much pain. She knew about his childhood – they all did – about the murders, the escapes, the hiding and the fear. But he had survived and nothing would stop him now he was a man. Could a union with the house of Flanders and the French royal blood wipe out the last taint of bastardy and take him to the height of greatness? She thought of Judith's words and smiled inwardly: better this than an old, fat bachelor set in his ways.

And William needed love, especially after the life he'd led so far, and, remembering his grey eyes that betrayed an lonely emptiness beyond the arrogant hauteur, Matilda thought that she could be the one to love him.

'I'll take him,' she smiled to her parents.

*

'She says yes,' said William.

Will FitzOsbern smiled at his delight. Never before had his lifelong friend been so utterly stricken by a girl. He'd returned from Lille boiling with passion for the girl he'd asked to marry, and had waited now for three weeks for the reply. In that time, he had endlessly repeated the girl's virtues, her glossy tresses of black hair to her waist, her flawless white skin and pouting little smile.

'I'd go mad if she'd refused me,' said William. 'You should see her, Will!'

'I know,' said Will patiently. 'So you've said many times – and even to her, if I remember.'

William laughed. The memory of his words to Matilda, so mortifying at first, had become a legend in the ducal household.

'It'll be a good alliance,' said Will.

William nodded, but wasn't thinking of the politics of it all. He was thinking of the mass of dark hair, and the flushed, perfect skin of the tiny girl-woman standing by the horse. 'Yes,' he said absently, to keep Will happy, 'It'll be a good alliance for Normandy and for Flanders.'

*

Word of the proposed marriage between William of Normandy and Matilda of Flanders spread rapidly across Europe. The threat of an alliance between the two states moved the pope, Leo IX, to condemn the marriage at the Council of Reims in October of that year, on the grounds of consanguinity.

William was angry at the news. 'If I can't marry her soon, I'll go and have her before the wedding.'

'No, don't do that.' Will urged. 'It would be foolish and dangerous. Although you're betrothed, her virtue mustn't be in question until the wedding.'

'I know,' said William impatiently. 'What does Baldwin say?'

'He suggests we should wait awhile.'

William cursed softy. The ban wasn't entirely unexpected, of course, because of the alliances in Europe, but he'd not thought to fall in love with the girl.

The pope, everyone knew, was in the pay of the emperor of Germany, who had told the pontiff to ban the marriage in the hope that the alliance between France, Flanders and Normandy would collapse.

'It's Geoffrey I fear most,' said Will.

'He's our greatest enemy,' William agreed. Count Geoffrey of Anjou had seized the city of Tours and pushed into Maine and Touraine, the principalities south of Normandy, and in this year he had captured the bellicose bishop of Le Mans and imprisoned him. Geoffrey seemed more determined than ever to expand his territory at the expense of his neighbours; his marriage to Agnes, widow of Duke William of Aquitaine, had led him to pursue interests in the south, in Provence, Lorraine, and even Italy.

'We can't go to war against Geoffrey with Guy still on the loose,' said Will. To defy the papal ban and marry Matilda would bring the wrath of Rome down on the duke, and his enemies would be justified in usurping him.

William sighed heavily. 'Then we must leave the wedding until my position is more secure. We'll send word to Baldwin and suggest the marriage be postponed until next year – we'll not give Geoffrey an excuse, nor Mauger the chance to begin another rebellion.' William's voice hardened. 'But come the summer we'll go to war without fearing the consequences. It's time cousin Guy was uprooted. He's a running sore on the lips of Normandy. We'll finish him when the spring comes.'

The siege of the castle of Brionne had begun soon after the victory at Val-ès-Dunes, but at a pace severely constrained by the lack of resources at William's disposal, and while Guy remained at large, there would be no peace in the duchy. So, they would muster troops – some from Flanders and France – train them in the winter months, plan the campaign, and strike in the spring. There was, after all, a woman and an alliance to fight for now.

*

The castle at Brionne sat on a sheer rock cliff high above the river Risle. There Guy had fled after the defeat at Val-ès-Dunes, leaving his army to drown in the Orne. William's ensuing blockade of the castle had no great effect, and when King Henri returned to Paris he left few men behind, barely enough to encircle the fort. As a consequence, food and supplies had got through, and Guy had frequently escaped to Rouen and returned with fresh troops and high morale, which could only dampen the spirits of the besiegers.

The situation changed in the spring. With five hundred men and a team of carpenters and masons, William set about building a series of small wooden forts on the opposite bank, under the eyes of the guards in the tower of the castle above. From the beginning of May, he was able to direct catapulted stones onto the more vulnerable areas of the walls without fear of counter-attack. On the third week of the bombardment the master-mason, Roger of Catteville, found the duke in his command-tent and told him that the wall of the castle hall would soon be breached.

'When?' William snapped. He was tired and irritable and time was short; Guy had no doubt sent for reinforcements from Rouen since the bombardment began. If they were not careful, the besiegers would become the besieged.

'Three – maybe four days, sire.' The mason grasped his cap tightly, anxious to please the duke and very nervous in the presence of some of the great men of the duchy.

William smiled briefly. 'You have done well, Roger of Catteville; come to me the day you finish.'

When the mason had left the tent, William turned to his advisors. There were several men who had made their stand for the duke over the winter. Ralph of Tosny, Roger of Beaumont, William of Vernon and Hugh of Montfort-sur-Risle were all men who had survived the anarchical years of William's minority. The houses of Tosny and Beaumont were by far the most powerful, established in the reign of William's grandfather, Duke Richard I, and Duke Robert, William's father. Both had survived a blood-feud between their houses, and had joined William after Val-ès-Dunes. Vernon was a lesser house, established by Robert, and Hugh Montfort depended upon William's patronage. All were young, energetic and had good faith in William's abilities.

'Well, what shall we do, gentlemen?'

'A night attack, sire.' Roger of Beaumont was the eldest of the assembled lords and spoke with a gravity that commanded attention. He was tall and powerfully built, with close-cropped black hair and a thin face. 'Weaken the walls and go in at night.'

William looked at the others. He wanted a unanimous decision, not something half-hearted that could go wrong, resulting in blame and confusion. The loyalty of these men was not yet solid; it would take a victory – or a defeat – to decide them. Ralph of Tosny's opinion would be vital, also. Roger of Beaumont had killed Ralph's father in the wars that had dominated William's youth, and William was uncertain how he stood with Roger; old feuds were not forgotten so easily.

'I agree,' said Ralph, glancing at Roger. 'The walls by the hall are so weak that we should attack there with ladders and under cover of darkness. But it'll be difficult and the attack must be co-ordinated carefully. There are a lot of things that could go wrong...'

'Will?' William turned to Will FitzOsbern.

'A sound plan,' Will nodded agreement. 'We don't have much time.'

Two days later, William's scouts reported a small army approaching Brionne from the direction of Rouen. Guy had sent for reinforcements, and he may even have been among the group, as they weren't entirely sure that he was inside the fortress. William increased the bombardment, but he knew that they would have to attack very soon or not at all.

'We cannot wait any longer,' Roger of Beaumont insisted after his return from a patrol. 'Guy's troops will be on us tomorrow.'

The moment had come. William would have to risk the loyalty of Roger and Ralph. 'We attack tonight, then. Prepare the men now.'

They assembled soon after sunset, under the dim light of the flickering candles in William's tent. Roger, Ralph, Hugh and William of Vernon were all there and had their men ready. As William had not ruled out the possibility of a last-minute betrayal, their presence was in itself cause for relief.

William's plan was simple. All the best plans were the simplest. Roger of Beaumont would attack the main gateway to the fort, causing a diversion whilst the main party under William's command would breach the weak walls at the rear, by the hall. No one disagreed with this, though most of the men in the tent had far more experience of war than William, having seen action in the succession of sieges and counter-sieges of the civil wars. William had seen only a wet, confused battle between groups of cavalry. But they listened to him now; his was the right to command, and God willing, he would be right.

Roger began the attack.

Any doubts William had about the lord of Beaumont's loyalty would have to be cast to the winds now, as a blistering trumpet blast rent the night air. Its aim was to rouse the defendants and bring them to the gatehouse. There was no moon, and the air was warm and clear; the lack of rain had left the ground dry and veterans of Val-ès-Dunes thanked God there would be no mud. The thudding of hundreds of feet on the hard earth, accompanied by roars and screams, announced that the attack was under way. The attackers made the maximum amount of noise in order to lead the defenders to believe they were being assailed by many thousands, not a few hundred. William turned to the waiting men along the bank beside him, and drew his sword.

'*Now!*'

There were no trumpets for the duke; the success of this attack was entirely dependent upon surprise.

Swords slid silently from oiled scabbards as William gave the order to move forward. The river water was shockingly cold, and reached up to their armpits. William shivered and grinned at Will next to him; but not one man made a splash. Daylight reconnaissance had marked out the shallowest areas and the interrogation of a local fisherman had confirmed it. All was going to plan, but never before had William felt so vulnerable; concealment was everything, and it would take only a glint of sword-metal to be seen by a guard on the walls and the arrows would come hissing down to bring sudden death in the dark.

William pulled himself to the bank and resisted the urge to shake himself like a dog. The sounds of battle from the gatehouse grew ever louder - Roger of Beaumont would lose a lot of good men up there, another debt for William to repay and William cursed his own lack of faith in him when he was risking death for only a diversionary attack.

'William!' Will FitzOsbern whispered, pointing to the short cliff and the breach in the wall above it; it appeared to be unmanned.

Behind them came a splash followed by loud curse.

The men froze. 'Who was that?' William hissed. 'I'll have his guts – who was it?'

He never found out. A trumpet call answered him instead. Shouts came from above, and the clamour of many men.

'Up there!' Will pointed to the breach.

They were discovered. Ralph of Tosny ran a wet hand through his hair.

'What do we do, sire?'

The men were waiting for William's decision. The sound of running feet above them grew louder as the defenders pulled back from the gatehouse.

The diversionary action had fulfilled its purpose but was fast losing its advantage.

There was only one thing to do. William pulled the horn from his belt and blew hard, praying that it was not water-logged.

With a roar the men surged forward, all pretence of secrecy thrown to the winds. William dropped the horn and replaced his sword in its scabbard, gripping his dagger between his teeth. The cliff was short, but sheer, and finding a way up with wet hands was slippery and dangerous; but it was the safest place to be, as the archers above could not fire down at them. There were several screams from those still in the river caught by the arrows, but most of the men were grimly climbing the cliff.

The dark saved them. It had got them across the river unseen and unnerved the defenders. William reached the breach first, to find it deserted. The hole in the wall was wide enough for five men.

'Will – are you there?'

'Yes.' Will's voice sounded small in the darkness. 'I think they've retreated to the courtyard.'

'Form the men up ready for a general assault,' ordered William. 'It's too late to go back now.'

They were ready in minutes. Roger of Beaumont had pulled his men back from the gatehouse and was crossing the river, but they could not wait for him. William drew his sword and led the waiting men into the torch-lit courtyard. Instantly, a storm of arrows greeted them from the dark walls and the yard became a killing ground. The night was suddenly filled with screams of the wounded and the dying. William crouched by a wall, searching for the archers, but could not see them. The arrows continued to rain down, so that the men were pinned to the ground with the hail of missiles.

The attack had failed.

'What do we do now, sire?' Ralph of Tosny spat out the words in the darkness.

'Pull back,' said William.

He stood up, but a searing pain ripped into his leg, hot as a branding iron, and knocked him to the ground. The black night became a red mist; he fought for breath, and when the air cleared, he saw twelve inches of ash protruding from his thigh. A voice far away was saying, 'I'm hit, by the Mass, I'm hit,' and someone closer to him was shouting, *'The duke is down! Save yourselves!'* and the men around him were running back, scrambling past him and jumping into the water. The panic became a rout and the rout was in danger of becoming a massacre. But William saw none of this, heard none of the screams of terror and didn't smell the sharp stench of sweating, terrified, retreating men: he was unconscious.

*

Will saved him. In the minutes of panic, he kept a cool head and hoisted the duke onto his shoulders and carried him through the rout of cursing soldiers diving into the river. Will lowered him down the cliff, and carried him over the river before the defenders realised the full extent of the retreat and came down from the walls after them.

William was lucky. The arrow had pierced the fleshy part of his thigh without damaging the bone or the nerve; he would walk and ride again. He woke long after dawn back in his tent away from the castle, in a cold sweat and sick in the stomach.

'Drink this.' Will bent over him with a flask. He gulped down the fiery liquid and lay back against the straw pallet.

'How do you feel?'

William looked at Will's anxious, pale and unshaven face and said, 'As bad as you look.'

Will grinned. 'Then it's as well that you have not seen yourself, my friend.'

William struggled up in the bed. 'Why didn't Guy counter-attack? He could have pushed us back and killed us all.'

Will shrugged. 'Most of the men are still with us.'

'Ralph – Roger...?'

There was real dread in William's voice, but Will reassured him. 'They're unharmed.'

But the attack had failed completely. It was only the speed of the panicked retreat – far quicker than any ordered withdrawal would have been – that had saved the men. And the reinforcements for Guy would be arriving later in the day.

'And I have ordered that we raise the siege,' Will said after reminding William of this last fact.

'Damn you, we cannot pull back now!' William struggled upright in the bed, furious with his oldest friend and ally.

'There's no other option left to us, now, William,' said Will. 'It took me all night to come to the decision, watching you lying there with the physician digging about for the arrow-tip somewhere in your leg. I cannot let you be taken captive.'

William lay back on the bed and smiled a wan smile. 'You were right, Will; forgive me for questioning your judgement.' Outside, a blast of the horn echoed across from the walls, and the familiar sounds of the camp – the jingle of horse harness, busy soldiers on the move, cursing and joking, sharpening swords and hammering chain-mail into shape – filled the silence in the tent. 'I wonder why Guy did not counter-attack,' William mused. 'He could have had the lot of us, including me.'

Then Roger Beaumont burst into the tent. 'Sire, the gates of the castle are opening and Guy –'

Ralph of Tosny pushed past after Roger, smiling hugely beneath his black moustache. 'Guy of Burgundy submits to you, Duke William.'

Guy was taller than William remembered. Maybe it was because William was seated in a wicker chair, his left leg encased in a huge bandage.

He'd come with three men and, as tradition dictated, held the keys to the great doors of the gatehouse where so many of Roger's men had died, at the point of a lance. He was thinner than William remembered too, thin to the point of starvation, as were the men flanking him.

'We haven't eaten for days,' he said. 'We were expecting reinforcements, but they haven't come. That's why we did not finish you off last night.'

William nodded, feeling the pain in his leg grow worse. The physician said it would not become gangrenous, but he'd not mentioned the pain; each second was a hammer blow on his nerves, but he breathed deeply, trying desperately not to faint.

Guy knelt at William's feet. 'I beg your mercy, my gracious lord.'

William wiped his face and looked at Guy. He was different from the boy with the books who had shouted across to him in the yard at Conteville – *bastard, bastard* – that sunny afternoon so long ago. They were men now, and treachery was a man's deed. Guy had taken up arms against him, fought a battle against him, and kept alive a rebellion in the castle of Brionne for three years. Treachery was a man's crime and deserved a man's punishment.

There could be no mercy.

William gritted his teeth against the pain in his leg. It was coming in waves now, and would soon carry him off into unconsciousness. 'All your lands are forfeit to me, as are your chattels, your titles and other possessions. You shall remain in my court with promise of safe-conduct, but any further rebellion shall merit death.'

Guy hung his head; both cousins knew that he could not be exiled – William did not have the power to do that to his kin – but he would in effect be an exile in court; landless, penniless and hated. And watched at all times for any sign of betrayal.

'Now get out,' William hissed; he could bear the pain no longer. 'Get from my sight, you snivelling wretch.' Guy jerked his head in acknowledgement and left the tent.

The last words William managed to hear before slipping into unconsciousness was Roger Beaumont's triumphant boast that Guy had missed the fresh reinforcements from Rouen by a matter of hours.

Chapter Fourteen
Eu, Normandy, August 1050

Baldwin of Flanders brought his daughter to the town of Eu for the wedding.

There wouldn't be a better time than now. With William's defeat of Guy in May, and the dispersal of the alliance between the pope and Henry of Germany, it was a safer time than any to defy the papal ban.

The fall of Brionne marked the end of all concerted resistance to William. The lords of Normandy were by no means all behind him, but not one dared to oppose him openly. Since his victory at Val-ès-Dunes, barons had been coming forward to recognise him as their rightful duke and seeing in him a way to end the civil wars. Guy's fall was crucial, and his disgrace and subsequent departure from the court to Burgundy told everyone who did not yet understand, that the base-born son of Duke Robert was here to stay. The marriage to Matilda of Flanders, daughter of the powerful count and niece to the king of France would put a seal on that.

*

'It must have hurt dreadfully,' said Matilda. She was studying the wound on William's thigh. An ugly scar was all that remained of the arrow tip that had ripped into his flesh at Brionne. It had left a clean wound, but it had been weeks before he was allowed to ride.

'It did,' said William, stroking her hair.

It was their wedding night, and Matilda felt that she was beginning to know him. That he was not a man of finesse and grace had been clear from the start. He could hardly read or write; his court etiquette, in which her French mother had schooled her, was non-existent, and he was a man of few words. Yet he intrigued her. It was a shock to encounter such a man (an animal hardly tamed, Judith had said), as all her other courtiers had been simpering, perfumed dandies. They had come from the whole of France, from Burgundy, Maine, Anjou, Aquitaine, Brittany, and from England and Germany to woo her, but none bore the stamp of character that this man had.

After the feasting and revelries – paid for by Baldwin – William had taken her to bed with an ease which surprised him. At first, he was afraid of hurting her, she was so small and delicate, but she responded with a fiery passion that had her lithe body leaping and rearing above him with an energy that delighted him.

'When did you get this?' Matilda fingered a small scar on his shoulder.

'Someone tried to kill me, a long time ago.'

'I cannot imagine what it was like,' she said, setting her head on his chest. 'I've heard so much about the murders.' She looked up and saw the pain in William's eyes. 'But I will say no more, if it hurts you.'

William smiled and kissed her. 'I love you for that. I will tell you, as we are man and wife now, and must share everything if we're to succeed together.'

He began at the beginning, with the lonely boy who'd seen what grown men were capable of doing to each other. He told her of the narrow escapes, the murders and the years of hiding; his fear of the dark, the recurring nightmares and his distrust of all but those closest to him.

Matilda sat silently through it all and when he finished, there were tears in her eyes. 'I still dream, now and then,' he said, kissing her wet cheek, 'so you must accustom yourself to being woken occasionally. But at least you can teach me to read.' He laughed, trying to make light of it.

'What will you do now?' Matilda asked, huskily.

'Rouen,' he replied, his face grave again. 'I'll go to Rouen.'

Mauger.

The churchman was older now, his hair thinner under the mitre. The years had taken their toll, but not the toll of honest labour or worry; rather the toll of good food and lack of exercise. He turned from the window and crossed to a table, his long purple surplice trailing in the rushes.

'What are you going to do?' he said, selecting an apple from the dish on the table. He began to peel it, looking occasionally at his brother as he did so.

William of Arques had the brown eyes and black hair of his brother the archbishop, but there the similarity ended. Where Mauger was grossly overweight, William was powerfully built; where Mauger's jowls quivered as he ate the apple, William's face was lean and tanned a leather-brown colour from the years spent outside on horseback. His mouth turned down into a sneer of disgust as he watched his brother noisily eating the apple.

'It is unripe,' said Mauger, spitting out a pip.

'Of course it is. It's only the beginning of the season.'

Mauger shot his brother a look of exasperation.

'So, what are you going to do?' he asked again.

'Leave.'

'Leave?' Mauger set down the knife. 'Are you sure?'

'Yes.' William's mouth was set. 'I'm a soldier and I don't make hasty or half-hearted decisions. My mind is made up, unlike you men of the church who mediate beyond all the limits of patience and then put it down to God's will.'

Mauger gave out a snort. 'Where will you go?'

'Arques. Until the time is right. And you?'

Mauger paused and fingered the sleeve of his robe. 'I will remain here.'

'Stay?' William scratched his jaw. 'Is that wise?'

'My decision is final.' Mauger selected another apple. 'The bastard can't touch me, and he knows it. He may come to Rouen in all his glory like a Roman emperor returning after a victorious campaign, but he cannot touch me, Mauger.'

'Yet,' said William.

'Ever,' Mauger countered. 'Richard of Gacé is dead – I have seen to that. The bastard's support is still very thin on the ground, and though he has wed Baldwin's daughter, he still relies on that fool Henri Capet; king of France in name, but in truth no more than the king of Paris. William is base-born and nothing can change that. And in any case, I am a man of the church. I am safe.'

'I wouldn't press that point too far if I were you,' said his brother, his leathery face breaking into a grin.'

Mauger scowled. It was a little-known fact that Mauger, like many other churchmen in the duchy, had never received the pallium, his badge of office, from the pope; if this were found out, it could prove very damaging. 'I'll take my chance,' he said.

'As you wish.' William walked to the door.

'Wait.' Mauger waddled after him. 'What did you mean "until the time is right"? What time might that be?'

William paused. 'The bastard has no future. The only real power in our part of the world is Geoffrey of Anjou. When the time comes, he will crush the so-called duke. I intend to be on the winning side. What about you, brother?'

Mauger watched him go and shivered. Was this his conscience pricking him? He snorted at the absurdity of the thought. Not after all these years – never.

*

Every bell in every church rang to the duke's return to Rouen. Work ceased, shutters and doors were thrown open and the people lined the streets to greet the duke, his wife and Count Baldwin of Flanders. The narrow cobbled streets teemed with people, and the army William had brought with him had to fight its way through the crowds. It was a day of celebration, of feasting, and a day to banish the memories of those dark days of war. Few could remember the day when the boy-duke had fled the town that evening when the old archbishop died, but many boasted of prophecies come true, of tradition and folklore and the miracles of Christ. One old woman claimed to have been the duke's wet-nurse and told how she had found the baby one night crawling amongst the rushes on the floor, grasping everything within reach into his little hands, and the people saw it as a sign that he would one day seize all that was his. An old retainer of Duke Robert's told of a dream the Lady Herleve had when the duke was but a seed inside her. In her dream, the seed became a tree and its branches spread over all Normandy and beyond, across the sea...

These tales were not true, of course. People knew it, but did not care; they believed in what they wanted, and the return of the son of Duke Robert after so many years against all the odds was prophetic enough. They believed and rejoiced; Rouen was saved, Normandy was safe at last.

William found the castle empty.

'He left yesterday,' said Baldwin. The hall showed signs of a hasty departure. The overturned chairs, chests left half-full and the ashes of the fire kicked carelessly across the filthy rushes also told of neglect. 'I'll order a clean-up,' said Baldwin, sharing his son-in-law's disappointment; he had long looked forward to the day when he could put the overmighty count of Arques in his place.

'Mauger is in the palace.' William felt saddle-sore and thirsty. 'I would like to see him.'

Baldwin took his arm. 'You can't touch him, boy.'

'I know,' said William bleakly. 'But I will see him now.' Baldwin nodded and began to move to the door, but William stopped him. 'Alone,' he said.

He took Baldwin's household troops with him and carved a path through the cheering crowds. Baldwin had ordered that the day be made over for feasting, and had provided the roast oxen and the wine now being consumed on the streets.

William saw none of this. Numb to the events surrounding him, he was only vaguely aware of the clatter of hooves on the cobbles, the palace guard opening the gates without hesitation and dismounting in the yard. He left the men there and walked on alone, his head crowded with mixed emotions. Half-afraid, half in a torment of rage, his heart raced, but outwardly he forced himself to remain calm and detached.

The great hall of the archbishop's palace seemed empty and dark, in stark contrast to the castle hall, where a frantic departure had left the fire still warm, and a pot of food above it; here there were no signs of habitation, recent or otherwise. It was cold, dark and unfriendly.

William cursed softly; Mauger, wherever he was, was not here after all. But as William turned to leave, a voice, no more than whisper, came from the shadows.

'Did you come to see me?'

William stepped back into the room, and let the door close with a thump that echoed around the walls of the empty hall. 'Who speaks?' he asked, but he knew very well who had spoken.

Mauger stepped from a darkened corner of the room. 'So you have grown into a man,' he said, walking towards William.

William recognised the face. Though undeniably older, it was the same face that had peered down at him in so many nightmares. 'Yes, I have grown,' he said. 'In spite of your attempts to cut me short.'

Mauger looked away from the grey eyes that blazed loathing and asked softly: 'Do you hate me, then?'

William gave a low laugh. 'A naive question from one such as yourself. You expect me to love you?' Mauger said nothing and William continued, 'No, though it may surprise you, no, I do not hate you.' Mauger frowned. 'I have no energy left, Mauger. My youth was consumed by hatred and revenge, and what I am today is the product of that hate.' William moved closer, close enough to smell the wine on Mauger's breath and close enough to spit the next words into his face. 'I despise you,' he said. 'I no longer have the energy to hate you, but I will destroy you. You are nothing to me – nothing.'

William stepped back, fighting to control the anger inside him. 'You're nothing,' he said again, the anger suddenly gone, burned out, the battle within him won. He pushed the churchman away from him and strode to the door.

'You cannot touch me, boy,' Mauger jeered, seeing the duke walk away, and thinking that the boy had done his worst. 'There is no evidence, no proof; they will never touch a man of the church – the archbishop of Rouen!' Mauger was shouting now, sure of himself, stabbing his finger at William's departing back.

William stopped at the door. 'The archbishop of Rouen, you say? You are right of course; they will not touch the archbishop of Rouen.' He walked back to Mauger. 'But you are not the rightful archbishop, as you have never received the pallium from the pope.'

Mauger's face drained of all colour. 'How did you know?' he whispered. 'How did you discover such a thing?'

'It matters not.' William thought of all those who had died at this man's command. 'I will destroy you, though, and all your lackeys.'

Mauger felt a chill along his spine. He was cold again, but this time knew it to be fear. 'What is it you want, William?'

William's grey eyes flickered.

'Retribution,' he said.

Chapter Fifteen
Westminster, August 1050

Edith saw Edward dismount in the courtyard long before she heard the knock on the door. He rarely spoke to her these days, and when he did, conversation was so tortuous and contrived that she wished he wouldn't bother to make the effort.

Five years of a stale and fruitless marriage hadn't blunted Edith's natural optimism. She was a Godwin, and proud of her parentage, much though Edward might belittle her, and although her youthful dreams of a happy marriage had vanished, Edith refused to bow to the king's crushing coldness towards her. She was still a virgin; he had never once come to her bower at night, or at any other time of day for that matter. At first, she had been tempted to take a lover – she could always deny it – one of the handsome soldiers in the king's household guard – or even Ralf of Mantes, for she had caught him looking at her with an expression of guilty lust. But the risk was too great: the threat of a child that was not Edward's was too dangerous. So she turned to God for her sustenance, and gave donations and alms to the poor and sick. She was beginning a costly rebuilding programme at Wilton, and devoted her energies to that.

If Edith had accepted that her marriage was to be one of estrangement, then Godwin had not. The earl had ceased to blame Edith and had sown the seeds of hatred against Edward and his advisors which would one day reap a bitter harvest. And it would be directed at the Frenchman, Robert Champart.

The bishop of London had judiciously increased his power within the court, securing both secular and ecclesiastical appointments for his friends. His delight at Swegn's crimes and misdemeanours was clear to see, and the murder of Beorn, as far as he was concerned, left one less Godwin to deal with. Everyone knew that Robert wanted for himself nothing less than the archbishopric of Canterbury, the highest office of the church in England. The day when Eadsige died would reveal his open desire for the post, and would be cause for the hatred of the two sides to come out in public. Nobody looked forward to that day.

Edward came into the chamber, and bent politely over Edith's hand. He was never discourteous, or offensive – except that once on their wedding night. He had never struck her, but nor did he touch her in any other way; he was aloof, polite and cold.

'My dear. How are you today?'

'The same as most days, Edward: well, thank you.' Edith was sorely tempted, as she had been on all the other days when he asked her the same question, to say: *I am with child*, just to see his tight mouth drop open with shock and put an end to his annoying serenity.

'Good.' Edward's eyes glittered; he was uneasy, and fiddled with the window pane. Edith watched him, and could hear there was a tautness in his voice as he talked about the weather, and how good the hunting had been these past weeks. She detected a hidden excitement within him that he was trying, without success, to control.

Since Beorn's murder, the atmosphere at court had been strained and tense. Shocking though it was, not everyone was sorry to see Beorn die, and there were some who hoped to benefit from a curb in the power of the overmighty Godwins. The distribution of Swegn and Beorn's lands had created further cause for tension in the court. Ralf of Mantes had taken more lands in Herefordshire so that he had most of the shire, and governed it with Norman soldiers based in castles along the border. Harold, Tostig and Gyrth were apportioned some of the estates.

At that moment Edith's chambermaid entered and announced that Earl Harold had arrived. Edward tensed, and ceased his smalltalk.

'My apologies, lord king – I didn't know that you were with the queen.'

Harold had walked straight in and was clearly taken aback by the king's presence.

'No matter,' said Edward graciously, and flashed a rare smile.

Edith watched them carefully. She knew that Harold respected Edward, and the respect was mutual, but Harold no longer revered his sanctity as he had done at the time of Edward's coronation. They all had at first, she thought bitterly, but now they knew better, though the common people still believed Edward was a saintly man.

'How is the earl of Wessex?'

Harold looked up sharply at Edward's query, but could detect no malice in the question. Edward was sincerely asking after Godwin's health.

'He is well, thank you,' he said guardedly.

'Good. I am pleased to hear it.' Edward gave another smile. 'If you will excuse me, I am sure you have a great deal to discuss with your lady sister on a fine day such as this.' He bowed and walked away quickly.

Harold watched him go and said: 'The king seems full of uncharacteristically good cheer today.'

'You noticed also?'

'What is it, Edith?'

'He appears excited about something – I do not know what,' Edith explained, pleased that Harold had seen through the king's odd behaviour in their brief exchange. 'He's been talking in whispers with the bishop of London, as if he didn't know I see him doing so.'

'There's nothing new in that, surely?' said Harold dubiously.

'I don't know,' said Edith quietly. 'There is something afoot.'

Several days later, the king struck.

The alliances of England, Germany and the papacy had gradually broken up. Edward had disbanded much of the fleet and returned the remaining ships to the ports of Sandwich, Rye, Hastings, Hythe and Winchelsea, a decision made at the mid-Lent council. Nine of the fourteen ships were paid off and the remainder were given only a year's contract.

Godwin wasn't happy with this. England needed a fleet, and had had one since the days of the great King Alfred. England's position as an island was both its strength and its weakness: a fleet was essential. But Edward refused to acknowledge this, and most of the ships were laid off. This had done little but increase bad feeling, and the anger felt by the king's refusal to send aid to Svein in Denmark still lingered. Only Magnus' death had saved both Edward and Svein, as the Hardrada had recently sent messages of peace to England. But this, Godwin was sure, was only to allow himself the leisure of crushing Svein and then turning his attention to England, and then where would they be?

Edward didn't listen to Godwin. He had no interest in Godwin's Danish relations and had no wish to embroil himself in such matters, even though Godwin insisted that the safety of the realm was at stake. The fleet had gone, and with it, the last connection with Canute. Edward looked to the mainland – France and Normandy – and forged his links with the place where he'd spent so many years in exile. Godwin guessed, correctly, that the king was secretly relieved that the alliance with Denmark and Germany, which had opposed Normandy and France, was at an end.

But the matter of the fleet and the king of Denmark was only the beginning of Edward's assault.

'Two days ago,' he said, 'it was brought to my attention that an exile had returned and pleaded for clemency.'

Bishop Robert, who had been skipping about like a man on hot coals throughout the earlier business, now leaned forward eagerly. Harold, standing by Godwin, noted this, and with a quick dread remembered Edith's word of warning just as the king announced to the council:

'Swegn Godwinsson has asked that I reverse the sentence of nithing passed last summer after he murdered Beorn Estrithsson.'

Harold gasped, and beside him, he saw Godwin close his hands into fists. Many men cast shifty glances at the earl and his son; neither man seemed to breathe.

'I have done so. Earl Swegn has been reinstated.' Edward could not suppress his smile of triumph now, and Bishop Robert was skipping on the dais again.

'But sire, you cannot...' Godwin's eyes bulged in rage and disbelief at the king's calm announcement. Swegn pardoned, forgiven, reinstated – after what he'd done. It was a deliberate insult to the earl of Wessex, a direct contravention of the decision the family had made. It was a ploy to create dissent in the house of Godwin.

'Sire, I protest!' Godwin shouted above the roar of the astonished council, who fell silent to let him speak. 'Lord king, I object to your decision. He is *nithing* - beyond pardon. My sons and I – with my nephew the earl Beorn – made the decision that after he raped the abbess he was not worthy of your consideration, and then he most cruelly murdered my nephew...I beg that you reconsider.'

'My decision is final.'

Edward's look at Bishop Robert told Godwin what he needed to know: that the Norman had persuaded the king of the advantages to be had from Swegn's secret return.

'Sire, I beg you...'

Harold had seen the look and grasped his father's arm, fearful that matters could become out of hand.

But Godwin shook himself free of Harold and advanced towards the king.

'I beseech you, sire,' he said in a low voice, but the Edward shook his head, smiling slightly behind his hand, and before Harold could stop him, Godwin bellowed loud enough for those at the back of the hall to hear: 'Then damn you to hell, you and your Norman whelps!'

'Jesus, father! What are you saying?' Harold said, catching his arm. But then he noticed that Godwin's face was purple with apoplexy. 'Father...?'

Harold caught him as he staggered and assisted him from the chamber. The councillors, horrified at the outburst, watched in silence, avoiding the glare of the king and the bishop of London.

Godwin lay speechless for two days at the house in Southwark. On the third day he sat up and asked to see Swegn. Harold, who had assembled the family at his bedside, including Eadgyth, wiped the man's brow.

'Is that wise, father?'

'I would see him.' The old man's voice trembled, but brooked no argument.

Swegn was almost unrecognisable. He looked years older than his thirty summers. He was haggard and thin-faced, the once jaunty eyes had dulled, and the grin was gone. The year in exile had aged him twenty years, not one, and he approached Godwin's great bed and knelt, tears running unchecked down his cheeks. This, Harold felt bitterly certain this time, was true humility.

Godwin sat up in the bed with difficulty and stretched out a shaking hand. The illness had taken the colour from his hair and face and he looked terrible. Gytha crouched by the pillow and held his other hand.

'Father,' Swegn whispered, taking the hand.

'My son.' Godwin embraced him.

Of all the family gathered around the bed, only Harold saw the look that passed between Godwin and Gytha as he held Swegn.

Chapter Sixteen
Guildford, January 1051

The winter had so far remained mild. The soft rains of autumn had quite definitely heralded the end of summer, but the expected cold and snow had not succeeded them. The leaves turned gold, brown, then left the trees to spindly solitude. The countryside around them was enveloped in a warm, wet fug that held until after Christmas.

The earl of Wessex was pleased the snows held off; he didn't think his old bones would bear the chill. The mild winter kept the wolves at bay, and Godwin would rather have damp logs hissing on the fire than the company of wolves howling in the freezing night.

Since Swegn's pardon last summer the family had returned to something resembling normality. Godwin had insisted that Swegn be accepted by the other members of the family, emphasising the need for unity in the face of Edward's continual enmity. With grudging respect, they accepted the head of the family's wishes, but they rarely addressed Swegn, and saw him only at Christmas and Easter, when the family gathered at Guildford. Although Swegn was restored to Edward's favour, most of his lands were not returned to him. This did not worry Swegn, for he was a changed man. Old before his time, his arrogance and brash confidence had gone, and he rarely appeared at court, said little, and lived modestly.

The fragile peace at court was shattered at the end of October by the death of the ancient incumbent at Canterbury, Archbishop Eadsige. Christmas was tense and uneasy, as it was clear to all the court that Robert Champart, bishop of London, would surely now achieve the position he had coveted for years, and then use the immense power that came with it to attack the Godwin family.

'It isn't a foregone conclusion, father.'

Harold found the earl staring gloomily into the fire after a day of hunting. The sport hadn't been good, as the rain had made it too muddy, and put the hounds off the scent.

'You should support Aelric, your kinsman,' he urged, bringing his father a cup of warm mead. In November, the monks of Canterbury had elected Aelric to succeed Eadsige. The monks had an ancient right that allowed them to choose the next archbishop, but their choice had yet to be verified by the king, who could veto it, if he wished.

'If I do so, the king will accuse me of putting my family interests before those of the church and the crown,' Godwin said bitterly. He drank his mead and moved closer to the fire.

Harold drew up a stool next to his father. Godwin relied on him increasingly these days. Harold advised on the running of the earldom and counselled on the thoughts of the king and the Normans, and now that Eadsige had died, his support was needed more than ever before. But Godwin, crouched by the fire, seemed to have surrendered the fight against Edward before it had really begun. Beorn's murder had aged him, and had taken away from him the final spark of defiance that was needed now. Betrayed, he had said, betrayed from within. There was a feeling in the family, and Harold found himself sharing it, that the earl would never fully recover from what Swegn had done.

The news wasn't all gloomy, though. Negotiations had progressed on the proposed marriage of Tostig to Judith, second daughter of Baldwin of Flanders. Godwin had wanted her for Harold, but Harold had refused, seeing Eadgyth tearful at the prospect of his taking a wife and putting her to one side. Godwin cursed Harold, but agreed eventually, and Tostig was put forward, there being no question of suggesting Swegn. Immediately after England had withdrawn from the hostile alliance against Flanders, Godwin had written to Baldwin, and after hearing of the brilliant marriage William of Normandy had made with his eldest daughter, Matilda, he pushed all the more for it. Baldwin had accepted and, all going well, the nuptials would be celebrated in the coming weeks.

Two days later, news arrived at the household that was to throw them into further consternation. On 22nd January, the archbishop of York died. The two foremost offices in the church were vacant and awaiting the choice of a king who was unsure whose advice to take.

'It's not the right time to have these appointments in the church,' Harold said to Eadgyth after he'd returned home. 'Father seems to be unable – or unwilling - to control the king's Norman friends in the court. He relies on me and Tostig to bear the weight of his position.'

'The business with Swegn has broken him,' said Eadgyth.'

'But he's still the most powerful man in all England,' Harold said with a confidence he didn't feel. 'His lands stretch from Kent to Cornwall; his daughter is wife to the king - although it is a stale marriage she is wife no less - Swegn has lands in Oxfordshire, Gloucester, Herefordshire, Berkshire and Somerset; I am the earl of East Anglia, Cambridgeshire and Huntingdonshire. The king cannot afford to ignore us.'

*

But the king did.

In March, at the mid-Lent council, Edward rode roughshod over local interests and court unity. Every promotion went to a royal favourite. Robert Champart became archbishop of Canterbury; Cynsige, a royal clerk, archbishop of York; Spearhavoc, abbot of Abingdon and the king's goldsmith, became bishop of London and was succeeded in Abingdon by Rothulf, a kinsman of the king's.

The king had pleased himself. He had opposed local connections and influence, refused advice and stunned the opposition with his bare-faced arrogance. The views of the monks at Canterbury and their ancient privilege of choosing a successor had been utterly disregarded, and Bishop Ealdred should by tradition have been translated from his see at Worcester to York. In Abingdon, the monks made it clear that Rothulf was unwelcome.

The king had flouted tradition and the members of the house of Godwin were deeply insulted, but they could do little except retire to their lands and hope that the king would not be disproportionately advised by the new archbishop of Canterbury.

*

It was an unhappy time for the Godwins, similar to the period following Canute's death, when Godwin had been out of favour with Harold Harefoot and his mother, Aelfgifu. The house of Godwin was definitely out of favour in Edward's court. The archbishop did not remain content with his new position, as some hoped he would, but harassed the earl and deliberately opposed his advice in the great council. He then began to accuse Godwin of appropriating land belonging to the cathedral of Canterbury, and then a rumour began to circulate in court that the earl of Wessex had had a hand in the murder of Prince Alfred and that even now he was plotting to murder the king himself. Godwin was informed that the rumour was first put about by the archbishop.

'I am powerless to do anything,' he said on returning from the council with his sons.

'We knew it would come to this,' said Swegn.

Godwin rounded on his eldest son. 'Yes, damn you, if you hadn't...'

'Father.' Harold laid a hand on the earl's shoulder. 'We can't argue amongst ourselves again. It would be fatal – and exactly what Edward wants.'

'Aye, boy, you're right.' Godwin looked at Swegn. Only a few years ago, his eldest sons would have risen to the bait and by now they would be at blows. 'I'm sorry, lad; it would have come to this whatever you had done in the past.'

'What we must decide,' said Tostig, speaking for them all, 'is what to do now; not what we have done or should not have done.'

'But why does it always come back to Alfred?' asked Swegn.

'I wish to God he'd not come to England that January day,' said Godwin bitterly.

'Wulfnoth hanged for the murder of Alfred, and you swore a public oath to Harthacanute proclaiming your innocence, and that should be an end to it,' said Harold, remembering the snow and the horses, and the dreadful decapitated head held up high by one of Wulfnoth's followers.

'But it's the rumours and the lies that do the damage.' Godwin's eyes were bloodshot and intense, like those of an old boar. 'Not the truth, boy, not the truth itself. The truth harms no man; it is the half-truths that turn him out and hound him. And the archbishop and the king are like those hounds that scent blood.'

*

The crisis came in late summer, but was not directly the doing of the new archbishop or the king.

Count Eustace of Boulogne's visit in late August was a brief one to convey messages from Edward's allies on the continent. But as the son of Edward's sister, Godiva, Eustace was the king's nephew and his stay was prolonged beyond official business. Godwin, already alienated, was further put out by the favour bestowed on the rather arrogant nephew of the king, and was again excluded by the foreign element in court.

When Eustace finally departed from Westminster, he and his men arrived at Dover with the intention of crossing the English Sea the next morning.

They found the ancient town closed to them.

'What's this?' asked Eustace on seeing the deserted streets and the boarded windows. His troops, numbering some thirty mounted men, looked around in weary bewilderment. 'We're to be entertained here – those were the king's orders,' said the count, a plump, red-faced man with a short temper. 'It seems that the earl of Wessex has seen fit to order the contrary.' He turned to his men. 'Prepare arms; we'll put on a show for these English scum.'

'My lord,' one of the knights moved forward. 'The men are tired and the sun is beginning to set. Should we not go elsewhere and report this matter for the king to deal with?'

'My honour has been impugned, and I'll seek restitution for myself,' Eustace spluttered. 'You,' he pointed to a man-at-arms. 'Find one of the town burghers and bring him to me. Take four men.'

Minutes later, Eustace's men were armed, swords and spears at the ready. The horses fretted and pawed the dust, sensing that all was not well as one of the town burghers was brought before them, shaken at the sight of so many men with swords.

'What is it you want from us?' The burgher asked tentatively.

'We want food and shelter for the night. On the king's orders.'

'You cannot have it. I have orders from the earl of Wessex.' The burgher was sweating with open fear now.

Eustace smiled. 'You are a brave man to say such words.' He drew his sword, and was followed by his men. Now will you change your mind?'

Though faced by a forest of blades, the burgher stood his ground. 'I cannot go back on the earl's command,' he said.

'Even if you defy the orders of your king?'

The burgher shrugged.

At this, Eustace's face went dark with rage. 'Name of God!' Then, to his men he shouted, 'Break open that door!'

The burgher watched, unsure what was going to happen, as one of the mounted men backed his horse to a small door of a house nearby. He twitched his spurs into the flank of the animal so that it kicked out and lashed a large hoof through the door, which splintered into a dozen pieces. Eustace shouted further instructions, whereupon three men dismounted and went into the hovel and emerged minutes later dragging a townsman into the street. A sword flashed down and cut short his writhing protests.

'No!' The burgher, realising too late the effect of his obstinacy, ran forward in horror. There was a scream from a woman further along the street and the sound of doors banging. Eustace held up an arm to steady his men. Then, dozens of townspeople swarmed into view, armed with stones, sticks and axes, filling the street.

'Hold!' shouted Eustace, realising that the situation had got rapidly and dangerously out of control. The crowd got closer and closer, and before Eustace could stop him, a burly citizen armed with an axe broke free of the crowd and ran up to the knight by Eustace's side. Hemmed in by his fellow horsemen in the narrow street, the knight had no space to manoeuvre away from the axe, which took his leg off at the knee.

The sight of the cascade of blood stopped the crowd, who backed off, awed by what had happened and satisfied that vengeance had been done. The knight slumped from the saddle and fell onto the cobbles, already unconscious; in a few minutes, he would be dead, the life-blood pumped out of him all over the street.

'Christ Jesus!' Eustace screamed, all attempts at restraint gone. 'Kill them! Kill the bastards!'

Seeing their dead comrade in the gutter, his men needed no second bidding, and urged their horses into a canter. Instantly the street became a killing ground, as the heavy horses trampled men, women and children into the gutters, huge, flashing blades despatching any who remained upright. Those alive retreated, leaving the fallen where they lay, and Eustace, seeing the dozens of people gathering ahead, and hearing the sounds of movement in the alleyways behind, knew that the time had come for them to leave.

'Retire!' Eustace shouted. 'If they surround us, we shall be torn limb from limb.'

Once the men had regrouped, they moved as one down the dusty street, and left behind them the women weeping over the bodies of their children in the stunned and shocked streets of Dover.

The king was at Gloucester with his court when the news reached them a few days later. Immediately he summoned a meeting of the council to see what should be done.

Godwin was infuriated by the Frenchmen's attack on his people; they were overbearing, arrogant and must be stopped now, once and for all. Harold agreed that the king must now take a firm line against Eustace, nephew or not.

Edward considered this carefully when Godwin suggested it at the council and said at length, 'I think that in this case the people of Dover are at fault.'

Beside him, the archbishop of Canterbury nodded sagely. Siward of Northumbria and Leofric of Mercia stood impassively, taking neither side.

'But sire...' began Godwin.

'I gave the command that Eustace should be given food and shelter at Canterbury and Dover and a passage of safe-conduct was guaranteed,' insisted

Edward. 'They received food and lodging at Canterbury but were refused them at Dover. Indeed, one of their number was killed outright with an axe.'

'Sire, they intimidated a burgher of the town and killed a citizen before his wife and children!'

'And why was that?' asked Edward. 'It came to my ears that the earl of Wessex had sent word to the men of Dover that they should not entertain the count and his men.'

'That is not true, sire,' Godwin answered back.

Edward was not to be drawn. He leant back into the throne, reluctant to become involved in a series of accusations and counter-accusations. He addressed the council as a body: 'It is my command that the town of Dover be harried. Earl Godwin, as the town is in the confines of your earldom, I command that you see to it.'

It was a harsh and savage punishment. King Edgar had once ordered a harrying of Thanet because some traders from York had been killed there, and everyone could remember the more recent harrying of Worcester by Harthacanute after the inhabitants murdered two of his housecarls. It was a punishment that amounted to setting armed soldiers against civilians to sack the town, and scarred generations to come.

This was too much for Godwin. 'No, sire, I will not do it,' he looked steadily at the king, whose brow creased.

'You will not...?'

'No, sire, I will not. Eustace killed many of the townspeople – including women and children – and I consider that to be punishment enough. They are not in the wrong, and I will not cause them further misery.'

'Do you disobey the command of your king?' Edward was standing, his pale face towering over Godwin from the dais.

'Yes.' Godwin glanced at Leofric and Siward, and knew there was no help from that quarter.

Harold stepped forward. 'It is over-harsh, sire, and I beg you to reconsider.'

With his son standing by him, Godwin's confidence grew. 'It is a hasty decision, made unjustly and with evil advice,' he said, feeling the resentment of the whole year boiling inside him. The hated Norman's appointment to the archbishopric, the other royal favours, the lies and slander put about the court, and now this. It was the last straw. 'I will not tolerate your government at the hands of these Frenchmen,' he said, waving at Robert and Ralf of Mantes. 'They have taken over the court, monopolised the king's favour and poisoned your mind with their counsel.' Several nobles around Godwin nodded in agreement. 'I will not punish the people of Dover merely because your kinsman was in the wrong and you seek to cover for his mistakes.'

'This is tantamount to rebellion, sire,' said the archbishop.

'Be silent, you wretch!' Godwin could contain himself no longer. He turned to the king. 'Yes, sire, if that is what it is, then that is what it is.' He walked to the door, followed by Harold and Swegn. At the door he stopped, and addressed the court.

'I am heartily sick of the king's total disregard for the wishes of this council and the traditions of the people. We all know what they called his father; Ethelred the Unwise – the same might apply to his son.'

The assembled council gasped and with that parting shot, Godwin walked from the hall, leaving the king shocked at the comparison with his usurped and deposed father.

The declaration had been made.

Chapter Seventeen
Beverstone, near Gloucester, September 1051

Harold left his tent and looked at the army with growing disbelief. Row upon row of tents stretched across the fields into the distance, interspersed with groups of men huddling under the shade of the trees. Arms and armour glinted in the September sun as the men played cards and dice while their masters decided their fate.

So it had come to this. An armed rebellion in the face of the king.

Immediately after Godwin's departure from the council meeting, the earl summoned his levies from Wessex, Harold's from East Anglia and Swegn's from Berkshire and Gloucestershire. Day by day they arrived, the most loyal from the south coast, where the earl was revered. His stand for the people of Dover had brought the sea-crews of all the coastal towns out in strength. The king's reply had been to summon his army to Gloucester, and there it increased daily. Both Siward and Leofric had called for their levies, though no one knew for sure whose side they would take.

What their fate would be, Harold did not know either. He didn't want to fight, nor did Godwin, and they were sure that the king did not want to either.

A trumpet blast halted shattered the quiet peace of the camp. A small party of horsemen was approaching the centre of the field; it was Leofric of Mercia. Godwin strode from his tent and welcomed the earl with a stirrup-cup, which he drank gratefully, and Godwin waved his sons across.

'The king wants to treat,' said Leofric. 'He offers you safe-conduct to talk near Gloucester.'

'He sees reason, then?' Godwin said quickly.

Leofric shot Godwin a look of sympathy. 'No – I fear the king hasn't backed down. Rather, his resolve is strengthened. He offers to talk – and no more.'

Edward arrived first, and seized the shade of the tall oak tree in the centre of the meadow. With him were Robert Champart, Ralf of Mantes, Eustace of Boulogne, and Osbern Pentecost, another Norman lord with lands in Herefordshire. They were accompanied by twenty or so housecarls.

Godwin arrived a little later, immediately furious that Eustace was present.

'You've got a damned nerve, showing your face here after all you've done,' he said, ignoring Edward's greeting.

Eustace opened his mouth to curse an angry reply, but the king silenced him. 'My nephew has given me a full account of the fracas at Dover, and it has served to vindicate my judgement which you have chosen to disobey.'

'His account, yes,' said Godwin. 'But I doubt whether you have heard it from the women and children trampled to death by his horses –'

'Messires, we have come here to talk and negotiate our problems, not to tear each others' throats out like wild beasts,' said Robert Champart, clasping his hands in prayer. 'I urge a sense of decorum.'

'The archbishop is of course, correct,' said Godwin. Robert bowed his head at Godwin's gracious comment. 'We are not here to fight, but to talk. We are, after all, Englishmen, and we do not butcher one another like Norman savages.'

Harold hid his smile behind a hand and Swegn, like the Swegn of old, sniggered openly. Robert's head snapped up and he shot the earl a look of pure hatred, but Godwin merely smiled back.

Noting the tension between them, the king said: 'Your grievances clearly run deeper than the incident at Dover – whoever was to blame.'

'I'm glad that you see that, sire,' Godwin said in a tone of deep irony. 'My terms are these: I will call off my army and swear a public oath of allegiance to you if you surrender Eustace to me and reconsider your choice of archbishop of Canterbury.'

Godwin's terms struck at the very root of Edward's power. To give in to them would be to allow the earl of Wessex to dictate to the king how to govern, but to refuse... The king paled, and behind him Ralf of Mantes ceased fiddling with his swordbelt and said to Godwin in a low voice, 'Are you mad, man?'

But Edward held up a hand and said in a tired voice: 'I will consider your terms, and let you know of my decision, through the earl of Mercia.'

*

The day after the talks, the men began to desert.

'We can't hold them,' said Harold to his father. 'They have a dual loyalty; you're their overlord, but the king has the supreme authority and they fear his wrath. The men of the coast will stay loyal to us, as will my men of East Anglia, but the men of Oxfordshire and Gloucestershire...'

Godwin nodded. Those drawn to the king would be the thegns, the fully trained gentry who, though owing immediate allegiance to the earl of Wessex, saw the king as the greater force, with divine authority. The men from Cambridge came from the heart of the old Danelaw, many of them of Danish descent with a healthy dislike of the English kings.

They knew Harold Godwinsson was half-Danish and would stay with him, but they were not well trained and did not number very many.

Swegn entered the tent and broke the silence. 'Leofric is here again.'

Leofric came in almost immediately after Swegn and said without preamble, 'He rejects it all, Godwin. The king refuses your terms.'

'All of them?'

'Yes. But there is more. The king has outlawed Swegn. His says that his pardon last summer was merely conditional, and that his part in this rebellion has forfeited his right to that pardon.'

'Sweet Jesus,' said Swegn. 'That means my men from Berkshire, Gloucestershire and Oxfordshire will go over to the king. They won't stand by me if I am wolf's head.'

Leofric nodded grimly. 'I do not want to take sides in this, but I do fear for you, Godwin.'

'Do you? Do you really?' said Godwin bitterly. 'Join us then, and rid the realm of these grasping French bastards!'

Leofric shook his head. 'You know I cannot. God knows, I am sympathetic to your position, but if I did join you, my men would not follow me against their consecrated king. Siward says the same.' He laid a friendly hand on Godwin's shoulder.

Both had risen to high office in the reign of Canute, along with Siward – a Dane himself – and each had past disagreements, but never before had it come to this. Godwin nodded. 'You're right, of course. Under Canute, it was different.' He sighed and said: 'What are the king's terms, then, if he refuses mine?'

'Not to your liking, I fear.' Leofric ran a hand through greying hair. 'He suggests that we repair to London, where you and your sons will appear before the council and answer charges.'

'What charges?' frowned Godwin. 'What does he mean – charges? Is this to be a trial and if so, what are we on trial for?'

'I don't rightly know. The king didn't state specifically the charges.'

'Will he disband his army?'

'No, I don't think that he will.'

'Is there more?'

'No.' Leofric, clearly uncomfortable, moved to the entrance of the tent wanting to go. 'I'll come back tomorrow to hear your reply. I'm sorry there is nothing else...'

Godwin smiled and muttered his thanks. Leofric nodded and walked out, and Godwin's smile vanished and he said bitterly: 'Whoreson liar.'

'What do you mean, father?' Harold asked.

'I sometimes wonder whether he ever forgave me for standing by Emma and Harthacanute after Canute's death,' said Godwin. 'I know he had the victory with Harold Harefoot, but the real victory was mine, with Harthacanute, and then with Edward. It is I who have sons who are earls, and it is my daughter who married the king – not Leofric's.'

'But surely he would not...'

'Maybe not.' Godwin shrugged. 'Perhaps I'm being too harsh on him. We're too old for this, both of us. Canute would never...' He stopped himself running away with the past, aware that the needs of the present were greater. There were decisions to be made before it was too late.

*

They were still undecided when Leofric returned the following day.

More troops had deserted during the night, and those remaining were dispirited and nervous. The men of Gloucestershire and Berkshire had gone over to the king on hearing of Swegn's reinstated outlawry, and Ralf of Mantes had poached Swegn's troops from Herefordshire.

'Your position is hopeless,' said Leofric as he dismounted. 'I urge you to accept the king's offer of a trial. He has arranged it for the twenty-first.'

Seemingly, the decision had been made for them.

'The king appears a little regretful of late,' said Leofric. 'He says that he and his advisors acted out of anger and emotion rather than calm judgement over the Dover business. He admits to being hasty and will consider your case carefully and fairly. It is quite an admission.'

Godwin nodded, still hesitant, and said: 'The king does not want to fight. He does not want a war between his people.'

'The king doesn't but his Normans do, and if it comes to battle, I fear you will lose.' Leofric leant forward. 'Accept it, Godwin. It is your last chance.'

Godwin met his stare and relented. 'Tell the king we accept. We shall meet in London on the twenty-first.'

'A wise choice,' said Leofric, smiling with relief. 'I'll tell the king immediately.'

As they watched Leofric ride off, Godwin said, almost to himself, 'Flanders.'

'Flanders? But what of the trial?' asked Swegn.

'Do you really expect us to attend Edward's mockery of a trial?' Godwin rounded on his elder son with sudden anger. 'Don't be a fool, boy. We must leave. Where are the women?'

'Mother is at Southwark, with Judith,' said Tostig.

'Eadgyth is with them also,' added Harold.

'Good,' said Godwin. 'And Edith is at Westminster. Edward may be a fool, a weakling and half-French, but he won't harm a woman – even the daughter of Godwin.'

With that, Godwin gave the order to strike camp and prepare for the long march to London.

Chapter Eighteen
Southwark, September 1051

Gytha and Eadgyth knew nothing of the gathering armies and negotiations at Gloucester until an exhausted and dusty messenger thundered at the door of the Godwin town house in Southwark late one night. Although they had known of the fracas at Dover, and guessed that there might be a confrontation, neither had dreamt it would go so far.

Gytha's first thought was for Godwin's health. The physician had warned that another seizure like the last one would be fatal if the earl forgot himself in a heated argument and lost his temper. She did not worry too much about her sons; they could look after themselves.

Tostig's young bride had joined the household and spoke only a little English. She had settled happily into the house, but did not understand what was happening. The next day, another message arrived. Godwin had penned the note himself, and it told how his army was deserting day by day, and that the king showed no sign of relenting. It was with sick dread that Gytha told Eadgyth and Judith that they might have to prepare for exile.

Godwin and his sons arrived three days after the last message. Gytha saw instantly from Godwin's weary expression that the news had worsened. 'The king's army lines the north bank of the Thames,' he said, slumping into a chair, 'and mine is on the south and diminishes with each hour that passes.'

Gytha looked to Harold and Tostig, and saw by their expressions that it was true. 'Time is on Edward's side,' said Swegn. 'And I am once more wolf's head. Nobody in their right mind would fight by the side of one so worthless as I.' As he spoke, Gytha felt a stab of dismay at the defeat Swegn had given in to. Where was the old Swegn, the arrogant, haughty son who would have shrugged off the king's declaration and laughed his way to the brothel? She caught Harold's eye, and could tell that he was thinking the same. Swegn sat at the table with sagging shoulders, old before his time and defeated.

The bishop of Winchester was announced soon after noon.

'I come from the king,' he said hesitantly.

Godwin rose from the table. 'It is Stigand, is it not? The old queen's cleric and now the intermediary between the king and his rebellious earl.'

Stigand nodded. 'I would that it were not so. I have indeed risen far, but I did not expect to have to do this.'

Godwin gave a hollow laugh. 'One must expect to do anything in the service of the Lord and his king.'

'The king commands your presence and that you transfer your thegns still with you over the river to him,' said Stigand.

'You may tell the king I will send him the remaining thegns under my command, but I will only follow them on this condition.' Godwin paused, and added: 'If I have a guarantee of safe-conduct and hostages to prove it,' Godwin replied.

Stigand bowed, and left as quickly as he had come.

Godwin turned to his waiting family and said quietly: 'I do not think the king will comply with my offer. Tostig, have the horses prepared. We shall be travelling very soon.'

Stigand returned one hour later. 'The king summons you once again to appear with your sons before the great council,' he said.

'Does he guarantee us safe-conduct through the city and back?' Godwin asked.

'No.'

'And have my thegns gone to him?'

'Yes, Lord Godwin. You have only your household troops with you now. I am sorry, Godwin.' Stigand was genuinely moved.

'Do not blame yourself, bishop. Send word to the king that I shall come only when I have a guarantee of safe-conduct.'

Stigand nodded and left again.

'I fear not only a hostile court, but that I will be forced into swearing oaths and even the prospect of assassins in the streets,' Godwin explained to his family. 'Now that he has us on the run, the archbishop will stoop to anything.'

'It's too dangerous to go without a passage of safe-conduct,' Harold agreed.

Godwin turned to Tostig. 'Are the horses prepared?' Tostig nodded. 'Dismiss the servants, then.'

Stigand came again late in the afternoon. The sound of his horse's hooves on the street outside broke the silence within the house. With a sinking heart, Gytha knew that the news was bad as soon as the bishop entered the chamber.

'Well?' said Godwin, sitting at the table with his hand on Gytha's.

Stigand took a chair at the opposite end of the table and surveyed the waiting family. 'The king says he cannot guarantee a passage of safe-conduct or give hostages.'

'I knew it,' said Godwin. 'We're ready to leave. Is that his final word?'

'He said...' Stigand swallowed, reluctant go on. 'He said that you can have your peace and pardon if you can restore to him his brother Alfred and all his companions...'

'Christ Jesus.' Godwin blanched. 'Did you hear that?' He turned to his family. 'They would kill me if I went.' Gytha nodded, close to tears. 'It always comes back to Alfred.' The earl closed his eyes for a moment, then opened them, startling the bishop with his sudden stare. 'You may tell the king that I do not trust my life in his hands. Tell the king that though I do not come today, I shall be back another day.'

Stigand stood from the table. 'That is your final answer?'

'It is.' Godwin's mouth set in a hard line.

'You know that by refusing the king's third summons, you will be contumacious, outlaw and exile?' said Stigand.

'I do.' Godwin rose from the table and grasped the bishop's hand. 'Get from here, Stigand, and tell the king my answer. But I would ask you to delay your return a little, so as to allow us a some time...'

Stigand nodded. 'Of course. I would not allow the Norman archbishop the satisfaction of taking you captive.'

'Thank you,' said Godwin. 'God go with you, bishop.'

'And with you, Lord Godwin, and with all your family.' Stigand walked out of the hall.

Godwin thumped the table. 'There is no time to be lost. I knew months ago that it might come to this, and I have prepared for it. Swegn, you will go to Bosham and take a ship to Bristol. Harry – take Leofwine and head for Bristol overland. Meet Swegn there and go to Ireland; you will be well received in the court of Diarmaid mae Mael, king of Leinster.

The rest of us will embark at Thorney Island for Flanders.'

When Harold saw the sparkle in Godwin's eyes he knew that the old fox had life in him yet.

'The womenfolk will come with me to Flanders,' Godwin confirmed, looking at Judith, who understood very little of what he was saying, but smiled at the mention of her homeland. 'And there we'll seek asylum with Count Baldwin.'

Harold went to Eadgyth whilst she was packing clothes into a chest. She saw him approach but turned away quickly.

'Eadgyth – I must go now.'

Harold took her arm gently, but she resisted. He pulled harder and she faced him, her face streaked with tears.

'And when will I see you again?' she sobbed, shaking uncontrollably.

'Soon,' said Harold soothingly.

'But how will I know that you are safe?'

Harold sighed. Going to Ireland was the hardest part to bear. He was going to raise ships and men for their return, but this did not console Eadgyth; she would be in Flanders, many hundreds of miles away. 'I will be safe there, and will send news as soon as we arrive.'

'Harry!' Swegn was at the door, flexing his riding whip.

'I must go now.' Harold bent and kissed her; she held him tightly, willing him to stay, wetting his cheeks with her tears. 'I love you,' he breathed.

'And I love you, too,' she whispered, as he broke free of her embrace.

Harold walked to the door and looked back briefly. 'I will see you soon.' He nodded reassurance and left. Swegn and Tostig were in the yard, Swegn holding the reins to his horse, grinning with some of his old insouciance. 'Time to go, Harry,' he said. 'The devil's on our tail and there's nothing ahead but danger and difficulty.' He laughed and led them from the yard.

Swegn was right; there was nothing ahead but danger and uncertainty in exile, while the king reigned supreme with his hated favourites. The waters from Bristol to Ireland across the stormy seas would be as dark and uncharted as their future.

Chapter Nineteen
Westminster, September 1051

The following day dawned bright and sunny. Edith rose from her bed in the palace of Westminster and remembered with a sudden shock the events of the previous day. Even now, with the sun warming her cheek, it was hard to believe. She dressed with care, wondering where her maids had gone, as they usually attended her toilet. She went to the windows and looked out. The realisation of what had happened sank into her like a damp autumnal evening. Father, mother, her brothers, all fled. The confrontation had come and gone, and her father had been defeated by her husband.

The door to Edith's chamber swung open and Ralf of Mantes strode in; he was dressed for battle in mail hauberk and coif with a heavy sword strapped to his side. 'My lady, you are to prepare to leave the palace at once,' he said.

Edith caught her breath, astounded that Ralf should come into her chamber like this. 'What do you mean by this? How dare you come into the queen's chambers unannounced and alone?' As she spoke, Edith became aware that Ralf was eyeing her body with slow deliberation, and she felt very alone.

Then Ralf grinned, baring small, white teeth. 'I shaved especially for you, my lady. I bring the king's orders. We cannot find your father, and it seems that he has taken ship to Flanders. The great council has this morning proclaimed your father and brothers wolf's head.'

Edith gasped and reached out for the table. The room was suddenly stifling, and Ralf seemed to sway from side to side. 'My lady?' he called.

He caught her just before she fell. Holding her tightly, he lifted her to the bed and handed her some wine, his eyes full of concern. 'Drink this,' he said softly, holding the goblet to her lips.

'That is not what I ordered, Ralf.'

Edward was at the door. Ralf stiffened and said quickly, 'The queen feels faint, sire. I am helping her calm her nerves.'

'I am better now, thank you, Ralf.' Edith moved from the bed and smoothed the front of her gown. 'I see that you have seen fit to exile my entire family,' she said to the king.

'Not all, no,' was Edward's measured response. 'Only your father and brothers. The others would have been quite safe, but they chose to leave.'

'Where have they gone?'

'Harold and Leofwine headed for Bristol.' Edward smiled. 'I sent the bishop of Worcester after them, but I think he will temper duty with discretion.' Edith nodded in relief; Bishop Ealdred was a family friend and would not hurry to catch Harry. 'Your father and the rest have gone south, where they will take ship, either for Denmark or Flanders. I suspect Flanders, as the sea is too rough for the passage to Denmark. I have sent the archbishop of Canterbury in pursuit of them.'

Edith tried to hide her dismay. Robert Champart would certainly not temper duty with discretion; he would do everything within his power to catch his arch-enemy now that Godwin was outside the protection of the law. She felt relief too, that she would not have to face that odious man in his hour of triumph, but the relief was instantly replaced by guilt; she would rather face Robert for her father's sake than let him catch Godwin.

'Ralf said I must prepare to leave,' she said.

'Yes...' Edward paused, looking at her coldly. 'We have decided that you shall be sent away to Wilton Abbey, your old school. There you shall reside until I decide further.'

'You are sending me away?' Edith felt the room grow uncomfortably hot again, and her heart thumped faster and faster. 'You are banishing me?' She had heard of kings who sent their wives away, condemning them to years of imprisonment in nunneries, but not for one moment had she thought it would happen to her. She grasped the bedstead to steady herself, and saw Ralf start in concern.

'Come, come.' Edward walked towards her and jerked his head at Ralf, who bowed and left. 'You know that our marriage is a sham.' He bent close to her and said: 'I have exiled your father and now I exile you.'

'You cannot do this. It is not your doing, anyway; it is that Norman, the archbishop; it is all his doing!' To her horror, Edith felt tears well up and begin trickling down her cheeks before she could stop them.

Edward shook his head. 'No. In fact he counselled divorce, but I will not have that.' He stepped back from the bed, oblivious to her distress, and said: 'You shall go to Wilton and remain there, with only one or two select servants. You shall leave most of your movables here.'

'No, please, Edward! I beg you not do this to me!'

But the king ignored her and walked to the door. As he opened it, he said over his shoulder, in a tone of pure malice: 'Your father should have thought better than to put one of his bitches in my bed.'

With that, he left, and Edith knew his triumph was complete. She was utterly alone, the house of Godwin scattered far and wide and exiled, her marriage to the king now renounced publicly and all of them shamed.

The bachelor king had won.

Part Two

The King's Choice

Chapter Twenty
Rouen, Normandy, February 1052

'Will you go?'

William considered Roger of Montgomery's question carefully and said, 'Yes. I'll go, providing that the seas aren't too rough.'

The fall of the house of Godwin had come as a great shock to the states of northern Europe. Many could not believe that one so powerful as the earl of Wessex could fall victim to the weak and mild Edward. But events had shown that the earl was not so mighty, and that Edward had a greater powerbase than previously thought.

Soon after Godwin's departure, William had received an invitation to Edward's court, to discuss an alliance and renew their bonds of kinship. Until now, William had had few dealings with England, and had opposed Edward in the alliance between Baldwin and France against Germany, England and the pope. But all that was over now, and it had only been a theoretical alliance with no call for war. Edward's invitation had drawn William into new considerations; it would be a delicate business, as Godwin – outlaw and enemy of Edward – was seeking refuge with Baldwin, William's father-in-law, and Tostig Godwinsson was married to Matilda's sister. He would pledge no allegiance either way, and he would have to tread very carefully indeed.

'I'll sail next week, all being well,' he said, just as Matilda entered the chamber in time to catch his last words.

'Sail next week?' she asked, smiling. 'Where are you going?'

William hesitated before answering. Matilda had quickly proved to be a forceful and headstrong woman, easily matched to his own determination.

They were qualities he admired and sought after in a woman, as he had wanted a wife who would help him govern, and not merely be content with being governed. He needed a wife for another purpose too, and in that she had not failed him either: producing a son and heir, Robert, three months ago. But there were times when Matilda's advice was a shade too forceful, especially where her family was involved, and this could be one of them.

'I am going to England,' he said, carefully.

Matilda's face fell. 'Why – what business is it of ours? You know that my father is sheltering Godwin and that therefore we are on Godwin's side.'

'I am aware of that.' William tried to avoid sounding impatient. 'But Edward is my kinsman, through his mother Emma, who is my great-aunt. So we're cousins, and I'm paying a visit to renew that kinship.'

Matilda could see that William's mind was set on the matter, but it didn't put her off. 'My father and King Henri of France have both interceded on Earl Godwin's behalf.'

'Don't worry,' William said, 'I shall tread carefully. Remember – Edward has repudiated his wife and as yet, he has no heir.'

The king was at Gloucester for Christmas and it was there William found him soon after Epiphany.

William had told few people of his visit, and to this end, only two ships docked at Southampton Water after a smooth crossing. He found Edward in a congenial mood, enjoying his triumph to the full. At last he was free from the cloying legacy of Canute and his Danish favourites, and he embraced William warmly and spoke in Norman-French to his cousin.

'It has been too long since we last met,' he said.

'I was but a boy,' William said, remembering the time he'd last seen this man. It had been at Rouen, before the old archbishop had died and all hell had been let loose on Normandy. Edward, an English exile, had stayed briefly for Christmas at Rouen on his ceaseless travels in search of a home and an inheritance. He had been as he was now, tall and gaunt, with brilliant blue eyes. Now the hair was turning white, the stoop pronounced, but the eyes remained piercingly blue. At the time of their first meeting, Edward had already been an exile of some twenty years, and soon afterwards had gone to England to visit his mother. Shortly after that, his brother Alfred had met his dreadful death, leaving Edward alone and bitter, his hopes dashed; and after that, William had fled, running away from murderers in the shadows of anarchy. Both knew what it was to be afraid, to be hunted, and to know that life was cheap.

'You are a man, now,' said Edward, breaking the silence. 'A man, and duke in your own duchy.'

'And you are king as your father was, and his father was before him,' replied William.

Edward smiled, and Robert Champart beside him followed suit.

William had noted with some surprise that there were no English nobles present. They were all Norman-French; Robert Champart, Ralf of Mantes, now earl of Herefordshire, Gloucestershire, Oxfordshire and Berkshire; Eustace of Boulogne, another of Edward's nephews, and Osbern Pentecost, Ralf's vassal. Matilda's fears were unfounded: Edward had established a court of Norman kin and would be no threat to Normandy. 'It pleases me that you have your own kin to advise you on government, and not the men of Canute's realm,' he added.

William had said the right thing. Ralf and Eustace moved forward to embrace him, and all at once they were all talking together, enquiring as to news from Normandy, the weather, the women and King Henri of France, and more importantly, the growing threat of Geoffrey the Hammer of Anjou.

On the third and final day of William's visit, Edward took him to a quiet chamber in the upper levels of the palace, where he insisted they have a private conversation.

'I would like to know exactly how strong your position in Normandy is at the present time,' he said, taking a window-seat. 'Be truthful – I must know precisely how matters stand.'

William nodded, aware that Edward would not appreciate boasts and bravado. If there ever was a time for straight talking, it was now.

'I'm not yet safe, sire,' he began. 'Geoffrey of Anjou is the greatest threat to us. Last year I clashed with him on the southern borders of the duchy. He's taken Le Mans now that Hugh of Maine is dead, and he threatens my castles at Domfront and Alençon on the border. He only retired from Maine after King Henri protested.'

'And what are your plans for the summer?' Edward asked.

'To take Domfront and Alençon.' William's face was set. 'I can't risk a lengthy siege, but they must be defeated. He cannot be allowed to occupy my borders. Castles are everything in Normandy; control the castles and you have power in Normandy. You do not have them in England.'

'England is a land of peace,' smiled Edward.

'Would to God Normandy could be so. I cannot rest until Geoffrey has been defeated; like Guy of

Burgundy, he is an encouragement for other enemies to take up arms.'

'So you will eject Geoffrey's men from these castles in the spring?'

'God willing, yes.'

'And then your position will be safe?'

William looked at his cousin, wondering where all the questions were leading. 'Safer, yes, but I shall never been entirely safe , I fear, until Geoffrey is dead.'

'And what of King Henri?'

William hesitated. 'He has helped me in the past...'

'But...?'

'He's interested only in the survival of the kingdom of France, at the expense of the independent duchies and counties that owe him allegiance.'

Edward laughed. 'It is a fault of kings, cousin. I shall, of course, be glad to offer any financial aid you require. I can afford it, and there is nobody to tell me otherwise.'

William smiled at this reference to the Godwins, but Edward wasn't laughing now. 'There is more,' he continued. 'I would offer you more.' Edward took his hand and squeezed it. 'I would offer you the throne itself if you could assure me of your ability to keep it.'

*

Matilda had just put baby Robert to sleep when William walked into the bower. Like all noblewomen, Matilda had wet-nurses and chambermaids, but she preferred to care for the boy herself as often as she could, and in times of William's absence she found him a special comfort.

'You spoil that boy,' he said from behind her.

'William – I didn't expect to see you so soon!' Matilda turned and ran into his arms. 'But is there something wrong?'

Seeing her surprise turn rapidly to consternation, William held her tight with reassurance. 'I bring news of such importance that it couldn't wait.' He had planned to travel to Caen and Falaise before returning to Rouen, and was not therefore expected for at least another week.

'Well, what is it?' Matilda demanded, searching his face for some clue as to the nature of the news.

'King Edward has offered me the throne of England.'

Matilda stiffened with shock and stepped back from him. 'But he can't – you do not...how can he? You cannot accept!'

William grasped her hands and pulled her close. 'It's a surprise, I know – but I've had time to think it over. You'll get used to the idea, given time.'

Matilda shook her head. 'It is a ridiculous idea – you will never be accepted by the English.'

'I will,' said William, and described how the chief advisors to Edward were mostly Norman now that Godwin had gone.

'But what of Ralf of Mantes and Eustace – they are Edward's nephews through his sisters, and closer in blood to Edward than you.'

'I asked him that. Edward said that Ralf would never be accepted because he is tainted; he is one of the Norman favourites, a supplanter of Godwin. He has no real power, apart from his levies in Herefordshire on the Welsh border. And as for Eustace – Eustace is an outsider, like me, but he is a fool.' William permitted himself a grin. 'Unlike me. Eustace caused all the trouble at Dover and he's not a man with the confidence or integrity to inspire leadership.'

'And you are?'

William looked at his wife, unsure whether she was teasing him or not. 'Edward thinks I am the man,' he said quietly, 'And that is good enough for me.'

'What of the Godwins? Had you forgotten them? They're bound to make a bid to regain all that they have lost, supported by my father. And we all know that Godwin wants his grandson for king of England!'

William held up his hands. 'I know, I know.' Matilda had asked these questions as coolly and searchingly as if she'd had days, not minutes, to consider the news. 'I've thought about that,' he said, though in truth he had concluded nothing until now. 'Earl Godwin is a force not to be denied, I agree, and if – *if* – the family returns one day to England, he will, without doubt, oppose my election as Edward's heir. If there is no child forthcoming from the marriage between Edward and his daughter – and it seems not – then he'll put forward his own nephew, King Svein of Denmark, to succeed Edward. But I don't think that Godwin's sons have the same loyalties as their father. When he is gone, everything will change.'

'Edward won't live forever, either,' said Matilda. 'Are they of an age?'

'Godwin is the older of the two, and was ill with a seizure last year.'

Matilda fell silent, her mind filled with the growing thought that it might, after all, be possible. But would the English ever accept William as their king?

'I must see Will and tell the others the news.'

'Not now – it's too late,' said Matilda, pulling him to the bed. 'Not tonight. Tell them in the morning.' She bent and kissed him, and blew out the candles before he could protest.

Chapter Twenty-One
Domfront, Normandy, April 1052

All William's hopes concerning England were quickly dashed, for in the spring Count Geoffrey of Anjou struck again. Moving from Le Mans, he took the castles of Domfront and Alençon, claiming them for Maine and Anjou. Both were strategic towns along the border and Geoffrey's advance was a clear signal that he meant to threaten William's own position in the duchy.

William moved fast. He established siege machinery at Domfront castle and appealed to King Henri of France to exile Geoffrey from the duchy. William was fortunate in having the loyal support of Roger of Montgomery, whose marriage to Mabel of Beléme brought him the rich frontier palatinate of Beléme. But Henri made no move to reply to William's call, and William's rapid response brought no results. The siege at Domfront dragged into May, and threatened to repeat Guy's prolonged defence of Brionne, which had lasted three years. A plan to end the stalemate would have to be devised, or time would begin to run out once Geoffrey mustered more troops south of the border.

It was Will's idea. He found William in his command tent, absorbed in polishing his helmet.

'Can't you find a squire to do that?'

William looked up, irritated. The boredom and frustration of the siege were beginning to tell on him. 'It helps me to think,' he said, returning to the rag.

'I have a plan.'

William stopped polishing. 'What do you have in mind?'

'A night attack.'

'We tried that at Brionne and it did us little good,' William said darkly, and continued with the polishing.

'Not here; at Alençon,' said Will.

William looked up again. 'Tell me more.'

'Well...everyone knows that the duke is entrenched in the siege of Domfront castle,' said Will, warming to his theme. 'Under cover of darkness we march to Alençon, which is only a fortified town, and strike at dawn. They'll never expect us, because they believe we're here at Domfront!'

William rubbed his jaw. 'It's a sound plan, but we'll need a guide to take us there – secrecy will have to be paramount – and we can't leave until it's too dark for the guards in the castle to notice our departure. 'Can we make the distance before dawn?' William continued, leaving nothing to chance.

'If we ride hard with the best horses and horsemen, we can be in position before the sun comes up,' said Will.

William was silent for a moment. Will had thought carefully about this. 'It is a risk, of course,' Will added, 'but we have to break the deadlock before Geoffrey strikes again.'

'It's dangerous,' murmured William, feeling the old thrill tingle his spine at the thought of action. 'We can only take the best, and that limits us to about two hundred men at the most. And if we fail...' William left the sentence unfinished. If they failed to break into Alençon, they would be left stranded, the army cut in two, and leaderless. Easy prey for Geoffrey to destroy. 'But we'll do it. Go and pick the best horsemen we have, but tell them nothing, only that they must be on the edge of the camp – by the copse near the river – just after sunset. Leave everyone else to their business. Remember: tell them nothing. Surprise is our weapon.'

They left as soon as it was dark.

Leaving Roger of Montgomery to continue the siege as if nothing had changed, William led the horsemen, stripped of all excess harness and weapons, into the night. All shields and lances had been left behind, and the men had only swords and daggers. In any case, lances and shields would be cumbersome and of little use in the close-quarter fighting they would have if they gained access to the narrow streets of Alençon.

William had no illusions about the risk they were taking. He'd told Edward that he would take these castles and keep them, and that he would defeat Geoffrey. Then, Edward would be able to nominate William as his heir to the world, without fear of the consequences. William had been planning this all winter, and he had won Will over with his eagerness. Will had been extremely sceptical of the king of England's promise, but William had won him round to a grudging support. Matilda, too, had been wary of Edward's promise, saying that there was nothing in it. There was no telling who might be the heir to the throne of England with Godwin still waiting in the wings. William had been forced to agree with that, but it was May now, and there was no sign of the old earl yet. There was so much at stake, too. If William were to die in this campaign, then he would leave Normandy no better off than when his father had left the seven-year-old bastard as his heir. Mauger was still at large, Geoffrey was waiting like a crouched cat for his chance, and Henri of France, for all his boasts, was in no position to stop them. So much to lose; and when they left Matilda at Falaise, she told William that she was with child. Another son, he hoped; a man always hoped for several, in case the first sickened.

The horse stumbled, and William cursed as his stomach jolted against the pommel of the saddle. They were in a part of Normandy he hardly knew. The great forest of Andaines stretched to the left, and reached almost to the town of Sées, where it met the forest of Écouves, to the north of Alençon. The huge trees cloaked the small army in total darkness, shielding them from the pale light of the moon. Only the torch of the guide ahead indicated their direction. That aside, they were invisible, unseen and unseeing.

They made good progress, and the dawn came quickly. The rising sun peeped briefly above the grey skyline before bursting into a red disc of fire. The mist on the river Mayenne, whose winding trail they had followed some of the way, vanished as the sun clawed higher in the sky, turning from red to yellow, and the sky about it stretched cloudless and blue into infinity, mocking the slowly disappearing moon. A few minutes more, and it would seem as if night had never been.

As Will had promised, they had beaten the dawn. Not pausing to admire the glory of the sunrise, William positioned the men. Alençon was a walled town and though the inhabitants would not be expecting an attack, the gates would be manned and guarded carefully. William's plan was simple; they would wait under the cover of the trees on the edge of the Écouves forest, hard by the south gates until they were opened for travellers or tradesmen from Le Mans, on the southbound road. Then, at his signal, they would mount up and charge the unsuspecting guards and force an entry.

Meanwhile, they would wait in the shade of the trees as the sun climbed higher and higher in the hot sky, and catch up on sleep. William ordered that all helmets be hidden from view, and hauberks stripped off, so that they would not flash in the sun, and the men settled down to doze in the bushes, rotating the watch on the town gates.

Crouching beneath his horse, William was assailed by doubts. If the defendants back at at Domfront woke to realise how thin the ranks of their besiegers had suddenly become, and counter-attacked, then they would be finished. Roger would continue the siege as if nothing were amiss, but it seemed to William as he sat in the shade, that it was painfully obvious that the forces were depleted, and that the defenders must notice. And here: would his men be noticed?

There was so much that could go wrong.

It was not until nearly noon that Will crawled through the undergrowth and woke William.

William licked his dry lips and reached for the wine-flask on his saddle. The growth on his chin itched unbearably, and he had cramp in his neck. Will looked equally rough, but his face was red with exertion.

'Jacques les Moulins reports a series of large wagons approaching the gate,' he whispered. 'They'll be here very soon.'

William got to his feet. 'Order the men to prepare their arms.' Will disappeared into the undergrowth, and William strapped on his hauberk and comforted his horse.

The road leading to the gate was clearly visible from the trees, but the edge of the forest ended long before the gates, as the townspeople had cleared the area to build on. But that had been before the Norman duke and Angevin count had decided to go to war. Now it was a stretch of wasteland, parched hard by the sun. Remembering Val-ès-Dunes and the horses braying and screaming in the mud, William was relieved that the same thing would not happen here.

'The men are ready!' Will called softly across the glade.

William waved back, and saw Will's teeth flash briefly beneath his great nasal guard. His chest tightened, but he knew that his apprehension would soon be replaced by an urge to get started. He could see the wagons rounding the bend and the guards at the gate preparing to open up. There were four wagons, all big enough to ensure that both gates were opened. They had some fifty yards of ground to cover, and the open gates would leave William's men some twenty yards to charge through; less, when the guards saw them coming, and began to close them. And if they were not fast enough across the wasteland, then some would get through, and others would be cut off and slaughtered in the town.

They would be fast enough! These men, like William, had been riding horses for as long as they had been walking; riding was as natural as talking and making love.

There was the timing to consider. Should they charge before or after the wagons had been admitted to the town? When would the gates be at their widest and the guards fully occupied? Endless debate with Will during the night ride had left them with the decision to leave it to instinct: William's instinct. He had insisted on taking full responsibility and judging when the time would be right. But today there would be no trumpet calls and no darkness to conceal them.

The wagons were very near the gates now. William made out the long beard of the merchant riding at the head of the little convoy. Some merchants employed armed escorts to deter bandits, but there was none here, and William heard the merchant shout up to the guards to open the gates. Wool was the likeliest content of the wagons; wool from Le Mans, enemy territory. But the gates hadn't yet opened, and the gap between them and the wagons grew smaller. William gripped the pommel of his sword, aware that his hands were clammy with sweat. Why didn't the gates open? He hoped he would not slip as he mounted, letting go of the reins in a sweating welter of fear.

The gates opened, swiftly, and with a clang. Both swung wide open, and the town of Alençon was as defenceless as a virgin in a brothel.

Now.

William heaved himself into the saddle and drew his sword. The men, having watched his every move, were mounted alongside him in seconds. The great war-horses thrashed in the undergrowth, making a row fit to waken the dead, and then they were out of the trees and spurring across the wasteland.

They made little sound save the drumming of hooves. The wagons continued to trundle through the gates and as the leading nag nosed into the gateway, a shout went up: they had been seen.

There was no need for secrecy now, and with the exhilaration of the ride, and the pent-up tension of the night-march and morning wait, they shouted their fear to the winds. William shouted with them, laughing like a madman as the thrill of fear, anger and an inexplicable sense of freedom ran through him.

The guards at the gate were also shouting, in panic, as they tried to close the gates. But the leading nag had her nose between the walls and refused to budge back, despite the wagoner laying on the whip with frantic violence. Seeing the charging horses heading straight for him, the wagoner and the merchants jumped from the carts and fled into the town, leaving the guards helpless at the entrance.

They were all but bowled over. The small army that had emerged from nowhere crashed through the gateway, wave upon wave. William was dimly aware of the arrows thudding down, too late, the gaping faces of the watching guards, rooted to the spot, and then they were through, into the streets, making for the castle. There, the guards at the bailey gates had no chance, and they swept on. The surprise was complete and the guards, surrounded by the snorting, blown horses, threw down their weapons, and only then did they realise that it was the duke of Normandy himself who had come for them.

Alençon had fallen into William's hands like an overripe plum.

Scores of castle guards were walking to the bailey, unarmed and subdued, shocked by the attack and stunned by the presence of the duke himself. A well-dressed merchant leading a dozen others similarly attired, walked through the gates.

'Come to surrender the keys to the town,' Will murmured.

Behind them, townspeople crowded the streets, staring disbelievingly at the conquering troops and hopeful that the town would not be sacked. The knights nearest to William formed a human wall, creating a path to the duke, while behind them the prisoners stood sullen and resigned.

The leading merchant approached William and knelt humbly.

'We surrender the town and wait upon your mercy, Duke William.'

The crowd waited, watching the hardened young man on the large black horse to see what he would do.

William was in no mood for mercy. 'You had ten years of misrule while I was a boy, merchant, to do as you wanted. Yet I claimed the duchy five years ago and defeated the rebels on the field of Val-ès-Dunes, and since then most Normans have recognised me as their duke. Five years ago. Why do you rebel now?'

The merchant flinched at William's words, wondering what could possess a man of such youth to make him harbour such resentment.

'It was Count Geoffrey,' he said. 'He forced us to recognise his overlordship, claiming that Domfront and Alençon are not in the realm of Normandy.'

'I don't believe you.'

'It is true, my lord duke,' he babbled, 'I...we did not know what to do when the count garrisoned troops on us –'

'You could have closed the gates to him and sent for aid from me. I would have come.'

'We were afraid –'

'Liar!'

One of the prisoners stepped forward and said, 'The fat merchant is lying to save his greasy skin – pig!' The soldier spat at the feet of the merchant.

'What do you mean by this?' William asked the soldier, perplexed by the accusation.

'The merchants consented to an alliance with the count so that they could be assured of trade.'

'Do you deny that?' William asked the merchant.

The merchant hesitated a fraction, then shook his head. He couldn't lie to this man whose grey eyes saw everything.

William raised his voice and called out: 'Round up all the Angevin troops!' When this was done, he announced: 'I spare the town.'

Those nearest him gasped, and spread the word across the bailey and into the town. Within minutes the sound of loud cheering filled the area; the bells were rung at the two churches.

The merchant bowed over William's hand, smiling his relief.

'But not the merchants.'

The fat burgher's head snapped up with shock.

'Lord duke, but...'

William regarded with distaste the clammy fear written over the quivering jowls of the man below him. 'You've eaten one good meal too many, my fat friend,' he said. 'Only you and your kind could profit from an alliance with Geoffrey, not the common folk.' He turned to Will. 'Seize him, and nine other leading merchants of the town.'

'What will you do to us?' The merchant blundered forward, scrabbling for William's hand.

'I mean to hang Count Geoffrey's men,' called William to the crowd. 'They are the enemy and will be treated as such. But the merchants are Normans, and have betrayed me, so they will have their hands and feet cut off.'

'Sire, no!' The fat merchant stumbled forward, but was seized by one of William's soldiers. 'Sire, you cannot...!' he gasped. 'I beg mercy!'

Even Will FitzOsbern, ashen-faced, grasped William's arm, saying, 'William, you cannot do this – it is too dreadful.'

William shook his arm free. 'I will do it, and I order it so, even if I must wield the axe myself! And,' he added, 'the rebels at Domfront shall hear of it, and I think they will reconsider their own position.'

One hour later, William was ready. In the centre of the bailey stood a chopping block and beside it, a gallows. A large crowd of townspeople stood, silent and expectant.

William swung up on his horse and waved to Will.

'The soldiers first.' He rode up to the crowd. 'Twenty of Geoffrey of Anjou's men shall hang. The remainder shall go free to tell their master who I am and what I have done here today. The Norman troops are free to go, on condition that they swear an oath to me.' There were groans of relief at the last announcement. As William had surmised, there were friends and relatives of the Norman soldiery in the town, but the people would not be sorry to see the foreign troops die. He signalled to Will, and the first of the soldiers was led, kicking and screaming, to the noose. William watched impassively as he dropped, choked, and died.

When all twenty had hanged, he waved the merchants forward. They too, were unpopular with the people, and there were jeers as they approached the block. There was clearly no love lost between the townsfolk and these merchants, who had grown fat on Geoffrey's goodwill.

'Chop off their hands and feet,' he ordered to the soldier by the block, the largest and toughest man that had come with them from Domfront, a butcher's son who knew how to wield an axe.

The leading merchant was to be first. On stepping up to the block, he turned to William and said: 'What kind of man are you, Duke William? What are you?'

And William, avoiding Will's horrified look, replied, 'You should know, merchant. You, and others like me; you made me what I am.'

The merchant stared back, uncomprehending, and shrugged as he was led to the block.

Within minutes, he was dragged away, screaming and weeping as the other Normans bound his wounds so that he would live, and remind the town of the fate of a traitor. The second merchant kicked and wept as he was led to the block, but William watched impassively as the axe fell repeatedly, thudding through bone and flesh, ignoring the screams for mercy and the piteous cries of agony. The crowd's jeers gradually ceased and they watched in stunned silence, as all ten of the merchants were mutilated, and the ground beneath them grew slippery with blood.

Within days of hearing the news of the capitulation of Alençon and the atrocities committed therein, the people of Domfront surrendered the castle and town to the duke's mercy. They received it, and the two towns with their fortresses became powerful additions to William's defences on the southern border of the duchy.

But Count William of Arques chose that moment to renounce his allegiance to the duke. Despising his nephew's bastardy, he left for eastern Normandy, where he aimed at no less than establishing himself as an independent ruler east of the Seine, and his marriage to the sister of Count Enguerrand of Ponthieu provided the means to support him.

At the same time, Count Geoffrey of Anjou had reached a reconciliation with the king of France; William's erstwhile protector seemed set to abandon and possibly even oppose his former ward. With his uncle in open revolt, his overlord the king in alliance with his greatest enemy, and his father-in-law, Count Baldwin, harbouring Earl Godwin, the enemy of King Edward, the young duke would have to prepare for a summer of hostilities. His hopes of presenting himself as the legitimate heir to the king of England were fast receding under the shadows now being cast over his duchy.

Chapter Twenty-Two
Bruges, Flanders, May 1052

For Godwin, the spring brought hope rather than fear. The winter had been a bleak one, the bleakest so far in his long life. Edward had ignored all pleas for a reconsideration, Godwin's correspondence with the thegns and ealdormen on the Wessex coast had so far proved fruitless, and the stormy weather discouraged any possibility of a sea-crossing.

The marriage alliance between Tostig and Judith had proved invaluable. Count Baldwin of Flanders, a man much feared and respected across northern Europe, had generously housed Godwin and his family at Bruges, and as well as finding money and shelter for them, wrote to Edward, as did the king of France, pleading that he review the sentence of outlawry imposed on the earl and his sons, but to no avail.

In March, they heard of the death of Emma. It was a bitter blow; she was old, very old, but had survived so much over so many years that she had become a talisman of invincibility. Now she was dead, and Godwin, her oldest and only trusted friend, had not been there with her at the last. She had died alone, with the shadow of disgrace hanging over her from her letters to Magnus, her only comfort the memories of past glories and her dreams of what might have been, if Harthacanute had not died when he did.

In April, Harold arrived in Bruges with Swegn and Leofwine, and nine ships crewed by Irish-Norsemen. He had found shelter with King Dermot in Dublin. He didn't stay long, but left Swegn in Bruges and headed west to recruit men and seek out support. Until they were sure of support in the coastal towns of Sussex and Kent, they would be exiles still. The only person pleased to be where they were was Judith, Tostig's young bride. Surprised at leaving England so soon after her wedding and returning unexpectedly to her homeland, she took pleasure in seeing her family again.

Then, one day towards the end of May, word reached them that Harold's ships had been driven off the coast of Somerset. Sailing up the Bristol channel with Tostig, he'd landed at Porlock, near the Devon border. There, they had met fierce resistance from the thegns of Earl Odda, who was the chief beneficiary from Godwin's fall in the West Country. Harold was driven off, and sailed round Land's End and up the English Sea.

Godwin was more shaken than he would admit. It was the first attempt any of them had made to recover their losses, and it had met with unexpected resistance. The possibility that they might never return to England became a very real one, but Godwin refused to allow that to put him off. Now that the fine weather was here, and Harold needed him, they would take action, and quickly, for Odda's fleet might capture Harold in the English Sea.

'Where shall you head for?' said Gytha, when he told them all in the great chamber of the manor Baldwin had given to their use for the duration of their stay.

'Portland. We'll meet Harry there.' Godwin squeezed her hand. The months in exile had not been kind to Gytha, and she had aged beyond her years with the worry and tension. Her blonde hair was totally white now, and she looked tired, her eyes reddened and encircled by dark rings; new lines had appeared around her delicate mouth. She had, by her constant efforts, kept them all going through the winter, while he had sat and moped by the fire. Now the spring was here, it was his turn to act.

'But first, we'll land at the southern ports and recruit men loyal to me. News is that England is becoming heartily sick of King Edward's Normans.'

The last was true; reports had been coming in of Archbishop Robert Champart's increasing arrogance. He placed his own men in power and even expelled Spearhavoc, bishop of London, replacing him with a Norman cleric, William. 'We'll find our cause more favoured in Kent than Somerset and Dorset,' he added. Turning to Swegn and Gyrth, the youngest of his sons, he said: 'So, we shall embark as soon as the ships are ready and go to meet Harold.'

'Not I, father.'

Godwin stopped at Swegn's words. He glanced at Gytha, wondering whether she knew any more than he did. But she shook her head, puzzled. 'What do you mean – not coming?' he asked angrily.

'I've decided that I must make my peace with God,' said Swegn. 'It has been a hard decision to make, but these months in exile have made up my mind for me. I am going to make the pilgrimage to the Holy Land, to the holy city – to Jerusalem.'

'Good God – you cannot go now, boy.' Godwin's face suffused with colour. 'I need you...'

'Do you, father? Do you really need me? I have been more trouble to you than some of your worst enemies, father. I am no good; I am useless, a liability –'

'You are my son,' said Godwin hoarsely. 'My flesh and blood.'

'Harold and Tostig are better commanders than I – they earn the respect of the men, they have integrity; I have not. I will stain your cause with my past deeds,' said Swegn.

Godwin faltered, hearing the truth in Swegn's quietly spoken words. Godwin knew that Swegn had changed so much since his return after murdering Beorn. He had become quieter, more subdued and reflective. But he had never guessed that Swegn would contemplate the pilgrimage to Jerusalem. After all, he'd never bothered with God much before so why now?

'I have thought long and hard on it, father. It has not been an easy decision. I cannot return to England until I have fulfilled my vows.'

'You always let me down when I needed you,' Godwin hissed, slumping into a chair.

'It's not like that, father...'

'Get out, then – go, damn you!'

Swegn moved to the door. 'Do I have your blessing, father?'

Godwin hesitated, and for a minute it seemed that he would turn away, but instead he rose from the chair, and embraced his son.

'The journey to Jerusalem is long and hard. Pray God you return safely,' he said.

'Pray God that I do,' replied Swegn. But the look in his eye told Godwin that even if his eldest son survived the dangers of the pilgrimage, he would never seek his home in England again.

*

Gytha too, was shocked by Swegn's sudden announcement, and his departure soon afterwards left her with a deep sense of loss. With Swegn gone east, Harold, Tostig and Leofwine away at sea, there was only Gyrth left, and Godwin would take him when he went. Godwin shared her sense of loss, and felt his age now that his only company was a young son and the womenfolk.

The evening before their departure for England, Godwin got Gytha alone and told her he would send word as soon as they made progress.

'What if you fail?' Gytha's face was a mask of apprehension. It was a question she did not want to ask, but one that would have to be answered soon enough.

'I have made provision for that. There is treasure hidden in the crypt of the church at Bosham. It can be reached by whosoever of us is not harmed.'

'Does Harold know of this?'

'Yes, and so does Tostig.' Godwin sat beside Gytha on the bed. 'If the worst happens, you can remain here – Baldwin will not let you down. Or you can go home to Denmark. Svein will welcome you with open arms.'

Gytha nodded. Odd to think of Denmark as home, though. She would be welcome there – there was no doubt about that – but it would be strange, foreign. It was over twenty years since she had been back, with Godwin and Canute. Twenty years...

'But we shall succeed, my love.' Godwin broke into her thoughts and wrenched her out of the past. 'And I'll have my revenge on Edward and all his fawning Norman bastards.'

*

The wind was set fair the following day and Godwin made no nonsense about the departure, and before they knew it, they were away, the weeping women tiny on the horizon as the ship sped them towards England. In his tunic, Godwin bore a letter from Eadgyth to Harold, and the memory of her dark beauty, wet with tears, set him thinking of the days when he'd been young, and chasing Gytha across the seas. He thought with a flash of anger of Edith, as fair as Eadgyth was dark, but denied love by her soulless husband. Was it better not to have known love than to know it and lose it? He held Gyrth tight as he pondered over the question, the large ship pitching and heaving across to England – the boy loving every minute of it – and decided that there was no answer.

They headed for Dungeness. Once there, they would take on provisions and begin to recruit men loyal to their cause. Godwin didn't wish to mount a full-scale war against Edward, but a show of force was necessary. And after the king's high-handed dismissal of him and his family, and the subsequent arrogance of his foreign advisors, Godwin felt that feelings had changed in England. Last time he had raised forces against the king, his men had deserted because they were afraid to oppose their consecrated king, but now they might not be so confident in Edward Ethelredesson. The sea-crews and foot-levies of the sea-ports were the men Godwin was relying on now, men who'd had no chance to be with him last time, and men who surely would back him to the hilt after his refusal to harry Dover.

If they did not support him, then there was money enough to pay mercenaries and the Irish Vikings to fight; Harold had those men with him now, but for choice, Godwin would rather have the inexperienced Englishmen on his side.

'Land ahoy!'

'Dungeness, father!' called Gyrth, his face bright with excitement. The boy had his mother's blond hair, and it was tousled by the wind.

'Raise the flag, Gyrth.'

Gyrth ran to the main mast, pleased to be chosen to run up the banner of the earl of Wessex, the dragon of Wessex. He did it, with a little help from the captain, and ran back to his father. But Godwin no longer had eyes for the boy; he was staring intently at the cliffs below the grey-white clouds as if there was a message written on them for him.

Dungeness welcomed the earl of Wessex warmly. Scores of cheering people lined the quayside at the sight of the familiar flag fluttering in the breeze, and their cheers became one roar as the earl was rowed ashore.

'A sight you'll tell your grandchildren about, eh, boy?' Godwin smiled at Gyrth, awed at the waving, shouting people.

Godwin shipped the oars and jumped nimbly up the steps, helped by eager hands. The crowd parted, and a finely dressed thegn stepped forward.

'Edric of Lydd at your service, my lord of Wessex.'

Godwin grasped the outstretched hand and grinned wolfishly.

'It is fated,' he laughed, suddenly feeling younger than he had done for years. He studied the bearded, well-dressed man opposite him and decided that here was a man he could trust. 'I ask you to despatch ten men across the area, telling the news that the earl of Wessex is home to claim his own.'

'My pleasure, Lord Godwin. I hope that you will honour me by staying in my town house whilst you are here?'

Godwin nodded. 'Of course; lead on.'

They did not stay long.

Soon after finishing supper, supplied by Edric's wife and daughters, the door crashed open, and Edric himself rushed to the chamber where they were bedded down for the night.

'Catch your breath, man,' said Godwin, rising from the fireside. He could see that the thegn had ridden fast. He handed over some wine, but Edric refused.

'You are in grave danger,' he gasped. 'Ralf of Mantes and Odda of Deerhurst have set sail and intend to trap you here, at Dungeness.'

'Damnation,' Godwin swore. 'I thought the fleet had not seen us. It's at Sandwich, and I thought we'd avoided it successfully.'

'There is more,' said Edric. 'A land army is near – at Hythe; that was the latest report.'

'Have we been betrayed?'

'No, my lord,' said Edric. 'It is merely your misfortune.'

Godwin's energy washed out of him. It was over before they had even begun. Then he saw Gyrth, sleeping by the fire. With the boy with him, he could not give in now, not ever. 'Rouse Osric, my steward, and tell him to round up all the sailors and men from the taverns and brothels. Send some of your men with him, as they'll know where to look. Tell him to hurry, and if the men don't come, then Ralf will kill them.' Godwin stooped and woke the boy. 'I thank you, Edric, for your help.'

'Where will you go?'

Godwin stopped at the door. 'Pevensey.'

*

They didn't reach Pevensey.

All the men returned to the ships, fearing for their lives at the mention of Ralf of Mantes, and after a restless night, they set course for Pevensey. Once they reached the open sea, however, the royal fleet caught up with them before they could turn to the safety of Pevensey. By noon, it was evident that they were going to engage in battle.

It was Ralf of Mantes. Godwin's heart sank when the banner of the king's French nephew became visible. There would undoubtedly be a battle now. Had it been Odda, a fellow Englishman, they might have come to a compromise, but not Ralf; he would take pleasure in destroying Godwin with his superior ships.

'The wind's getting up,' said Jurgens, the Danish captain. Jurgens was a giant of a man, with a beard to match. Godwin took pleasure in speaking the Danish tongue that had once been part of his life. Jurgens was a mercenary, and as long as he was paid, he wouldn't ask too many questions; he could be trusted to stand firm. The Dane pointed to the Godwin banner above them, flapping wildly in the breeze. 'There may be a storm this evening.'

If we live to see it, thought Godwin. Ralf's fleet consisted of some thirty ships. Godwin had ten, and most of them were mercenaries.

The sky turned a darker shade of grey. The sun showed no sign of breaking through the monotony of cloud, yet only yesterday the horizon had been an untainted blue, the sun as glaring disc of light above them. It was a reminder of how changeable the weather was out here in the English Sea.

Ralf's ships were close enough for Godwin to see the Frenchman leaning excitedly from the prow of his flagship. None of Godwin's ships had battering rams attached, but Ralf would come alongside and board them, and there would be a bitter hand-to-hand struggle on the decks. Godwin would have to surrender, because Ralf had so many more men, and the mercenaries would be hanged without qualm, from the mast.

Then the rain came, hissing quietly out of the grey sky with no warning. The ship lurched violently, sending Godwin against the side.

'The storm will be upon us soon.' Jurgens had reappeared.

Godwin watched, soaked already, as the rain grew heavier and Ralf's line of ships tossed and pitched not two hundred yards from them.

'Look there, my lord.' Jurgens pointed to the distant shore.

Through the curtain of rain, a mist was developing as rapidly and as unexpectedly as the rain before it. It became a fog, and came towards them like a great, white, blanket.

'In a few minutes, we'll not be able to see the prow of the ship, let alone the enemy,' grinned Jurgens.

Godwin was speechless. They were saved. The mist would envelop them like a witch's cape, and they could vanish across the sea.

Jurgens laughed, reading Godwin's thoughts. 'There'll be no battle today, my lord of Wessex.'

*

The storm left them in the night. The tiny fleet was scattered in the fog, but of Ralf, there was no sign.

'Where to now, my lord?' Jurgens was by Godwin's side. The sky was clear now, and he would be able to set a course by the stars.

Godwin hesitated. Where to, indeed? Go on, or retire, to lick their wounds and think again?

'Set sail for Bruges,' he said finally. Harold was not due to meet them for several weeks yet, and they needed time to rest and gather more men. More mercenaries, he thought; men bred and hardened to war, who would teach Edward a lesson, and who would see Godwin return to England in triumph.

It had been a lucky escape, but when was all said and done, they were no nearer England and restoration than they had been all the winter.

Chapter Twenty-Three
The Solent, August 1052

'There!'

Harold followed the direction of Tostig's outflung arm and squinted in the sunlight. Where the blue sky met the sparkling sea, a line of dots was just visible.

'Spithead,' said Leofwine. 'It's father.'

Pray God it is, thought Harold, clenching his fist. They'd met, briefly, at Portland, and Godwin had recounted his near miss with Ralf off Dungeness Head, and then they'd separated, to raise their armies and avoid Ralf and Odda, both at large in the English Sea. It wouldn't do to be caught all together; that would be a catch for Edward indeed.

Since April, nothing had gone right. Bad weather, deserting crews and the fight at Porlock. Not much more than a scuffle – a mere skirmish – but a dangerous one at that. What shocked Harold most was not the violence – and he had an ugly scar from a sword-thrust to prove it – but the force of the rejection by the local thegns. True, they were not the loyal people of Winchester, and the east Downlands of Hampshire, Sussex and Kent, but Harold had expected some support. The man who'd come at him and wounded him had cursed the house of Godwin for the deaths of Prince Alfred, of Harold Harefoot, of Harthacanute even, and shouted that they would one day bring ruin and slavery on the kingdom.

Porlock left them shaken and disillusioned, and they had retired to Dublin to take on more mercenary crews, and then headed for the south coast.

'I can see father's banner now – the dragon of Wessex,' said Leofwine.

'Your eyes are better than mine.' Harold peered through the haze. 'Are you sure? There do seem to be a great many ships.' There were, too. Strung out in a line, some thirty ships rocked gently on the horizon, growing closer by the minute.

For the first time since leaving Bruges, Harold felt a surge of confidence. This time they would succeed.

'It is Harold,' agreed Godwin, rubbing his eyes and acknowledging Gyrth's grin of delight.

When the ships met, Harold ordered ropes to lash the ships together.

'Harry! Leof! Tostig!' Gyrth was waving and shouting. Harold grinned and waved back, laughing with pleasure.

The three brothers fought to clamber aboard. Harold won the struggle and heaved himself on to the deck first.

'Father!' He embraced Godwin. 'You look well.'

Godwin smiled back. 'The weeks on deck in this warm sun have given me new hope.'

'You have many ships – are they all mercenaries?'

'Most are, but eight of them come from the coastal towns. People are beginning to join us now.'

'We have two ships with local men aboard,' said Harold. 'Men from Wareham and Lyme, but none from Cornwall.'

'Aye – it's the Sussex and Kent sea-crews who'll turn out in their hundreds for us, as soon as the word gets round.'

'Where's Swegn?' asked Tostig, having clambered aboard after Harold.

'Where is he?' Harold asked. 'Is he sick?'

'I wanted to tell you all later,' said Godwin, looking at his sons in turn. 'But I see that I cannot delay it. To be brief, Swegn has taken the pilgrim's vows. He is walking to the Holy Land, to Jerusalem.'

'But why now?' Leofwine asked, as bewildered as Harold and Tostig.

'He has much to pray for,' said Godwin dryly. 'His sins are heavy enough, God knows, and now he feels that he cannot return to England until he has endured all the hardship that the journey to Jerusalem entails. It is his way of doing penance. I have you fine young men with me,' Godwin surveyed his four sons proudly. 'United, we shall succeed.'

There was a chorus of agreement, and they all began to talk at once, swapping tales of their various adventures, looking ahead to a bright future, Swegn forgotten for the moment.

*

Godwin's call to arms in the south-east of England was answered with a speed and enthusiasm that astonished everyone, the earl most of all. There was no sign of Ralf and the royal fleet, as the victory over Godwin in May had made the king complacent, and the fleet had rested at Sandwich too long. Within three weeks of meeting Harold, hundreds had joined the rebel fleet, and before long, a land army would be large enough to start the campaign.

It was the question that had formed on everyone's lips: what would Godwin do next? And when Leofwine asked it, Godwin assembled his sons and told them of his plan of campaign. 'We'll head up the coast and down the Thames and force Edward's hand. I don't wish to give battle, and in all probability, Edward doesn't want to, either. Now we have all the sea-crews with us, I have sent word to him that I wish to negotiate. We have a strong bargaining position – strong enough to make him listen this time.'

By-passing the king's fleet at Sandwich, the favourable wind took them to Sheppey, where Godwin ordered the sack and burning of the royal manor at Milton; he wanted to show the king that there would be no defeat this time.

On 14th September they arrived at Southwark, almost a year to the day since their departure. The fleet weighed anchor on the south bank, and Godwin despatched Harold and Tostig in search of the thegns at the head of the citizenry. 'Will you allow us a safe passage through London Bridge?' he asked without preamble when they arrived.

The two thegns, Ulric and Oswald, were quick to give their consent. 'Archbishop Robert's arrogance has been insufferable,' said Ulric, 'and we wholly support you. We are honoured that you asked us to proceed.'

'I like to have the consent of the people when I take decisions,' Godwin smiled.

'We wish you luck, Earl Godwin.'

They didn't need any luck this time. Edward had called for reinforcements at Sandwich, but panicked on hearing rumours about how Godwin's vast army was growing far faster than the royal levies were. He ordered the depleted royal fleet to Westminster.

Early on the morning of the fifteenth, Godwin ordered his ships to close in on the city defences, keeping to the south bank of the river. The streets were crowded with well-armed thegns and levies, all eager to support the earl of Wessex.

'Will Edward fight?' Harold asked as the royal fleet came into view.

Godwin wasn't sure. A few weeks ago, he had said no, but a few weeks ago he hadn't dreamt of the support he had now, and that Edward would make his stand in London. Cornered like a wounded boar, he might now fight to the last.

Godwin halted his ships within arrow-shot of Edward's fleet, and within hearing of the royal army yelling obscenities at them from the north bank. He was about to send a messenger across when the bishop of Winchester came alongside in a rowing boat.

'So turns the wheel of fortune,' said Godwin, helping the churchman to the deck.

Stigand grinned. 'You have the devil's own luck, my lord of Wessex.'

'God's fortune, I prefer to say,' Godwin smiled back.

'It is always the same. God's favour when you are in a strong position, and the devil's misfortune when things go wrong.'

'Am I then, in a strong position?'

'Oh, yes. There's no doubt that it is you who have the king in difficulty today.'

'Will Edward capitulate?' asked Godwin quickly, seizing on the prelate's words.

'No,' said Stigand steadily. 'At least, not immediately. He is arguing with the archbishop.'

'And what does the archbishop counsel?'

'War.'

'Damn him to hell,' hissed Godwin. 'He would, as he has nothing to lose. He'd not hesitate to see Englishmen spill their blood for him and his Normans. Tell the king this: I demand the restoration of everything. Lands, titles, money, and my reputation, for which he can apologise. All that I lost last year.'

Stigand nodded. 'What of hostages, conditions...?'

'None. I would see my family restored. No more, no less.'

In the palace across the river, Edward considered Godwin's message. Stigand remained by the door, unsure of himself in this room full of apprehensive Normans.

'You may leave, bishop.' Robert Champart was white with anger, and vented it on Stigand. 'Now!' Turning to the king, Champart urged: 'We must fight, sire. Godwin has only a rabble of mercenaries at his dubious command; you must not surrender.'

'I *must* not?' Edward rose from his chair. 'Are you telling me, archbishop, what I must and must not do?'

Champart flushed, and took a step backwards. 'Edward, I...'

'I do not wish to see blood spilt,' said the king firmly. 'And you are wrong, or you would wish to deceive me. Godwin has a great many more Englishmen under his command than you care to admit. The men from Sussex and Kent have turned out in full support of him. We have on our hands the making of a full-scale civil war in the realm.'

'My men will see them off, sire,' Robert FitzWimarch said from the window. 'The English do not have the stomach to fight. They have been soften by the years of Viking invasions.'

'I doubt it,' answered Edward. 'Godwin's following obviously value loyalty. Something you don't understand.'

FitzWimarch reddened at the reference to the renunciation of his own vassalage to the duke of Normandy for the lure of better rewards in Edward's court. Before he could frame a response, Ralf of Mantes walked into the chamber.

'Sire: in answer to your refusal to comply with his demands, Godwin has moved his ships to encircle your fleet. Your ships are trapped, sire.'

'But I gave no such reply! Stigand must have told Godwin that I said no, curse him!' Edward sat on the throne and raged his dismay. 'What do we do now?'

'We fight,' said the archbishop. 'We have no choice.'

After Godwin had ordered the encirclement of the royal fleet, he wondered what the king would do in response. If there was to be a battle, it would be horrific; flights of arrows would massacre the crews as they stood on the open deck, and any close-quarter fighting would be bloody and inconclusive. Godwin did not want to fight. They were his people, and it was his country, but would Edward, a half-Norman exile, feel the same? If it came to war, the city of

London would surely be destroyed in the maelstrom of violence that was bound to ensue and the memory of the traditional rule would forever be dishonoured.

Behind him, the cheers of the Kentish men grew louder, and Godwin guessed that Tostig had told them to prepare for war. 'The men are ready, father,' said Harold. As yet, there was no response from the royal ships. 'What do we do now?'

'We wait.' Godwin stared at the ships and the shouting, running figures on the opposite bank, no longer yelling obscenities at the rebels, but fearful for their lives.

Above it all, the September sky threatened rain.

Siward and Leofric pushed past Ralf of Mantes and approached the king at the dais.

'Our men refuse to fight, sire,' said Leofric.

Robert Champart stepped forward. 'Your men or you, Earl Leofric?'

Leofric ignored the archbishop's supercilious query and said, insistently, 'Sire?'

'What of the housecarls?' Edward asked.

'I don't know, sire. But I doubt that they will countenance bloodshed, lord king.'

'Then what do I pay them for, God damn them?'

'You must treat, sire.' Siward was undeterred by the king's wrath.

'Treat?' whispered Edward. 'Treat with...an outlaw who invades England like a foreign lord seeking conquest, and with an army of Vikings? Good Christ – and you tell me to treat?'

He shouted the last words, flecks of spittle on the king's beard repelling Siward who countered: 'Sire, the situation is very different from last year. Godwin seems to have the upper hand; events have turned in his favour. He has more men, and they believe he has the right. You'll have to see him.'

Edward slumped back into the throne, the colour drained from his face. When he finally spoke, it was to the archbishop. 'It is over. Godwin has won. I always knew that he would come back...he was too powerful for us. It couldn't last...'

Robert Champart stared at the king for a moment, the realisation gradually dawning on him that Edward was not going to see it through, after all. 'But you know what this means,' he said slowly. 'I shall have to go – Godwin will never spare me. Edward, you cannot do this. I beg of you...!'

'Do not tell me what I cannot do!' Edward rose from the throne. 'Perhaps you should have not have been so greedy, so presumptuous and high-handed in your hour of triumph.'

Robert had no answer to this. Standing transfixed, mouth agape, he knew then how weak Edward was, and how mistaken he had been. Not only had he misjudged Edward, but he'd misjudged the kingship to which Edward was consecrated. He turned on his heel and regarded the other Normans in the chamber with irritation, as if surprised to see them standing there still.

'Well?' he rasped. 'Go – get out! Go on, leave this godforsaken country while you can, and return to your own! It's over, finished!'

FitzWimarch, William of London and Ulf of Dorchester all moved silently to the door, casting reproachful glances at Edward's unmoving figure on the throne. Ralf moved to follow them, but was halted by Robert. 'He won't harm you,' Champart jeered, his thin mouth a line of twisted hatred. 'You're quite safe – the king's nephew.'

With that bitter parting shot, Robert Champart stormed from the palace and out of England, never to return.

The great hall was echoingly empty when they arrived. Godwin led the party, flanked by Siward and Leofric. Behind him were Harold, Tostig, Leofwine and Gyrth. At the rear, Ralf of Mantes and Odda of Deerhurst kept a silent counsel, Stigand with them, watching and waiting for events to unfold.

Edward was alone, seated on the throne on the dais, his face set in calm resignation. Godwin halted the group a few yards from the dais and stepped forward alone.

'Lord king.' He knelt.

Edward rose from the throne and walked from the platform. Godwin kissed the proffered hand and Edward embraced him. The movements of both men were silent, slow and deliberate: both seemed aware that that they were acting out a part predestined for them. Two old men bowing down to fate, reconciled, for the moment, to what had to be.

'Your terms?' Edward asked briefly.

Godwin did not gloat. 'The restoration of everything; titles, lands, reputation for me and mine. You must inlaw us, and in return, outlaw Robert Champart, Eustace of Boulogne, Robert FitzWimarch, Osbern Pentecost, Ulf of Dorchester and William of London, restoring Spearhavoc to the bishopric of the city.' He glanced at Ralf. 'But leave Ralf untouched; he is your nephew and has caused us no real complaint.'

'How magnanimous of you.'

Edward's sarcasm was lost on Godwin, who continued: 'We do not seek vengeance, sire. Merely to restore our positions in England and at your court. That includes, the queen, too, my daughter. She must be brought back from Wilton. I repeat that we have no blood-feud with you, only with your evil counsel.'

'I accept your terms,' Edward said. 'You are hereby inlawed and returned to your position before September of last year. The council will ratify it tomorrow.'

Godwin moved his gaze from Edward's face and said: 'It is all that we want; no more, no less.'

Godwin knew that he would get no more. Siward and Leofric would see to that. Just as they had stood by a year ago and let events take their course, they stood by now, and watched the events move in Godwin's favour. But they would not, however, tolerate the complete humiliation of the king. A settlement for all would be reached, and harmony of a sort returned to the royal household.

Godwin turned to his sons and smiled at them. They would be safe now that the Normans had gone, their future restored. Gytha would come back, and Edith would be accepted again – who knows, he might yet have a grandson who would one day grace the throne of England. It was an optimistic thought, but Godwin was in the mood for optimism, though consummating the marriage with his daughter was the one thing he could not make Edward do.

And, despite the unspoken restraint of Leofric and Siward, there was no doubting that the victory lay with the house of Godwin.

Chapter Twenty-Four
Vitry-aux-Loges, France, September 1052

In September of that year the king of France held his court at Vitry-aux-Loges, east of Orléans. Late in the month, the arrival of the duke of Normandy was announced, and after concluding a grant of land to the bishopric of Sens, Henri consented to see him.

'William, my boy.' He rose and embraced William.

William regarded the ageing French king coldly, but respectfully. He found it difficult to contain his anger at Henri's dealings with Geoffrey of Anjou but had to somehow remain civil with the man he called his overlord in spite of the rumours.

The long, hot summer had been fraught with a tension that had bubbled but had not boiled into open war. In August, William heard news of a formal reconciliation between Henri and Geoffrey at the royal court of Orléans. Following Geoffrey's constant threats after William's seizure of Domfront and Alençon, and his uncle William of Arque's defection, William decided to approach the king before the winter set in, and confront him with what, it seemed, was an astonishing *volte face*.

William bowed, and forced the events of the summer to the back of his mind. There was still hope, but when he straightened, the look in his eyes was steel. If Henri noticed, he showed no sign of it. 'We must talk in private,' William said tersely.

Henri was taken aback by William's peremptory tone. William felt the battle for goodwill slipping away from him at the sight of Henri's fat grin taunting him openly.

'Why is it,' William asked when they were alone, 'that you have reconciled - no, allied, even - with Geoffrey of Anjou?'

'There isn't an alliance between us.'

Henri's eyes no longer showed the bonhomie with which he had welcomed William. His patience had been tried enough by the young man's demand to speak with him alone, and he was unused to being addressed to in such a manner by a vassal.

William detected the irritation, hearing the unspoken 'yet' at the end of Henri's sentence, and checked himself. Perhaps all was not lost between them. He said quickly: 'Forgive me - I did not mean to be so brusque. I am tired after the journey from Falaise, and have not slept well recently. My wife has, by God's grace, given birth to another healthy son: Richard.'

Henri's face broke into a genuinely warm smile. 'Congratulations, my boy! But why did you not say so immediately?' For the first time, Henri noticed the grey pouches beneath the younger man's bloodshot eyes. 'And Matilda? Is she well?'

William grimaced. 'It was a difficult birth, truth be told, but yes, she is recovering quickly.' He did not tell Henri that she had nearly died in his arms, and was so weak now that he didn't dare linger away for long, and that it had been Matilda who'd begged him to go and see the king, and that it was this king whose double dealings had, after all, caused much of the tension leading to her premature birthing. And the lad might not live... He said nothing of that, but his heart hardened at the memory of that night, and the reason he was here, and he set his jaw in a look that Matilda would have recognised as utterly unmoveable. 'I cannot stay long...'

'Yes, yes, of course.' Henri was all apologies.

'But before I go, I must know the arrangement that you have with Geoffrey.'

'It was merely a treaty of friendship,' Henri said defensively.

'Why?' William saw that Henri was on uncertain ground and pushed the point further. 'You must know that Geoffrey is a great threat to us all – to you as well as myself.'

Henri nodded. 'He is, and I aimed to thwart that threat.'

'To ensure that he could not threaten you but that he might continue to harangue the borders of Normandy? Is that it?' William's bloodshot eyes glowered down at the French king. 'The price of your security in the Île de France is whatever lands in Normandy Geoffrey of Anjou can help himself to. Am I correct?'

'I do not care for your tone, Duke William,' Henri snapped.

William jabbed his finger at Henri's chest. 'And I do not care for your diplomacies, King Henri. For many years you have stood sworn-protector to Normandy and her base-born heir. I thank you for that, from the bottom of my heart, and I hoped that together we should fight Geoffrey and his Angevin dogs – but I was clearly mistaken.'

'You were,' said Henri evenly. 'A king should not ally himself overmuch with one subject at the expense of his relations with the others.'

'I was right, then,' William whispered. 'I knew it all along. You're scared half to death by Geoffrey, but by making an ally of him, you know he won't attack you. You know that with my uncle in open revolt, my position in Normandy remains as precarious as ever?'

Henri nodded.

'And you know that my uncle could, at any time, instigate that revolt? And that, were Geoffrey to invade, I would face two deadly enemies at once?'

Henri nodded again.

'Then curse you for playing the puppetmaster!' William's rage finally exploded into the open. He'd said enough, and seen what he'd wanted to see. He turned to leave.

'I am aware of your ability to put down revolt and extinguish your enemies. I know about Alençon,' the Frenchman said, before he could walk away. Was there a hiss of indrawn breath after the king spoke, a ghost of a frightened laugh at the daring of what he'd said?

William's grey eyes flickered, but he didn't flinch, saying in a low voice: 'Then be careful I do not employ such abilities in your direction, lord king.'

Henri paled, and opened his mouth to rage against such insolence, but William turned on his heel and walked out. Henri closed his mouth. It would be unseemly for a king to shout after a vassal. Curse William. Curse Geoffrey.

They didn't know it, but that would be the last time William and Henri would meet in peaceful circumstances.

Chapter Twenty-Five
Winchester, April 1053

It had been a quiet, almost listless winter in England. The euphoria following Godwin's triumphant return quickly evaporated as the court settled back to normality. Several Normans came back: William, bishop of London was allowed to retain his bishopric, and Robert FitzWimarch retained his lands unmolested. Robert Champart, they heard, hurried to Rome after fleeing England and pleaded his case to the pope, but to no avail, and he died at Jumièges, a broken-hearted man. Stigand was chosen as his successor at Canterbury, a man acceptable to all parties, and the once-humble cleric from Norwich was now one of the most powerful magnates in the land, especially as he retained his bishopric of Winchester.

Soon after Michaelmas, in the middle of November, news reached the court of another death – Swegn's.

He had died on the return journey from Jerusalem, near Constantinople, and nobody was sure why, but illness caused by the extreme physical hardship of the journey seemed likely, or even murder by one of the many bandits in the Anatolian mountains.

Godwin was devastated. Swegn's death meant far more to him than Robert Champart's - he was too old and tired to gloat, now - and Edward felt the same, sending the earl his condolences. The two deaths had, in some way, made things equal between the earl and the king; but Godwin's health was shattered. He spent the winter at Guildford, ruminating on the past, and relying on Harold and Tostig - mostly Harold - to advise the king and relay the news back to Guildford.

The king, for his part, did not feel ill-disposed towards Godwin and his sons. His own interests were increasingly directed towards his new church at Westminster, and to that end, he seemed content to let matters rest at court. It was true that the past could never be entirely forgotten, but when the opportunity to widen the rift arose, neither had the energy or interest to pursue it.

In order to keep the peace, and to honour the promise made to Godwin on his return in September, Edward took Edith back as his wife. She, too, had learnt the hard lesson of those momentous months, perhaps more than the others in the Godwin household as she had suffered alone, and she emerged a stronger, more reserved woman, resigned to what Edward was. For the marriage, although resumed, remained unconsummated, and there was nothing Godwin could do about it, but accept the fact that no grandson of his would ever be king of England.

*

The lack of an heir was the chief subject Godwin wanted to discuss with the king at the Easter court at Winchester. With the cold winds of the winter come and gone, the earl felt rejuvenated again, as he always did when spring arrived, and was well enough to travel from Guildford to Winchester for the Easter court. He was held in high regard in the ancient town, and with the familiar streets around him, he felt able to confront Edward with the subject that had nagged him throughout the winter months. He had accepted now that Edith would never carry Edward's child and heir. Who, then, would Edward nominate as his heir?

'Ralf of Mantes is a possible choice.' Harold said this as he, Tostig and Godwin were entering the king's hall to go to dinner.

'Never,' snorted Godwin, leaning heavily on his stick. Harold had presented his father – amid plenty of laughter – with an intricately carved walking-stick at Christmas, but the good humour and jokes scarce concealed the fact that he needed it, often.

'But Ralf is Edward's nephew,' Harold persisted, holding Godwin's arm. 'He is Norman-French, but he is a good man – and we bear him no grudge for his part in the Champart affair.'

Godwin grunted again, and they pushed through the crowd of courtiers invited to dine with the king, and made their way to the dais at the end of the hall. Edward was already seated at the centre of the high table, but stood graciously as Godwin sat next to him, as was his right. Tostig and Harold sat on Godwin's left, and to the other side of Edward, Archbishop Stigand half-rose and gave a nod at their arrival. Edward clapped his hands, Stigand uttered grace and the first course, lamb broth, was brought in by the servants.

Edward broke the bread at his side and said without preamble to Godwin:

'You wished to address me on a matter of urgency, I believe, Lord Godwin.'

Godwin swallowed some wine. He'd not meant to talk of it here, but now that the matter was raised...'Yes.' Godwin set the goblet down firmly on the table. 'I am concerned as to the matter of your heir, sire,' he began slowly. 'At present, you have chosen nobody to take your place. And if I may be so bold as to say...you are not a young man, and I fear my daughter will not have issue in your marriage.'

On the other side of the king, Stigand set down his knife and cocked his head for the reply, in an unashamed act of eavesdropping.

'I admire your candour in this matter,' said Edward. 'It is indeed of importance, and as my chief councillor, it is with you that I should discuss it first.' He glanced at Stigand, who hastily resumed eating. 'Because of what you say – and it is quite true – I have in fact a man in mind to succeed me.' Edward spoke candidly and without hesitation, but quietly, so that only those nearest could hear. 'William of Normandy is my choice,' he said coolly, 'a man of strength and determination, and although not entirely secure in his own duchy yet, he will...'

Godwin's fist hit the table with a crash. Several goblets jumped at the impact and a flagon tipped over, spilling the blood-red wine into the rushes.

'How dare you suggest a Norman bastard to succeed you to the throne after the events of these last two years – how dare you!' Godwin had leapt from his seat and was shaking uncontrollably with rage. All around them the conversation froze in mid-sentence.

'Sit down, father.' Harold tugged at his sleeve and on the lower benches, somebody laughed, a short, nervous laugh, and the conversation started up again.

'Never William of Normandy,' muttered Godwin, drinking more wine, sitting back down unsteadily.

'Never a base-born Norman whelp on the throne of England. Never.'

Edward eyed him coldly. 'He is my kinsman. Remember that when you talk of him.'

'The council will never ratify it,' Godwin said quickly.

'That is a question neither you nor I will be here to influence,' Edward replied.

Harold signalled to a servant-boy to bring some more wine. The fragile peace had been destroyed in that last exchange, and the mood might well turn worse before the night was out. Some wine could ease the tension.

The servant-boy was nervous at having to approach the king's table so soon after Godwin's outburst, and stumbled on the steps of the dais. The tray containing a flagon of wine and cups slipped to one side, but with his other foot, the boy managed to regain his balance, and the wine remained on the tray. Those at the end of the table clapped a little at the boy's dexterity, and Tostig called, 'How right it is that one foot should support the other!'

Godwin leant over to Tostig and said: 'So should one brother help another, and a man support his friend in time of need.' He looked meaningfully at both brothers.

'So would my brother have helped me if Godwin had allowed it,' said Edward from his other side.

The king's words carried loudly and clearly across the high table, the accusation in his voice obvious to all. For the second time that evening the conversation stopped dead.

'I know very well that you hold me responsible for your brother's death,' Godwin said.

'Father...' Harold began.

'I know very well also, that you do not disbelieve those who say that I was traitor to him and to you,'

Godwin continued, ignoring his son's interruption. Godwin snatched up a crust from the manchet loaf on the table. 'Let God who knows all secrets be my judge!' he shouted, dark with rage. 'May this crust which I hold in my hand pass through my throat and leave me unharmed to show that I was guiltless of treason towards you, and that I was innocent of your brother's death!'

Aware that all those on the dais and those on the nearby tables were watching intently, Godwin thrust the crust into his mouth and chewed hard. After swallowing, he took up the goblet and took a deep draught of wine.

'There,' he began, but got no further, as he was seized by a paroxysm of coughing.

'Sit down, father,' said Harold, annoyed by such an unnecessarily public display. Godwin continued to cough, and waved Harold away. Harold slapped him on the back, and the coughing ceased abruptly. Godwin opened his mouth to speak, but no words came out, and he crashed to the floor, his face purple, his mouth working like a fish.

Harold was on his knees, unable to believe what he was seeing. 'It's a seizure– the old fool!'

'God's vengeance,' muttered Stigand. 'God has spoken.'

Those at the high table sat back, awed and breathless, shocked sober by the sight. The news spread across the hall and soon everyone was silent, whispering prayers and curses in the same breath.

Harold turned on Stigand. 'Shut up, you damned fool!' He looked down at Godwin; he was still alive. Harold's mind was filled with the memory of another feast eleven years ago, in another hall, where another man lay prone in the rushes, dead.

The memory of Harthacanute's death stirred him into action.

'Stand back; let him have air,' he said sharply. He turned to Tostig. 'Fetch Gyrth - quickly.' Tostig moved off, pushing roughly through the watching crowd. Harold looked up and caught Edward's stare. Was there a glint of triumph behind those impenetrable blue eyes?

But Edward was in no mood for vengeance. 'Take him to my rooms. They are closer than your town house.'

So they carried the stricken earl through the hall to the king's rooms and set him down on the bed. All they could do now was send for Gytha and Edith - and pray.

Godwin collapsed on the Easter Monday but showed no sign of recovery, not speaking or showing any signs of life, and on Thursday his condition worsened. Stigand administered the last rites to the dying man and the entire family gathered in the candle-lit room to wait until the end. Stigand finished the unction and left them. Harold, as the eldest, stood by Godwin's side, with Gytha on the other side. She was quite composed and, it seemed, resigned to the inevitable.

Some minutes after Stigand left them, the earl stirred and opened his eyes. Harold felt Gytha's hand tighten on his, and hope flared; it was the first sign of life since Monday.

'Harold,' whispered the earl.

Harold bent down to the level of the bed. 'Father?'

'I've been thinking, boy,' said Godwin. His words came out in short breaths. 'Do you remember the fox, Harry?'

Harold remembered it well, seeing the white snow bespattered with mud churned by the horses' hooves, the scarred man with no nose, and the decapitated head...how could he forget?

'They killed the fox, father.'

'And do you know why, boy?'

Harold shook his head, unable to check the flow of tears streaming down his cheeks. Godwin's breathing was slow and uneven, and the light was going from his eyes.

'Trust, boy. The fox had too much trust.' Godwin lifted a heavily veined hand and shook it at Harold. 'Don't you trust Edward.' he whispered. 'Don't trust him, or he'll do for you.'

Godwin fell back onto the pillow, exhausted by the effort, but still breathing steadily.

He died at sunset. After those words to Harold, he didn't speak again, reserving his last sight of the earthly world to be his beloved Gytha.

He was greatly mourned.

The people of Winchester had lined the streets in silent vigil since Monday, the day of his collapse, and when Harold announced his passing, the grief of the common folk was plain to see. He had been a good lord and ruler to the people of Wessex; a fair man, harsh when necessary, but never cruel.

He was buried on Saturday in the Old Minster, alongside Canute and Emma, the two people whose lives he had shared in the old days, the time of his own youth and greatness. His widow Gytha made generous gifts to the church for the redemption of his soul, and prayers were said every day for that purpose.

The evening following the funeral, Edward summoned Harold to him for a private interview.

Edward was in a congenial mood when Harold entered his chambers. 'Sit down, Harold.' He handed Harold a cup of warm mead. 'We all feel the loss of the old earl. Indeed, many of the townspeople feel that they have lost a father.' He smiled ruefully and continued, 'For some years after my coronation, my place on the throne was insecure. Despite our differences, it was chiefly due to your father that I remained king. His help was crucial, and I never properly thanked him for it. I now need your help.'

Harold did not hesitate to answer the question forming on Edward's lips. 'You have it, sire.'

'Good.' The king smiled. 'Then we must talk of the succession.'

'Sire, people say that William of Normandy visited England during the winter of our exile. Is it true? And did you offer him the throne then?'

'I shall be frank,' said Edward. 'William did indeed visit during the winter and I suggested that he might be my heir – but on condition that he was to be strong enough in his own duchy first. He is not, yet, so I cannot propose him formally as my heir until I can be assured of his total supremacy in Normandy. I believed at the time that renewing my relations with him was a useful thing to do. He may one day be a great power, and England will need to be with him, not against him.'

'So the duke of Normandy isn't your final choice?'

Edward shook his head. 'No, not by any means. England is an ancient, established kingdom. William is but a suitor after the heiress, and must wait upon my decision. One of several suitors, I think.'

Edward's analogy was a clever one, and it was reassuring to know that William of Normandy was by no means confirmed as Edward's heir.

The other business Harold discussed with the king was of a more immediate nature. Now that Harold was earl of Wessex, he was to relinquish his earldom of East Anglia, and Edward had decided that Aelric, son of Leofric of Mercia, should have it, on condition that he too would relinquish it on inheriting the earldom of Mercia. Harold had hoped to press a claim for Tostig having his old earldom, as he had no lands to call his own yet, but Edward had decided, and Harold had privately thought that he could not disagree, as Leofric and Siward would want to be assured that the house of Godwin was not becoming over-mighty. In return, Leofric would hand over Somerset and Berkshire. Harold hoped that Tostig would not take it too hard; he would have to wait, that was all.

'It will allow us to take stock,' he told his mother when he returned to the Godwin household after seeing Edward. He made no mention of the question of Edward's heir.

Gytha had accepted Godwin's death with no bitterness and few regrets, and made it clear to Harold that she intended to devote the rest of her life to ensuring the happiness of her children. She was happy in that, and Harold was pleased.

Edith was not so easy to please. The exile at Wilton had changed her immensely. She had become deeply religious, and on her return had come to a reconciliation with Edward, both finding common ground in their beliefs. She had fought her struggles alone, and was apart from the world now because of it. She had, Harold realised, been alone since the day she married Edward.

'I am sorry about Tostig's earldom,' he said.

Edith gave Harold a haughty stare. 'Did you try very hard with Edward?'

'He is a difficult man to persuade – as you well know,' Harold smiled apologetically, 'but Leofric and Siward are behind all this. I cannot afford to upset them.'

Edith shrugged. 'Tostig is a grown man now. He ought to have lands fit for one of his station. He has made a good marriage, and has children of worthy birth...'

She stopped, aware that she had gone too far. Harold let go of her arm and said angrily: 'I know that Tostig is wed to the daughter of Baldwin, count of Flanders, while I have three bastard boys by my mistress – you need not remind me of the fact, sister. But I am afraid that I cannot – and will not – jeopardise the peace at court so that Tostig has an earldom. He finds it difficult enough to manage the few lands he has already, God knows.'

'The lands you see fit to give him, in your charity!' shouted Edith.

'Calm yourselves.' Gytha was between them, urging peace. 'We must not fight amongst ourselves.'

Edith sat still for a moment, then walked from the chamber without a backward glance.

Harold watched her go, feeling wretchedly guilty. 'I cannot understand her, mother. She had so much promise before she married...'

Gytha said quietly: 'I was against it.'

'The marriage to the king?'

Gytha nodded. 'Your father was all for it. He was so hopeful for his little girl...' Her voice trailed off miserably into silence.

And now he's dead, thought Harold, and they were going to miss him dreadfully. Harold most of all, as the weight of responsibility for the family fortunes was now squarely on his shoulders.

Chapter Twenty-Six
Gloucester, July 1054

Bishop Ealdred of Worcester was a congenial, energetic man of immense intellect. Harold respected him greatly. Ealdred was exactly the man required for the mission he had been chosen for.

When Canute had seized the throne from Edward's elder brother, Edmund Ironsides, he had been advised to kill Edmund's sons, and so he sent them to the king of Sweden with the express purpose of having them murdered. But the Swedish ruler had passed them on to King Solomon of Hungary, and the eldest son, Edward, had married Agatha, a daughter of Emperor Henry of Germany, and was now living in Hungary.

Nobody was certain who had thought of Edward's forgotten nephew as a candidate for the throne. Certainly Earl Leofric had taken up the idea with enthusiasm, along with Ealdred, and Harold had been quick to see the significance of such a person. It was, they agreed, an excellent choice to put forward, and would continue the Old English line to the exclusion of foreign intervention.

As the rumours in the royal court grew, it became clear that a sizeable number of the courtiers favoured the plan. When Harold made it known that he too, would support it, the proposal was taken to the king. Would Edward countenance his long-lost nephew as his heir?

Edward was reluctant at first, but under pressure from his earls and the queen, he gave his assent for an expedition to seek out the prince and offer him the throne. The council ratified the decision, and the eminent bishop of Worcester, accompanied by Abbot Aelfwine of Ramsey, would lead the expedition. They would take with them rich gifts for various rulers in Europe, as it was to be a diplomatic venture as well as a search for an heir.

Harold made it his business to see the bishop before he left. He knelt and kissed Ealdred's hand. 'I wish you well on your venture into Germany, my lord bishop.'

'I thank you for your kind words,' said Ealdred. 'I will not keep you from your business, just as you would not hinder me from aiding my flock.'

Harold smiled. 'Do you see Prince Edward as one of your flock, then? Or perhaps a lost sheep?'

'The people of England are my flock, Harold, and I would seek to serve them as best I can...God aiding me, by finding the heir to the blood royal and thus preventing any further foreign intrusion.'

'Wise words, Ealdred, and well spoken.' Not for the first time, Harold sincerely regretted that this man was not archbishop of York, a post he so richly deserved. Edward had vetoed Ealdred's promotion after the death of Aelfric Puttoc, and had put forward Cynsige. In the ensuing confrontation over Robert Champart's appointment, the fact that Ealdred had been passed over had been forgotten, and Cynsige had remained. Ealdred was a humble man, and did not press his case, though his very humility and wisdom were what made him such a popular choice.

'Wise words, maybe,' said Ealdred, 'but will the king listen to them?'

'My sister the queen wields much influence over the king. She herself is in favour of the king's nephew coming back to England.'

'If I reach him,' Ealdred countered. 'And if he chooses to come. If I do not and he does not – what then? We've been unlucky since Canute. Insecure successions have made for insecure reigns. You were but a boy when Canute died at Shaftesbury. He nominated no heir, and it was left for Harthacanute and Harold Harefoot to fight it out. Perhaps we are still paying for Canute's indecision.'

'But, as you say; if not Edward the Prince, then who?'

Ealdred met Harold's question with frank openness. 'William of Normandy isn't the only foreign choice, Harold; King Svein of Denmark may lay claim as a kinsman of Canute. If he does, then Harald Hardrada certainly will do so also, by virtue of the treaty made by Harthacanute with Magnus, Hardrada's nephew. If William of Normandy thinks that he has a right, then the foreign claimants will see that their claim is as good as his. Edward would back William, as they are kin, and Svein will look to you, his cousin, and the earl of Wessex, for help and support.'

'But you are forecasting double, no, triple invasion – and bloodshed that would tear the realm apart for generations!'

Ealdred nodded. 'But if the choice is from within the country, if he is a man of the English blood royal, then the foreign princes will have no justification whatsoever in claiming the throne.'

'Then you must succeed in your quest.' Harold held out his hand and the bishop took it. 'God go with you, bishop, and for England's sake may you bring back the last English prince from exile.'

Ealdred nodded. 'For England's sake.'

*

William, when told of the bishop of Worcester's expedition to Hungary to find the last English prince, was speechless with shock.

'Why?' He finally exploded in the chamber to Matilda when he could find the words. 'Why has he betrayed me?'

'He hasn't betrayed you,' said Matilda, wary of William's rage. 'He's simply misled you. And in any case, we don't know for sure whether he is going to offer the prince the throne.'

'He is,' rasped William, 'and he did promise me, damn him; he did!'

'He did no such thing.' Matilda, though she would never admit it, was secretly glad that Edward was searching for another heir. The possibility of William becoming king of England filled her with doubts and fears – God knew, there was enough to govern in Normandy.

'He told me that if I made myself secure in the duchy, then I would be king!'

'You may have to face the prospect that he only offered it to you so as to make a new ally – and it was at the time when the Godwins were exiled, and his Norman advisors had the supremacy.'

'So he would dangle me on a string like a puppet? If the prince accepts, and comes back alive, then I'll have no say in the matter. Curse Edward for betraying me.'

*

Harold was at Guildford when he received the first letter from Bishop Ealdred, four weeks after his departure in July.

'Tell me what he says.' Edith leant across his shoulder and peered at the parchment.

'He is in Cologne,' read Harold. 'The emperor welcomed him with gifts and he in turn gave the emperor gifts from Edward. The journey from England was uneventful. Baldwin gave them a magnificent welcome at Lille, and he has some gifts from Baldwin for Judith. They are now deciding on how best to find the prince...'

Harold stopped, puzzlement creasing his brow.

'What is it?'

'He says that the Magyars in Hungary have been in revolt against the emperor for some years, and earlier this year, they invaded Carinthia. Ealdred thinks that all communications between Germany and Hungary have been sundered.'

'Oh,' said Eadgyth. 'What will he do now?'

'He plans to wait. He's in no hurry, and he says that the emperor's hospitality extends indefinitely, thanks to the alliance we had against France and Normandy in 1049.'

Harold looked at Eadgyth. 'I think that whatever happens, it will be some time before we receive any positive news from Ealdred.'

Several days after hearing from Ealdred, Harold was accosted by the archbishop of Canterbury whilst at Edward's Winchester court, and accepted an invitation to the palace.

Seated in a luxurious chair with a glass of fine wine, Harold admired the trappings that adorned Stigand's chambers, and reflected that Stigand had done very well for himself. The humble cleric from Norwich had risen far, first under old Queen Emma, then – after betraying her over the letter to Magnus and being pardoned by Edward – rising to Winchester, a rich enough living. After the exile of Robert, Stigand had seemed the right compromise, but had retained Winchester on acquiring Canterbury. The wealth he had accumulated was legendary, and his power was undoubted.

Harold set down the delicate glass and transferred his gaze from the magnificent interior of Stigand's chambers to the archbishop himself. The cleric from Norwich lived better than the earl of Wessex, but Stigand's invitation to Harold was a reminder that the power and wealth he had accumulated were not necessarily permanent. Robert Champart's abrupt departure had shown that. Stigand needed the ear of other powerful men.

'Have you heard from Bishop Ealdred recently?' Stigand asked.

'Not since he wrote and told of his arrival in Germany.'

'I had news only yesterday. Ealdred writes that he has been advised to stay in Cologne if he values his life. But he adds that he's going to press ahead and continue the search for the prince.'

Harold shifted in his chair. 'Will he go to Hungary?'

'Not yet, but he will have to if his letters and messages bring no positive news.' Stigand swallowed some wine. 'Clearly a determined man, Bishop Ealdred.'

Harold glanced at Stigand with some distaste. Stigand was happy to let a man like Ealdred do the work, and then reap the benefits from his efforts. 'I hope then, that he succeeds,' he said.

'Do you?' said Stigand quickly. 'You would rather have an exiled prince from Hungary than the duke of Normandy?'

'I don't think Edward was seriously proposing William as his heir. He has made no formal offer, no treaty has been signed, no hostages given over; all the things that normally happen in the nomination of an heir. In any case, William wouldn't be accepted by the earls and ealdormen of the country –'

'Would you accept him?' Stigand leaned forward, intent upon Harold's reply.

'If King Edward willed it, and the council ratified it, then yes, I would,' said Harold.

Stigand nodded, apparently satisfied at Harold's answer. 'Let's discuss the earldom of Northumbria. Siward hasn't long on this earth and he has no adult son to succeed him.'

Earlier in the month, Siward had led a fighting expedition into Scotland, defeating Macbeth, and in the process losing his only adult son, Osbern, and his nephew, Siward.

'Siward's only surviving son, Waltheof, is a boy of three years of age,' Stigand continued. 'He cannot succeed Siward. The north would never stand such a long minority. But I know who can succeed Siward: your brother Tostig. A good man, and without the lands which his status demands. He would rule the north well enough. What do you think?'

Harold shook his head. 'The north won't accept Tostig. He's a southerner, a Godwin.'

'They would accept him if he had the full support of the church behind him,' said Stigand forcefully. 'I will back him; they cannot ignore the archbishop of Canterbury.'

Harold hid his expression of doubt behind his wine glass. 'And what would you want from me in return?'

Stigand permitted a faint smile to cross his lips, and said: 'Your help in securing for the me the papal pallium for my appointment as archbishop.'

Harold nodded. It was reasonable enough. 'But is it wise to do this? Won't Leofric protest?'

'Leofric has his own designs on Northumbria. He wants it for his son, Aelfgar. You must get there first, Harold.'

Harold wondered whether Stigand was elaborating on Leofric's designs in order to persuade him to support Tostig, but it occurred to him that if he didn't agree to Stigand's deal, then what was to stop Stigand going to Leofric and throwing the weight of the church behind Leofric's bid for the north?

There was too much at stake to allow the house of Mercia to expand. Harold felt that it was better to have this man as an ally than as an enemy. He grasped the archbishop's hand: 'I accept.'

When Harold approached Tostig with Stigand's proposal, Tostig was gripped with enthusiasm for the scheme. For too long he had been deprived of lands fit for one of his status, and he had not been blind to the possibilities opened by the death of Siward's only adult son. Edith too, expressed an eagerness to press Tostig's cause when the time came.

The three of them gathered one afternoon in late September in Edith's apartments in the palace of Westminster to discuss the matter further. Edith had already approached Edward in private; she had a powerful influence on the king nowadays, who in turn was increasingly interested only in his new church at Westminster. The foundations to the church had been laid, and the building of the ground floor was in progress. It would be finished, according to the master-mason's report, in just over ten years' time.

'I can persuade the king easily enough,' said Edith.

'It's a case of the council ratifying his decision,' said Tostig. They both turned to Harold, and Edith added: 'It is you we are relying on, Harry.'

Harold saw their hopeful looks and shrugged. 'I'll do what I can. I have written to the pope, asking him to bestow the pallium of office upon Stigand.'

'Will Stigand honour his part of the agreement?' asked Edith.

'Yes,' said Harold, still wrestling with his doubts over Tostig's suitability for the task. He gave up, and said: 'But do you really think it wise to press your claim, Tostig? The north is unruly and unpredictable at the best of times. Siward was a Dane, and was appointed by Canute, and he ruled a large population of Danes. They might not take too kindly to a southerner, especially one from Wessex, displacing Siward's dynasty. It might, after all, be best to allow Leofric and Aelfgar have the north, and all the problems that go with it.'

'I sometimes think that you want all the power to yourself, Harold,' Edith snapped.

Harold flinched, and said: 'I merely wish to consolidate our power in the south, in Wessex, rather than overstretch ourselves...'

'You may well say that, Harry,' said Tostig, his face twisted with envy, but you're the earl of Wessex, and I...I have very little to call my own. It is my chance now, and I beg you to allow me take it!'

A silence fell across the chamber following this plea, for a plea it obviously was, and Tostig's voice was raw with emotion. Harold relented, but against his better judgement. 'I agree, then, that we shall follow Stigand's proposal, although I believeit is not a wise course to take. However, I promise that I'll do all I can to help.'

Tostig's face dissolved into a grin of gratitude, but the look on Edith's face told Harold that all he could do might not be enough.

Chapter Twenty-Seven
Lisieux, Normandy, November 1054

When William heard of Ealdred's safe arrival in Cologne, he decided to let events take their course. Matilda stated her belief that it was unlikely that the prince would be found, and that if he was, he might not wish to return to England, which would seem to him a foreign country. This didn't convince William, though, because Edward himself had returned hom after over twenty years in a foreign exile.

William devoted his energies during the summer into building up further support in the duchy. His position within the duchy was greater than ever before; he was supported by men from the shores of the Cotentin to the forests of the Seine far to the east. Peace, at last, was predominant in the duchy, and people devoted themselves to securing it, happy in the knowledge that at their head was a man equally devoted to restoring prosperity to the land ravaged by so much war.

Now that he was sure of himself, William could also press forward to finish the last enemy left within his lands: Mauger.

The only way he could do that was to use the law. Just as he had defeated the rebels and Henri on the grounds of their illegal stance against the rightful duke, he would use the support of the church, which was in turn eager to use the duke as the mouthpiece of the new reforms emanating from Rome, in order to extinguish clerical abuses and overmighty prelates. Mauger was one of these.

William had spent the summer preparing to mobilise his supporters, and the arrival of Pope Leo's legate, Bishop Erminfrid of Sitten, provided him with the justification to act.. Erminfrid agreed to hold a council, and to formally depose Mauger as long as William agreed to certain other reforms which would benefit the church. William did not quibble: he would agree to almost anything to see Mauger deposed, and the final revenge for all the murders of his youth complete.

Erminfrid, on seeing a list of the numerous clerical abuses Mauger had committed, did not present a case defending him. He had never received his pallium of office as archbishop of Rouen; he had committed the sin of simony; he had sired several bastards, and still kept at least two mistresses on wealth plundered from the coffers of the church. It was enough to be rid of him, Erminfrid promised. There would be no charge of murder and he could only be expelled from the church on the grounds of his abuses. It didn't do justice to Turold, Osbern and Richard, and the countless others, but for William, it would have to be enough.

On the middle Wednesday of November, in the presence of Erminfrid, Hugh the bishop of Lisieux, Odo the bishop of Bayeux, William's young half-brother by Herluin and Herleve, and many other bishops from provinces all over Normandy, Mauger was formally deposed. William himself did not attend. Mauger was replaced by Maurilius, a churchman with an ardent desire to see reform done.

*

'It's over then,' said Odo, the day after the council.

'Yes.' William felt strangely empty. He couldn't bring himself to attend the council – at least, yesterday's proceedings, as Erminfrid's business was due to continue into the weekend. 'After all these years, it's over.'

A servant knocked on the door. 'Sire. The archbishop is here to see you.'

William grunted. 'I didn't expect to see Maurilius until tomorrow.'

The servant reddened. 'No, sire...I did not mean...it is Mauger who would see you.'

'Shall you see him?' Odo asked.

'I shall. But alone, Odo, if you wouldn't mind.'

'Of course,' Odo said, and left the room, palpably glad to be gone.

Mauger was finely dressed in a blue tunic, riding breeches and polished leather boots. No longer the clergyman, he looked like a wealthy aristocrat, which he was. It was rumoured that he had chests of treasure hidden away and was ready to start a new life in the Byzantine empire with one of his concubines.

'You've won then, boy.' Mauger advanced several steps towards William. 'You have taken from me everything I coveted. I am the last enemy on your progress to power, and you have finished me off.'

William didn't trust himself to speak. The tone in Mauger's voice was anything but humble and beaten.

'I concede defeat, William,' Mauger went on. 'I should have done so years ago...I told your uncle to do so, but we hung on.' William doubted this, but kept silent. At his nephew's refusal to speak, Mauger moved closer and, touching William's arm gently, said, 'Couldn't we be friends, now it's all over?'

William lashed out with all the force and pent-up fury he could muster. The heavy ring with the ducal seal on his middle finger tore Mauger's plump flesh with surprising ease, leaving a jagged, bleeding gash on his jowl. Mauger was knocked flat to the ground, sending a chair flying. He put a hand to his cheek, felt the wet blood, and searched for a handkerchief to staunch the flow. A black bruise was already welling up over the side of his face. He stared up at his nephew, eyes wide with fear, his brow glistening with sweat in anticipation of more violence.

Remaining in the rushes, he said quietly: 'Aye, I can well believe what you did at Alençon, boy.'

William raised his fist and stood over his prostrate uncle. Mauger flinched at the blazing grey eyes, and half raised his hand to ward off the blow he thought would come, uttering just the one word in a barely audible gasp: 'William...?'

In that pathetic plea for mercy, William saw Mauger for what he was: defeated. Torture and death couldn't destroy Mauger, but the knowledge that he had no power would destroy him.

William took a deep breath and felt for the first time that the debts had been paid. It was not the blow, but Mauger's plea , that exorcised the anger and the fury from him.

William bent his head close to Mauger. Seeing the sweating, pallid face, the ceaselessly flickering eyes, William knew that from now on, there would be no more fear: only pity.

'You made me what I am,' he said. 'You made me, and now I have destroyed you. You are nothing. Leave the duchy of Normandy and never return as long I or my heirs live.'

He stared into Mauger's face for one more long moment, then turned and walked away.

Truly, he had won.

Chapter Twenty-Eight
Westminster, March 1055

Early in the new year, news reached Edward's court of the earl of Northumbria's death. Siward died at York, and word had it that he ordered his servants to dress him in full armour and place his sword in his hand, so that he might breathe his last prepared for Valhalla.

Siward was not mourned for long in the south, for the problem of his successor was uppermost in the minds of the courtiers in London. Rumours spread through the court to the effect that Leofric of Mercia aimed to thwart the ambitions of Tostig Godwinsson by pressing the claim of his son, Aelfgar. But it was known that Leofric himself was not long for this world, and if Aelfgar should have Northumbria and then succeed to Mercia, then the greatest powers in the land would be concentrated in the hands of one man only. Harold and Edith spoke to the king, and Edward agreed to speak for Tostig in the matter.

But before the council convened to decide on the succession to Northumbria, several letters arrived from Ealdred. He had found the English prince, who was living in Bratislava, married with three children. He spoke no English and was to all purposes a Hungarian, and would have stayed in Hungary but for the wars between Germany and the Magyars taking a new and dangerous turn. It was possible, wrote Ealdred, that the prince would accept his offer as a means to escape the wars. It was good news indeed – but the business of the earldom of Northumbria was, to most people, more important.

*

Stigand was the first person Harold saw when he entered the great hall adjoining the council chamber. There was no avoiding him, and the large churchman pushed towards him through the milling councillors.

'Have you heard the news from Ealdred?' he asked, his eyes bright with jubilation.

'I have,' Harold smiled back. 'It's good news indeed, but there's much that can happen before the prince arrives safely in England.'

'You believe he'll come, then?'

Harold shrugged. 'From what Ealdred says in his letter, it seems more than likely.' A loud gong sounded at the entrance to the council chamber. 'Shall we go through?'

Stigand led the way through the crowd, waving aside petitioners with a heavily bejewelled hand.

'The king has pledged his support for Tostig,' said Harold.

'And you have my support in the matter also,' said Stigand. 'Have you had word from Rome, yet?'

Harold remembered Stigand's anxiety over the lack of acceptance from Rome in the matter of his archbishopric. He shook his head. 'No word yet.'

Stigand pursed his lips and left Harold to find his way to the dais, where he sat alongside Tostig. Tostig, having seen Harold enter with Stigand, said quickly, 'Will he stand by me?'

'Yes.' Harold flashed his brother a grin. 'Don't fear, brother; Northumbria will be yours.'

Edward entered some moments later and took his seat between Harold and Stigand. He rapped his staff on the floor. 'The business of the new earl of Northumbria must be decided. Siward departed this earth but six weeks ago, may his soul rest in peace.' Growls of assent followed Edward's tribute to the old

Dane. 'He will, I feel assured, find his seat at God's right hand.'

'Aye, and in Valhalla!'

'Be that as it may,' Edward said sharply, the reference to the old faith not unnoticed. 'He's dead and both his first-born son and heir, Osbern, and his nephew, Siward, perished on the Day of the Seven Sleepers in battle last July. He left only an infant son, who cannot take the reins of the government of the north.' He paused, aware of the tension in the room. Most of the councillors present didn't know of his decision to support Tostig; they knew only that he was one candidate amongst several.

'I therefore propose that Tostig Godwinsson be appointed earl of Northumbria, to succeed Siward, in the stead of his infant son.'

The reaction was mixed. Tostig twitched with relief now that the king had kept his word in public, but Earl Leofric of Mercia, also on the dais, shook his head in disbelief. His son Aelfgar, down with the other councillors, was open-mouthed with rage.

Then Stigand rose from his seat. 'The king has proposed the new earl of Northumbria and I, Stigand, support this. Tostig has also the full support of the church of York, under my lord Archbishop Cynsige. May God grace his rule with peace and prosperity.' He sat again, and Cynsige nodded sagely at his words.

Edward leant over to Harold and said: 'Will you speak, Harold?'

Harold was about to rise, but was cut short by a shout from the front row of the massed councillors on the benches below.

'No! I say no to the appointment of Tostig Godwinsson as the earl of Northumbria!' Aelfgar had found his voice and was waving his fist at Tostig, who went white with shock. 'The appointment of a

Godwin will spell disaster for the north,' shouted Aelfgar. 'He knows not how to handle the people – he is a southerner!' Several councillors beside Aelfgar were nodding in agreement, and Harold, deep down, was forced to admit that Aelfgar was probably right.

'Say something,' hissed Tostig.

Harold cleared his throat. The crowd below hushed to hear what the lord of Wessex had to say.

'I know that Tostig is my brother, but as the king's chief councillor, I have thought long and hard over my own council. Tostig is a good man, with a wife of noble and royal birth and a growing family. He is godly and will govern the north conscientiously. I fully endorse the king's decision that he should succeed Siward and put his talents and energy to good use.'

When Harold finished, the chamber erupted into cheers and clapping from the councillors, and Edward leant across and said, 'Wisely spoken, Harold.'

Aelfgar, with some of the other councillors, wasn't cheering. Leofric stood up and banged his staff repeatedly on the floor until the excited councillors fell silent again. 'Let my son speak!' he roared.

There was complete respect for the old earl of Mercia and Aelfgar said: 'I must protest that the earl of Wessex speaks falsely...' He got no further, as the roar of the angry councillors drowned him out.

'Silence!'

It was the king who had shouted. His outburst, a rarity from him these days, commanded instant obedience. 'Continue, my lord of East Anglia.'

Aelfgar bowed his head in gratitude. 'The earl of Wessex wishes only to increase the power and wealth of his own family,' he said, his face flushed deep red. 'He doesn't care for the peace of the realm. Tostig will never be accepted, he...'

Tostig leapt from his seat and would have jumped from the dais had Harold not stopped him in time. The councillors roared like a crowd at a cock-fight, and Aelfgar, delighting in Tostig's rage, screamed: 'Godwin's ill-gotten brood will rule the kingdom if they have their way!'

'Enough!' Edward was on his feet again, but this time his wrath was directed solely at Aelfgar. 'You have said enough, my lord of East Anglia. Leave the chamber now, and cool that hot head of yours.'

Aelfgar stood speechless for a second, then looked to Leofric for support. 'Father...say something – tell the king what you said, what I was going to do if...'

Aelfgar broke off, horrified at what he had begun to say.

'You fool,' whispered Leofric. 'You stupid fool.'

'What is this?' asked Edward, turning to Leofric. 'What does your son speak of, Leofric?'

Leofric looked at Edward, but shook his head slowly and deliberately. 'I do not know, sire.'

'Father!' Aelfgar ran to the dais, but stopped short of climbing the steps.

'The lord of East Anglia speaks of treason, I think, sire,' said Stigand, with a malicious glint in his eye.

'Treason? Aye, and you may be right, my lord archbishop,' said Edward, his blue eyes blazing bright with anger.

'No, lord king,' pleaded Aelfgar, 'We did not mean, I...' Aelfgar fell silent, suddenly aware of the dread silence filling the chamber. He found his seat, and collapsed into it, white with horror.

'You have spoken too much,' said Edward. 'Your tongue has run away with your ardour to attack the house of Godwin. It is treason you implicate yourself in, and I banish you from the realm for it.'

'My lord king, I protest...' Aelfgar was on his feet again, begging. 'Father...?'

But Leofric was not to be drawn into supporting his son, remaining slumped in his seat beside Harold and Tostig, a mottled hand over his forehead in resigned despair.

'The king has spoken,' rasped Stigand. 'Do as you are bid – or face further consequences.'

Aelfgar bowed his head, aware of what the archbishop alluded to: excommunication. His soul would burn in hell for eternity, and would be irredeemable from the flames.

'Very well,' Aelfgar said. He bowed, tight-lipped, and left the chamber.

The open door revealed for a moment the excited courtiers in the hall outside, intrigued to know what the shouting was about in council, then it was closed tight again.

It was wrong, Harold knew. Not merely because Tostig wasn't the right man to govern the north, but because the exile of Aelfgar did the realm no good at all, and would surely leave his grievances to fester like a wound in the hot sun. He found the king in Edith's chambers, and Edith greeted him with intense pleasure – as well she might, as her wish had been obeyed.

But Harold ignored her and addressed Edward. 'Sire, I beseech you to reverse your decision made yesterday in banishing Earl Aelfgar from the realm. It can only bode ill for our unity of purpose.'

Edward eyed Harold pensively. 'I can only do that if I reverse the decision to appoint Tostig as earl of Northumbria. Your sister, I fear, would never allow that.'

Judging by Edith's sweet smile of triumph, it was clear to Harold that she had already foreseen his arrival and had persuaded Edward to stand by his hasty decision to exile Aelfgar. 'The feud between the house of Godwin and Leofric stretches back many years, sire,' Harold said, patiently attempting a new approach. 'My father was often at odds with Leofric before your reign began – especially after the death of Canute, when Leofric favoured Harold Harefoot over Harthacanute, and forced Godwin out of favour. I fear that if we are not careful, all the old wounds will be reopened.'

Edward laid a friendly arm on Harold's shoulder. 'They're all dead, Harold,' he said gently. 'Your father, Canute, Harthacanute – and Leofric will soon be following them to the grave. He has no wish to become embroiled with his son's intrigue during his last days. If Aelfgar continues his senseless behaviour, then Leofric will nominate his other son, Edwin, as his heir. I envisage no damaging break-up of any house. It is wise to let Aelfgar cool his head outside the realm for a while, until Tostig is settled in the north. I shall pardon him when the time is right. Stigand agrees with me, and I have my good wife here for advice also.'

Harold bit back a response and bowed out, accepting defeat; he might have guessed Stigand would contribute his opinion. They were all together: Stigand, Edith, and Tostig; they would tear the country apart, those three, if God allowed them.

Edward's optimism was ill-founded. Aelfgar stormed out of England bound for Ireland. There, it was said, he hired eighteen Viking mercenary ships and was last seen off the north coast of Wales.

Aelfgar's dramatic departure was overshadowed by the return of Bishop Ealdred from Germany. When Harold greeted him, Ealdred presented Harold with a silver locket made in Cologne and fashioned with an intricate design. Harold slipped it over his head. 'I shall wear it always, thank you. Tell me about the prince.'

'He has a wife, Agatha, and three children: Edgar, Margaret and Christina.'

'Will he come to England?'

Ealdred smiled. 'It's the question on everyone's lips, and one that I have pondered over for a long while. I think that yes, he will come. Hungary is now involved in a full-scale war with the emperor. Prince Edward won't be safe for much longer. I've arranged with Emperor Henry for the prince's safe passage with his family out of Bratislava, to Cologne, Lille and thence to London.'

Not for the first time, Harold marvelled at the capability of Ealdred; he had indeed been the best man to carry out this task. 'Do you know when he will come, exactly?'

'It will be some months, maybe over a year before they arrive. I can't be more certain than that.'

'You have done well, Ealdred,' Harold said. 'The king is pleased?'

'He is – and so is Stigand.'

'And so he might be,' Harold grinned, for they both knew how important it was to Stigand that an outsider was not appointed heir. He could see Stigand across the room now, and nodded to him, but Harold's thoughts were filled with the last prince of the old blood who might one day put England at her ease.

Chapter Twenty-Nine
London, January 1057

Eadgyth woke late and turned sleepily on her side, reaching for Harold's warmth. But the other half of the bed was cold and empty: he wasn't there. Eadgyth opened her eyes and remembered that he had left her at first light: he had gone to meet the prince. After all these years in exile, in Hungary and Germany, the last English prince was returning to England, bringing his wife and family. The wars with the Magyars had made it too dangerous to stay, and he must have seized Bishop Ealdred's offer as a drowning man does straws.

The importance of the return of the prince, so long awaited in Edward's court, could not be underestimated. That much Harold had impressed upon Eadgyth again and again after council meetings and private talks with the king. Edward's long-lost nephew and namesake was the final hope for an heir from the old line: making him heir would silence all the foreign princes who believed they had a claim to the throne of England.

In November, Harold had been despatched to St Omer to meet the prince and make the arrangements for his crossing to England. Now all London buzzed with excitement, and some people remembered another little-known exile, King Edward himself, who had come and taken the throne after years in the wilderness.

Eadgyth shrugged herself free of the bedclothes and began to dress, hurriedly, for the chamber was cold and the winds swept mercilessly along this stretch of the Thames. Calling for her maids, she chose her jewellery with care, wondering what the prince's wife looked like, and how she would react to the English court. Perhaps she, Eadgyth, could make a friend of her and help her settle into her new home.

*

Harold stood on the pier and cursed the wind again. The combined forces of the icy blast and the low temperature were hellish. He wrapped the thick cloak tightly around his shoulders and wished to God he'd brought another one.

With him were Leofwine, Tostig and several of the king's stewards. Edward himself was waiting at the palace. Gyrth was with the prince and was to escort him from St Omer; late last night he had sent word ahead that the small fleet was at Dover and would be at Westminster soon after dawn if the wind was right.

It was now long after dawn and there was no sign of the ships. Several barges had passed by as the shipmen began their day on the river, but the shivering huddle of men on the pier hadn't yet seen what they were waiting for. Harold passed round the flagon of wine he alone had had the good sense to bring, and it was drunk gratefully.

'This is madness,' Tostig exploded, passing the flagon to Leofwine. 'We'll all die of cold. We should go back to the king's hall and wait by the fire.'

Harold said: 'We should be here, to welcome the prince...' He broke off as three large ships hove into view around the sharp bend in the river.

'Is it them?' asked Leofwine.

Harold had told Gyrth to hoist the dragon of Wessex banner on entering the mouth of the Thames. It fluttered at the head of the leading ship, and he said: 'It's them. It is the prince.' He turned to one of the stewards: 'Go and tell the king he's here.'

The small crowd tensed as the ships grew closer, aware that this was an historic homecoming. The cold wind, still buffeting the weary timbers of the pier, was entirely forgotten for the moment as all eyes watched the ships, scanning the prow of the foremost vessel for a glimpse of the prince who might be on deck to survey his new land.

'I can see Gyrth,' said Tostig, pointing to the leading ship. Gyrth was at the stern, holding the ropes ready to fling onto the pier, but of the prince there was no sign. 'Why is the prince not on deck? Is he not eager to see his homeland after so many years?' said Tostig. 'Of course; he's probably in his cabin, in the warmth; no doubt Gyrth advised him to stay out of the wind.'

They were all eager to see him, but they would have to wait. Another gust of wind whistled past and the ships rocked in the swell.

'Pass me that flagon,' Harold said. 'Gyrth will need some.'

Tostig passed the flagon over.

Gyrth shouted a warning and the ropes came flying across. The quayside servants made them fast and Gyrth stepped onto the pier.

'What is it, Gyrth?' Harold sensed that something was wrong.

Gyrth, deathly pale, said in a hoarse voice, 'The prince is sick. The physician says he has not long to live. He may die very soon.'

Edward sat patiently as Gyrth described the sea-crossing to Dover. The prince had been in good health when they left the Flemish port of Wissant, but had fallen ill very suddenly once they were at sea. They stopped at Dover, sent the messages on to London and hoped that the illness would pass. Instead, it grew worse, and was now a raging fever.

'Was the crossing rough?' Edward asked when Gyrth had finished.

'Not unduly so,' said Gyrth. 'Not nearly enough to make a man sicken like this. We must hope that your best physicians can cure him.'

'Can we see him?' Edward asked.

'No, sire,' said Gyrth. 'The physician insists that the prince be left undisturbed.'

Edward grimaced, but the answer seemed reasonable enough. 'Then at least show his family in.

I would like to meet them.'

The prince's wife, Agatha, and the three children, Edgar, Margaret and Christina, were ushered into the hall. They were tired and apprehensive at the strange faces and the foreign tongue. Agatha, a German-Hungarian princess, knelt before Edward, who rose from the throne and embraced her.

'Tell the princess that she and her children are welcome to live in my court for as long as they please. Now, the children. How old is the boy?'

'Three, sire,' said Gyrth. 'I have spoken to them all on the boat. The girls are ten and six – Margaret is the eldest.'

'We will look after them. Tell them not to fear,' said Edith. She was seated by Edward's feet and hadn't spoken until now.

'Sire.' It was Elgan, one of the king's household stewards. His face was bitten by the cold and an icy draught followed him into the hall. He had come direct from the ship, and the crowd in the hall fell silent.

'What is it, Elgan?' the king asked calmly.

'The prince is dead, sire. He died just now, after he had been shriven. I...I am sorry to be the bearer of such news, lord king.'

Edward crossed himself, and others in the room followed suit. If Elgan's words needed translation, then that was more than enough, for the princess broke down and wept, clutching her children close and telling them in their strange, guttural tongue that they would never see their father again.

'See to it that they are provided with comfortable quarters,' Edward motioned to the weeping princess and her children.'Spare them nothing.'

As Elgan led the grieving family from the hall, Gyrth said quietly: 'I imagine that they wish that they had stayed in Bratislava and braved the wars against the Magyars.'

Tostig hissed: 'It's all very well saying that, but it's too late. What are we going to do now?'

Tostig had gone to the heart of the matter. The boy Edgar was far too young for Edward to designate him as his successor and once again, England was bereft of an heir for her throne.

*

The prince was buried at St Paul's, alongside King Ethelred, the grandfather he had never known, and in a city and country he had never seen.

Nobody suspected murder. Foul play was ruled out, but the will of God was not. It seemed that it was God's will that no heir would be found for Edward until God decided that the time was right. Until then, they would have to wait.

'Harold, I would speak with you.'

Harold, walking down the steps of the church after the funeral service of the prince, stopped and turned to face the archbishop of Canterbury, who was blowing into his hands to warm them from the cold. 'Very well,' he said, 'But not here.'

They walked quickly back up the steps past the departing members of the court, and sought shelter in one of the chapels of the church.

The church was warm from the recent mass of humanity, and many candles still glowed from the service. Priests moved back and forth round the prince's coffin by the high altar, preparing the process of entombment.

'We have a great problem,' said Stigand, dropping his mitre on the bench. 'There is no heir to the throne.'

'What of the boy, Edgar; he could be nominated Edward's successor, couldn't he?'

'Too young,' said Stigand quickly. 'If Edward dies tomorrow, what then, eh?'

'We could act as regents...'

'Impossible. The duke of Normandy would never accept that. A grown man succeeding Edward, maybe. But a boy – no.'

Harold had thought it over again and again since the death of the prince and could think of no alternative but to choose the boy and hope that Edward lived long enough for the boy to grow to a man. But Stigand had hit the nail on the head: if Edward died sooner rather than later, what then?

'What do you suggest then, archbishop?'

Harold, who was wondering what scheme the man had dreamt up now, was well aware that Stigand had the most to lose by the arrival of a foreign king; he would be removed from his archepiscopal throne immediately. Stigand's face had turned a garish yellow in the light of the flickering candles, and he said in such a matter-of-fact voice that Harold wondered if he had heard him correctly: 'I suggest you, Harold Godwinsson. You could succeed Edward.'

In a far-away chapel, a choir of boys sang a mass for the soul of King Ethelred, as they did every day, and had done since his death forty-one years ago; and it seemed, as the voices rose and fell and diminished into nothing, that they were mocking Stigand's proposal.

'I have no right,' said Harold. 'I don't have royal blood in my veins – how could you think of me, I...'

'That is no matter.' Stigand grasped the front of Harold's cloak. 'It was always going to be Edward's son by Edith, but that never was; then it was going to be the prince, but now he's dead, and his son is too young; there is nobody left now. But you – you are the earl of Wessex, like your father before you, the seat of the ancient kings of the West Saxons; you are liked and respected, as Godwin was. Your brother is the earl of Northumbria and Gyrth and Leofwine will undoubtedly be belted earls one day; your sister is the queen, loved and respected for her generosity and purity. Through your mother you are descended from Danish aristocracy and related to Canute. The Godwin family is more powerful now than it ever has been, and it is popular and in the king's favour. You dominate the court and the country. Earl Leofric of Mercia is not long for this world and his son is exile and outlaw. What matter that no royal blood flows in your veins? The people would rather have you than some foreign bastard with a vague, distant ancestral connection, or another Viking hellhound from Scandinavia. They will have you, because you are a good man. It is not at all unreasonable that you, my lord of Wessex, should consider yourself a candidate for the throne of England.'

Harold stared into Stigand's eyes. He was deadly serious – there was no doubt that he had meant every word he'd said. 'I had not thought of myself,' he said slowly, 'but the events of these past days open new doors of opportunity.' It was a shock, too, to think of himself as Edward's successor. 'But surely it can only be a possibility –'

'A very feasible one,' rasped Stigand.

'But to be king...consecrated by St Peter...'

'You could do it, Harold.'

Harold nodded to himself in the dark. He could do it, and now that he was over the initial shock of the idea, he felt the excitement – spiced with guilt – grow at the thought of it.

'But Edward would never choose me,' he said.

'Who else would he choose then, Harold – who else?' Stigand's face glowed yellow again in the candlelight, giving him the appearance of a ghoul.

'Think on it, my lord. King of England. With my full support. King Harold.'

Stigand got up and walked away, leaving Harold in the semi-darkness, clenching and unclenching his hands, which were wet with sweat at the thought of it. King Harold.

Haroldus Rex.

Chapter Thirty
Rouen, Normandy, March 1057

News of the death of Prince Edward reached William while he was at Rouen. He was jubilant. 'Now,' he said to Matilda, 'it must be me. There is no one left but me. Edward must designate me his heir.'

Matilda wasn't so sure. 'What of the dead prince's son?'

'A boy. A mere infant,' said William, 'Edward wouldn't dare to declare such a young boy as his heir.'

William had good cause to rejoice. The Christmas festivities at Rouen had celebrated the end of a good year; the news from England could only advance William's cause further. William had garrisoned the castles of Mont Barbet and Ambries on the border with Maine. In response, the powerful family of Mayenne, headed by Geoffrey, appealed to Count Geoffrey of Anjou, whereupon William marched south and took him prisoner. The price of Mayenne's release was his avowal of loyalty to the duke of Normandy. This was done, and another overmighty family was tied to the ducal house.

Matilda could only express doubt as to the whole venture of the English succession. But William wouldn't listen to her, and soon afterwards he departed for Breteuil, where he had instructed Will to fortify the town and begin building a castle.

She found a more sympathetic ear in Odo, William's half-brother, and put to him William's dream of succeeding Edward.

'It's just that,' said Odo. 'A dream. It keeps him going, and drives him against his enemies. It'll never come to pass. Such a thing would be impossible,' he said. 'The ruling aristocracy of England are unlikely to accept my brother, and Edward knows it. Nothing short of a full-scale invasion would persuade them.' Odo smiled and gave a chuckle. 'And that is well nigh impossible; the lords of the duchy have more than enough trouble holding their own with Geoffrey and Henri on the doorstep, let alone holding lands in another country.'

'But Henri and Geoffrey won't live forever,' protested Matilda.

'Nor will any of us. Our interests lie to the south, with Maine, not in England. William knows that well enough.'

'But what if the earl of Wessex is supportive of any decree Edward might make? Harold Godwinsson is known to be scrupulously fair; he is very powerful and holds a place of great influence at court. Letters I have from my sister Judith say how widely respected he is, and how people listen to him. She is envious, as her husband Tostig has none of the charms of Harold...'

'That may be true,' said Odo. 'But have you thought that when the time comes, Harold might forfeit that trust and seize the throne for himself? If he is anything like his father, he may do that.'

Matilda hadn't thought of this. 'Or perhaps Edward might leave the throne to him?'

Odo shrugged. 'Who knows? Either way, it is not our business to meddle in. We have enough to deal with here.'

Matilda's conversation with Odo left her feeling much happier; of course it was possible that Harold would take the throne, and even likely that Edward would leave it to him. It would solve all their problems if that happened. It would be so simple, so conclusive, that William would have to forget the idea of becoming king. She was comforted by that. He could never contemplate an armed invasion then. Never.

As spring arrived, the question of Edward's succession was put aside again as William's spies and scouts reported the mobilising armies of Count Geoffrey and King Henri; it was clear that they were going to invade the duchy.

But William was ready this time. The majority of Norman barons were with him, his family and close friends were in control of the churches and towns; there were no enemies within the duchy who would stab him in the back. He had the support of the pope too, who saw in him a ruler who would implement the church's reforms. Odo was already bishop of Bayeux and Robert, William's other half-brother, was newly invested as lord of Mortain. They had wealth, land, power and confidence.

William was ready and men would fight to the last for him. He had no qualms about facing in battle the man who had once acted as his protector and betrayed that trust.

William was hunting outside the town of Falaise when a messenger arrived from Will FitzOsbern, telling him that King Henri and Count Geoffrey had entered the duchy on 27th July and were heading north. Will seemed to think they would march for Bayeux and Caen.

William pulled at the reins of his horse. 'Call off the hunt. I'll issue commands for the army togather at Falaise. We'll wait there and see what they do.'

Four days later, the small town of Falaise was crowded with troops from all quarters of the duchy. Men from the Cotentin, from the Eure valley, the Orne, Calvados and from the east of Rouen and the south, Chartres; they all came, and continued to come, eagerly flooding the town in their desire to serve the duke and, if need be, to shed blood for the oath they had sworn to him.

On the seventh day, William judged that his army was at maximum strength. He assembled his council. All the faithful barons were there: Ralph Tosny, Roger Montgomery, Hugh Avranches, and his half-brothers Odo and Robert, the latter two excited at being involved in their first campaign. And of course Will FitzOsbern, who was on edge with nerves and tiredness, not from the strain of preparation for battle, but from worry for his young wife, Adeliza, who had just given birth to a daughter. It had been a difficult confinement, and Will had come from Breteuil only late last night. Adeliza was Ralph Tosny's daughter, but Ralph showed no concern. He was a hard man, but Will loved his wife with a tender passion.

'Henri and Geoffrey are marching north ,and were last seen at Vire, two days ago. We'll hound them, chase them, panic them, and wait for their defences to come down; and then we'll smash them.'

William surveyed the barons, searching for signs of disagreement, but there was none.

'We leave at dawn. I've sent on scouts to Thury-Harcourt and Aunay. When we catch up with the invading army, God willing we shall give Henri of France a day to remember,' he added bitterly.

Will was watching him from across the table. 'Amen to that,' he said quietly, and the meeting came to an end.

Chapter Thirty-One
Varaville Ford, Normandy, August 1057

Henri regarded the count of Anjou with profound distaste. He had often wondered, with good cause, why he had found himself allied with Geoffrey; God knows he harboured enough doubts as to the wisdom of this invasion of Normandy. He was hot, tired and old. At least, too old to be leading an army into the heartland of the duchy without coming to some sort of grief. Geoffrey too, was sweating like a pig beneath his heavy mail hauberk. His red face glistened.

'What exactly do you mean?' asked Henri belligerently. The sun was at its highest point, and beat down mercilessly on the weary, straggling army with all the heat of a relentless furnace fire.

They were at Dives, a small town on the river bearing that name, close to Varaville. During the weeks of marching across the duchy, north to Bayeux, and east past Caen, the troops had grown glutted with food, wine and women, all plundered without mercy. The leaders had become less sure of the purpose of their invasion, as William had not come out to give battle, as they had hoped. The duke had stayed out of sight, but Henri knew he was waiting and watching their every move, and this served only to add to their lack of purpose. And now Count Geoffrey had ridden up from the rear and announced that the entire rear of the army was too drunk to ford the river, and would have to wait on the east bank to sober up.

'I mean what I say, lord king.' Blustering Geoffrey stood his ground. 'Too much good food, women and cider. They beg for a day's rest before pressing on.'

Henri hesitated, restraining his instinct to curse. Despite the heat, he was tempted to give the order to advance and damn the drunkards who could not keep pace: they could stay and rot. And damn Geoffrey too, for dragging him into this, for the campaign was fast becoming a debacle, thanks to the count insisting that they march on – though his men picked fights with Henri's men – and thanks to the cunning patience of the duke for holding back his forces.

But instead, for reasons he could not explain but would later regret bitterly, Henri replied: 'Very well, then. Order a general halt on the bank. We'll cross later.'

'Thank you, my lord.' Geoffrey bobbed his head in an obsequious bow, but before he could vanish back to his Angevin escort, who were loitering restlessly around the king and his own guard, Henri added: 'And bring me the guide.'

The guide appeared almost half an hour later. He was having difficulty in finding Henri's tent. Henri had placed his command quarters in the shade of a group of trees near the riverbank. The bulk of the army was by now scattered through several fields and around the town, sleeping off another night's drinking and rape. There was little Henri could do to prevent their unruly behaviour, so he resigned himself to waiting in the shade.

The guide was drunk. He staggered across the field, slipping and stumbling in the long grass, weaving a circuitous path to the king. On reaching Henri, he bent double and vomited copiously into the river. The vomit formed a small slick on the surface of the water and there it stayed, unmoving. Flies buzzed furiously towards it. There was a horrified silence as the king looked away from the vomit to the guide.

The king was not amused. 'This man doesn't know who I am, let alone where we are,' he said.

The guide, recovered somewhat now he had retched his guts clear, knelt in the grass at Henri's feet, unshaven, unkempt, and with dribbles of puke running down his chin: not surprisingly, Henri did not offer his hand for his subject to kiss. The guide grinned inanely and tried to stand, but was defeated by the effort and swayed headfirst to the ground, where he lay like a man poleaxed.

'Oh, for God's sake, take him away.' Henri waved a hand, more irritated than anything, and three soldiers began to drag him off.

Watching the guide's face bump along the ground and away to the nearest water trough, Guy of Sens said: 'It was Count Geoffrey's men, sire; they filled him with cider.'

'I might have known it, damn them to hell,' said Henri. 'I don't want to know the finer details, but I do need to know the times of the tides so that we can cross this damned river. With or without Geoffrey.'

The Dives was a tidal river and could only be crossed at low tide. There was a ford, but not a large one; wide enough for eight or nine men only.

'The guide told me that the tide will be out between the hours of three and six, sire,' said Guy.

'Was the man drunk or sober when he told you that?'

'He was sober, sire.'

'How can I trust his judgement? When he sobers up, I want him flogged. Take the skin off his back, d'you hear?'

'Yes, sire. I'll find another guide, shall I?'

'You do that, Guy. Find a fisherman, someone who knows the river well. Hurry – I'm sick of this waiting around.'

Henri sat back in the shade, satisfied that something was being done at last, and at someone else's initiative. He drank some of the wine that had been kept cool in the shade, and settled down to wait.

'Strange.'

William scratched his chin and looked at the scout. Why should Henri halt his troops by the river at Dives? The report was comprehensive enough: the entire French-Angevin force had stopped on the west bank of the Dives near Varaville, but they weren't in battle formation, and since they were loose in the town, they didn't appear to be preparing to cross the river, either.

'Strange?' echoed Will. 'Good God, it's our chance, William. Surely God has given it to us and we should take it. Order the advance and we shall smash Henri and Geoffrey once and for all.'

William shook his head. 'But surely Henri knows we are here, at Caen?'

Will checked his restless horse as it gave a snort, irritated by the flies at its mouth, and said: 'After all these weeks of us following him, he doesn't expect us to attack him.'

The soft jingle of harness announced the arrival of Roger Montgomery from the rear. 'Why have we stopped?' he asked, panting. 'Has the king been sighted?' He was hot and a little annoyed by the halt.

'Henri is at the ford on the Dives, by Varaville,' said Will. 'He's resting on the west bank, doing nothing.'

'Then we'll have him!' exclaimed Roger.

'I'm not sure,' said William. 'Does Henri know something we don't?'

'Now we can finish them both.'

'It might be a trap,' said William.

'Then let me and FitzOsbern lead the army,' Roger urged.

'No,' said William forcefully. 'I won't abdicate my responsibility as the duke and leader of this army against the invader. We'll go on, and if we find him still on the bank then it is God's will, and...'

'....we'll attack? 'said Will.

'Yes.'

When Henri awoke, the tide was out and the sun had sunk considerably lower in the sky. He cursed himself for becoming as lax as the men in the town, and struggled to his feet.

The shallow crest of sand and shingle that made up the ford was easily visible from the hundred yards distance to the king's tent. The road, little more than a rough track baked stone-hard by the heat, ended abruptly at the bank and continued on the other side into the distant trees, leading to Pont L'Évêque and Honfleur.

'How long has the tide been out?' Henri demanded of a nearby servant.

'Nearly two hours, lord king.'

'What of the lord of Sens and the new guide?'

'There has been no sign of them, sire.'

Henri rubbed his back, stiff with the sleep, and decided what he would do.

Joinville, a lord of Champagne, wandered over. A thickset man, he spoke with a slight lisp. 'Sire, what is it?'

Henri turned to him and pointed to the ford. 'You: order the men across. We're going over.'

Henri watched the orders go out to the five hundred men of his own guard who were lolling in the field. They at least had obeyed the order not to go into the town and rose, sun-soaked and grumbling, and began to splash across the ford. The water at that point was some hundred yards across. Ten men at a time could fit the narrow causeway and as they walked across, Henri watched with increasing impatience. 'Get a move on,' he muttered to nobody in particular.

Guy of Sens came running through the grass, pushing through the shuffling soldiery who were making their way to the ford. Henri watched Guy with grim satisfaction and when he reached him, said: 'I'm sending the men across. I'm sick and tired of this delay and bad discipline. Geoffrey has disappeared –'

'He's in the tavern, sire,' Guy got a word in.

'– and you've been gone for hours.' Henri continued as though Guy had never interrupted. 'In the tavern with the count, no doubt?'

Guy reddened, and grinned sheepishly. 'Sire, I didn't think that there was any particular hurry to bring the guide along.'

Henri eyed him coldly for a moment. 'So I have given the order to cross, as the tide is out. Geoffrey and his drunken Angevin scum can rot.'

'Very well, sire, I shall command my men to follow the guard.'

'Where is the new guide?'

'He's somewhere behind me, sire.' Guy pointed to the mass of soldiers.

Henri sighed. 'Go and get him, and tell them to go faster,' he said, snapping his fingers. His sword-belt was handed over and he buckled it on and walked to his horse.

When they saw the king coming, the men parted to let him through, giving a great cheer. As Henri reached the opposite bank and steadied his horse, he turned to a squire and shouted in a voice that betrayed his growing impatience:

'Tell them to hurry, damnation!'

The waters of the Dives were running faster now, stirring even the laziest of eddies among the reeds into a current.

Then Guy of Sens reappeared by the water's edge and began shouting at the men at the back to go faster. They began to run, pushing and shoving those in front of them to a greater speed.

Guy himself forced a passage across the ford, and slipped into the shallow waters at Henri's feet.

'Sire,' he gasped, heaving himself to his feet. 'The guide says that the tide will turn at any moment. We must get across now, or run back, before it's too late.'

'Surely it's hours before the tide turns?'

'No, sire. Not at this time of year. It turns earlier and changes very rapidly.'

'But...' For once, Henri's bluster failed him and he left the words hanging in the air.

'The army will be cut in two if we are not quick enough, sire,' Guy persisted.

'How many have crossed?'

Guy did a rapid calculation and said: 'All the household troops are over, my men from Sens, the men from Berry, Orléans and a few from Anjou.'

'Most of ours, then?'

At that moment the the count of Anjou emerged on the opposite river bank, shouting at Henri. He plunged into the water and expertly swam his horse across the river, ignoring the yelling mass of infantry on the ford. Other horsemen were doing likewise, leaving their arms and armour behind to reduce the risk of drowning.

'Christ Jesus, Henri, what are you doing?' roared Geoffrey. He whipped his stallion through the mire. 'Do you want to kill us all?' He had reached the king and faced him soaked, sober and furious; he didn't care whether Henri was a king or a recalcitrant servant. 'The tide is about to turn and you didn't inform me of your decision to send the army across. What the hell is this? Treachery?'

Henri studied the enraged count with quiet disdain.

'You were, I believe, in the tavern; drinking all afternoon and whoring. Too busy to aid me in conducting this campaign. Quite aside from that, you address me as if I were something that had lodged under your boot. I...'

Henri's voice tailed off as a cry from the ranks of men on the ford became a scream of terror. The tide had turned and was now rushing with a vengeance to swallow up the small crest of the ford. The troops began to panic as the word spread, and those at the rear surged forward; men were trampled and shoved helpless into the swirling torrent at their feet.

Henri's face had gone ashen grey at the scene of pandemonium before them. In a few minutes the ford would be gone. 'How many men have yet to cross?'

There were hundreds - any man could see that from a glance - all pushing to get on to the ford, many jumping into the water and drowning. There were those running from the small town, suddenly very, very sober.

'Now you see what you have done?' Geoffrey shouted. 'We'll have to wait until tomorrow before the army is rejoined. You bloody fool!'

Henri recoiled. No man had ever spoken to him like that - ever. 'This army will never rejoin,' he snapped. 'The alliance is at an end, and should never have been. God knows what I'm doing here with you.'

Geoffrey stared at the king for a minute, then realised the full significance of Henri's words. 'But most of those men over there are mine. They're Angevins. You can't just leave them.'

'Mercenaries and hired killers, all of them,' Henri said. 'They can hang.'

'Damn you then,' said Geoffrey. 'I should have known that the man who betrayed his own vassal – aye, his own ward – couldn't be trusted.'

Henri reddened. 'You talk of trust, you...like your father, you're an unworthy dog, Geoffrey. One that feeds off the rotting carcass that is war.'

Henri stopped, feeling that this exercise in trading insults had gone far enough. There was an army to be regrouped and the long march home to be planned. Geoffrey could go hang.

But then, the sound of a shrill trumpet blast reached them, and out of the woods on their left a long line of cavalry broke forth. With couched lances and raised swords, the cavalry charged towards the Angevins in the fields near the ford.

All Henri's nightmares became reality in that moment.

'God have mercy,' breathed Geoffrey.

It was William.

The Norman cavalry charge hit the fleeing Angevins with all the force of a tidal wave smashing a flimsy boat. Some, drunk and terrified out of their wits, were cut down where they stood. Others, staggering half-dressed out of the town brothel, gaped in horror and ran back inside to hide from the slaughter of their comrades. The Normans hacked and stabbed until their arms ached, until their horses were blown and their sword-grips too slippery with blood to hold, and by then there were no more enemies left alive.

On the opposite bank, Henri watched the destruction of the rest of his army with sick horror. It wasn't a battle. It was a slaughter ground. Those who survived the swinging swords and jabbing lances of the Normans leapt into the river, taking the gamble in full armour; but the tide was now at its highest, and they were swept away, never to be seen again.

At sunset, when it was too dark to kill any more, William regrouped his horsemen and found that there had been only one casualty: a knight who had slipped from the saddle and twisted his ankle. The victory was complete.

Henri watched until the end; even the men hiding in the town were winkled out and put to the sword, and the whores they had been with were supplied with new clients from William's victorious troops. Henri ordered the retreat to Paris. Geoffrey, still cursing his king to hell and damnation everlasting, gathered the remnants of his shattered army and headed back to Anjou.

It was the last invasion of Normandy by either of them.

Chapter Thirty-Two
Gloucester, December 1064

Eadgyth slept badly the night before Christmas. It had been an exceptionally mild winter so far, and the chamber was hot and stuffy. She lay awake, listening to Harold's steady breathing beside her, and wondered whether he would one day be king.

When Harold had told her what Stigand had said that afternoon in the church of St Paul's, she had laughed; then she had realised that Stigand had been serious, and not only that, but he had planted an idea in Harold's head which had taken root like a seed.

It was more than possible now. Both Leofric and his son Aelfgar were dead. Aelfgar's son, Edwin, had inherited the earldom of Mercia but was only eighteen years old, and was a ward of the king. Ralf of

Mantes had died, too, leaving the house of Godwin supreme in King Edward's court: Tostig held Northumbria, Gyrth had been made earl of East Anglia, Leofwine given lands in Suffolk, Surrey and Kent, enough to give him a place on the council. The king was happy to leave the reins of government to Harold, who had added the lands of Herefordshire to his earldom in Wessex. Edward himself spent his time pursuing his lifelong dream of completing his abbey at Westminster. He would be buried there, and would ensure that his name outlasted all others in piety and godliness.

But Edward still hadn't named his heir.

Uncomfortable in the hot bed, Eadgyth turned over several times before finding the right position. Harold slept on, undisturbed. Eadgyth looked at him; his fine blond hair was beginning to grey a little at the edges, but he was as healthy and muscular as ever. He could beat any of the young bloods in the housecarls at swordplay and wrestling, and their respect for him was enormous. Eadgyth reached over and traced the line of his jaw with her finger. His hand automatically found hers, and he grunted in his sleep. She smiled; after all the years, he still found her attractive, and to her knowledge, had never sought his pleasure in another woman's bed. She was proud of her figure; the ravages of childbirth had by good fortune left her with a smooth stomach and a slim waist. And her hair remained glossy and long, and he still loved to bury his head in it and breathe in her scent.

He slept undisturbed, but by day Eadgyth knew that he had worries. He harboured his desire to succeed Edward like a boy hiding a secret, but doubts still made him guilty and hesitant. He shared them with her, of course, and she knew what, or rather, who, his greatest doubt was: Duke William of Normandy.

Three years after the news of the shaming defeat of Henri and Geoffrey at Varaville Ford had reached the courts of Europe, they were both dead. Geoffrey left chaos in his wake in Anjou and Henri left a young boy in France. Since William's father-in-law, Count Baldwin of Flanders, was acting as regent for Henri's heir Philippe, William was the undisputed master in northern France. Would he assert his claim to Edward's throne more forcefully now, or would he remain content with what he had already?

Harold stirred in the bed and Eadgyth saw him watching her.

'How long have you been awake?' she asked.

'Long enough to hear you moving about like a mole,' he said. 'What is it?'

For a moment Eadgyth was tempted to tell him what she feared, and to urge him to forget making a claim to the throne. They had enough to contend with, hadn't they? But then, what would happen when Edward died? The boy Edgar was still too young and if a foreigner succeeded Edward, what would Harold do?

'Nothing,' she said at last. 'I'm hot, that's all. Go back to sleep.'

Harold rolled over and lay silent. Soon, his breathing became relaxed and grew deeper; he was asleep.

Eadgyth closed her eyes and hoped that she would find sleep as easily, and allay the demons of fear and doubt, but she couldn't. Nevertheless, the dawn would inevitably arrive, and for another day there would be an escape of a different kind.

*

No expense had been spared for the Christmas feasting. The king of England was one of the wealthiest monarchs in Christendom and did not stint his courtiers where food and drink were concerned. Roast ox, swan, beef, lamb and boar adorned the tables of his hall, followed by sweetmeats and washed down with as much wine and beer as a man could take.

Unusually for him, Edward was jubilant and talkative on the high table. The latest report from the master-mason of the abbey indicated that good progress was being made; it was declared that the builders were on schedule and projected that the church would be completed within three years; by 1066, with God's grace.

After they had eaten, the minstrel sang for them. He began his repertoire with *Beowulf* as he always did, and after the monster was finally dead, he went on to the second most popular song; the 'Song of Maldon', the heroic tale of Ealdorman Brihtnoth defeated by the Vikings in Essex, but defended by his thegns who stood by him and died to a man.

These songs were virtually obligatory, and plucked the heart-strings of all the young housecarls in the hall. Harold smiled at their cheers as Brihtnoth urged his men on: 'Thoughts must be the braver, hearts more valiant, courage the greater, as our strength grows less!' Then the minstrel sang some lullabies and finished with a poem called 'The Happy Land', which was one of Harold's favourites. With the king seated by the fire, and his queen at his feet, and his chief earls around him, the minstrel began:

I have heard there is hence
That bright bower as the tallest hill,
 Which white and bright gives the world light
 And shines to men under the shining of the stars
 Far away from the world
 A nook in the East, a noble plain,

Great, and girt with gallant trees,
Which the Lord from living men
Has shut tight, shielded quite,
Since he formed first the world.
That victorious plain pleasant shall remain,
With no pain and no rain,
No showers to steep, no rime to creep,
No hot sky, no screaming hail;
Always the plain is a pleasant place.
For there are no mountains high and proud,
Nor any stone cliffs, starving clefts,
Precipices leaning up, precipices leaning down,
But the noble plain never fails to stand
Even and open, unanxiously perfect.

There was a soft applause at the conclusion of the poem, to which the minstrel bowed, delighted that he had pleased the king's company.

They were a contented court. Tostig and Judith were present with their three children; Eadgyth and Harold's boys were of course present; his other brothers Gyrth and Leofwine, the latter with his wife, Agnes, who was with child; the young Earl Edwin of Mercia and his brother, Morcar; the eleven-year-old Prince Edgar, with his mother and sisters, all wards of the crown. And at Edward's feet, Queen Edith, devoted to the king like a daughter, her past estrangement from him nothing but an ugly blur in her memory. Harold's mother Gytha too, was there, her beauty undimmed by time, sharing a joke with Stigand, who persuaded himself that she was flirting with him. It seemed that all the enmities of the past had resolved themselves – and perhaps they had. It was a contented, extended family at peace with itself, from the boy-prince to the ageing, gracious king at the head.

And the power at the heart of it all was Harold.

As he grew older, Edward had delegated more and more control over the governance of the realm to Harold. Along with Tostig and Edith, Harold exerted most influence over the court and council, while Edward, content with Harold in command, devoted his energy to his abbey. In this aura of peace and prosperity, the question of Edward's succession had been set aside, as if they would go on forever, undisturbed and at peace.

*

One morning after Christmas Day, the king summoned Harold to a private audience.

'It is about the vexed question of my heir,' Edward explained. 'I will die soon and I have not declared my heir to the world. Several men hope to succeed me: Duke William of Normandy is one. He is related in blood to me and indeed I have already suggested to him that he might have my throne.'

Edward smiled briefly. 'But that was a long time ago, when your father was alive. King Svein of Denmark was another, but I fear that it is Hardrada of Norway who will press his claim more strongly.' The years of rivalry between Denmark and Norway had erupted into a bitter war, with Hardrada heavily defeating Svein in battle at Nissa.

'Finally, there is Prince Edgar, an eleven-year-old boy. The boy is my most direct heir and he is of the old blood, but he is terribly young and if he should sicken...'

Harold waited for the king to finish, scarcely able to breathe. Would it be him, after all? But in the second the flames of Harold's hopes flared, they were damped out.

'I think the boy will have to succeed me, Harold.'

Harold cursed himself for having thought that it could be him; it could never be – how could that fat fool Stigand have suggested otherwise? It would be the prince, of course, the boy with the old blood running through his veins. Harold noticed Edward watching him with a curious glint in his eyes. 'It's the best possible solution, sire,' he said hastily. Did Edward think he had hoped...? Maybe Stigand had whispered the thought into the king's ear? Damn Stigand! 'It will be agreeable to all sides,' he added. 'The church, the north and south, the court and country.'

Edward said: 'You, Harold as the most powerful man in the realm, will stand by him and be his guardian, will you not? You will see him reach manhood and judge when the time is right to put the crown on the boy's head?'

'Of course, sire. It will be my great privilege, to keep the throne safe.' Harold's mind was racing. He would be regent, king of England in all but name for possibly years. The house of Godwin would remain the greatest power in the land with Edith as dowager queen, the brothers Harold, Tostig, Gyrth and Leofwine ruling the shires; it was as much as Godwin could ever have dreamt of...

'So you will see the boy into a new age?' Edward was asking.

'I will,' Harold said. 'I swear it.'

'Then I must ask you to undertake one great mission for me.' Edward grasped Harold's cloak to emphasise the urgency of his request. 'Only you can do it, for you are the man all of Christendom knows is England's guardian in my dotage.'

Harold met the king's gaze and automatically answered: 'Anything, sire. I am your man above all else.'

'It will be dangerous. I am asking you to go into the lion's den and possibly put your head into the jaws of the lion itself. You may not return, Harold.'

'I am yours to command, sire.'

'Would that all my men had but half of your loyalty!' Edward released Harold's cloak and looked away, struggling to contain himself. Harold waited patiently. Where was he to go - Wales? Scotland? Perhaps even Rome -

'Normandy.' Edward said. 'I want you to go to Normandy and tell the duke ... tell my *cousin* the duke that he will never be king of England. Tell him that I have decided that my great-nephew of the old blood, Prince Edgar, is to be my successor. You can go in the spring, when the seas are safe to cross.'

'Yes, sire.' Harold said, the colour draining from his face. It was a terrible mission; those Norman bastards would tear him apart. But it would resolve the succession once and for all. His very presence would ensure Edward's sincerity. Nobody else could go; after all, the Normans didn't read documents, so it was up to him to take the message. He *was* the message.

'We have to take the risk that if you are harmed by Duke William or any others across the water then no invasion would succeed because of the outrage caused by your demise. The pope will condemn any assault on your person, but I cannot guarantee your safe return home.'

Harold appreciated Edward's candour. It was all very well the pope condemning Harold's murder, but that wouldn't bring him back. But the message would be delivered and that was what mattered most.

'I'll do it,' he said, recalling the dark days following the death of Canute, the struggles between Harthacanute, Harold Harefoot and the murder of Prince Alfred. He would go to Normandy to prevent that happening again, in the name of Prince Edgar, the last prince of the old blood and in the name of peace.

Even if he died in the attempt.

Chapter Thirty-Three
Rouen, Normandy, April 1065

'Richard! Richard, come here. Now, please.' Matilda grasped the boy's arm and wiped his mouth with a damp cloth. 'Sticky face. I've told you enough times.' She looked up, and smiled. 'Go and see your father, then, there's a good boy.'

Richard ran off, his five-year-old legs running as fast as they could across the rushes to the far side of the long hall.

William swept his son into his arms and laughed, tickling him mercilessly. They'd named him after the first Richard, who'd been born too weak to survive. This Richard, though, was a healthy handful. William would never admit – not even to Matilda – that Richard was his favourite. But she knew him well enough to know that, anyway. He gave the boy a last hug and put him down; he ran down the steps and into the courtyard, yelling for Robert.

'Have you finished your business?' asked Matilda, walking towards him.

'Yes.' The sparkling humour went from William's face. 'It's finally resolved,' he said, and dropped a kiss on Matilda's forehead.

Just over a year ago the boy-count of Maine, Herbert, had died of the ague. By the terms of a treaty made by William, in the event of Herbert's death without issue, the county would pass to his son Robert, who had married Herbert's sister. That had happened, but of course Robert was too young to govern Maine for himself.

'I am the master of Maine in all but name,' said William. It had been left to him, as he had hoped for years, to take actual control over Maine, thus securing the southern borders of Normandy. It had taken the greater part of the previous year to subdue the lords of Maine, but he was confident that this was done now. And with his old enemies Geoffrey of Anjou and Henri of France four years in their graves, William was truly master of northern Christendom. 'Do you know what they're calling me now?' he asked Matilda. 'They call me "the Conqueror".'

'The Conqueror?'

'William the Conqueror,' William said. 'My father was Robert the Magnificent – or Robert the Devil if you were his enemy – Geoffrey of Anjou was Geoffrey the Hammer, and I ... I am William the Conqueror.' He bent and took Matilda's face between his hands. 'No longer William the Bastard.'

Matilda saw in William's eyes the acceptance he had been searching for all these years, and she said softly: 'Then perhaps we shall have some peace at last, my lord Conqueror.'

'Peace? I hope so.'

'I had a letter from Judith this morning.'

'Is it the first letter you've had since last autumn?'

Matilda nodded. 'The storms in the English Sea cut off all but the hardiest of ships this winter.'

'Then what does she say about Edward?'

'That he is well, and he thrives. His chief ambition is to complete the abbey at Westminster before he dies.'

William grunted. 'Am I mentioned in the letter?'

'Judith sends her love, but that is all.'

'No news from Edward, about his heir?'

'No. Only that the Prince Edgar is a healthy boy of some eleven years of age. You should accept, William, that the boy is the rightful heir to the throne of England.'

'No!' William shook his head. 'Edward promised the throne to me, Matilda; he told me it would be mine if I was secure and strong enough in my own duchy. You know that I am now. France, Anjou and Maine pose no threat to the borders of the duchy now.'

'Edward promised the throne to you a long time ago when he was surrounded with Norman councillors. Now he is old, and Harold Godwinsson is his deputy, and an English boy, a prince of the old blood, has been found to succeed him.' Matilda took William's hands in hers. 'You must forget England; there is Maine to secure, the duchy to govern, and as you said only yesterday, there may be trouble in Brittany. You cannot afford to shatter this fragile peace by laying claim to England as well.'

William stared at his wife for a long moment, before saying: 'Hell and damn it; you're right, as always. I'm foolish to depend on the words of an old man spoken thirteen years ago.'

Matilda felt a surge of relief at William's capitulation. Perhaps now, he would forget this obsession. 'It would have been different had Godwin never returned to impose his influence on Edward again,' she murmured. 'And had Edward kept his Norman favourites in control, then yes, you would have had been a good choice. With the prince alive and well and the power of the Godwinssons as it is, we should leave England well alone.'

William wavered, and couldn't find an answer to the sensible logic in her speech. He smiled at Matilda. 'You're as wise as you are beautiful. Thank God I have you for my wife; I wouldn't have succeeded but for you.' It was a rare admission for William to make, and he added hurriedly, as if to conceal a moment of weakness: 'I wonder what kind of man Harold Godwinsson is?'

Matilda fingered the letter in her hand. 'Judith speaks highly of him. He's brave, a great warrior, and a wise councillor to the king. Alongside his brothers and his sister the queen, he is the unacknowledged ruler of England. He will be regent of England when Edward dies, and he'll govern the realm until the boy comes of age.'

Willam set his jaw and with dread Matilda recognised the familiar stubborness: she hadn't won after all. 'Edward hasn't declared Prince Edgar his heir yet,' William concluded. 'Until then, there's still hope. I could still be king of England one day.'

Chapter Thirty-Four
Rouen, Normandy, June 1065

The Norman summer came and banished the spring rains, leaving the orchards dry and the forests parched. William held court at Falaise in May, at Coutances in early June, and was at Rouen at the end of the month, satisfied that the border regions of Beléme, Mayenne and the Vexin would give no trouble in the campaigning months of the summer.

In Brittany there was a rebellion, and William decided to support the rebels against Conan, as Conan was becoming too powerful for his own good on the western flanks of the duchy. Messengers were despatched to all corners of the duchy, ordering the barons to prepare for war, so it was with surprise that William greeted Will FitzOsbern when he arrived at the ducal palace in Rouen early in the morning.

'Will – you're supposed to be at Breteuil. I need your men with me when we go into Brittany.'

'No fear of that, William, but the news I bring is too important for me to stay away.' Will said. 'Guy of Ponthieu is holding Harold Godwinsson prisoner in the castle of Beauvais.'

*

It had gone wrong from the beginning.

The weather was fine, the wind fair, and what better way to travel on the mission than in one of the king's vessels? So it had seemed on leaving Bosham, but near Eastbourne, off Beachy Head, a sudden squall had blown up and drifted the ship off course and into one of the worst storms Harold - and many of the crew - had ever experienced.

Dawn heralded a cloudless sky and a new coast: northern France. Low on food and water, Harold ordered that they put into the nearest port for supplies. It was a port called Montreuil, and there Count Guy of Ponthieu had seized them and cast them into a dungeon in his castle at Beauvais, for no particular reason, and without heeding Harold's threats. There they stayed for two days, and were now beginning to wonder if they would ever leave.

The heavy door swung open and light flooded the small cell, blinding the man crouched in the filthy, stinking darkness.

'Out!'

Harold stumbled to his feet, shielding his eyes from the bright flame of the torch. 'My men - where are they?' He tried to restrain the anger in his voice. Maybe his life was in danger but his men deserved better. But the jailer simply jangled his keys and slammed the door shut behind Harold. He jerked his head to the stairs winding upwards to further light and voices. Harold rubbed his wrists where the chains had taken the skin off, and climbed the steps, supposing that his crew and his steward, Wulfric, were locked away in another cell. The steps led to a corridor, and as the jailer indicated that he should walk along it, the voices grew louder and it became clear that there were two dominant voices, and that they were vehemently at odds with one another.

The corridor led Harold to more steps, and a hall. They were above ground, and he blinked again, this time at the natural light. The shouting ceased as he emerged, and he stood at the entrance wondering who they all were. He recognised Guy of Ponthieu, their captor, walking towards him. Behind Guy stood three tall men, dusty and grimy from hard riding, with cropped hair and foul-tempered expressions. The tallest was in the centre, and he dwarfed the others, though they were tall in their own right. His mouth was a tight line beneath cold grey eyes, and he seemed to be fighting to contain his temper.

'I have been ordered to set you free, my lord of Wessex,' Guy was saying, unlocking the chains. 'I am sorry for any trouble. There are many pirates along our coastline.'

Guy had spoken in a tone that was anything but apologetic, but Harold nodded his thanks, accepting the goblet of wine Guy handed him. Guy gestured to the tallest of the three visitors. 'My lord the duke of Normandy will see you now.'

Harold swallowed the wine and put the goblet down. This was William of Normandy, then; bastard child of Duke Robert and fugitive who had fought his way back against all the odds to become duke after his father. His enemies had called him William the Bastard, and now they called him William the Conqueror because he had no enemies left; they were all dead. And this was the man to whom Edward had once promised the throne of England, and who Harold now had to inform that the promise was withdrawn. He could well be back inside that dungeon before he knew it.

William carried himself well, and was as broad as an ox. The flat, wide nose was haughty and gave his face a brutal look, but the grim gash of a mouth broke into an unexpectedly friendly smile as Harold bowed and said in French: 'I thank my lord of Normandy for assisting me and my men.'

William returned the bow. 'I must apologise for the count of Ponthieu's behaviour. He will be dealt with.'

He spoke with a grating, nasal voice that tended to rasp, and that would brook no dissent. Harold met the cool, grey eyes with what he hoped was an equally frank appraisal. Two days in a dungeon was not the best of preparations to meet this man of whom he had heard so much. Looking into those eyes told him that what he had heard was true. Not only what he had suffered, but what he had made others suffer.

William gestured to the men on his right. 'Allow me to introduce my cousin and lifelong friend, the lord of Breteuil, Will FitzOsbern.'

The last man to be introduced was Odo, the bishop of Bayeux. This threw Harold; looking at Odo, he'd expected him to be another warrior. In England, bishops were usually old men who wore their robes of office all the time; but Odo was clad in the same rough riding-wear as the other two, wore the same cropped hair, completely shaven at the back and cut to half an inch at the front. He was young to be a bishop, much younger than the duke and the lord of Breteuil.

'I hope you will honour me with your presence at my castle in Rouen, my lord of Wessex,' William said.

It was what Harold had been waiting for, but looking into those grey eyes told him that it was hardly an invitation, and that had he might have exchanged one prison for another.

Chapter Thirty-Five
Rouen, Normandy, June 1065

William's first impression of Harold Godwinsson was of a quiet confidence that belied the good looks and the light-hearted banter that accompanied them on the journey to Rouen. At Neufchatel-en-Bray, he rode ahead to supervise the welcome and prepare a feast in Harold's honour.

After the feast, which aroused much interest in the strangers and was much enjoyed by Harold and his men, William led Harold to his private chambers to meet Matilda and to talk in confidence.

'My sister Judith speaks highly of you,' said Matilda, offering Harold a goblet of their best Burgundian wine. 'She tells me that you are the foremost councillor, and the king's general in the realm.'

Harold, better for being washed and dressed in clean clothes after the two days in Guy's stinking dungeon, bowed graciously: 'I thank you, Lady Matilda, I am flattered.'

William was too impatient to listen to niceties between his wife and Harold.

'What news from England, Lord Harold? How is my cousin, the king?'

This was the moment. At least he felt safer here than in Guy's castle, surrounded by men-at-arms. Surely the wining and dining in William's hall would soften the blow?

'The king of England sends all his good wishes, Duke William. Indeed, he has sent me on a mission of secrecy and utmost importance to see you directly.'

'Oh? Then we are flattered to receive you.'

'My ships were diverted by the storm to Guy's lands and we never intended to stay there ... I am in your debt.'

'Think nothing of it, Lord Harold. Tell us what the king of England has to inform me.' William's eyes glittered. Now at last he was to be confirmed Edward's heir, and by no less than the most powerful and trusted man in the realm, Harold Godwinsson himself. 'There are no secrets between my wife and me,' he added, seeing Harold glance at Matilda. 'You may speak freely.'

'Very well, then. King Edward means to declare Prince Edgar his heir to the throne of England.'

William hid his disappointment well, but Harold saw his knuckles whiten as his grasp tightened on the goblet he was holding. Matilda's glance of sympathy to Willam confirmed Harold's suspicions, and he added quickly: 'I am aware that Edward promised you the throne many years ago, but times have changed. I beg you not to take offence.'

'How do we know he is serious with the prince?' William's face was set angrily. 'He's but a boy...'

'As you were, when your father departed for the Holy Land, my lord duke. Edward intends to leave the boy under my guidance –'

'And what of the other Godwinsson brothers? They have earldoms in the realm, too.'

'And sister.' Harold smiled briefly. 'My sister Edith, the queen, wields much influence with Edward.'

'Do you not think that a woman should speak her mind?' asked Matilda.

'I do, my lady,' said Harold, suspecting that Matilda had no small say in William's government. 'Indeed, the history of my country has been much determined by women. The old queen, Emma, was wife to two kings, to Ethelred and Canute, and mother to Harthacanute and Edward; she was always busy with affairs of the realm. And there was Canute's mistress, Aelfgifu of Northampton, who insisted that her base-born son should succeed Canute.'

'And there was my own mother,' said William softly, his anger fading at the memories. 'The beauty of a simple peasant girl washing her clothes at the stream changed Normandy forever.'

'It did, for certain,' Harold agreed, relieved that they had moved away from the question of Edward's heir. 'We in England have heard the story of your rise to power in Normandy and your epic struggle to regain your father's duchy from those treacherous relatives who tried to kill you. We salute that bravery and marvel at the stories,' Harold added, feeling that a little flattery would not go amiss.

'It is the stuff of legend,' William admitted, secretly pleased that this man had an appreciation of what his childhood had entailed. 'My father saw my mother from the bridge at Falaise castle and asked that she be brought to his chambers that night. He was not yet eighteen; she was sixteen, the virgin daughter of a tanner. It was not merely a night of lust on my father's part, for my mother remembered it always, and they fell in love. She came to live in the castle and was his wife in all but name. Then he went on a pilgrimage and he made me, a seven-year-old bastard, his heir. It was thought that he was mad. I thought so too, when I grew old enough to understand what he had left me.'

Harold leaned forward. 'Did you hate him for going?'

William nodded. 'Yes...at first, certainly. I hated him for condemning me to years in exile, on the run, in hiding, betrayed by those nearest me, for all those murdered in my service...how could I not hate the man who left me that? But now that all the hatred has gone and I have defeated my enemies, I try to understand why he went; he needed to salve his conscience.'

'My brother also died on the return journey from the Holy Land. He had done some terrible things...'

'So did my father,' said William. 'As I grew up, I began to learn that Robert was not the man of honour I, and many others, had supposed him to be. He had a reputation for largesse and generosity aplenty, but to many people he was Robert the Devil, and it is said that he was poisoned by one of his many enemies in revenge for the murder of his own brother.' William drained his cup. 'I'll fetch some more wine.' He kicked the fire into a blaze and went down to the hall.

Harold glanced at Matilda. She was not only a very attractive woman but a shrewd influence upon William's affairs; a woman to talk to honestly, and now was his chance before William returned. 'Does William desire the throne of England?' he asked.

'He did once,' said Matilda. 'Very much.'

'But not now?'

'How can he, now that Prince Edgar is Edward's heir?'

Harold detected a note of satisfaction in her voice; she at least was pleased that Edgar would succeed, as it meant peace. Perhaps her husband would at last lay to rest the demons that had driven him since he was abandoned and betrayed by all those closest to him. He asked, 'Would he fight for it if he thought his was the right?'

Matilda saw in Harold's eyes her own fears for the future. 'He has fought all his life for what he considers to be his. I...I do not think this would be any different.'

Harold was taken aback by the palpable fear in Matilda's voice. It confirmed his suspicion: she didn't want any involvement with England. But if she had a powerful influence over William...

Then William was in the room again and the moment had passed. 'Wretched servants are all abed.' He poured some more wine and said: 'Two days ago, I received word from Riwallon of Dol, pleading for my help against the count of Brittainy, Conan, who's growing over-mighty. I have agreed to help Riwallon.' William looked straight at Harold. 'We live in a warrior age, Harold, and we are two of the greatest warriors in Christendom. What say you to leading an army with me into Brittany?'

*

Brittany. Like Wales, land of the Celts, another home of Arthur, the last true king, and the last outpost of the Britons. And like the Welsh, the Bretons were fiercely proud of their independence, boastfully free of the Viking-Normans and the Germanic French. They were a bellicose people, either very loyal or utterly mercenary; either way, they made good warriors.

The evening before they left Falaise, where William assembled the army, William presented Harold with a mail hauberk and breeches with a body-length shield. Harold was honoured and was looking forward to seeing how the Normans went to war. English arms and armour, he explained to William, were similar to these, but few could afford such expensive protection.

Castles, however, were completely new to Harold; he had seen the timber forts erected by Ralf of Mantes in Herefordshire, but the stone fortress of Falaise was awesome.

'Built by my grandfather, Count Richard I,' said William proudly, showing Harold the towers and the high walls. 'There is the little bridge where my father saw my mother all those years ago,' he added when they reached the gatehouse. Harold gazed at the stream gurgling under the bridge through the ditches, the sunlight dancing and twinkling on the water; he could well believe how a man could be bewitched by a beautiful girl in such surroundings. 'My own courtship was somewhat more conventional,' said William. But he told Harold about the ban on his marriage to Matilda, and the first meeting when he mistook her for a stable-wench. Harold had laughed at that, and promised not to repeat it at Edward's court.

The first week of the campaign was uneventful. William led the army on a rapid march to Dol, to relieve the rebel Riwallon, but Conan fell back on hearing of his approach, and the small town went to William without a fight. Conan retreated to Rennes, but William decided to take the castle of Dinan nearby, to add weight to his campaign and further weaken Conan's position. By fostering opposition to Conan, his flanks of western Normandy would be more secure than ever before.

*

The castle of Dinan lay in a small valley above the banks of a river. It was a timber fort constructed above a high mound, and encircled by a timber palisade and ditch; very different from Falaise, and far less formidable. Viewing it from the crest at the head of the Norman army, Harold thought it looked vulnerable, and asked William what his plan of attack would be.

'There can't be more than fifty men in the fort,' said William. 'A full-frontal charge should batter down the gates, and then we'll have them.' He grinned at Harold. 'Someone's for the chop; there shouldn't be anyone in the fort at all, the idea being to pull all the men out at the sign of an army such as this, and let us through. When we are deep into enemy territory, then they attack and harry our flanks.'

'Are you sure it's garrisoned?' Harold asked.

'Do you see the smoke from the huts?'

'A trick?' Harold suggested.

William scratched his jaw. 'It's possible. But when we questioned a woodcutter an hour ago, he told us the garrison had doubled, but as far as he knew, it hadn't moved.'

'Did he speak the truth?'

'With a sword at his throat and his comely wife tied to the kitchen table, I should think he didn't dare lie to the duke of Normandy's men.'

'Well then,' said Harold, 'I thank God that I am not inside that tower.'

William laughed, but Harold wasn't in the least fooled. This entire campaign was doubtless an elaborate means of showing Harold the might of the duke of Normandy. And maybe more...did William hope that he might be killed in battle? Without Harold to guard the prince, could Edward really leave the kingdom to a boy?

William clicked his fingers and the bugler blew a long blast. The horses moved forward as one. There were no infantry with them, nor archers, as William wanted a speedy in-and-out raid. There were four hundred mounted troops, each with a lance raised for throwing, or couched for stabbing, and a broadsword at his side.

'Watch out for the archers!' William shouted. Harold could see men-at-arms scurrying about on the ramparts of the fort.

Harold was exhilarated by the charge. The horses were bred especially for warfare; William had told him that they were trained to flail their great hooves into the hapless bodies of the enemy, and use their teeth to bite the face of any man still standing. William had also explained how, although the cavalry appeared to move as a single mass, in fact it was made up of many small groups called the *conroi*, each with a leader, usually the overlord, who had a pennant to signal to the group. In one minute they could be a tight force with all the penetrative power of a sledgehammer, the next, a series of small parties wheeling about and confusing the enemy and assaulting the various objectives of the attack. The whole charge was an example of tremendous discipline and skill. And there was nothing like it in England.

Harold saw the first arrows coming and raised his shield. The shafts seemed to hang in the air for seconds before shooting past in a spray not unlike rainfall. He prayed that none would hit him or his horse – the horse was trained to ignore the shafts whistling past – for if he went down now, he would be trampled to a pulp by the raging mass behind him.

The charge broke up on reaching the palisade, breaking into the separate *conroi*, so as not to allow the defending archers too dense a target. Some groups milled around the outside, searching for a weak spot, where the ditch had fallen in, or where the timber had rotted, but William led his group to the gates; Harold followed, marvelling at the way the arrows missed him. William led his horse to the gates, and while the troops around him hurled their lances up at the archers, who were too close to shoot effectively at them now, pricked his horse cruelly in the side so that the great beast reared up and kicked at the gates, which splintered into firewood. William was first into the breach, scything his sword deep into the neck of a horrified archer. Harold followed and peered around the near-deserted bailey. Another archer, too slow to run to the inner ward, was caught and skewered in the back by a lance. Two women, one of them clutching a baby, ran to the only stone building in sight: the chapel. They would not be pursued; William had expressly forbidden the slaughter of women and children in this raid.

Already, several huts and stables were burning. William had brought oil, and some soldiers had bows. They set light to pieces of cloth that were wrapped onto the arrow-tips, and were firing these into the buildings. But most of the defenders had fled into the keep beyond the second palisade and on the top of a sharply inclined mound; that would be the hardest part of the fort to take.

It was the crucial moment. Will was rallying the groups, and arrows were still flying down from the tiny windows in the walls of the keeps. There was a steady drain of casualties from these, with no hope of retaliation, and many soldiers had dismounted and were crouching by the burning hovels, watching for William to make the next decision. 'You!' he shouted, to one of the soldier-archers. 'Fire the roof!'

The first archer was picked off as he took aim with a burning arrow. But other flaming arrows were hitting the roof of the keep. Harold watched anxiously; if the keep didn't burn, then how else would they take the fort? William had said that weeks of food and supplies were housed down below the keep, where there was a well. There was no time to besiege the castle, as William had only enough supplies to get from Dol and back, and in any case, Count Conan would be on their backs in days.

They waited, lungs burning with the smoke from the burning buildings around them. Each minute a horse or soldier was hit by an arrow.

Then a cry went up, and a soldier shouted: 'Sire, the roof is afire!'

It was indeed. 'God's wounds,' William swore, his face splitting into a grin. 'The stupid bloody fools forgot to dampen the roof.'

However wet the thatch and turves on the roof of the keep had once been, it was high summer and they were now dry enough to burn merrily. Small tongues of flame grew into a raging inferno. Smoke billowed out from the tiny window-slits and the flow of arrows ceased. Silence fell, broken by intermittent coughing, retching and cursing. Then a rope was flung from the top window and one of Conan's men swung from the window and dropped down into the ditch. He was followed by another and another, until the ditch was filled with choking defenders lying at swordpoint.

The smoke cleared a little, and the doors of the keep, on the first floor, opened and a raised lance thrust into the air. At the end of it hung a large key.

'What's that?' asked Harold amid the cheers.

'The surrender,' laughed William. 'And that is how we in Normandy conduct war.'

Chapter Thirty-Six
Mont St-Michel, Normandy, August 1065

They left Brittany the following day, William having decided that they had achieved what they had set out to do. The castle of Dinan was a burning ruin and hostages were secured at Dol. On the way back into Normandy they passed through Pontorson, where William explained to Harold that he had spent several years in hiding, and then, leaving the bulk of the army with Will at Pontorson, they went north to visit the abbey of Mont St-Michel, a remarkable building perched on a rocky outcrop reached by a narrow causeway.

The abbot welcomed the duke with open arms and, William and Harold were invited to stay for the night in the monastery. They sat at the abbot's table and ate his food, but when they were shown to their chambers William touched Harold's arm and said: 'I have some wine to finish. Will you join me?'

Harold followed William to his chamber, where a single candle flickered beside the hissing fire. The room was high up on the rock, and peering through the window slits Harold could see the sea and the silver shadow of the moon on the water far below them. 'A most interesting place,' he murmured.

'So I used to think when I was a boy, staring at it from the land,' said William, passing him a cup of wine. 'I stayed in the village and we used to watch the monks come by on their horses. I was taught how to wield an axe, to cut wood, trim it, and build houses. I grew to know the common folk – the labourers, the carpenter, the miller, cobbler, smith and tanner. A few of them, including the abbot, knew of my presence, but they never breathed a word, though there were men out looking for me, who would have come for me with daggers in the dark had they known. That was my education; rough and ready. Not what you'd expect for a duke, eh?'

Harold thought of his own childhood – the warmth of the family home at Guildford, the training in arms, the learning of letters, Latin and French in the draughty school-room – and they had thought that a hardship – and above all, a feeling of security. Everything he'd had, this man had been deprived of. 'I cannot begin to understand what it was like for you,' he said.

William gave a low laugh. 'I'm not asking you to. Nobody does understand, except Will FitzOsbern. Only once did he go against me – at Alençon.'

'Is it true, then, what happened...at Alençon?'

'Do you know what I ordered?'

'We did hear something of it, yes.'

'Then I'll tell you the rest. But I'll begin with a bastard boy frightened for his life. Will you listen?'

'I shall.'

So William told Harold everything until the candle spluttered to its end, and until the grey light of dawn tore a crack in the sky over the sands. Only then, when William had finished, did Harold think he could understand this man.

*

The dawn saw the island abbey reunited with the mainland and after a brief breakfast, they bade the abbot farewell.

As the small party progressed across to the shore, Harold thought of the previous night's conversation with William. And of Edward. How much longer had the old man to live? He must be past sixty now, an age that was seldom reached in these times; Godwin had been just over fifty. Would Edward stick by his decision to make the prince his heir? Surely he would, but where would William stand, this powerful and charismatic duke they called the 'Conqueror', a man driven mercilessly by a troubled past and goaded by constant treachery? He had said last night that since claiming the duchy, he'd campaigned almost every year of his life since Val-ès-Dunes against an enemy of some sort. Small wonder that Matilda prayed for peace. War in England was unheard of. Wealth and talks were the English way; force and brutality the Norman way. Now that Maine was secure, would William rest easy, or would he want England? Despite talking to him all night, Harold was still uncertain as to how William felt about Edward's plans for the boy-prince to succeed him, with Harold as regent. Surely to God, he would have to accept it.

A shout from the rear of the party startled those at the front. Harold saw the reason first. A horse was floundering violently, its rider trapped in the saddle, and sinking fast into the treacherous quicksands. The party were but thirty yards from the hard soil of the shore and above them, the blue sky reached into infinity over the vast stretches of sand. The abbot had warned them about the quicksands, but it didn't seem possible that death could touch them on this quiet morning.

Harold didn't hesitate. Wrenching at the reins, he kicked his horse back onto the sand, ignoring William's bellowed command to come back. The sand yielded under their weight, and the horse grunted with terror, but the sand held firm beneath the soft upper layer. Harold dismounted and began to walk forward. Behind him, the rest of the group sat frozen on the causeway. Ten yards ahead, the horse had sunk into the sand up to its neck. It thrashed and whinnied in horror, and the other horses screamed their sympathy. Seagulls screeched overhead, sensing the danger.

'Help me, for pity's sake,' gasped the knight, who was called Bevin.

'Hold steady,' Harold shouted, though he was only fifteen paces away now, and crawling cautiously forward. The horse was about to disappear beneath the sand.

Harold moved forward until the sand began to collapse under him and he could go no further.

'Oh, God, I don't want to die,' shouted Bevin. The horse was going under the sands and Bevin's legs were sinking quickly.

'Nobody is going to die today,' Harold shouted back at him. The shield on his back would have to do. He unstrapped it. 'Listen, Bevin,' he said. 'I'm going to throw the shield onto the gap between us. As soon as it lands, you must jump onto it and crawl forward and reach for my belt. You must do it quickly. Do you understand?'

Bevin nodded frantically. Harold held the shield in both hands and threw it. It landed flat between them and rested for a moment on the sand.

'Now, boy, now!'

Harold's roar galvanised Bevin into action. The young knight thrust himself forward onto the shield and spread his body across its length. As he did so, his horse finally vanished, leaving the sand undisturbed as if it nothing had happened. Bevin now lay sobbing on the shield, which now began to sink with gathering pace.

'Come on, boy; crawl forward,' Harold urged, holding out his belt and moving as close to the shield as he dared. Bevin obeyed and stretched for the belt-buckle at the end of the shield.

'Got it,' he gasped.

Harold pulled hard, but Bevin was sinking rapidly into the sand.

'Holy Mother of God,' whispered Harold, pulling again, but to no avail.

Then strong hands were around his waist, pulling him back, Bevin with them at the end of the belt. When Bevin was on the firm ground, they stopped pulling and all three of them collapsed to the ground. The men on the causeway were cheering, but Harold lay back heaving for breath and stared at the blue sky, at the circling gulls mocking them. Death was like a bird of prey, and might swoop down on them at any moment.

'You're a brave man,' said William from behind him.

'You pulled us back?' Harold asked stupidly.

William nodded. 'That was the bravest thing I have ever seen.' He held out a hand and hauled Harold to his feet.

'Brave – or foolish?' said Harold, dusting off the sand from his mail breeches.

William flashed him a smile. 'Sometimes there is little to choose between the two. Today you were brave.'

The bells of Bayeux greeted the victorious ducal army with thunderous peals from one end of the town to the other. Bishop Odo rode out to the gates with a richly attired escort to meet them and lead them as his guests of honour to his luxurious palace close by the cathedral.

When the horses were stabled, the men fed and changed, William led Harold to Odo's great hall, where he introduced him to his other half-brother, Robert of Mortain, and to Roger of Montgomery and Roger of Beaumont. Harold was honoured to meet them.

'I sent word that we were coming,' William explained. 'I would like to publicly announce my appreciation of your help on the campaign – in particular your act of saving the life of one of my men.'

Harold studied the faces of the warlords standing in the hall; Odo he had met already, though he looked quite different in his bishop's robes – most incongruous, in fact. Will he knew too, but the others were strangers, and eyed him with strangers' suspicions. They were tall, clean-shaven, with close-cropped hair that marked them the world over as Norman. They had brought their men with them, a few dozen, all alike. Their clothes were homespun and simple, the tunics ridiculously short at the knee, hitched in by a belt from which hung the inevitable broadsword. They fidgeted and looked uncomfortable in clothes not geared to war. In England, Edward had forbidden the wearing of swords in his hall, and the wielding of a naked blade in the king's presence was an offence for which exile was the minimum punishment. Here, it looked likely to be the norm.

William unbuckled his sword-belt and held out the sword to Harold. 'My sword,' he said to the assembled crowd as well as to Harold. 'It was my father's and his father's before him. It is yours to keep, now.'

Robert of Mortain stepped forward, his face flushed with anger. 'William, you cannot!' he exploded. 'Mother kept it safe all those years until you were old enough to claim the patrimony...'

'Be silent, Robert,' William said.

Harold said: 'I am honoured to accept this gift from you, Lord William.' He took the sword and strapped it to his waist. It was heavy and ugly, but it was a weapon for a warrior. William smiled and held out his arms. They embraced, and Harold felt the strength of the man who had pulled him and Bevin from the quicksands of Mont St-Michel.

'There is something I would ask in return,' said William, releasing him.

'Anything within my powers,' Harold said.

In a prepared manoeuvre, two servants carried a table to the centre of the hall. On it were two chests. William opened them and beckoned the audience nearer.

'These chests contain holy relics – saints' bones,' he said. Harold peered inside. A jumble of finger-bones, ribs and several skulls leered back at him. 'Lord Harold,' William said softly. 'Would you be prepared to swear on these holy bones that you will support me in my claim to the throne of England, in the event that Prince Edgar does not succeed?'

The assembled warlords waited with intense anticipation, and in that moment Harold knew that this had all been planned. The barons had not come to Bayeux merely to celebrate the successful return of the duke, and Odo's ostentatious priestly garb suddenly made sense on this carefully rehearsed stage. How had he thought William would give up Edward's promise of the throne so easily?

Harold met William's stare, aware of the warlords looking at them both – they were witnesses to the oath he must swear. Must, because he had no choice. Matilda was nowhere to be seen. She, a voice of reason and influence, had been kept well away from this. He was not exactly a prisoner, but it was clear that if he swore the oath, he could return to England. And if he didn't swear...?

'I'll swear,' he said.

The satisfaction was apparent amongst the assembled company; triumph blazed in William's eyes.

'... but only if Prince Edgar's claim becomes untenable. If Edward nominates him, then I am bound to stand by the boy.'

Harold placed his hands over the relics and swore, loudly and clearly, to uphold William's claim based on those conditions. When Harold had finished, William took his arm and said: 'It has been a pleasure having a man of your bravery and integrity with us. I'm glad that we've ended your visit with a formal agreement.'

'We have refitted your ship and provided the crew with food and supplies,' said Odo. 'They're waiting off Arromanches, just north of here.'

So all the loose ends were tied up nicely, even down to the departure. William must have sent out the orders before the Brittany campaign; Harold couldn't help but admire the way he'd kept his nerve – and his temper – following Harold's announcement on the succession.

Anyhow, his allegiance to William only counted on Norman soil; he had delivered his message from

Edward. The boy would succeed to the throne of England and he, Harold, would hold the reins of government. As Godwin had been fond of saying, oaths were like pie crusts – made to be broken. It was done now and couldn't be undone. It was time to go home.

*

Edward was furious.

'You had no right!' he shouted, shaking his staff.

'Sire, calm, yourself, for the love of God,' Harold urged, astonished at the king's reaction. The king was red-faced and shaking, and looked fit to collapse if he didn't quieten down. 'I had no choice, sire. I was a prisoner, and they wouldn't let me go until I swore the oath.'

'Nonsense.' Edward slumped back into his chair, scratching his long, white beard with agitated, emaciated fingers. 'You could have refused. You had no right, as I had not authorised you to swear any oath in my name.'

'But sire, I swore it in my name, for me,' Harold insisted.

'You swore it in the name of your king and the realm of England; you are my subject and therefore you had no right to do so.'

'It was only an oath – there were few witnesses and no hostages.'

'It was an oath made before God, made on the bones of the holy saints!'

'It won't matter once Edgar follows you on the throne,' snapped Harold, finally losing his patience with the old man.

'But I don't rightly know if Edgar *will* follow me,' Edward retorted. Harold's jaw dropped and Edward went on, and in a tired voice: 'It is such a responsibility to lay on the boy's shoulders. So much depends on the support of the earls, and I do not think the lad will bear the weight.'

'You sent me to tell William expressly that Edgar is your choice.'

Edward waved a hand dismissively, rising from the throne. 'That is my prerogative. It is not for you to re-interpret as you see fit.'

'But sire...' Harold uttered, his mind racing. If not Edgar, then who? If Edward chose Svein of Denmark, or the Hardrada of Norway, then he, Harold, would be bound by his oath to support William. If Edward chose William, and the other earls didn't agree, then he alone would have to support William because of the oath. Either way, it could tear the country apart. And what had Matilda said about William? *He has fought all his life for what he considers to be his; I do not think this would be any different.*

'My God, what have I done?' Harold asked, but Edward had already walked out of the room, leaving him alone in the chamber with the empty throne.

Chapter Thirty-Seven
Gloucester, October 1065

The oath at Bayeux was forgotten in the autumn because the thegns of Northumbria finally rose up in rebellion against the rule of Tostig.

Since becoming earl of Northumbria, Tostig had striven for peace in the unruly north. At first, his appointment had been fiercely opposed by the native populace, who deeply resented a southerner succeeding Siward, the Dane whose rule had been almost that of a sovereign. But Tostig had persevered and managed to establish some sort of compromise with the independent thegns; he based his government at York. Recently, however, the grumbles of dissent had grown louder – old feuds had flared up, new alliances were formed and his position had become precarious. He dealt with them as best he could, but all too often he was heavy-handed, and that only united them against him.

The rebellious thegns all voiced one main grievance: the severity of Earl Tostig's rule. They claimed that he had used the law to deprive his enemies of life and land, that he had despoiled churches of their property and that he had taxed the whole of Northumbria heavily and unjustly. But most serious of all the claims made against Tostig was the accusation that he had murdered several prominent men, namely Gamel, son of Orm and Ulf, son of Dolfin – killed by treachery in the earl's own chamber at York when they were there under a promise of safe-conduct. Another, darker, rumour was circulating too: that Gospatric, who'd died of a fever the previous December, had in fact been poisoned at the royal court by Queen Edith for the love of her brother Tostig.

The rebels progressed south, calling on the aid of the brothers Edwin and Morcar, and making Morcar the new earl; they exiled Tostig and marched through Derby, Nottingham and Northampton, where they then encamped, waiting for the king's word on the matter.

The rumours grew uglier; the leaders of the rebellion had conspired with Edwin and Morcar long before coming out into open revolt; it was said that Earl Harold had even started the revolt himself, and when Harold received large estates in Mercia it was whispered that this was his payment for helping the brothers Edwin and Morcar against his own brother.

None of the rumours were true, but whatever the truth of the matter, it was accepted that relations between Harold and Tostig were severely strained and the revolt could only rub salt into a festering wound. Although the people didn't want war and the old king wished only for peace in his last years, there were plenty of foreign princes who would watch eagerly for England to tear herself apart after the old king died childless.

*

When Harold discovered that Tostig was in the queen's bower in the palace at Gloucester, he waved aside the guards and entered without bothering to knock.

Tostig, with his back to the door and in midsentence, spun round at Harold's entrance. Edith was sitting on the bed, her face flushed with anger.

'Harry –' Tostig began.

'You stupid fool.' Harold cut him short. 'The rebels have killed all your thegns in York, plundered your armoury, ravaged your land and outlawed you. Morcar is the earl they want. Did you think I didn't know, or would never find out?'

Tostig shook his head. 'Know what?'

Harold had his hand on his brother's neck before Tostig could blink. Tightening his grip, Harold said through clenched teeth, 'Don't play games with me any longer, little brother. Gamel. Ulf. Gospatric. Don't these names mean anything to you?'

Tostig's eyes flickered wildly across to his sister. 'It was Edith,' he gasped, trying to free himself from Harold's grip, but his brother was too strong for him. 'She did it...she told me to. It's all her fault!'

Harold released him so quickly that Tostig staggered and reached for the wall to support himself, gasping for breath. Turning to Edith, Harold demanded: 'Is it true? Did you have these men – sons of important thegns in Northumbria –murdered at your behest? Because you are the queen, and no man dare defy you?'

Edith gave Harold a stony stare. 'I admit that Gospatric's death was in some way my doing – but as to the others, I deny any action in their deaths.'

Harold hesitated, surprised by the cold-blooded detachment in his sister's voice. He was inclined to believe her about Gamel and Ulf. They'd died in York, far away from the royal court and Edith. But she had admitted to involvement in Gospatric's murder. And she didn't care about it, either.

Tostig lurched forward, his face ugly with rage. 'You lying bitch! How dare you sit there and deny it!' He raised his fist above Edith's horrified face.

Harold was quicker and grabbed Tostig's arm, twisting it behind his back. Tostig roared with pain and humiliation, but Harold ignored his cries, forcing him into a crouching position, not letting him go this time. 'Don't ever speak to our sister like that again,' he said into Tostig's ear. 'Do you understand?' Tostig nodded, his eyes wet with tears.

'Harold, Tostig, please God, stop!' Edith was between them, her slim body pushing against Harold's angry strength. The sound of their hard breathing filled the bed-chamber.

'What have you done?' Harold looked at them both in turn. 'Christ, you've destroyed us for sure. I know it.'

Edith slumped onto the bed and began to weep. Neither brother moved to comfort her.

'You should never have become earl of Northumbria in the first place,' Harold said to Tostig, above Edith's gasping sobs. 'But for her –' he jerked his head at his sister '– and Edward, this would never have happened. You were never right for the north; I said so at the time. A West Saxon, a son of Godwin – hated and feared in the north, thanks to Siward – and chosen by a king who favoured Normans, to rule over a largely Danish people and all the other savages in the north. It never made sense, and I knew it – but you wanted your lands, didn't you Tostig – and at all costs, it seems.'

'They'll take me back,' said Tostig defiantly. 'I'm sure of it.' He glared at Harold, his mouth tight as a trap, and Harold was reminded of Swegn, and what a fool he'd been, and how his actions had brought down Godwin and destroyed the old man's health. There was much of Swegn in Tostig.

'Shut up.' Harold said, hardened by the memory of Godwin. 'How you believe you can get Northumbria back is beyond me, but how you thought you could get away with killing men so well known and not cause trouble God alone knows, for I cannot credit it. And neither can the thegns coming for your blood. This isn't Normandy, where anarchy rules and men die screaming in darkened dungeons – this is England. And those men want revenge. Do you think they'll listen to you now?'

'If we treat with them,' Tostig stuttered, 'then they'll have me back.'

'You stupid bastard,' Harold realised that Tostig was serious. He really did think he could get the north back. 'You're finished, Tostig. Edwin of Mercia has put forward his brother as the new earl for the king to decide upon. If he has any sense, he'll accept, to preserve peace in the realm.'

'But you will counsel my return, will you not, brother?' Tostig asked.

Both Edith and Tostig waited for his answer, but Harold, unable to trust himself to speak, simply shook his head.

When the king judged that the time was right he banged his staff on the floor-boards of the council chamber. The chattering courtiers hushed as Edward rose to speak.

'We're gathered here in Britford to discuss how best to end the divisions that have arisen in the realm of late. We hope to reach agreement with the rebels so that they can leave Oxford in peace and go home.'

There were angry murmurs at this. Many councillors wanted the rebels punished, not allowed to go home in peace. But the king didn't want the rebels to go just for their sake – he wanted peace for himself, too.

'I have been to speak with the rebels at Oxford and at Northampton,' Harold said, raising his voice a little to drown out the hecklers. 'They have no quarrel with the king. They want the removal of Tostig and the appointment of Morcar in his stead. They want Tostig to be exiled.'

At that moment, the doors of the chamber were flung open and Tostig strode in, surrounded by heavily armed guards. He pointed to Harold on the dais, and shouted: 'It is all the fault of the earl of Wessex! He's made a devil's pact with Edwin and Morcar to get rid of me!' The council was in uproar now, and Stigand was muttering about armed men in the presence of the king, whilst Edward merely sat grey-faced on the throne, a hand on his forehead, in no state to speak. 'I accuse my brother the earl of Wessex of the most heinous treachery and of disturbing the king's peace. I demand satisfaction!'

'Can you answer these charges, Harold?' asked the king.

'Yes, my lord king, I can. Councillors, my brother is sadly misled, and, I fear still suffering from the events of these past days which have clearly upset him. I swear on the Cross that I have had no part in this rebellion, and no dealings with the rebels, or the brothers Edwin and Morcar. The rising was solely due to the my brother's misgovernment, and he must accept the consequences.' As Harold spoke, Tostig stared back at him, eyes ablaze with rage.

The councillors murmured assent at Harold's statement and Tostig, seeing which way the wind was blowing, walked out of the room, calling as he went: 'I will be back, Harold of Wessex - I'll come for what is mine!'

*

The following day the king sent an ultimatum to the rebels at Oxford, telling them to lay down their arms and that he would give them a fair, impartial hearing. They did not do so, sending back an ultimatum to the king instead: if Tostig Godwinsson was not dismissed from the court and exiled from the country in punishment for his brutal governance of the north, then they would make war on the king and his followers.

Harold found the king alone in his chamber, holding the letter from the rebels. The fire had almost died and it was bitterly cold.

'What will we do now, sire?'

'Summon the levies, boy. We must confront the rebels.'

'No, sire.' Harold was shocked to see how the past weeks had aged the king. 'I can't sanction war, or even armed confrontation, and nor will the other councillors. The levies won't come, anyway, sire - Englishmen will not fight each other. They have wives, families...'

Edward gave a sad smile. 'You defy me, then, Harold?'

Harold looked into Edward's lined and exhausted face. His expression, as ever, was difficult to read, the blue eyes dimmed now, gazed back with - what? Disappointment? Or perhaps admiration? Harold nodded. 'I will defy you, sire, if the unity and peace of the realm are at stake. Tostig will have to go in order to preserve that peace.'

Edward stood up, accepting Harold's helping hand. 'You were right,' he said, his voice as quiet as a summer's breeze. 'Tostig should never have been made earl of Northumbria. I should have listened to you, Harry.'

Harry. Harold blinked. It was the first time Edward had called him that. 'Don't trouble yourself, sire,' he said. 'The realm will remain at peace. There won't be war in England.

Edward squeezed Harold's hand. 'See to it, then. Give us peace.'

When Harold told Tostig what Edward had said, Tostig gave a slow smile. 'The king is yours to command, Harry, isn't he? An old man, glad to have you manage the government of the realm for him, tell him what to do, maybe even tell him to appoint you as his successor if he doesn't do it anyway, and give a title to the power you already wield. King Harold. That's what you would like, Harry, isn't it?'

Harold opened his mouth to deny it, but the words failed to come out. He had thought about the crown for himself, God's truth he had...

'You got rid of me quickly enough,' Tostig continued saying, too absorbed in his hatred to notice Harold's hesitation. 'You waited for the rebellion which you knew was bound to come. You've deliberately refused to call out the army; you say it's in the name of peace, but in fact you know it'll finish me. So if I go, the peace will be restored. I'll be left to rot. How very convenient.'

'It's not like that at all, Tostig,' Harold said, pleading with his brother. 'I cannot support you now. It would bring ruin upon the realm. If you go away for a year, to Flanders or Denmark, and wait until the fuss has died down, then Edward will call you back, and you will have other lands. But for now, we must keep the peace. Surely to God you understand that?'

For a moment Harold thought he had succeeded, until Tostig said: 'I understand well enough, Harry. You want to get rid of me, and I'll never be allowed back, just like Swegn –'

'Yes!' Harold shouted, finally losing his temper. 'You're just like Swegn, damn you! A fool, a liar, a coward...and God knows, a murderer!'

Tostig paled. 'Devil take you, Harry –'

At that moment Edith appeared in the doorway and there were tears streaming down her face.

'What is it?' asked Harold.

'It's the king,' sobbed Edith. 'Edward has had a seizure.'

He had collapsed soon after leaving Harold. The strain of the rebellion was too much; once again in his long life, events were beyond his control and he could not give orders with the knowledge that they would be obeyed. The world still had as much hate in it since he'd learnt the meaning of the word, and he'd had enough.

They'd carried him to his chamber and there the physician proclaimed that the king would survive the attack, but his health was failing fast.

'You cannot see him now,' said Edith. 'He's sleeping.'

'Have you sent word to Stigand?' Harold asked. Stigand would know what to do – despite all his faults, the man was vital at a time like this.

'Yes.' Edith dried her eyes.

Harold turned to Tostig. 'Will you stay with us?'

'No, I shall not.' Tostig didn't meet Edith's glance.

'Where will you go then?'

Tostig pursed his lips. 'Flanders, to seek asylum with Count Baldwin.'

Harold smiled with relief. Tostig could return when things had quietened down. Everything between them would be alright, after all.

But the small hope Harold harboured was quashed when Tostig added, not without a hint of scorn and with enough conviction to tell Harold that it was a final decision: 'And then I'll go to Normandy, and make my peace with the duke.'

Chapter Thirty-Eight
Rouen, Normandy, December 1065

William received Tostig Godwinsson in his private chambers and studied him with undisguised interest.

He was as tall as Harold, with the same blond locks and grey-blue eyes, but there the similarity ended. Tostig wasn't as broad in the chest as his brother and didn't carry himself as proudly – though that might be a consequence of his exile – and his facial features weren't quite as defined as Harold's. But most of all William noticed the look about him of a man hunted, a desperate look William had seen many times before.

Tostig bowed to the waist, saying carefully in his best French, 'Count Baldwin sends his kindest regards, Duke William, as does my wife Judith.'

William nodded, accepting the politic references to his family as a matter of course from this English nobleman. 'Have you news from England?'

'Yes, my lord duke. The king is grevious sick, and may even be dying.'

William glanced at Matilda. 'Are you sure of this?'

Tostig nodded. 'Yes, sire, but my brother has most treacherously turned against me and stood by while I have been exiled by my own people. I am here to petition your support, as your kinsman and, I hope, as your friend. I must also warn you, Duke William, that my brother has designs on the throne of England for himself.'

'And what evidence is there of this, Lord Tostig? How do you know Harold will take the throne when Edward is gone?' William was intrigued and angered by Tostig's claims. The question at the root of this was, how much was true and how much was Tostig's own miscalculation?

'I just know,' Tostig said falteringly. 'He has complete control over the old king and is waiting, ready to seize his chance –'

'But he put the peace of the realm over and above the loyalty and love he held for his brother, didn't he? And you suggest that he might jeopardise that very peace by claiming the throne for himself, in the face of other claimants from outside the country – Harald Hardrada, Svein Estrithsson and –' William looked hard at Tostig '– myself, as you well know.' William sat back in the chair, adding, 'and that of course does not include Prince Edgar, who has a better right than the rest of us.'

'Harold's greed is obvious, my lord. I am certain...'

'You are certain of nothing,' William said. 'The earl of Wessex has ensured peace in the realm by not supporting you. The king lies dying and we know that his heir-apparent is the prince. Harold will support the boy. The greed comes from you, the former earl of Northumbria. Your brother is a man of honour and loyalty.'

With such daming words, Tostig knew that his cause was lost on the duke. He made to leave, but William motioned him to remain where he was while he had the last word.

'Who else were you going to petition after me? Would it be King Svein, perhaps? Or maybe even the Hardrada?'

Tostig paled. It was exactly what he had planned to do. William had read his mind like an open book – except this bastard duke could hardly read.

'We have heard much from Judith on that score,' said William, enjoying the discomfort on Tostig's face. 'Have a care not to return to St Omer with evil thoughts against her, either,' he added quickly, 'or else you will have me to contend with as well as the whole of England. Now leave us.'

Tostig fought back the tears of rage. Who was this man? Nothing but a heavy-handed, illiterate peasant-spawn inured in bloody violence. He turned on his heel and strode to the door, his cheeks stung red with shame as he heard the stifled laughter and sniggers from those around the fireplace – the humiliation! – and when he reached the doors, his lip was bleeding where he'd bitten it to silence his rage. By Christ, Harold would pay for this – if it was the last thing Tostig Godwinsson did on God's earth.

*

'At first I thought him to be like Harold,' William said to Matilda. 'He's similar in looks, but has no integrity; he is shallow.'

'He has been a good husband to Judith,' said Matilda. 'To be fair, he has had much harm done to him.'

William snorted. 'He's suffered nothing. There's a deep-seated resentment against Harold, something that's festered like a wound for years, I'll wager. He is jealous of the goodwill and respect that Harold commands amongst the court and the people of England. He knows Harold was right to back down to the rebels and not side with Tostig. That must have been a decision forced upon Harold

Godwinsson by the very devil himself – I'd not envy him that. But Tostig won't see it that way and he'll never forgive Harold for it.'

'What will Tostig do now?'

'If he's sensible, he'll wait at St Omer under Baldwin's protection – God knows, your father has been patient enough with these Godwin people – then he'll return to England in the summer, when all the fuss has died down.'

'And if he's not sensible, William – what will he do instead?'

William was used to his wife's directness. There was nothing he could hide from Matilda. 'He'll go to Svein,' he said slowly, 'possibly to Harald Hardrada. In fact, probably to the Hardrada.'

'And when Edward dies?'

Matilda saw on William's face the look of intense excitement she had come to dread over the years. His eyes burned with his obsession more now than ever before.

'It's unlikely that Edward will nominate Prince Edgar as his heir now. With Tostig Godwinsson on the loose, rebellion in the air and the young and inexperienced earls Edwin and Morcar in command of Mercia and Northumbria, it would also be impossible to set Harold the task of being regent. It must be me: Edward must name me as his heir.'

Chapter Thirty-Nine
Westminster, January 1066

By the first week of December, Edward was well enough to undertake the journey from Gloucester to Westminster. The great abbey at Westminster was finished. Edward had lived long enough to see his life's work and joy completed, and would now see it consecrated. Almost all men of standing had travelled to London from the shires to attend the ceremony of consecration and to celebrate the birth of Christ. Bishops, abbots, earls, ealdormen and thegns crowded the narrow streets, renewing old acquaintances and gazing in wonder at the abbey. But it was not the abbey they had come to see alone, nor the Christmas festivities, for normally the lesser men would stay in their own halls in the shires with their families to do that. It was for word of the king that they had come, and the state of his health was on everyone's lips; everyone knew, even the beggar-boys and whores in the stews, that there was no heir for England, and that the king was very ill.

On Christmas Eve the stricken king suffered another seizure, but on Christmas Day he was well enough to participate in the ceremonies, and the banquet on Boxing Day. On Wednesday, the Festival of the Holy Innocents, the great abbey was consecrated, but Edward was too ill to attend. Two days later, he became delirious. The end was very near.

Since the arrival of the king at Westminster and the flood of nobles and churchmen into the city of London, Harold had been busier than ever before in his life. There was the king's business to attend to, matters of church and state, matters of his own earldom to attend to, land disputes to settle, charters to witness, taxes to raise – all the business Edward would have done, and more, as all the landowners present took the opportunity to settle quarrels and petition for various rights now they were together at the king's court. But all the while there rested at the back of his mind the question of the succession.

Archbishops Ealdred and Stigand, the Godwin earls Gyrth and Leofwine were there to assist and advise. Queen Edith was too broken-hearted at

Edward's sudden decline and sat at his feet, praying for his recovery, which most people now accepted would never come.

Christmas came and went, the New Year with it – 1066 was ushered in with little celebration – but two days before Epiphany, word came from Edward's physician, Abbot Baldwin of Bury, that the king had recovered consciousness.

Leofwine brought the news. Harold was with Stigand and Gyrth in the crowded hall. There had been such an influx of courtiers that the hall, chapel and even the kitchens had been utilised to house the guests. The people of the city had done brisk business, putting up their homes for lodging, while Harold had accommodated the bishops of Exeter and Wells, Leofric and Giso, in the Godwin house at Southwark.

'The king orders that the household and councillors be assembled in his chamber,' Leofwine said into Harold's ear after battling through the throng.

'He's talking, then? Making sense?'

Stigand said to Harold: 'He will make his last will and testament.' He grasped Harold's arm. 'You must be there, Harold.'

The king's chamber was hot, stuffy and crowded. The air was heavy with the scent of herbs prepared by Baldwin, but beneath the sweet smell, Harold could detect the stench of sweat and vomit of a dying man.

Edward was propped up on several pillows in the centre of his great bed. Queen Edith sat at his feet and Robert FitzWimarch supported his head. Edward smiled faintly at Harold, the once startlingly blue eyes now milky, bloodshot and dulled with age.

'Lord King.'

Harold knelt and kissed Edward's hand. It was as light as a feather. Harold placed it gently onto his chest, which rose and fell slowly with each unsteady breath. Behind them, members of the council filed into the room – William of London, once exiled but returned to favour, and now in tears; Walter of Hereford, Leofric of Exeter, Giso of Wells, Ealdred of York, Ralf the Staller, Eadnoth and Aethelnoth, ealdormen from the north, Gyrth, Leofwine and Edwin and Morcar, the young earls of Mercia and Northumbria and the Prince Edgar.

'What day is it, Harold?' Edward spoke softly, but clearly.

'Wednesday, sire, the fourth of January.'

'It is the New Year, then?'

'Yes, sire. It is the Year of Our Lord, 1066.'

'A new year, Harold. A new beginning. And without me, I fear.'

Harold tried to smile. 'We do not know that, sire.'

'But we do. Is everyone here?'

'Yes, sire.' The chamber was packed. Outside, weeping and praying crowds lined the passageway into the hall and out into the streets, where the city had come to a standstill in the wait for the king to do his dying.

At Edward's feet Edith sobbed quietly. 'Do not weep, my child,' he said to Edith. 'Pray to God for my soul and give me leave to go to Him. He who allowed himself to die will not permit me not to die.'

Edith nodded through her tears. She had come to love this man, as they all had, after so many years of peace. Others in the room, too, choked back tears.

Edward cleared his throat. 'I have had a vision, my people. It concerns you all and the fate of this nation. In my vision, I met two monks I knew in my time in Normandy, both of whom are long dead now.

They told me that all the earls, bishops, abbots and thegns in England are not the servants of God, but are of the devil. God has cursed this kingdom. I tell you, my people, that God has cursed us and that a year and a day after my death you will be delivered into the hands of the enemy, so that devils will come through all of this land with fire and sword and the havoc of war. But, my people, I will bring you all to repentance and ask for God's mercy, which, surely, shall not be withheld. But the monks I knew in Normandy said to me in my vision that the people would not repent and that God could not pardon the people; He will only cease to punish England for her sins when a green tree, a tree in full leaf...'

The people of the court were transfixed by the king's speech. Many were openly weeping and praying.

'...which had been felled halfway up the trunk and the part cut off carried three furlongs away should by its own efforts, without the aid of man or any kind of stake, join up again, and through its own efforts and rising sap, break into leaf and bear fruit. Only when that marvel has happened, will God's anger be stilled.'

Harold felt a tug at his elbow at this point and moved his gaze from Edward's face. 'He is rambling,' hissed Stigand. 'He's insane, talking rubbish.'

Harold studied Edward's face, saw the grey complexion glistening with sweat, and the thin trickle of saliva running from the corner of his mouth down to his white beard, and was inclined to agree with Stigand.

Edward, utterly exhausted by his speech, sank back into the bed. Baldwin of Bury wiped Edward's brow and the king drank a little water.

'And now I make my last will and testament,' Edward addressed the room again.

This was what people had come to hear the king say, and there was a palpable change in the atmosphere of the room; it was at last time for the king to pass on his greatest legacy: the crown of England.

Edward gestured to Edith. 'May God repay my wife for her dutiful and loving service, for she has been a devoted servant to me and has been at my side like a beloved daughter. May God's mercy reward her with eternal joy in heaven.' Then his hand reached out to Harold. 'I commend this woman and all the people to your protection. Remember that she is your lady and sister, and serve her faithfully and honour her as such for all the days of her life. Do not take away from her any honour that I have granted her.'

'Sire.' Stigand pressed forward. 'The throne, sire. To whom do you leave the throne?'

The room waited, holding its breath, but Edward ignored Stigand. 'I also commend to you, Harold, all my foreign vassals and servants and I ask that you either offer them service or grant them safe-conduct if they refuse.'

'Sire, the kingdom...'

'Have my grave prepared in my Westminster, in the place which will be shown to you. I beg you not to conceal my death, but to send out the news promptly to all parts, so that all the faithful can beseech the mercy of Almighty God on me, a sinner.'

'Sire: who shall be king after you?'

Finally, Edward acknowledged Stigand's question.

He sighed, and said: 'It is a question that has dogged me for years.' His voice was quieter now, less clear, like the departing wind in the dead of winter. Stigand crouched closer, and so did Harold and all those around the bed, others behind them straining to hear the king's last words.

'I had hoped that it would be Prince Edgar, but the rebellion in the north has divided the realm and laid us open to invasion from overseas that always plagued us English as it did my father.' Edward beckoned Prince Edgar to come closer. 'I am sorry, my boy, but England needs a strong arm, a grown man of skill, experience and determination to ward off the evil that awaits her. I have made my choice and it is for the good of the whole people and you must accept him and stand by him. That I beseech you all to do.'

There followed an agonising silence, and it was thought that it was too late, that Edward had lost the power of speech and that they would never know who the heir was. But then he spoke his last words, loudly enough for those at the back of the chamber to hear him, and with an effort that was painful to watch, pointing his hand to Harold:

'To you, Harold Godwinsson, my brother, I commit this kingdom and this people.'

Part Three

The Devil's Inheritance

Chapter Forty
Westminster, January 1066

Harold heard Edward's last words as clearly as anyone in the room, but all the same it took a few seconds for their meaning to register.

'The king has at last decreed who shall be his heir,' Stigand announced to the assembled group. 'His last will and testament is that it should be Harold Godwinsson, the earl of Wessex. The council will now convene in the hall. The king must be shriven.'

Stigand grasped Harold's upper arm and pulled him to his feet. 'You will be accepted,' Stigand murmured, as they walked out of the bedchamber. 'The people respect you and you command their loyalty. Men of good standing, from all over the country, from all different loyalties heard the king utter his last words. No man can deny that. And they remember your father, Earl Godwin: a good man, loyal and true to the realm.'

Father. How proud Godwin would have been to see this day! His son to become king of England, better even than a grandson by Edith, which was what he had wanted in the early days.

'The dying king has nominated you his heir,' Stigand continued. 'It is the custom of the English to pass on the throne in this way. But the council of elders will acclaim you the new king. They are all present and we shall see to that now. Finally, the coronation of the new king in the church of St Peter will serve as the sanctification and confirmation by God.'

The main hall filled with expectant councillors, courtiers and household men. All around Harold and Stigand people were bowing then standing back in awed silence as the news that Harold Godwinsson was the chosen king spread through the crowded palace.

At that moment Baldwin of Bury entered and a hush fell over the crowd.

'My lords.' Baldwin's voice was thick with fatigue and emotion. 'The king has just this moment gone to God.'

It was truly over, then. Edward was dead. Harold swallowed, clenching and unclenching his hands.

'I have been chosen by King Edward to succeed to the throne of England,' he said, hoping that the tremor in his voice wasn't too obvious. 'Do you, the representative body of the people of England, accept me as your new king?'

The affirmative roar was enough. The acclamation was done, quite simply.

'The king is dead! Long live the king!' shouted Edwin of Mercia.

The room thundered to the sound of applause and stamping feet. Grown men embraced one another, and alongside Harold, with tears streaming down his face, Stigand held the hand of the young Prince Edgar whose own face was lit with – what, exactly? Happiness and joy certainly, and relief perhaps, at not having the burden on his shoulders. It was Harold's now, and the realm of England was his to cherish, to love and to protect.

A new era had begun.

Epiphany. The first light of dawn on the new day, the day of Edward's funeral and of Harold's coronation. First, the funeral. Edward had lain in an open coffin in the centre of Westminster Hall, as custom demanded, and all day Thursday thousands of people filed past, silent with grief and awe, looking upon the king to confirm he really was dead, so that they could go home and tell their children and grandchildren what they had witnessed on this momentous day.

Edward's body lay on a richly embroidered pall. The corpse was packed with aromatics and a sceptre placed by his side, a plain gold crown on his head and a ring on his right hand. There were four choristers who would sing the anthem, and eight men who would carry the bier: four at the front, four at the rear, including the Godwinsson brothers Harold, Gyrth and Leofwine, and the brothers Edwin and Morcar.

The crowds – Londoners, courtiers and hundreds from other towns and villages – waited in silence beneath the cold grey sky, come to see their old king laid to rest. Edward had been greatly loved and respected in his time for the peace and prosperity he had brought to England after the terrible years of Danish invasion and rule.

The funeral procession arrived at the doors of the new Westminster Abbey. This, Edward's beloved conception, was built in the Romanesque style, a design from Burgundy which had spread to Normandy and had been brought to England by Robert Champart, whose own abbey at Jumièges exhibited most of the features now at Westminster.

The three master-masons, Leofsi Duddesson, Godwin Gretsith and Teinfrinth, had built a memorial for Edward that could not be surpassed. The nave consisted of six double bays and a presbytery of two bays under a timber roof. The central tower, claimed builders and churchmen from all over Europe, was sublime, reaching up spiral stairs to a lead roof and surrounded outside by a cluster of turrets. The entire building was dressed in Reigate stone.

It was a fine resting place for the man who had loved it and watched it grow like the child he'd never had.

A stone sarcophagus had already been sunk into the pavement in front of the main altar, and there Edward's body was placed. Prayers for the dead had been sung all the previous day and would continue throughout the following week. Alms had been distributed to the poor, and the widow-queen had contributed large sums to the needy.

The old and venerable king had gone to his final resting place with all the serenity he had pursued when he was alive.

Harold's coronation ceremony took the exact form Edward's had done, nearly twenty-three years before.

As old Eadsige had asked the crowd all those years ago, now Stigand requested: 'Do you, the people and the clergy accept this man Harold Godwinsson as your king?' And as before, they roared 'yes', the lords Gyrth and Leofwine at the front. Harold remembered himself shouting 'yes' to Edward. It was after he and Swegn had been told they were to become earls, that Edith was to marry the new king, and they would become uncles to the heir apparent. But there had been no heir apparent. And that was why he was sitting here now, the new king of England.

Stigand read the benediction: 'May God make you victorious and conquer over your enemies, both visible and invisible; may He grant you peace in your days and with the palm of victory lead you to his eternal kingdom...'

Peace. Could he bring peace to the realm, heal the wounds between the north and south? Would they together hold off any threat from the Norwegians and the Normans? With Edwin and

Morcar ruling half the country and fully supporting him, a royal house so quickly united was one that would withstand the storms ahead.

Vivat Rex! Vivat Rex! Vivat Rex in eternum! Amen!

The omens were good.

Chapter Forty-One
Quevilly Forest, Normandy, January 1066

Will FitzOsbern saw the messenger first.

It was cold, bitterly cold; so cold that parts of the Seine had frozen over and the townspeople of Rouen swore that it had not been so since the winter of 1043, when the streets had been lined with the stiff corpses of the starving inhabitants. Back then, though, there hadn't been a duke to speak of; only a greedy archbishop and a bastard boy in hiding. But now that the boy had grown into the adult duke, he saw to it that nobody starved in his capital, even though fuel and food were scarce.

The Christmas festivities in the ducal hall had been far from frugal, and it was to get away from the dancing, music and food that William insisted on going hunting. Only Will took up his offer, and together they headed for the forest of Quevilly, only a mile from the palace, leaving their families comfortable by the fire, falling asleep to the gentle strumming of the minstrel's lyre.

They hadn't killed anything yet.

'Christ,' Will muttered, his arrow thudding into the trunk of a withered tree, missing the stag by a yard and shaking the snow to the ground with a mocking hiss. Will blew on his reddened fingers. 'It's too damned cold for this, William,' He'd regretted the decision to go hunting almost as soon as they left the courtyard hours ago.

Then he saw the messenger.

The man jumped from his horse and came stumbling through the frozen mud and icy leaves, his breath making white clouds against the dark trees around him. He was shouting, calling a name, but was too far away to be understood.

'It seems as if they cannot be without us for long at the castle,' said William, seeing him too. 'I wonder what he wants?'

'He's not from the castle,' said Will, drawing his sword as the man crashed from the undergrowth and into the clearing. His face was raw with the cold, his breathing laboured, and he was a total stranger. William's bodyguards moved in on him quickly, patting him down for a hidden knife or dagger, but releasing him when it was clear that he was unarmed.

'My lord duke.' Free of their rough hands, the messenger collapsed onto the ground at William's feet. 'I come from Count Baldwin – from Lille.'

William frowned. His first thought was that Judith, Matilda's sister, had been taken ill – or perhaps that the young King Philip of France, under Baldwin's guidance, was ill – good news indeed, for a weak France only served to strengthen Normandy. But the messenger's next words dispelled both possibilities in an instant.

'I have news from England, sire,' gasped the messenger. 'King Edward died on the fifth day of the month. It appears that Harold Godwinsson is crowned his heir. Harold Godwinsson...is king of all England...'

The words struck William like a thunderbolt. As he stood there, speechless, the man continued, gabbling out the words in a flat panic: '...he was crowned the very day Edward was buried, sire, anointed king on the new minster church.'

The messenger was lying; it was a ghastly mistake, a terrible joke, anything but the truth. William dropped the bow, his head swimming. He could not believe it. In a lifetime of betrayals, this was the greatest of them all. William refused to believe it. It was absurd, even laughable. But there was nothing funny about this man standing in the snow shivering before him.

William grasped the messenger's cloak and drew back a clenched fist to smash the lies from that unshaven, bone-weary face.

'William, no!'

Will jumped between them, forcing William to back off. 'Leave him, William, for Christ's sake. He's only doing what he was paid to do, to bring the news...'

They were panting with effort, the three of them, their breath forming freezing clouds in the air.

'Take this,' sobbed the man, and slumped to the ground. Will took Count Baldwin's great seal from the messenger, 'It's Baldwin's seal. The message is genuine. It's not a trick!'

'You're right,' William said hoarsely. 'Jesus, I can't believe it...but it's true, isn't it, Will? Isn't it?'

'It is, yes.' Will gestured at the bodyguards. 'See that this man is rewarded for his efforts. Take him back to the hall and feed him before he returns to Flanders.'

They remounted and began the ride home to Rouen.

'I'll summon the great lords of the duchy and tell them. We must decide soon what is to be done,' said William, his expression twisting into a bitterness that Will, even in all the years he'd known William, found ugly in its intensity. 'I'll kill that Saxon pig and anyone who stands in my way to the crown.'

*

Through the narrow slit of the window, Matilda could see across the yard to the outer bailey, and over the town. Kitchen staff hurried to and fro, busily preparing for the night's feast, casting pitying glances to the guards on watch high up on the walls, who continuously had to stamp their feet to keep warm. And all the while, the same thought ran through her mind with a giddying intoxication.

It was over. It had to be. Harold Godwinsson's actions – right or wrong – were so utterly final that he could not go back on them, and in all truthfulness, William couldn't go on. He would have to accept that, much though he would hate himself for doing so.

The commotion in the yard below following William's early return from the hunt had sent one of her maids scurrying up to the chamber with the news, and Matilda had almost hugged the girl in her joy. Peace would be assured. The shared journey between England and Normandy, begun all those years ago when Emma had married the English king, had come to an end. The two states could go their separate ways in peace.

After a brief knock on the door, William walked into the bower with Will FitzOsbern. 'My love.' William bent and kissed Matilda's cheek, taking her hand. 'You have heard the news, I presume?'

Matilda tried to contain her obvious pleasure, ready to console and cheer William. 'I have heard the news,' she said. 'I am so sorry, William...'

'Don't be,' said William. 'It is war, now. If Harold Godwinsson will not relinquish the throne he has stolen from me, then I'll take it from him by force.'

'No, surely not,' Matilda whispered, her joy fading fast. In her mind she envisaged the scream of battle and William dead in some English ditch... In panic, she turned to Will. Surely Will wouldn't allow

William to gather the forces needed to invade England, he'd talk some sense into him. One word from Will FitzOsbern, lord of Breteuil, steward and chief advisor to the duke, would put a stop to this madness.

But Will shook his head a fraction and looked away from her pleading eyes. She knew then that it was going to happen.

*

Roger of Montgomery leant back against the wall and closed his eyes. Beside him, Hugh, count of Avranches, Lord Roger of Beaumont and his son Robert, and William's half-brothers Odo, bishop of Bayeux and Count Robert of Mortain, all sat in silence. Will FitzOsbern stood by the window, his arms folded, his glance ceaselessly flickering across the candlelit room, gauging the response of the most powerful men in the duchy. At the opposite end of the room, William was talking earnestly, outlining his plans, his rights and his claim to the throne of England.

They weren't interested. These were the men who had most helped and participated in William's rise to power, but they did not want to invade England – peaceful, wealthy, but untouchable England.

Will could see that; Roger of Montgomery appeared to be asleep, Robert picked his teeth, and even Odo was staring at the rushes, embarrassed by his brother's ardour for such an enterprise.

William finished his speech and looked at them expectantly for a response. But he'd been so enthusiastic in condemning Harold's seizure of the throne and proposing his theories for taking it back, that he was yet to realise how indifferent the Norman magnates were.

'It will never succeed,' said Roger of Montgomery, opening his eyes.

Hugh of Avranches grunted agreement.

William looked at Roger. 'Why not?'

Montgomery ran a mottled hand through greying hair and listed the reasons. A man of few words, but of great experience, he chose his words carefully, and in turn was listened to attentively by the barons gathered in the room.

'You'll never raise an army. There are Normans acquiring lands in southern Italy and Greece without much difficulty. Why then should we attack England, which will be well defended? We have no fleet to cross the English Sea. We will need horses; how do we get them across? If we raise a fleet, it will be picked off by the English one, far superior to anything we can build. If we do build a fleet and by a miracle slip past the English fleet, we go ashore – but where? On a beach massed with archers who'll cut us down before we even leave the boats, and if we get ashore, the housecarls will finish us off with their God-awful axes. And even if –' Montgomery raised a finger '– even if we succeed in all of those things, and we kill Harold in battle, the English will never accept you as their king, unless we want another twenty years of war. Harold is the crowned king of England; if he dies, Prince Edgar succeeds him. Forget it.'

The nobles stirred. It was a succinct and compelling speech, made all the more so by the overt threat of a long-term war. Normandy had recently recovered from twenty years of anarchy and bloodshed, and didn't need another twenty. The lord of Montgomery's speech had voiced their other objections perfectly and indeed, devastatingly. They looked to William for an answer.

But Roger's objections were what William had expected, and he would have been surprised if they had not been raised.

'Put in that way it does seem rather an impossible task,' he said when the muttering had ceased. They listened then, hoping that the duke had seen sense. William allowed himself a brief smile, but it vanished under a hard stare. 'But I tell you this: King Harald Hardrada of Norway has for many years harboured a claim to the throne of England. It is a claim based on the treaty made between his nephew Magnus and Harthacanute, that short-lived king of England before Edward. Harthacanute agreed to name Magnus his heir if he died childless and *vice versa*. Now that Edward has gone, the Hardrada may choose to press his claim, especially since his recent defeat of Svein Estrithsson in Denmark, which will leave him free to prepare an invasion force without the fear of exposing his own country.'

Hugh of Avranches opened his mouth to speak, but William hadn't finished.

'Normandy has never been so secure; Conan is under threat in Brittany, Maine is ours, Anjou is torn by civil war and France is under the guardianship of my father-in-law. Nearly every harbour from the mouth of the Couesnon by the Cotentin, up to the frontier of Flanders is mine, or under my vassalage. Both Guy of Ponthieu and Eustace of Boulogne will stand by me. We are in a better position than ever before.' William paused for effect. 'Well, messires, are we to allow Harald Hardrada to invade and conquer England and to be master of all the seas and threaten our coast, when we could have England for ourselves?'

There was a long silence whilst this was digested, and it was the duke's half-brother Robert of Mortain who finally spoke up.

'Is there any likelihood that Harold will step down from the throne peacefully if we threaten force?'

'I have written to him asking him to do so and I have said that if he does, I shan't punish him,' said William. 'And I have reminded him of the oath he took, of his perjury...'

'The oath!' Odo had stirred into action. 'We can use Harold's perjury against him in Rome. As rightful claimants we should act as the injured party and take our claim to the pope and ask him to judge who is in the right. The oath was taken publicly and sworn over holy relics.' Odo clapped his hands together. 'And who crowned Harold? Stigand!'

'He was Godwin's man,' said Will, sensing the growing excitement in the room. 'Rumour has it that he never went to Rome to receive the pallium and that he holds Winchester in plurality. The pope will readily condemn him.'

'We could argue that our claim is of a Godly cause,' said William. 'A holy war, to bring the reforms of the church to England, to rectify the errors of her ways. That might bring men from far and wide to fight under our banner, a banner blessed by Saint Peter...'

'We may never have to invade England,' added Roger of Montgomery. 'Harold will have to stand aside if his coronation is judged illegal.'

'I'll find a man and dispatch him to Rome immediately,' said Odo.

William met Will's stare across the room and his face split into his familiar triumphant grin. If God was on their side, how could they possibly lose?

*

Harold read the letter again, trying to detect between the formal Latin sentences couched in terms of polite outrage, exactly how William felt. Wronged? Certainly. Deprived and humiliated? Maybe, though Harold doubted whether others in the duchy felt the same way. William saw Harold's succession as a personal insult, but many of the chief councillors would probably disabuse him of that, as they themselves would not care too deeply. Acceptance? Definitely not. Though the letter was polite, William made it abundantly clear that by asking him in such a forceful way to reconsider his rash and hasty coronation, he was warning him that he would resort to less diplomatic means to gain what he believed was his inheritance. Would he, though?

What outweighed the shallow threats of the letter, which in themselves did not frighten Harold, was the mention of the pope, and that William was taking his claim to Rome. The current occupant of the papal throne was Alexander, a great reformer. But everybody was aware that the pope's chief advisor was a man whose interest in reform of the corrupt church and in curbing the powers of kings over the church almost verged on the obsessive, and who had powers as great as Alexander. That man was Hildebrand. Passionate, zealous, eloquent and overwhelmingly ambitious, Hildebrand was expected to succeed Alexander as pope.

Stigand was the problem. He made an easy target with his greed and contempt for Rome, not even bothering to obtain papal recognition for his archbishopric which had been made in the aftermath of the struggle with Robert Champart. It had seemed a good solution at the time, healing the wounds between Edward and Godwin, but now it had come back to bite them. Harold had thought for a moment that Ealdred of York should have performed the coronation; that was his instinct, but Stigand had been so persuasive, so supportive, that he deserved the task. But did it invalidate Harold's coronation and therefore his authority before God?

A clerk appeared at the door. He bowed. 'You summoned me, sire?'

Harold grunted. He had yet to become used to his title. And here in the state apartments of Westminster palace, it was hard to accept that his command was law, that the very ground he trod upon was not ordinary. For many years he had counselled Edward in the knowledge that whatever he said, the final responsibility had always lain with Edward; now it lay with Harold himself. And only now, barely a month after Edward's death and his own coronation, could he begin to appreciate the utter loneliness of power that had dogged Edward in his last years.

'Prepare a letter to William, duke of Normandy, lord of Maine.' The clerk sat at the writing desk. 'Greetings,' Harold began. What would he say? He wanted to remain polite – as William had – but imply also his strength and determination between the lines and show that he was not going to give in. It could be that William was bluffing, trying to bully him into renouncing the throne. But then he remembered the look of fright in Matilda's eyes at her husband's obsession with the English throne; he could not be bluffing.

'I have received your letter concerning our claim to the English throne,' he continued more confidently. 'We are sad to see that you have not understood that I, King Harold, was named heir to King Edward by the king as he lay dying before Epiphany. The great council then elected to ratify the king's dying wish and I was crowned in the new abbey at Westminster. Therefore, my right and claim as the legitimate successor to King Edward, may God have mercy on his soul, are correct and proper by the law of the English. Regarding the matter of contravening the oath I swore at Bayeux, I now state that it was sworn under duress and thus declare that it is null and void. The voice of the council and the will of God are greater, in any case, than any such case you put forth. I hope, therefore, that the good relations between our states that have existed in the past may indeed prosper in the future. Given at Westminster, on the twenty-ninth day of January in the Year of Our Lord, 1066.'

Harold watched the clerk scribbling frantically and the thought occurred to him that if William had written or sent a man to the pope, then why should he not do the same?

'Wait, please,' he said. 'I have another letter to send when you have finished.'

Once the clerk had prepared a fresh sheet of parchment, Harold began: 'Harold, king of the English, servant of God, to Pope Alexander, chief shepherd of the holy church, greeting...'

*

Will read Harold's letter to William and Matilda. When he'd finished, he set it down and folded his arms. Outside, the snow was falling heavily, casting a dense white blanket over the courtyard, bailey and town, as far as the eye could see, over the now frozen Seine. Time stood still. No horses moved in the yard; no townspeople ventured forth from the warm fires of their homes. It was as if the world had stopped moving and only this letter from a usurper king to a wronged duke could set it in motion again.

William broke the silence. 'Odo has found a man to undertake the journey to Rome. Gilbert, archdeacon of Lisieux; a good man, liked and respected. He's made the journey many times before.'

'Surely he cannot leave now, not in this weather?' asked Matilda.

William nodded. 'There's no time to be lost. He'll go south to Marseille and from there take a boat to Italy. That way he will avoid the Alps and the worst of the weather.'

'I suppose this letter ends all hopes of a peaceful resolution to the situation?' said Will.

'Yes,' said William. 'If Harold Godwinsson wishes for war, then he shall have it.'

Chapter Forty-Two
Oslo, Norway, March 1066

He was called the Hard One; in Norwegian, *Hardrada*, and was as hard as life had made him. His was a career of living legend that made up the sagas and myths of Norse folk-tales. At fifteen, he had escaped the massacre at Stiklestad which killed his half-brother, the mighty Olaf, and so many of the household warriors. He fled in exile to Russia, where he saw action in Poland, and then on to Byzantium, Constantine's magnificent city which straddled both Christian and Muslim worlds like the Colossus itself.

For as long as anyone could remember, the Macedonian emperors of Christian Byzantium had employed the feared and reviled Vikings as their household guards. The Varangian Guard, the Norsemen called it, just as they had their own word for Byzantium: Miklegaard. Rather than allow the pagan warriors from the icy wastelands of the north to pillage their city, the emperors had made them their employees, paying them to slaughter the enemies of the empire. Hardrada became captain of the guard on arriving in the Golden City.

His reputation was second to none. If a minstrel or a writer of sagas was to sit and compile a song or poem listing fantastic deeds and then ascribe them all to one man, he would not have to feel a twinge of shame if he named that man Harald Hardrada. Feared by Christian and Muslim alike, he had conquered as many women as cities, and had killed as many infidels as Christians. His was a life of blood;

he was baptised in it, born and bred to it, and he was the most feared warrior in the known world. And now he was going to conquer England.

Almost twenty years ago he had returned home from Byzantium to inherit his nephew's throne of Norway. Magnus ,had also left him the ancient blood-feud between Norway and Denmark. Hardrada immediately embarked on a decade of war, which only ended in King Svein's humiliating submission after the Battle of the Nissa gorge four years since.

There was also the long-forgotten promise between Harthacanute and Magnus, that whoever died first would bequeath their kingdom to the other. Harthacanute had reneged on that promise and an unknown English prince had taken England instead: Edward.

With Edward dead and the king of Denmark humbled, it was time for King Harald Sigurdsson, the Hardrada, to honour an ancient promise and bring the island kingdom of England back to the fold of her Viking partners.

*

'Father, you are too old.'

Hardrada looked at his eldest son, Magnus, and said: 'I am fifty, and in my prime. Look at me. I could beat a man half my age in battle.'

Magnus couldn't dispute that. For all the years of battles, travelling, woundings, his father still had the appearance and strength of a man in his thirties. He stood by the fireside, a giant of a man at nearly seven feet tall, as broad as an ox, his great beard streaked with grey. But the hard, blue eyes were young and alert, and the huge body well-muscled and fit. Most men of his age were either fat, and incapable of leaving their warm fires – or dead. This man was planning to invade England as if it were a stroll on a summer's day.

Magnus tried another tack: 'What is England to us?' He didn't hear the approach of his younger brother, Olaf.

'Wealth, fame, fortune and glory,' said Olaf. 'Is that enough for you?'

Hardrada beamed. His second son was so like himself, though not quite possessed of the extraordinary height. Magnus frowned, knowing that Olaf would agree with their father, and would encourage him in this idea.

'One last voyage, eh, father?' said Olaf, seeing the mood the old man was in. Had he not seen more in one lifetime than ten men in theirs?

'We'll leave in July and sail to Orkney, where we'll regroup.'

'And after Orkney?'

'Jorvik.' Hardrada clenched the cup in his hand so tightly that his sons thought that it would crack and smash to the floor.

Olaf nodded. Of course. Jorvik, or *York*, as they knew it in England. At one time it had been the capital of Viking England, as Scandinavian as longboats and Thor, in the heart of Danelaw England. Once there, they would be welcomed with open arms, take hostages, establish their capital and choose their moment to fight and defeat Harold Godwinsson.

'There is much to admire in Harold Godwinsson,' Hardrada was saying. 'He is the son of his father. Earl Godwin was as cunning as a fox and his son has learnt well from his master. But his is not the right.'

'And William of Normandy?' said Magnus. 'Does he not have the better right...better than ours?'

'Might is right, Magnus. Forgotten promises, oaths, blood-lines all mean nothing in the face of battle. And we shall fight the Normans if we have to.

They are a tough race, being descendants of us Norwegians. They make good warriors and that bastard-duke is not a man to be underestimated.' Hardrada's stone-blue eyes narrowed. 'When I was in Miklegaard we fought the Normans on the Greek islands. They fought hard but we defeated them, so they turned back to Italy and began to fight the pope. Can you imagine that Christian men would dare to fight the pope in his own land? And they beat him, as they did at Civitate. My God, they defeated the pope in battle! I think that they are more pagan and godless than we Norsemen ever were. They will join William in their thousands.'

'Then Harold Godwinsson is doomed?' asked Olaf.

'No,' Hardrada said. 'He'll have the wealth and might of England behind him. That will be formidable. But he'll be at a disadvantage with two invading forces coming at him in the same summer. It all depends on the wind and when we can sail. We could face either William or Harold in battle. Who knows?'

Who knows indeed, thought Magnus, as he watched his father stride from the hall shouting for his horse. One thing they could be certain of, though: by taking the throne of England, Harold Godwinsson had brought the wrath of the Northmen – both Viking and Norman – on his head, setting in motion a train of events that neither he nor anybody else could possibly stop now.

Chapter Forty-Three
Rome, Italy, March 1066

Gilbert was always overawed by the sight of the Apostolic Palace of the Holy See. He'd been to

Rome many times before, but still marvelled at its splendour.

The journey through France had been uneventful; with an escort of twenty knights, letters of safe-conduct to the various lords of Anjou, Aquitaine, Perigord and Toulouse, and his message to the pope, they reached Marseille where the weather was considerably better than in Normandy. Procuring a ship caused no difficulty, and after calling at Toulon, where the small merchant vessel acquired more passengers, and at Pisa, where they offloaded the first of their goods, they reached Rome in late March.

Leaving his escort of Norman knights to enjoy the pleasures of Rome – Gilbert was forced to admit that those pleasures didn't include the wonders of Ancient Rome but rather the whores – he walked quickly to the palace with two clerks in tow, one still clutching his stomach and still grey-faced after the sea-crossing.

They were expected and the pope was ready to receive them. Gilbert was suddenly nervous now that the moment had come. How much did the success of the duke's scheme depend upon his eloquence, his ability to persuade the pope to endorse the invasion? He did not like to contemplate the answer, but he suspected that it was a great deal.

The double doors swung open, and with a glance at the clerics standing with legs of jelly behind him, Gilbert stepped forward.

The palace was truly immense. It was greater than any lord's building in Normandy or anywhere else he'd been; this was the first time he'd set foot inside, as all his earlier visits hadn't merited his presence within the palace. At the far end, seated on the great throne, was the man he presumed to be Alexander, surrounded by hushed, whispering cardinals.

One of the cardinals stepped forward from the crowd and stretched out an arm in welcome. Gilbert recognised him instantly: Hildebrand.

'Gilbert, my friend.'

Gilbert knelt on the cold marble floor and kissed the cardinal's hand. Hildebrand raised him up and kissed both his cheeks, muttering a benediction as he did so. 'I trust that your journey was safe?' Gilbert nodded. Hildebrand went on, in a conspiratorial whisper: 'Alexander is, I think, favourable to Duke William's demands. He will possibly support William against Harold.'

Hildebrand gently propelled Gilbert forward to the papal throne. Two steps more, and he was before the pope. Scarcely breathing, he knelt and kissed the heavily jewelled hand. How they would envy him at the church of Lisieux for years to come, and how his fireside tales would arouse the awe of many! He heard the mutter of a benediction and got to his feet, looking into the face of Pope Alexander II.

'We have considered the duke of Normandy's proposals,' said Alexander. That was a positive sign; William had sent a string of messengers on ahead with the details of his request, stating that the archdeacon would arrive later to discuss them in person. Clearly the pope had taken the time to study the documents. 'But we do not wish to condemn England.'

Gone were William's hopes and dreams. The pope must have seen the disappointment etched onto Gilbert's face, for he continued with a small smile of comfort. 'But we do not condone King Harold's actions or indeed the corruption of the English church.'

'Holy Father, Harold Godwinsson is a usurper and a perjurer,' Gilbert blurted out. It was in the balance and he might just seize the advantage. 'He is forsworn. He pledged on holy relics that if the English Prince Edgar was not confirmed heir, then he would do all he could within his power to secure Duke William's succession. But he has gone back on that promise and claimed the throne for himself. Duke William demands satisfaction and asks that his cause be blessed by God.'

Gilbert drew a ragged breath and waited for the reply.

'It is an interesting story, archdeacon,' Alexander wasn't smiling now. 'But it's *your* story, the story of *your* duke and how he perceives himself to be wronged.'

'But...'

'I have here King Harold's version of events.'

Gilbert gasped. How in heaven's name had Harold got to the pope first? Out of the corner of his eye he saw Hildebrand make a sudden movement. Clearly, Alexander's announcement was news to him also.

'It arrived yesterday,' said the pope, reading his mind.

Even here of all places, Gilbert could have cursed out loud. One day too late! His mind went back over the journey, trying to think where they could have been quicker. Delays at Marseille, yes, but those had been unavoidable. The visit to the lord of Périgeux hadn't really been necessary, and stopping for two days at Pisa seemed disastrous now. The duke would finish his career for this. If only they'd pressed on, if only...

'Harold tells me that Edward chose him as his heir on his deathbed and that this was the last thing King Edward said in this life,' said Alexander. 'May God have mercy on his soul. Furthermore, King Harold states that his nomination as king was affirmed by his election by the great council. He was then consecrated king. The letter I have here is signed and sealed by Harold, and witnessed by Ealdred, Stigand, Edwin of Mercia, Morcar of Northumberland, William of London, and a dozen or so other nobles and bishops of the land. It seems that Harold's succession has been accepted and approved by all those of stature in England. They view his claim as entirely rightful.'

In the frozen silence that followed, Gilbert could only look at the ground, speechless with embarrassment. Why had Hildebrand said so clearly that Alexander would support William, when he so patently wasn't going to? Crimson-faced, Gilbert bowed and backed away. 'If that is your answer, your holiness, then I thank you and shall return forthwith to Duke William.'

But Hildebrand motioned Gilbert to remain where he was. 'Your holiness, may I be permitted to make an observation?' Without waiting for a reply, he continued rapidly, 'It appears, Holy Father, that the duke of Normandy is not asking you to condemn King Harold for what he has done, or indeed to make known any such displeasure from the papal curia. He is asking, instead, for us to bless his cause; whether we condemn Harold or not, he is quite set on invading England and seizing what he sees as his by right. We, therefore, would not be taking sides in the matter, but only blessing Duke William.'

It was breathtakingly audacious. For a minute Gilbert hardly dared to move, let alone take his eyes from Alexander's inscrutable expression. At a stroke, Hildebrand had removed all responsibility from Rome's shoulders; the church would neither condemn nor condone William's actions.

Alexander scratched his chin. 'And you suggest that by remaining impartial we would in effect be leaving it for God to decide?'

'Exactly, your holiness.'

Gilbert expelled some air, certain that the beating of his own heart echoed throughout the hall.

'But what of Harold Godwinsson? If we bless the ducal cause, then, in order to remain impartial, surely we ought to bless his cause?'

In answer to the pope's question, Hildebrand raised his shoulders and looked with feigned bewilderment around the hall.

'I see no such representative of King Harold's court, your holiness. But I do see Gilbert, archdeacon of Lisieux, here on Duke William's behalf.'

Alexander shot him a shrewd look. 'Very well, then. Since you put it in such a succinct manner, Duke William shall have our blessing.' He turned to Gilbert. 'You may take away the banner of St Peter for William to fly at the head of his troops. But if King Harold should send a man from England, he shall also receive our blessing.'

'You must also agree that the English church is in need of much correction, your holiness,' Hildebrand pressed on. 'King Harold's coronation, for example, was performed by Stigand, who has refused to come to Rome for his confirmation. Duke William, however, has done much to rid Normandy of corrupt practices. It would be a just war to take the banner to England and bring about reform, would it not?'

'I do not like the idea of the just war used on England,' Alexander said in a sharp voice that made Gilbert think that Hildebrand had gone too far. 'I gave a blessing to Norman warriors fighting a holy war against the Turks in Sicily and to those knights in Barbastro fighting the Muslims. I'll not sanction it against the English people. They are a Christian people, not infidels.'

'I accept that, your holiness.' Hildebrand spoke smoothly and calmly. 'I did not in any way intend such a movement against England. Perhaps then, we should keep to our original agreement, on the blessing of William's cause and the will of God.'

Gilbert wondered whether he dared to speak, but his tongue was as dry as a desert and the words died at the back of his throat.

Alexander grunted. 'Very well, then; God will provide.'

Chapter Forty-Four
Westminster, April 1066

Eadgyth regarded Harold with total disbelief. Her face was blotched and tear-stained.

'Marriage? Why – and to whom?' Harold tried to put his arms around her but she shook him off. 'How can you – after all the years we've been together? What of our children? Are they to be cast off?'

'My darling, you know that I love you and no other, but this is an important alliance, a political union.'

'Who is it then? Who must I share my bed with?'

'Gisla, Edwin and Morcar's sister. This marriage will be to serve one purpose only: to bring Edwin and Morcar into alliance with me, their king.'

'But they will also hope to have a nephew who will be king after you.'

Harold hesitated fractionally. 'That is what they may wish, of course. But it is what my father wanted from Edward and Edith – he never got it.'

'Do you mean...'

'... I do not have to bed the girl.'

'But surely Edwin and Morcar will suspect something?'

'Gisla is not a virgin. She's the widow of King Griffith of Wales. Once we're married, that will be enough to secure the earls' full support.' This time Eadgyth allowed Harold to embrace her. 'But you shall have to move out from the palace. You shall live at Guildford, with my mother. You'll want for nothing.'

Eadgyth knew that it was of no use to argue. In any case, she didn't like Westminster; it was too big, too formal. Guildford was familiar, cosy: home. 'I'll like living with Gytha.'

Harold was pleased that the matter was resolved. It hadn't been an easy task, but now it was done. 'This alliance is vital to me, you know that. The north is still unstable after the rebellion against Tostig last year, and I have news that King Harald of Norway is gathering an army to invade in the name of a treaty Harthacanute swore many years ago.'

It was remarkable how the past always seemed to haunt the present, constantly tugging at the sleeve of a man as he tried to move onwards. Father had never escaped the ghost of Alfred; it had killed him, some said. Now a long-forgotten pact between two dead men had reared its ugly head. 'I fear the summer will bring two of the greatest invasions this country has ever seen.'

'Have you heard from Tostig?'

'He sent me a letter some weeks ago,' said Harold. 'Attacking me for taking the throne, for usurping William. He is jealous, and believes that he should share the kingdom with me. And I doubt that William has taken any notice of him; if he had, Tostig wouldn't be languishing in exile in St Omer, living at the expense of his father-in-law.'

'It seemed that nothing could destroy England while the house of Godwin stood side by side. And now...and now Edith is at Winchester, and Tostig is overseas...' Eadgyth's voice trembled, a rush of hot tears spilled unchecked down her cheeks. 'What will he do? Would you pardon him if he returned?'

Harold nodded. 'Yes, I would. If only he would ask...until then I must ally with Edwin and Morcar by marrying their sister, little though we both like it. Kingship and love agree but ill together, it is said, and we are mere mortals caught in the web of fate.'

'I understand,' said Eadgyth, her voice betraying little of the bitterness she felt. Why could Harry not have remained earl of Wessex? Why did Edward have to point the finger at Harold and in his last dying breath condemn them all to this? Was it his final revenge on the house of Godwin he'd fought for so long and lost to? 'Things will never be the same again,' she murmured. She looked up, and caught Harold's bleak stare. He'd changed too, but not enough to disagree with that sentiment.

*

Harold's inner circle of government consisted of his two brothers, Gyrth and Leofwine, the brothers Edwin and Morcar, Stigand, and Ealdred of York. These were the men with whom he formed policy before putting it to the council. That way he could be sure of presenting a united front to the people; doubts were not to be allowed to ferment and any rumours of possible division were stifled at birth.

He called the group together two days after speaking with Eadgyth about the proposed marriage. With the exception of Ealdred, all were present. 'We shall be facing a double invasion this summer,' he told them. 'William of Normandy and Harald Hardrada have both made threatening overtures, with intent to seize the throne. So, I suggest this: the northern fyrd under the earls Edwin and Morcar will defend the north against Hardarda if he comes. I think he will head for York with the intention of taking hostages and making it his capital. I, in the south, with Leofwine and Gyrth, will call out the southern fyrd and stand ready to defeat William.'

'Our greatest advantage is the wind,' said Leofwine. 'The Hardrada cannot sail south if William is sailing north; the winds will not allow it. Therefore we must hope we can defeat the first invader, and when the wind changes, turn south – or north – and knock out the second. It is our best hope.'

'If the fleets survive the sea-crossings,' Gyrth said, picking up on Leofwine's optimism. 'Storms can scatter ships, drown and demoralise men and do as much – if not more – than we can, to end the hopes of an invasion. At best, we can pray that both invaders are repelled by the weather; at worst, that only one fleet will get through, and our warriors will destroy them.'

Harold scanned the expressions on the faces of the earls of Mercia and Northumbria and thought he detected an eager sense of purpose. It was good; his brothers had painted a picture of victory before the year was out. Now it was for him to ensure that the brothers Edwin and Morcar were going to support him, and he turned to them and spoke for their benefit.

'After I've been to York so that the northeners can see their new king, we'll celebrate Easter here at Westminster, and then I'll marry Gisla.'

Stigand stirred in his seat and spoke for the first time: 'And thereafter, we are in the hands of God.'

Nobody ventured a reply to that.

The city of York was still very much in a state of unrest after the rebellion of the previous autumn. Harold took the opportunity to halt at Northampton and Nottingham on the journey north, and at Lincoln on the return. Everywhere he was greeted with favour, though the love and loyalty of the men of his Wessex earldom could never be repeated here. His first act at York was to halve the cruel burdens of taxation that Tostig had levied, and leave some experienced stewards to advise Earl Morcar. This pleased the townspeople greatly.

Easter was duly celebrated at Westminster on his return and was followed by his marriage to Gisla. With that achieved, he knew that he could rely on Edwin and Morcar to the death but, please God, it would not come to that.

Two days after the wedding, Gyrth strode into Harold's bedchamber in Westminster palace.

'You won't find her here,' Harold said, noticing Gyrth looking for the bride in the other side of the bed. 'Not now - not ever. We sleep in separate rooms. But make sure Edwin and Morcar don't find that out, won't you? They need to believe that their nephew will be king after me.'

The wedding ceremony had ended with the traditional bedding, where all the menfolk had carried the bride to the bedchamber and locked her in with the groom, but Harold had remained true to his word and hadn't betrayed Eadgyth.

But Gyrth wasn't really interested in Gisla. 'Harry, there is a sight outside you must see. The people are saying that it is an omen, a sign from God. It is a star of some sort, burning through the sky.'

As he spoke, a commotion broke out. Shouts, screams and a muffled curse filled the morning air. Harold, now intrigued and not a little alarmed, pulled up his breeches and grabbed his boots.

'What is it, then?'

'It's witchcraft.' Leofwine, ashen faced, stood at the door. 'I don't like it; it is a portent of evil.' He strode to the window and threw the shutters wide. 'There...do you see it?'

Harold peered out of the window. The streets below were crowded with people all gazing in silent awe upwards, to where Leofwine was pointing.

'My God.' Involuntarily, Harold crossed himself. 'What's that?'

Far above them, but easily visible, was a moving star. Behind it, a long tail of light blazed across the sky.

Harold was filled with uncertainty. It was a sign from God - but was it a mark of approval? Coming so soon after his wedding and in the week following Easter, it could be a good sign. He caught the expressions of awe - and fear - written across his brothers' faces.

'They say it is a message from God.' Gyrth swallowed, and added, carefully: 'We fear for you, Harry.'

'Why?' asked Harold.

'The people...the people in the streets say it's a bad omen. They...they say it is God's displeasure, and that you should not have taken the throne.'

Harold called the council to order. The atmosphere in the great chamber was stormy and tense. There were grown men below him who were scared and did not mind showing it. After breakfast, he'd taken a short walk in the streets of London. People had looked away at his approach, some muttering prayers, only a few bowing respectfully; one had even made the sign of the devil's horns behind his back, thinking that the king would not see him. And all the while, the star with the long tail continued to blaze above them.

On the dais with him were his brothers and Stigand. It was Stigand who leant across and said:

'Tell them the star is a good omen, a sign from God that all will be well with us.' The sound of the ageing, familiar rasp of the archbishop's voice above the chatter was more than welcome. Harold should have known that Stigand was too much of a realist to spare time for omens and signs.

He got to his feet, grateful for the advice, and silence fell over the chamber. Light flooded in through the wide windows: April sunshine, mild at last; it was a reminder that summer would not be long in coming.

Spurred on by this thought of summer and all the dangers it would bring, Harold announced loudly and clearly: 'The disturbance at York has been settled. I have left the governance of the north in the capable hands of Earl Morcar and Archbishop Ealdred. I do not expect any further trouble from the north.'

'What news from Normandy, sire?'

'No news,' Harold said. 'I have sent word to Rome, as you know, and have told the duke of Normandy that my claim is an honest one and abides by the law. I have yet to receive his response.'

'And what of Harald of Norway?' called another.

'I have heard nothing. But we must assume the worst, and prepare for a double invasion in the summer. The northern fyrd shall wait at York, and the southern army at Winchester. The invaders cannot both come at once; the wind will ensure that we have plenty of time to deal with each independently and enable us to join our two armies and defeat the enemy. God will be with us.'

'God is not with us, lord king – He has forsaken us!' someone shouted from the back of the room. 'The star, my lord; it is a sign from God that we are doomed. England will be punished for her sins before the year is out!'

Stigand banged his staff and stood up quickly to quell any uproar. 'I tell you that it is a good sign, councillors; it is a sign that God favours us and will shine His good fortune upon us!'

But the councillors, though chastened by the archbishop's words, were not convinced. Stigand shot them an angry stare. 'Gullible fools,' he muttered. 'They'd believe the devil himself was on his way here if someone told them.'

'With the kingdom united, we can defeat any enemy who dares to oppose us,' Harold said, assuming control of the meeting again. 'God is testing us; He is putting us through a trial of strength. It shall be thus with the kingdom of England. God will set us a trial by battle; if He wishes us to win, we shall be triumphant. If not, we shall pay for our sins. The star above us now is a sign for us to prepare for the coming battles. Only then shall we know.'

The councillors seemed satisfied by his speech, and accepted the comparison with the law of the land. If God wished Harold to be king, he would win. If not...

In Guildford, Gytha and Eadgyth had also seen the star. Similar thoughts to those that many Londoners had entertained did not fail to cross their minds also.

'I have never seen anything like it in my life,' announced Gytha.

She had made Guildford her home since Godwin's death, and now that Harold was with the court at Westminster, Winchester or Gloucester, she had it to herself. The arrival of Eadgyth was welcome company she'd not expected, and the two were glad of it.

'People are saying that it's a sign from God,' said Eadgyth. Gytha saw the worried look on her face and did not know what to say. 'People have said that

Harold did wrong in taking the throne, that the English people shall be punished for their sins.'

'It's not true. You know it is not the case. Edward gave Harold the throne; he told the court that Harry was his heir, and the council confirmed it. He is consecrated by St Peter. Surely God would not have allowed it if He did not favour Harry?'

'But people are saying,' Eadgyth persisted, 'that many years ago, a dying abbot at Glastonbury foresaw that it would come to this. As he lay dying on his bed he had a vision of St Peter consecrating a bachelor-king – that was Edward – but when Edward asked who would succeed him to the throne, St Peter said: "The kingdom of the English belongs to God; after Edward He shall provide a king according to His pleasure."'

'Nonsense,' said Gytha, but her voice lacked conviction. 'We live in an age governed by omens, signs and the unpredictable will of God.' She paused, suddenly feeling the weight of her years. What would Godwin have said? He would have laughed it off, for sure. But he was dead, and she was old and alone. What else could she say? Maybe it was true; maybe it *was* a sign. The people in the streets seemed to think so.

And all the while, the strange star continued to blaze across the sky above them.

*

'Remarkable.'

Will FitzOsbern turned from the narrow window and said again: 'Remarkable.' The tower at Rouen afforded a clear view of the strange star in the sky, and Will had spent much of the morning peering at it.

'They call it a comet,' said Matilda.

'And the people say it is a sign from God; but is it to signal our good fortune or our doom? I hope that if they can see it in England, then Harold Godwinsson is quaking in his boots. It is an omen to say that he should not be king.'

Matilda snorted. 'Or maybe it is a message from God telling William to abandon his foolish plans to invade England.'

Will closed his mouth. He'd not thought of it that way before. He didn't know what had William thought of it. At daybreak, the duke had gone south to meet Gilbert of Lisieux on his return from Rome. There was much depending on Gilbert's mission and now this portentous comet had appeared in the sky.

Heavy footsteps broke into his thoughts. The oak door opened and William himself entered the bower. In his hand he gripped a banner with a white cross on a blue background. His wide mouth cracked into a huge grin of delight, like a child with a new toy. 'From the pope. Blessed by Pope Alexander II and all his cardinals. It is the blessing of God on our mission, as is the star outside. God is with us.'

Will took the banner and touched the cloth. It didn't feel holy, or in any way spiritual. Just a piece of cloth, a flag. But at the head of an army, fluttering alongside the lions of Normandy, and in the heat of battle, when a man was scared of death, he would see this cloth and know that God was with him.

'With a little help from Cardinal Hildebrand,' said a voice from behind William. It was Gilbert of Lisieux.

William laughed. 'I'll wager the duchy on that man becoming pope after Alexander.' He turned to Gilbert. 'You have done well, archdeacon. We are in your debt.'

Later, when he was alone with Matilda, she said, irritably: 'I suppose now that God is with you, you cannot lose.'

'We cannot lose.' William put his arms around her, and at once – and as she knew she would – she gave in to his strength and warmth. He nuzzled her neck like a hungry horse and she had to smile. 'And when we go, I shall leave you in command.' He kissed her cheek.

'Me?' Matilda wasn't sure whether she had heard correctly. 'You would leave me ruler of the duchy – a woman?'

William smiled. 'Why not? You will be my regent and Robert shall be appointed my heir and invested as duke.'

'Who would listen to me? Obey my commands? I –'

'They all would.' William spoke with such certainty that she fell silent. 'You are hugely respected, and I know that you can do it.' He kissed her again.

'And if you don't come back?' She looked into his eyes but he avoided her gaze, not daring to admit to such a possibility.

'Of course I shall return,' he said levelly. 'I am the Conqueror. And God is on my side.'

He kissed her again and was so lost in his own thoughts of the coming victory that he didn't see the single tear drop from Matilda's eye and fall onto his sleeve, and vanish as soon as it appeared.

Chapter Forty-Five
The Solent, May 1066

To Tostig the appearance of the comet in the sky that Easter had been a final confirmation of Harold's mistake in taking the throne of England.

Together with Judith and his children, now grown, and one married, he had spent the winter at St Omer. Another winter, another exile; the parallel with the bitter winter of 1051 was not lost on him, nor on Judith, whose first winter with him that had been. And since the rejection by William of Normandy, he had raised his own small fleet from money loaned by Baldwin, his father-in-law.

He was not entirely sure what he would set out to achieve when the weather improved and the wind was set. Some sort of punitive raid on Harry's beloved Wessex, an expedition to remind the new king that he had a brother whom he had forsaken and who was not going to forget it. Because in typical fashion Harold had put the peace of the realm before his own brother's position.

Tostig would never forgive him for that.

'The men are ready, Lord Tostig.'

Tostig ran his eyes across the blue sea, counting out of habit the eight ships bobbing in the soft wind. The last time he'd been in this stretch of water, between the Isle of Wight and Southampton Water, he'd been with Harry and Leofwine, and they'd spotted their father's fleet on the horizon all those years ago after the rebellion. Swegn had gone on his pilgrimage and never returned; father had died soon after their triumphant defeat of Robert Champart.

Tostig's mouth twisted at the memory, the images of the past serving only to fuel the bitterness of the present. Why was he here now, an exile again? Was he like Swegn, never to return to England except as a nobody?

Tostig turned to his steward, one of the few who'd escaped the northern slaughter of the previous autumn, and the man blanched at the searing hatred in his master's eyes.

'The men are prepared, my lord,' the steward said again.

The steward waited for a reply and just as it seemed that there was none forthcoming, Tostig said: 'Go to the island. Burn the villages; kill the men. Rape the women. Make the children orphans. Do it now.'

The steward would not question the order, no matter how dreadful the consequences were going to be. He would pass it on to the captain of the mercenary dogs Tostig had hired and they would be unleashed: hounds of hell on the sleepy, unsuspecting villages that dotted the island.

Tostig turned his back on his steward and looked out to sea, wondering about the great star they'd seen in the sky. If that had been a sign from God to show that Harold was in the wrong, then he would be more than glad to prove it.

'It's begun,' said Gyrth to Harold. Edwin, Stigand and Leofwine were all with the king at his father's hall in Guildford. It was a good place to be, near the south coast and within reach of London. 'Tostig has sacked Wight, Dungeness and Sandwich. He's raiding and pillaging all along the coast and heading now for Humber.'

'Were they Duke William's ships?' asked Harold.

'No. Sea-wolves: Vikings, mercenaries and scum that will do anything if the money is there.'

'Is it time to summon the fyrd, Harold?' asked Leofwine.

'Most of the fyrd are peasants, and they'll need to bring in the harvest, said Edwin quickly.'We cannot keep them out for long, else there will be a mutiny.'

'Two months is the statutory limit,' agreed Harold. 'So it is too soon to call them out now. But I remember father telling me how Edmund Ironsides summoned the fyrd five times when Canute was at England's throat.'

'That was spread over one year,' said Edwin. 'My grandfather, the earl Leofric, was there too, and he always said that the most dangerous time is the harvest. The Danes had a professional army who lived off the land. We've had to get the harvest in, and the army collapses at that point. It'll be the same this time if we're not careful.'

'You speak truthfully,' Harold said slowly. Neither William nor Harald Hardrada would be hampered by such concerns; they would benefit from them.

'When is the harvest likely to be in this year?' asked Leofwine. The weather so far this spring had been mild; it was late May but summer seemed to be in full bloom.

'August, I'd have thought. At least in the south,' said Gyrth.

'They'll come long before then,' said Gyrth. 'With the weather as it is now, with a strong southerly wind, William must come first.'

'How many men can we raise altogether?' asked Leofwine.

Harold did some rough calculations. 'Seven thousand from the south, I'd say, as well as my housecarl troops.'

'I can raise about a thousand from Cambridgeshire and Norfolk,' said Gyrth.

'And I about the same from Essex,' said Leofwine.

'I can vouch for three or four thousand fromMercia,' said Edwin. And I expect my brother could assemble another three thousand at York.'

'With my housecarls, that's seventeen thousand men altogether,' said Harold.

There was an awed silence.

'It would be the greatest army this country has ever seen,' whispered Leofwine.

'But will they all come?'

Edwin's question was brutally realistic, but they couldn't afford flights of fancy in what would be the gravest danger facing England since the time of King Alfred. 'They'll stand by me to a man,' Harold asserted. 'Wessex has always loved us Godwins despite all our faults.' But as to the other earldoms he could not say. Both Edwin and Morcar were young men, new to their lands and people. 'In Mercia they'll come in your grandfather's name, if not your father's; they loved the old earl. But the north...' Harold shrugged. 'I like to think they will come, but if Hardrada lands safely, he will attempt to exploit the Danish blood which runs so strongly in the north. Siward was a Dane; his son Waltheof didn't follow him as many had hoped...' He looked up, caught Edwin's stare, and wondered for a moment if he'd been too rash in accepting Morcar's appointment as earl of Northumbria. Too late, he glanced away, inwardly cursing his insensitivity. They must trust each other; without trust, they would have nothing. Suspicion and rifts would grow, and the mighty army would never unite. 'But Waltheof was too young at the time,' he added quickly. 'I'm sure the people of the north will unite against Harald Hardrada. I'll draw up the writs to summon the fyrd and we'll assemble at Winchester in a fortnight. Edwin, I suggest you assemble your forces at Derby, and march to York and wait there with Morcar and Ealdred and the northern army until I send word.' Harold heard his own voice, brisk and assertive, and full of confidence: 'We'll stay south with the main force of ten thousand, so when William comes we shall be ready and waiting.'

*

If Harold's greatest problems were the harvest and the loyalty of the north, then William's was the lack of an army – let alone what to do with it. The fleet was being built at Dives, but the response to his call to arms was slow.

William based his operations command at Falaise, where the great fortress was central to the duchy. From here he sent out a stream of messengers to all corners of the duchy, and to Brittany, Flanders, and southern Italy, where Norman knights were carving out a kingdom against the Byzantines.

Will FitzOsbern peered out of the window. The courtyard below was a hive of activity. And above it, the lion of Normandy and the cross of St Peter fluttered in the gentle southerly wind. 'The wind is right,' he said, 'But there is no fleet and no army to fill it.'

'The latest report from the master ship-builder at Dives is that we have two hundred ships ready,' said William from behind him. 'And I've called for all boats over twenty feet in length to be requisitioned.'

Odo entered the chamber. 'The lord of Beaming isn't coming,' he said, waving a letter. 'He says he is too old. But he says his son Robert will come with five hundred knights.'

'And Roger of Montgomery; is he with us?' asked Odo.

'No.' William said to his half-brother. 'I've asked him to remain with Hugh of Avranches to aid Matilda in the government of the duchy. There have to be men I can trust to leave behind. Robert is only fourteen...'

The meaning of William's words was clear; they all knew what had happened when another duke had left the duchy to go on a perilous mission with few provisions for his duchy and heir.

'Oaths of allegiance are not enough. They were sworn to me when I was a lad and my father was foolish enough to believe that would do. I want to ensure that if I die on this mission then what happened to me will not occur again. If I don't return, I know I can trust Roger and Hugh to hold Normandy steady until Robert comes of age. It'll only be for two years. I was sixteen, nearly seventeen when I took command of the duchy.'

'We need to know how many are going to come with us,' said Odo. 'We're all aware of the might of the English fyrd and the numbers Harold has at his disposal.'

'Peasants,' said William, bluntly. 'Farm labourers, smiths, tanners and cobblers. That is what forms the bulk of the English army. Giving them a shield and spear does not make them soldiers. And when did they last go to war? The English virtue of peace will be their undoing. Normandy is well versed in the art of war. God knows we have seen enough of it.' William's mouth twisted into a bitter smile. 'Our knights are trained to fight on horseback. When Harold came to Brittany with me, he said they had nothing like it in England. We'll have some two thousand knights if they all answer my call.'

Odo's heavy voice cut in again. 'And how will we transport the horses? How will we get them across the sea? It's never been done before.'

'It has.' William nodded to Will. 'Tell him, Will.'

Will moved from the window. 'It's been done in southern Italy. Norman knights under Robert the Weasel – Guiscardo, as they know him out there – developed a method of transporting horses across the water in special flat-bottomed boats. We're building similar ships.'

'And I have written to the king of France, the emperor Henry of Germany and Robert Guiscard, telling them of our mission and informing them that I have the pope's blessing. Already, there are mercenaries from Brittany gathering at Caen.'

'I'm impressed,' said Odo. 'But it'll be nigh on impossible to keep such a motley force disciplined without the main core of it being men from Normandy.'

William had to agree to that.

'That's why I've summoned a great council to be held at Caen in the third week of the month. I'll be promising land and riches beyond the barons' wildest dreams.'

'You mean to divide England up?'

'Yes. It will be the only way to attract the men to my cause. They want land and I'm going to give it to them.'

'You realise what this means, don't you?' Odo said. 'The complete destruction of England. This is not what the pope has blessed us to do.'

'If that is what it takes to raise an army, then that is what we must do.' William was stony-faced. 'England has brought this upon herself.'

*

The southerly wind that would take William's ships to England drove Tostig's small fleet from Sandwich along the east coast of England. At Lindsey, they put ashore and put the villagers to the sword. Moving up the Humber they encountered Earl Morcar's army and beat a hasty retreat. They then regrouped and sailed for Scotland, where the king gave them shelter and told them of the impending arrival of Harald Hardrada.

Tostig decided to stay and await the Norwegian king and then join the Norwegian invasion of his own country.

Chapter Forty-Six
Reggio di Calabria, Italy, June 1066

There were two of them, brothers close in age. The elder one, Joscelin, was twenty-eight; the younger,

Philippe, twenty-seven. Both had the misfortune to be born younger sons on a small family lordship of Romagny, near Mortain in Normandy. The law of the land was unequivocal: the first-born son inherited the entire estate, the second son made a good marriage to an heiress, the third son was given to the church. Any daughters were married off to first-born sons of other families. Failing that, they too were given to God.

Joscelin and Philippe were the fifth and sixth sons. There was no land to inherit, marry, or buy and the church was glutted with young aristocrats.

At eighteen Joscelin left home to seek his fortune and win his bread by the strength of his right arm. He headed for Italy, where he had heard that Roger de Hauteville, another younger son – in fact the youngest of twelve – had come to carve out lands. Two years later, Philippe joined him and found his brother commanding thirty Norman knights under Roger and fighting the Turks in the south of the peninsula.

When Philippe heard of the planned invasion of England by Duke William, he went to Reggio to find Joscelin. Reggio had been captured six years earlier by Roger and his brother, Robert Guiscard, the Weasel. Philippe and Joscelin had been present at the fighting and both had shared the rich rewards.

A vast stone fortress had been erected on the clifftop of the town, looking across the short stretch of blue sea to Sicily and Messina, where Roger was determined to plant his banner next.

'There you are.'

Philippe had climbed the steep steps up to the tower where Joscelin was playing dice with the guards. It was a hot day with a cloudless blue sky. Philippe, wearing only a linen undershirt and breeches, was sweating slightly. His hair, bleached blond by the sun, was close-cropped in the Norman style and his young face tanned the colour of leather.

Joscelin looked up at the sound of his brother's voice. He too was a deep walnut colour after years in the sun, and had the same eyes, but a longer nose and leaner jaw than Philippe's marked him out as the elder.

'News from Normandy,' said Philippe. The guards lost interest in the game, studying the young lord anew at the mention of the homeland. 'Duke William is gathering an army to invade England. The pope has sent his blessing and William offers land and booty beyond our wildest dreams.'

'So?'

'Don't you want to go?' Philippe was dismayed to see the guards return to their game with grunts of derision. 'There'll be land – England is famed for her wealth – and the women...'

Joscelin smiled. A slow, patronising smile that signalled a speech from the older brother to the younger. 'He will fail. The English are good warriors and will fight all the more for their homeland. Anyway, the women are pale and cold. There is more to be had here if we wait.' Joscelin looked over the wall and out across the bay.

Philippe followed his gaze and couldn't deny the tempting beauty of Sicily that lay before him. From Reggio they could see the port of Messina and to the left, the great Mount Etna, always snow-covered and smoking, glowing at night like a forge from the very bowels of hell. Before it, the blue sea sparkled and shimmered, a mirror to the blue sky, stretching to infinity and beyond.

'But how long do we wait?' Philippe looked back at Joscelin. After taking Messina and Palermo with ease five years ago, the Norman advance had stopped dead. Halted by the massive Saracen stronghold at

Etna, all they could do was wait, seemingly for ever.

'I won't hold you back.' Joscelin was aware that he was being asked to release Philippe from his vow of homage. 'You can go. Take twenty of our knights. But first you must seek out Lord Roger at San Marcos and ask his permission. I see no reason why he shouldn't give it.'

'You aren't coming?'

'No. You'll be alone this time.' The sun had crept around the stone parapet and Joscelin shaded his eyes. 'I don't think Duke William will succeed, but you have my blessing.' He held out his hand and Philippe shook it, grinning his delight.

Philippe of Romagny was going home.

'The knights from Italy have been most informative,' said Odo.

'The Hauteville brothers ferried their horses across from Reggio di Calabria to Messina just five years ago. Roger and Robert have released many of their men to join us. I will send them my thanks.'

'But the waters of Messina are not those of the English Sea, William,' said Odo. 'We'll have ten times the distance to cover and there'll be no Italian sun shining on our backs when we do it.'

'It is a risk we'll have to take,' said William.

Will glanced uneasily at the two brothers. Tempers frayed all too quickly these days, and the warm weather didn't help matters. William was due to make the first of several speeches to an assembly of local lords to encourage them to join his invasion. Others were planned at Bonneville-sur-Touques and Lillebonne. Last week a great number of churchmen and courtiers had met here at Caen to take part in the dedication of the abbey of Holy Trinity, and William had not wasted the opportunity to seek out support from lords who attended, and to solicit aid from younger sons. To this end, Will had travelled back and forth across the duchy to drum up support, and at last, men were flooding into Caen and Dives in their thousands.

'What news is there from Harald of Norway?' asked Will, eager to calm down the flaring tempers.

William sniffed. He had his spies in England, relaying messages across the English Sea by way of fishing craft and other trading vessels. 'Nothing – yet. It is clear that he intends to invade England. That fool Tostig Godwinsson is at the court of King Malcolm of Scotland, presumably intending to join the Norwegians.'

'They'll never match our army. We have men from Italy, Brittany, Anjou and Poitou, and there are many good archers and crossbowmen amongst the Poitevins and Bretons,' said Will. 'And at least we have good supplies of food.'

It had been a stroke of genius, organising and ensuring that the assembling army didn't run out of food. A hungry army was a discontented army, and a discontented army deserted. That wouldn't happen, though; months of food provisions were stocked ready and waiting, paid for by higher taxes and deeper excavation of the fast-emptying treasury.

'All is going well,' said Will, putting his hand on William's shoulder. 'The forces are arriving as we speak, the ships are being built and God – I swear it – is with us.'

That night the wind changed.

Matilda noticed it first. William had brought her and their sons Robert, Richard and William to Caen for the dedication of the abbey the previous week. On the morrow the great lords of the duchy were due to begin swearing their oaths of allegiance to the duke's designated heir, his first-born, Robert. Matilda hadn't felt at all well these past days – a summer cold, the physician said – and her monthly flux had only made it worse. The noise and bustle of the small town of Caen – packed as it was with foreign troops awaiting the completion of the fleet –created a scene of confusion and insecurity she didn't want to face each morning. And a tear-stained letter from Judith in Lille had troubled her conscience. Should she have persuaded William to take Tostig with his army? Judith said in the letter that Tostig had beaten her badly after his snub at the court of the duke of Normandy – William Bastard, he'd called him – and left her bruised and bleeding, raging that his revenge on both William and Harold would be terrible. Since his departure she'd heard no more of him; only that he had sailed north in search of the Hardrada. Judith had consequently left St Omer, and taken her family to Lille to live with her parents. The beating was the end of the marriage. Tostig Godwinsson was a bad man, filled with hatred and burning with a desire for revenge and a misplaced sense of justice. He was like his brother Swegn; he had an evil streak in him.

The night was stiflingly warm. Matilda slipped from the bed and crept along the passage to the privy, thanking God that William had had the sensitivity to requisition the largest town house for her during the hectic preparations for the campaign. The wealthy merchant who owned it had been glad to leave the town for the countryside, getting away from the heat and soldiery and with the bagful of money slipped to him by way of encouragement.

On her return a creaking noise made her pause. Her first thought was: rats. But it was coming from outside. She moved to the window and pushed the shutter open a couple of inches. The first light of dawn was enough to illuminate the weathervane at the top of the church of St Martin across the street.

'What is it, my love?'

'The weathervane on the church across the street.'

William pulled back the sheet and stepped to her side, pushing the shutters wide open. A cool breeze washed around her waist and armpits and she luxuriated in it for a moment. The sound of laughter, a woman's throaty chuckle, floated up from the ground below. Another whore, no doubt, making more money than she knew what to do with from the massed soldiery in the town.

William withdrew his head from the window. In the pale light from the east Matilda could see that his face was as pale as whitewashed stone.

'Are you ill?' Matilda put a hand to his face: it was cold as stone, too.

'The wind,' said William. 'It's changed. It's coming from the north now. We can't sail for England with it as strong as this against us.' He licked a finger and held it up.

Matilda understood why the breeze was blowing into the chamber, cooling and refreshing them. It hadn't done so all the other nights.

'This means the Hardrada will come first.'

'What if the wind doesn't change again?' Matilda hardly dared to hope that the answer he would give would be the one she wanted.

It was. In a deadpan voice, William said: 'Then we shall not sail. And if not this summer, then never.'

Matilda let the hope flow through her like the very wind itself, and allowed herself a smile in the shadows of the dawn.

*

Eight days later, Matilda departed for Falaise with the boys. She was glad to leave the crowded streets of Caen, and told William so; he laughed at her concerns that the rough soldiery and the painted whores were a bad influence on his sons. He added that one day the boys would be drinking and whoring like any other members of the common levy. Matilda shuddered at the thought, and silently promised that for now at least, they would be protected from such pursuits.

William headed for Dives, taking Will and Robert Beaumont with him to supervise the shipbuilding. They arrived on 2nd July. The small port of Dives had been transformed from a sleepy fishing village into a vast shipyard. William had chosen it, chiefly because of the long beach and the spit of land which provided natural protection. Along the beach before them were rows of ships, especially designed for transporting horses.

'Reginald of Cabourg, the captain of my ship, has suggested that we sail along the coast when the fleet is fully fitted out, to Saint-Valery, at the mouth of the Somme,' William informed Will and Robert Beaumont. 'By sailing close to the wind, along the coast, we can do that. There, we can wait for a change in the wind and the crossing to England will be shorter.'

There was good sense in this. Robert said: 'Does the master-shipbuilder know for sure when the fleet will be ready?'

'Another month,' said William. 'And by that time the army will be fully assembled. Then we must pray to God that the wind changes in our favour and takes us to England and victory.'

Chapter Forty-Seven
Winchester, July 1066

The English fleet was out in force, the ports of Romney, Rye, Winchelsea, Dungeness and Hythe supplying ships to patrol the English Sea from Sandwich to Portland Bill. The men of Wessex were out, encamped in separate contingents in Dorchester, Southampton, Winchester, Lewes and Dover. No one knew where or when William would land, but Harold's spies had informed him that the Norman fleet was almost complete and that he could arrive any day, once the wind was favourable.

In the north, Edwin and Morcar were stationed at York, having beaten off Tostig's attempted landings. They were on the watch for Harald Hardrada.

Moving to Winchester had brought Harold into close contact with his sister for the first time since Edward's death. Edith had made her residence the palace that was traditionally reserved for dower-queens; Emma had had it before her. Harold, anxious to preserve the fragile peace between him and his sister, had allowed her the control of the town.

They hadn't met since Easter, and then Edith had seemed a pale shadow of herself, widowed at forty and marginalised from the decisions taken at the court she had once dominated. She had aged, too. On Harold's first sight of her, he was instantly reminded of their mother, Gytha; the greying hair that had once been blonde was drawn back severely and her dress was a simple brown gown, which made her seem older.

'I have a letter from Tostig,' was the first thing she said when he visited her private chambers. He's at the court of Malcolm and he says he will join Harald Hardrada when he sails for England.'

Harold took the letter she handed to him and read it through slowly. It was hastily written and steeped in vitriolic hatred for the brother who had first exiled him and then taken the throne that was not his by right. And as he scanned the lines, blotched and scored through where Tostig's emotions had got the better of him, Harold realised that Tostig would never come back peacefully.

'I bear you no enmity for Tostig's exile,' she said. 'At first, when he left, and Edward died and you – you became king, I hated you...but now I see that you were right. You did as Edward decreed and he was right, too; you are the greatest soldier and leader we have against the threat of two invasions.' Edith's voice trembled. 'But I wish to God that Tostig was with you, not against you.'

Harold squeezed her hand and said gently: 'At a time like this, the need for unity is greater than ever. But do not blame yourself; it will do us no good at all. I'd have him back tomorrow if he were to ask. I need him here, at my side, not hundreds of miles away in Scotland, where his hatred and resentment can only grow and deepen like a cancer.'

Edith's eyes were full of tears. 'It's not you I blame for all this,' she said huskily. 'It's Edward. I blame Edward for tearing us and the country apart.'

*

Saturday 12th August.

The fleet was at last ready and complete. There were almost seven hundred boats assembled on the beach at Dives. An army of almost ten thousand was gathered at Caen and the surrounding villages. It was estimated that there were over seven thousand soldiers; of these, two thousand were Norman knights, four thousand were foot-soldiers from Normandy and mercenaries from across northern France. In addition, over a thousand trained archers and crossbowmen made up the great army. The duke fed them by raising taxes throughout the duchy and paying out of his own coffers. To many, though, the prospect of lands and riches in England was enough to keep them there.

'Perfect sailing conditions,' said Will, sliding from his horse and sitting in the long grass.

It was the day the master-shipbuilder had declared the fleet ready and William was with Will on the cliff above Dives. The sky above the silent rows of ships on the sands was an unbroken blue. The sea was calm and the breeze constant.

'But for the wind.' William joined Will and picked a blade of grass, pulling it to pieces. 'Just think,' he said, staring into the sky. 'Not so long ago we wouldn't have had to build a fleet. My great-grandfather would have had his own. We were Northmen then, of Viking blood.'

'I suppose there must be cousins of ours preparing to set sail in the Hardrada's fleet.'

'We shall have to fight them as well as the English.'

'Maybe. Perhaps Harold will do it for us.'

Will sat up and brushed off loose bits of grass from his breeches. He looked at William and frowned. 'My God, you could do with some sleep.'

'A week of it,' William nodded. His eyes, puffy and reddened, stared back at Will from a pale, unshaven face that was, since Matilda's departure, unwashed. His cropped hair was matted and uncombed, bits of grass blew lazily around his shoulders. He was wearing a simple homespun woollen tunic fit for a peasant, and the filth on his breeches was ingrained.

'You don't look like a king to be.' Will grinned.

'I feel like a peasant.'

'Like our days in Pontorson.'

They remembered those days in silence for a few moments, then William said: 'And now we have a mighty invasion fleet in readiness to sail for England, like Vikings of old. My God, what we have done? And what if we should fail?'

Will held out his hands to pull William up. 'We shall not fail,' he said. 'We shall not.'

Leofwine came straight to the point: 'The food is running low, morale is non-existent, the harvest is here, and the men want to go home.'

The heat of August, indistinguishable from that of July, had meant only one incontrovertible thing: the army would not last much longer. Food was scarce and the gathering of the harvest, which accounted for most of a year's food supply, was not being done. Already, they'd slaughtered many of the cattle that in normal times would have been kept until Michaelmas, well into the autumn.

'These aren't normal times,' Harold forced himself to look his brother in the eye. The heat was oppressive. If only it would rain, clear the air, dispel the tension. He found himself praying for a change in the wind, so that William would come and he could meet him with the full complement of the Wessex fyrd and the navy. And Edwin and Morcar would come south and join forces; William would stand no chance. But the wind hadn't changed, and all the while the army sat in the heat and the crops dried and ruined in the fields. Several desertions had occurred. On Leofwine's advice, a public hanging had put a stop to them, but it had not made the king and his councillors popular. Morale was as low as the blistering sun was as high in the sky.

'We have the Hardrada to think of, too,' added Leofwine.

'I know that, damn you,' Harold snapped. 'But I've told you enough times that William of Normandy is the greater threat; he'll head for London.'

'And Hardrada can have York?'

'Yes – for the time being.' Harold went to the window and looked out onto the listless street. God be thanked for one thing. London in this heat would be dreadful; the stench of the meat and the waters of the Thames made it insufferable. With father they'd always come here to Winchester for the summer, and to Gloucester for Christmas. It was an established ritual, following the king's court from Westminster to Winchester and to Gloucester and back to London. The thought of Christmas at Gloucester was comforting. After the summer, after all this...

'Remember.' He looked at Leofwine. 'It is a trial. God is testing us – testing me. We must be patient, pray, wait. When the time is right...we'll strike.'

*

Two weeks later, Harold bowed to the inevitable. On 8th September, the Wessex fyrd was disbanded and the fleet dispatched to London. The weather cooled and Harold took the court to Westminster; the fyrd dispersed to their villages and the harvest was gathered. Harold was not convinced that William had given up hope, but he knew that his army could stand it no longer; the harvest had to be gathered and people fed. The English people were farmers, not warriors. They always had been, and now the harvest of the land took precedence over its defence.

It meant that the south coast of England was now totally undefended.

Chapter Forty-Eight
Saint-Valery, Normandy, September 1066

Sunset, Tuesday 12th September. William's ship took the gentle wash from the shore with ease and rounded the point ahead of the main body of the fleet. The fleet had left Dives and were on course for the port of Saint-Valery, where they would await the wind to bear them to England. On William's insistence, he had travelled alone with the crew and a select company of knights; Will and Odo were in separate ships, to avoid all of them drowning at once should they be shipwrecked. Whoever survived would hold the duchy safe with Matilda until Robert came of age.

William lit the lamp at the prow of the ship and marvelled at the soft glory of the sunset. Behind him, the fleet – his fleet – stretched all along the coast and God willing they would all weigh anchor outside Saint-Valery before it was too dark. He sniffed the sea-air. The salty tang made him tired, as it had all of them, but there was little time to sleep anyhow. The grey coast of Normandy lay ahead, broken by the estuary of the Somme river. The sun lit up the sky like a Viking funeral-burning. William heard the muffled shout and splash as the anchor hit the water and thought how his ancestor Rolf the Viking must have felt when he came to Normandy two centuries ago, to carve out a new land from the continent and populate it with Northmen: Normans. Well, the Viking blood still ran strong and they were heading once again for the ancient invasion ground of England.

William stepped into the rowing boat at the ship's side. The army would sleep on board the boats tonight, but their duke would rest in Saint-Valery, where Matilda and Robert were coming. From the small boat, he could hear the laughter in the ships around him, and the clinking of cups. Most of the men seemed in high spirits, pleased to be on the move. But unless the wind changed, they would go no further. It was a question of how long the high spirits of the men could outlast the wind.

The rowing boat bumped against the wooden pier and the two rowers shipped oars. The low jetty was illuminated by a series of oil lamps. William stumbled from the boat, wobbling a little and glad of the strong arm that reached out to him. He had already puked up his breakfast and was looking forward to standing on dry land. He gripped the side and pulled himself onto the boards. They creaked a little under his weight, but at least they didn't pitch and heave. It was quite strange. He felt dizzy.

'You're safe, then.'

Matilda was standing near the edge of the pier, a shawl wrapped round her huddled shoulders, the flickering lamps lighting her face, her pale beauty drawn and tired. Behind her, the sun had become a thin sliver of yellow. It would be gone in a moment.

'Of course I am.' William took his cloak and put it over her shawl. He stooped and kissed her forehead. 'Is Robert with you?' Matilda nodded. 'I want him to be here, to witness our departure.' His face darkened. 'If we do depart, that is. Otherwise my own son shall think me a fool.' It was quite dark now, the black waters occasionally punctuated by the bobbing lamps of the ships as they waited in the bay. 'If the wind doesn't change soon, the men will desert. I can't feed them beyond the end of the month. Many more weeks of waiting and they'll be at war with each other, all these Bretons, Angevins, Normans and mercenaries and God knows what else I've got penned up on this coast.' William's voice cracked in the darkness. 'And I don't honestly know whether I can hold them together much longer.'

*

The chamber in Winchester was bright from the flaming torches and the roaring fire in the hearth. Harold studied each of them in turn. Edith, trying so hard to be of help until the crisis was past; Eadgyth, come from Guildford with his sons, Godwin, Magnus and Edmund. His brothers, Gyrth and Leofwine. And Stigand.

'I tell you he is not coming,' Harold said.

Nobody answered, in dispute, agreement, or otherwise so Harold spoke again. 'He's not coming this summer. Not now, not ever. The wind isn't right for him, and he'll not keep his rabble of an army together for much longer.'

'I am inclined to agree,' Leofwine said.

'Gyrth?'

Gyrth looked up from the fire and said slowly: 'You speak good sense. It does seem that he's left it too late and that unless the weather changes I don't see how he can come.'

Since the disbanding of the fyrd six days ago Harold had been trying all sorts of ways to convince himself that William was not coming. There were many reasons: his men had backed down, the mercenaries wanted their pay, the wind wasn't right. He would not be coming this year. And if not this year, then not at all. This was the one and only chance William had. And he'd missed it.

'And the Hardrada?' asked Eadgyth.

Harold shrugged. 'There are rumours that he is at the mouth of the Tyne but nothing is certain yet. Edwin and Morcar can hold York for us until we arrive. The weather is against Hardrada, too.' Since the end of August, the weather had steadily worsened and instead of the interminable blue skies of July and August, grey clouds threatened rain.

Harold turned to Stigand. 'What do you advise, archbishop?'

Stigand glanced up at the king. It was not a look of assured friendship or comfort. Relations between Harold and Stigand had cooled considerably since the coronation. Over the tense months of the summer Stigand had made no secret of the fact that if Harold lost the kingdom, then he would lose his office as archbishop. Harold, in turn, had pointed out that where Stigand stood to lose his office, he would lose his life. Their fates were bound together whether they liked it or not, and when the great crisis was over, both sensed that the animosities would unravel, but until then they'd have to go forward together.

'I suggest we wait here,' said the churchman. 'You have three thousand housecarls with you. And once the fyrd has gathered the harvest in another week or two, you can recall them. It is your right to recall the fyrd in times of dire need.' Stigand smiled mirthlessly. 'And this is indeed a time of emergency. So ... we wait here and keep watch. We don't take action either in the north or the south until both armies can unite.'

'Wise words, archbishop.' Harold nodded his thanks. 'Then we wait. If need be, until Christmas.'

*

Harold didn't have to wait that long. On 16th September, Harald Hardrada landed off the river Humber with over three hundred ships. It was said to be the greatest Viking fleet ever to put to sea and was led by the undisputed legendary warrior of his age.

On 18th September the king of Norway was approached by Tostig Godwinsson, exiled earl of Northumbria, who pledged his lifelong loyalty to the king of Norway. Together, the rebel English army and Viking force pushed up the mouth of the Humber and landed the ships at Ricall.

They marched to York – where else? – wholly confident that the former Viking capital would remember her heritage and throw her gates open to the Norsemen. But when the town came onto the horizon on the morning of 20th September, they found the road was blocked by a vast army; the mighty northern fyrd under the banners of Mercia and Northumbria, captained by the young brothers, Edwin and Morcar. There was no other way to get into York than to fight that army.

Edwin took command. At twenty, he was the elder of the brothers. The news came from a messenger who had ridden from Goole, the main watch-post, via Selby. He reached York ahead of the main Norwegian army.

The brothers were ready. Fortified by the rumours of Hardrada's presence by the Tyne, his landing at Ricall was half-expected. Though the most recent word from Harold was that the southern fyrd had been disbanded, and that he was not expecting Duke William to come, the northern fyrd was still out and fortunately, was encamped on the flat floodplain of the Ouse at Gate Fulford, two miles from the town.

Edwin's immediate reaction was to send a message to Harold. 'It will take two or three days to get to him,' he assured Morcar. 'And he will be here in nine, at most. We must hold out for twelve days, then.'

But after two days of waiting with the army inside the town walls, it was clear that the townspeople feared a slaughter too much to await the attack on the town. The army would have to fight outside the walls.

On 19th September Edwin held a hurried battle-conference with Morcar and the ealdormen of Derby, Nottingham, Worcester and Northampton.

Alfred of Derby spoke first: 'It's clear that we should fight.' Although a small man, he stood proudly and if he recognised the agony of the dilemma, he showed no sign of it.

But Morcar was adamant in his insistence on keeping the army in the town. 'The people can rot,' he said. 'I say we sit tight until the king arrives with the southern army and together we smash the

Hardrada. With the two armies united, we'll be invincible.'

'And if Hardrada storms the walls of the town he'll have us like rats in a trap, and butcher us like cattle,' replied Alfred. 'There will be no quarter.'

The others nodded at Alfred's words. The thought of being trapped in the tight, narrow streets of York, of the cloying panic of screaming women and butchered men in the gutter was too real a fear. Better to stand in the open fields, where you could swing an axe or sword, see your opponent and at least have a chance to die with a sword in the guts rather than in your back.

'Edwin – the king. We should wait for the king.' Morcar pulled at his brother's sleeve, sensing the growing consensus of opinion forming upon the lips of the ealdormen. It was unfortunate that Archbishop Ealdred wasn't here to talk some sense into them all.

Edwin hesitated. He had the final word, entrusted to him by the king and no other. Morcar could see the light of indecision in his eyes and held his breath. Then a cloud passed over them and his mouth set firm. For good or ill, Edwin had made the decision.

'We leave the town at dawn and form up in the fields by Gate Fulford.'

Chapter Forty-Nine
Gate Fulford, September 1066

Tostig slept well. Since meeting the Hardrada two days ago he had felt healthier than he had for months. The waiting had begun to dispel the determination and sense of purpose he'd held on the Isle of Wight. Malcolm of Scotland had been hospitable – like any Scots king, always eager to cause and exploit dissent in England – lending him money and ships, but it was acceptance by the king of

Norway that Tostig was searching for. Only by joining the legendary Hardrada could he hope to regain his lost position as earl of Northumbria, obliterate the shame and humiliation and wreak his revenge on those who had ousted him. Hardrada had taken his sixty ships and accepted his allegiance.

News travelled from the Orkney Islands to the Highlands and thence to the court of King Malcolm, where Tostig had learned of the Hardrada's arrival. At Ricall he'd joined the greatest army ever to invade England's shores. For once – just for once – Tostig felt that that he had joined the winning side. He wouldn't be like Swegn – the perpetual outcast who had never come back, and who had died shamed and forgotten in a ditch in the land of the Turks. No, Tostig would be victorious.

The morning was clear and bright. The September sun hung like a gold disc in the cloudless blue sky. It was one of those autumn days when it seemed that God had forgotten that summer was over. They rose at first light, breakfasted on salted pork and left several hundred men to guard the ships. Of an army consisting of ten thousand, such a figure was a small loss. Nothing the northern fyrd could put up would equal that. And Harold was in the south, waiting for William. Let him wait.

The road from Ricall to York ran for ten miles on a direct route. The Norwegian army made rapid time, but not rapid enough; at Gate Fulford, south of York, they found that the northern army had chosen to make its stand.

And every man outside the gates of York knew then that beneath the blue sky, the grass would soon be stained red, and that the tranquil fields would become a roaring, screaming arena of death.

'It is his banner I fear more than his men.'

Edwin was staring into the distance, shading his eyes from the sun and trying to distinguish the banner of the Hardrada from the dust and men. The hot summer had baked the roads stone-hard, but the surface retained a fine layer of dust. The thousands of marching soldiers rendered the use of scouts unnecessary: Edwin and Morcar had seen the approaching Norwegian host from miles away.

'His banner is the Landwaster,' Edwin went on. 'It depicts a huge black raven. An image of death. And they will shout his name: Hardrada! Hardrada!'

'How do you know that?' said Morcar, searching for the banner in the dust clouds.

'Harold told me.'

'We should have stayed in the town, you know. Those were Harold's orders.'

'It's too late now,' said Edwin, but his stubbornness failed to mask the truth. 'The townspeople will never allow us back in. We must make our stand here.'

*

The message arrived in London at dawn of the 20th. Harold broke open Edwin's seal and read it quickly.

'Christ Jesus,' he swore softly. 'He's here.'

Shouting for Gyrth and Leofwine and a clerk, he dressed himself, seeing that the exhausted rider – the sixth in a relay set up between York and London – was fed and housed. The message had taken a day and a night to reach them.

Gyrth and Leofwine stumbled into the chamber, half-awake and half-dressed.

'He's here,' said Harold, waving the letter.

'William?'

'No. Hardrada. We leave at noon at the latest,' Harold said. He had been wrong, and he knew it. But there was still time. 'The fyrd can join us on the way.'

'What about William?' Leofwine's face was white. 'What are we to do if he comes...?'

'He won't come now. It is too late. Hardrada is here and we must fight him.' Harold's voice was iron-hard. 'Go and call out the fyrd; tell them to march to York at the greatest speed they can.' He turned to his secretary and said: 'Put it in writing that on no account are Edwin and Morcar to leave the walls of the city of York. *On no account.* Emphasise that. Tell them to keep the army in check until I arrive.' He clicked his fingers and the clerk nodded frantically, seeing the urgency of the moment. 'Hurry, man!' Harold dug his ring into the hot wax. It was his Wessex ring, and not the royal seal, but no matter. 'Take it now.'

The clerk finished writing and scurried off to find a rider. Harold watched him go. Pray God it reached York before Edwin and Morcar - both young snf headstrong - made an independent decision. *Pray God.*

*

The sun had gone behind the clouds. What had promised to be a day of warmth and brightness had darkened into a cold, autumnal day.

'Perhaps God knows there is to be a battle here today,' said Morcar, looking at the sky.

Edwin snorted. 'If He knew that, he would stop us killing one another.'

It was ten o'clock and Edwin was ready. He had spread the entire army along in a great line on the west bank of the Ouse, blocking the road to York. Less than half a mile away, the Norwegian army was busily preparing itself for battle.

Both armies would fight on foot. There were few archers and no mounted soldiers. Hardrada was lining up his army to face the English man to man. The two lines would come together and it would be a hand-to-hand struggle of the worst and bloodiest sort. There would be no escape, no scope for retreat, and any advance could only be over a dead body.

They could see the Landwaster banner now, fluttering in the very wind that had ushered in the clouds to cover the sun – as if hiding the eyes of an innocent from an act of evil.

'Will the men stand and fight?'

Morcar's question had haunted Edwin all night. At the sight of the Landwaster, the terrible realisation that the Hardrada was here in England, he'd thought it enough to break the men before the battle even started. But no; if they ran, where would they run to? They could only run to York, where they would die like rats in the streets. But give a man the chance to fight or die, and he'd fight first.

'They'll stand.'

Edwin tensed. For some moments now, the opposing ranks had been still. 'They're coming on to us,' he said, and shouted: 'Prepare arms!' The call was repeated along the line and where a man could afford it, he drew a sword; others wielded axes of varying sizes, but most held simple spears, daggers and clubs – not unlike those in the Norwegian ranks.

A trumpet blared to the front of them and a tremendous roar went up. The roar became a shout, a single chant, intense and deadly clear, just as Edwin had said: *Hardrada! Hardrada!* And the Norwegians came on, running across the field.

It had begun.

Tostig raised his sword with the others and felt a surge of elation flood through him. A trumpet blared and the roar went up. *Hardrada! Hardrada!* How could they lose? Hardrada was standing ten men away from Tostig, taller than any man in the field, his helmet gleaming in the daylight, his double-headed axe swinging alongside the banner, the Landwaster. They could not lose: they were invincible.

Tostig was swept along in the charge, screaming his leader's name with the rest of them. The rank stench of sweat and fear mingled with the euphoria that was the scent of battle all around him. Men dared death to come and take them. He ran, pressed shoulder to shoulder with the men next to him. The spittle dribbled down his chin, unchecked, outward sign of his fury and the battle-rage inside. His feet sank into the soft grass – it was a flood plain, he remembered – but they pushed on. Ten yards away the rigid shield-wall of the English army held firm. They hadn't flinched at the awesome sight of the coming Norwegians, instead locking arms and starting their own momentum forward.

The two armies met with a shattering crash of shields and clang of steel. So heated were the swords banging upon each other that Tostig was reminded of a smithy's forge. Now that both sides had finished their charge, men were choosing opponents for the man-to-man struggle. Tostig picked an opponent and swung his sword. The blow did not connect; instead, his shield shattered under a blow from the axe opposite.

The face in front of him was a mask of fear, his axe wet with blood, but not Tostig's blood. The man had already killed. Tostig kicked out, caught the man in the groin. He doubled up in agony, and never saw the sword that sliced into the back of his neck.

Tostig grunted, wrenched at the blade and bent to take the man's shield, cutting the strap clear from the dead shoulders. He looked around. The two forces had separated into groups and couples hacking at one another. The Norwegians continued to shout *Hardrada! Hardrada!* But the English were answering with their own war cry: *Out! Out!*

Above them, the grey clouds opened and a soft rain began to fall. God certainly did not approve.

Edwin had placed the housecarls at the front. They were the professional troops, men who lived to fight, trained from an early age for this moment. They would bolster the confidence of the peasant farmers, the mass fyrd behind them, and encourage them to stand.

But the moment the armies met, Edwin lost all control. Harold would have told him that all commanders lose control when the battle begins. His actions and commands were confined to the screaming, swearing group of men within yards of him, intent on killing each other; it was all he could do to stay alive. The roar of the Norsemen reached a crescendo, hammering into his ears until he thought they would burst. He shouted back, 'Out! Out!' and wondered for a second if it was Tostig's face he saw briefly by the Landwaster. The roar seemed to go and on, until he realised it was the rain.

It was pouring down. In minutes, the flood plain became a bog and the water-logged earth was churned into a bloody quagmire. Both forces stood still, unable to move forward or back, each fighting for the advantage.

It was a struggle to remain upright in the mud. The Norseman squaring up to him raised a wicked spear, but slipped and was down, face first in the mud in a manoeuvre that was almost comical but for the cry of fear that revealed his desperate position. Without mercy, Edwin capitalised on the man's misfortune and brought his sword down on his neck with such force that it was all but severed the head from the shoulders. He drew a ragged breath, gagging at the stench of blood and a disembowelled corpse nearby, and struggled back through the mud, searching for Morcar.

The line was holding firm and the way to York was still blocked.

Tostig peered at the face glaring back at him. The shield hid most of it, but the eyes were wide with shock and recognition.

'I know you,' said the warrior.

Tostig gritted his teeth and slammed his sword down on the wet helmetless head. It ducked, and the steel met the shield. The shield splintered, but the sword stuck fast in the wood.

Grunting with fear, Tostig wrenched at the sword, but it didn't move. It was stuck fast. The face reappeared and beside it, a great axe. Tostig almost dropped his sword when he saw the face.

It was Morcar.

They stared at each other frozen together in the roar of battle, immobilised by the moment of recognition. Then at once, both pulled at the shield and the sword. They came apart and the two men staggered back, stumbling and slipping in the mud.

'You destroyed my father,' said Morcar at last. His face was chalk-white, his eyes burning darkly. 'None of this would have happened but for you!'

Morcar held up his splintered shield but Tostig slipped round it, probing for the unprotected leg. This was too ambitious a manoeuvre in the mud, and he fell forward onto his nose, feeling something break. He twisted onto his back. He sensed the shadow of the axe hovering above him. He closed his eyes.

When he opened them, Morcar had gone. He rolled over, ignoring the water and mud. He felt the warmth of his own urine down his leg. There was no pain in his nose. Yet.

He looked round. The Norwegian army was running, free of the mud, and the English were backing off, retreating.

The line had broken.

*

Edwin sensed a movement to the left. He and his men were in the centre, and the right was holding. But the left was wavering. Morcar was on the left but he could not see him in the driving rain. The Norwegians to his front, also sensing movement, pushed forward with renewed vigour.

Then Morcar appeared, his face streaked with blood running from a cut above his eye. He stumbled against Edwin and sobbed for breath.

'The flank has gone, crumbled. Hardrada must have swum the river and come behind us...we're finished.'

Edwin's instinct accepted the truth. They should have stayed in the town and waited for Harold.

All around them men were running now, back to the town, away from the ditch and river.

'I saw Tostig,' gasped Morcar.

Edwin's guilt at disobeying Harold's orders turned to revulsion and hate. The pain he felt against himself he now turned on the Godwinssons: all of this was their fault, not his. 'Curse Tostig. And curse his brothers, including the king. God rot the Godwinssons.' Edwin was shouting now, and a man died a few yards from where they stood, one leg hacked off at the knee by a mighty axe, a fountain of blood drenching them. Edwin grabbed hold of Morcar's arm and hauled him to his feet. 'It's finished! The day is Hardrada's. Let's get away now.'

'We cannot leave the field yet. We could regroup, fight on...'

'No!' Edwin screamed. 'I refuse to die in a cause that is not mine, not yours. Let the damned Godwin brood kill each other.'

Tostig ran with the others, forcing his tired legs through the mud, hacking and stabbing at the unprotected backs fleeing before him. The rain had stopped, but his line of vision was unclear. He did not know how long the battle had been going on. He felt fit to drop.

English and Norwegians lay twisted in a deadly embrace. Many of the fallen were wounded, groaning and screaming for help, bloody hands clutching piteously at torn flesh, bowels, limbs and body parts all around them, the stench of excrement, blood and vomit nauseous in the extreme.

Tostig ran through it all, occasionally hacking downwards and ending a plea for help, breathing deep that stench which for him was the sweet smell of success. The narrow channel of the Ouse was jammed with bodies; the water itself was red with blood. Triumphant Norwegians hacked and stabbed at the defenceless English, drowning and eviscerating them in turn.

'Name of God.'

The words were squeezed from his lips without conscious effort. He stopped running, rooted to the spot, then dropped to his knees and uttered a prayer, shutting his eyes to the horror, seeking refuge in the only thing that seemed sane after this. This wasn't war. It was pure butchery.

'Tostig Godwinsson!'

Tostig jerked round, expecting a sword thrust to his chest. The Hardrada was advancing towards him, bearing a sword black with blood in his right hand, while the left held an axe with smeared blood and brains on the blade. Tostig stood up and allowed himself to be embraced.

'The slaughter is great.' The Norwegian leader smiled down at him. It is always so with the losing side in any battle.' He inclined his head to the river and the floating corpses.

'What now?' Tostig felt bone-weary. The elation had left him, like a spirit exorcised, leaving him empty and sickened.

'Jorvik. After this, the town will surrender immediately. We'll take hostages and rest. There'll be no killing in the town.'

In the darkening distance the surviving English kept running, but the gates of the town were closed to them. No quarter was being given; those too slow were cut down.

The killing would carry on long after dark.

*

Edwin dragged Morcar into the copse and wiped the blood from his eye. The bleeding, profuse a few minutes before, had slowed to a trickle, but Morcar would suffer in the days to come. 'The horses,' he gasped. 'Must get to the horses.'

He staggered on, Morcar following as best he could through his blood-soaked vision, praying that the baggage was untouched.

They had left the horses the other side of the village. There was no sign of them. The small group of hovels was deserted, the inhabitants having fled to the town the moment it was known a battle was to be fought.

'The smithy,' said Morcar. 'We'll steal some.'

It was a good bet there would be horses in the smith's barn, forgotten by the villagers and missed by the Norwegians.

There were. Edwin breathed deeply, inhaling the aroma of sweet-smelling straw and warm horse-sweat

– a welcome relief from the stench of battle they had come from.

'These will do.' Morcar passed him a bridle. 'We'll head for London and pray God we meet Harold on the way.'

Edwin was filled with silent dread at the coming meeting. It must happen, but he did not want it to. How was he to tell Harold that in one single day the entire army of Mercia and Northumbria had been slaughtered?

Chapter Fifty
Doncaster, September 1066

Noon. Sunday 23rd September.

Harold dismounted and felt his knees crack. The pain in his backside was enough to make a man pray for eternal sleep. The housecarls around him were likewise rubbing their sore limbs and cursing their leader for setting a pace fit to run from the devil himself.

It was two and a half days since the message had arrived bearing news of Hardrada's landing. During that time the three thousand housecarls had force-marched northwards from London at a speed they hadn't known was possible. They were ahead of the fyrd, the thousands of foot straggling along behind as best they could, but morale was high; they were – at last – going to war.

Leofwine pushed through the horses and resting men to Harold's side and took a deep drink from his flask. The people of the town pressed forward food and ale to the troops, promising to feed the infantry on their arrival. A girl kissed a housecarl amid cheers and blushes.

'The people rely on us,' said Leofwine, looking at the crowd.

'And well they might.' Harold smiled at his brother. 'I feel confident of victory. If we continue with this speed we'll catch the Norwegians half-asleep.'

Then the housecarls parted to let a rider through. 'I must see the king!' the rider was shouting.

'Is it Gyrth?' Leofwine craned his neck to see who was shouting so imperiously for the king.

Harold shook his head. 'Doesn't sound like Gyrth.'

The rider pushed through the remaining guards in his way and dropped to his knees before Harold.

It was Edwin.

Harold's face drained of all colour. There could only be one reason why Edwin was here. He would never have left his troops otherwise.

For a long moment the two stared at each other. Then someone in the crowd recognised the earl of Mercia's tear-streaked face and the whispered recognition became a roar of consternation.

Edwin's voice was hoarse. 'We shouldn't have left the town...the men fought bravely...the Norsemen were too strong for us.'

Harold crouched beside the young earl. 'What are you saying, lad?'

'We fought a battle – at Gate Fulford. And we lost.' Edwin choked and swallowed hard. 'The army is gone...completely destroyed.'

'My God,' Harold took a deep breath. 'Why didn't you obey my message, why didn't...?' He stopped. They had never got the message. It had arrived too late.

'We had no message,' Edwin confirmed. 'The battle was fought on the twentieth.'

'How many men do you have alive?' Harold helped Edwin to his feet and placed the flask to his lips.

After he'd taken a long drink, Edwin said, 'About two thousand survived. Mostly of the fyrd – they ran first. The housecarls stood and died. To a man.'

'Christ's wounds,' Leofwine spluttered. The worst possible had happened. The two armies of England were separated and one had been wiped out, its best troops gone in a day.

'I could not believe you'd come this far so fast,' Edwin said, rising to his feet.

'We'll be at Tadcaster in a day or so.'

'Surely not?' Incredulity showed through Edwin's exhausted features.

'Yes,' said Harold curtly. 'Our only hope now is the advantage of surprise. Hardrada won't expect us for at least a week. If we can catch him unawares, it'll make up for our fatigue and smaller numbers.' He laid a hand on Edwin's shoulder. 'You have done your duty for me, brother. You must rest.' He paused, and asked hesitantly: 'And Morcar, is he...?'

Edwin nodded. 'He survived, yes. He...he said he saw Tostig –'

'Tostig?' Harold's face hardened.

'Yes. In the battle.'

'Did he kill him?'

'No. The line broke; he had to fall back.'

'More's the pity.' Harold's mouth was tight with barely contained fury. 'Christ strike my treacherous bastard of a brother into pieces. I'll wager he survived, too.'

But it was pointless to dwell on the disaster. They had to be decisive before word spread and the troops lost their high spirits. Harold signalled to the trumpeter, who sounded the advance. 'Go back to Morcar and gather all the men you can find,' he said to Edwin. 'Join me when you can. We'll be at York, or thereabouts.' He remounted and winced as his tender backside touched the iron-hard saddle.

If Harold was on trial before God, then he had failed the first test beyond all doubt.

*

The small church of Saint-Valery was bare and simple. There were no statues, paintings or frescoes; merely an altar at the east end and a baptism bowl at the west. The villagers were too poor to provide anything extra. It was how William liked churches. It was how the house of God was meant to be.

William knelt. He prayed that the wind would change, that God would grant him victory, and soon.

It was 25th September and the wind continued to blow from the north. The weather vane at the top of the tower resolutely refused to change.

William finished his prayers and walked from the nave, genuflected at the door, and opened it. Will was waiting, as he had told him to, with express commands not to allow anyone to disturb his prayers. His face was serious.

'One of your spies has arrived, William. He says it is urgent.'

The advantage of the persistent northerly wind – and the only advantage – was that messengers could come rapidly from England bearing news of events. It was how they'd heard of Harold's decision to disband the fleet and the English fyrd, news of which had made the waiting all the more unbearable.

William recognised the man: Urse of Elbeuf, from near Rouen. 'What news is it you bring?'

Urse got straight to the point. 'The king of Norway has landed, my lord duke. He was heading for York, the capital of the north of England.'

William's hands involuntarily balled into fists. His prayers had been answered. The worst had happened – for Harold. Unable to feed his army, he'd disbanded the troops and now the Hardrada had come. 'When?' he asked.

'I heard on the twentieth. He landed some days before. King Harold –'

'He is not the king.' Urse flinched at William's rebuff. 'Do not ever call Harold Godwinsson king of England again in my presence.'

'The earl of Wessex left for the north of England immediately.'

Until now, William had been uncertain as to whether Harold would actually forsake the southern coast to repel Hardrada, but now he knew.

'Do you think he will give battle with the king of Norway?'

'I do, my lord duke.'

William said softly to Will FitzOsbern: 'Do you know what I am thinking?'

Will nodded, 'If the wind changes now...'

Both looked up at the weather vane, willing it to turn.

'Tell the men Hardrada has landed. It'll do them good to know there will be no reception for us in England when we get there.'

Please God make the wind change. Please God. William turned on his heel and walked back into the church. There were more prayers to be said.

Approximately four hundred miles to the north of Saint-Valery, Tostig Godwinsson stretched out in the long grass and basked in the warmth of the September sun. The morning of the battle at Gate Fulford had begun like this, but there were no clouds threatening the horizon today. He yawned and thought about the battle. Was it only five days since the horror of that grim meeting? His broken nose testified to the memory of the day; but it was a small price to pay for such a great victory.

After Fulford, they had marched on York, and, with no army to defend them, the townspeople had thrown open the gates without hesitation. Money and food were handed over and negotiations for hostages had begun. The Norwegian army was now at Stamford, east of York and near the royal palace of Aldby, where food and clothing had been requisitioned. One third of the army was with the fleet. Tostig had questioned the king on the wisdom of this, but though it seemed absurd to leave soldiers idly by, Hardrada insisted that the protection of the fleet, and thus the escape route, was almost as vital as waging war. The wounded from Fulford had been taken back too, to rest and recover. Casualties at Fulford had been fewer than two thousand; it was estimated that over five thousand English died in the mud and rain, or afterwards, hunted down in the dark.

A splash and a yell woke Tostig. He looked up and saw the men swimming in the river Derwent. Much of the army was on the east bank, in the meadows. Hardrada had put outposts out on the west bank but beyond them, the ground rose steadily upwards to Gate Helmsley, a small village now deserted by its frightened inhabitants. The west and east banks of the river were linked only by a small, timber bridge, wide enough for only a few men at a time.

Tostig looked enviously at the men swimming in the river. The water appeared cool and inviting. Most of the men around him had taken off their heavy armour – some had taken it back to the boats – and lay in the grass, playing cards, dice, or merely sleeping. Some were drunk. Even the guards up towards the hill seemed to be lolling about in the shade.

Tostig closed his eyes again. It would be good to have a woman now. He thought of Judith. When Hardrada was king, he would divorce her and marry a young bride. He smiled at the thought. Perhaps that was why the villagers had fled, crusty old fathers taking their juicy daughters with them. And well they might, for these Norwegians needed some girls.

Another shout. Louder, hoarser, more urgent. Maybe some idiot was drowning. Then a yell, this time of warning.

Tostig opened a lazy eye. The men in the river were splashing and panicking their way out of the water. The Norwegians up on the hill were running down the slope, screaming and shouting.

A moment later, Tostig saw why. The ridge of Gate Helmsley was lined with thousands of men. An entire army. The sun twinkled on the rows of helmets and hauberks in mocking delight. At the centre, two banners fluttered in the gentle wind: the fighting man and the dragon of Wessex.

It was Harold.

Harold was here.

The banners of the English army moved forward and seven thousand men charged down the hill and into the fields. The Norwegians posted on the watch were swept away. It was like the wrath of God.

Chapter Fifty-One
Stamford Bridge, September 1066

Harold had planned on staying at York after gathering the survivors from Fulford. They had left Tadcaster at dawn, but on arriving at York at nine o'clock they discovered how close the Norwegian host was, and Harold ordered the advance. The last thing the Norwegians would expect was the arrival of the southern fyrd and the king of England at its head.

The village of Gate Helmsley was deserted. The squawking of hens scattered by the soldiers' approach was the sole sign of life. The Norwegian army must be close now.

Gyrth rounded the bend, whipping his horse into a gallop. 'Over the hill,' he said urgently. 'They're resting in the meadows by the Derwent. There are outposts on the west bank – about a thousand men – but the main host is on the eastern side.'

'How many?' asked Harold.

Gyrth rubbed his chin. 'Five thousand at most.'

'He will have left men guarding the fleet. Now's our chance to take him whilst his forces are divided.'

A murmur of grim satisfaction echoed through the ranks of housecarls. Despite the cruel pace of the march, morale was high, and the thought of the Hardrada's men lolling in the sun evoked a glorious image of a blood-soaked revenge for Fulford. Harold gripped the reins of his horse tightly, hardly daring to hope that the march from London could end in this, a complete surprise.

The road took them out of the village and into a small wood at the summit of a hill. Harold spurred forward and cantered into the trees, eager to see what Gyrth had seen. All the agonies from the march were forgotten in this one moment of hope. At the edge of the wood he reined in. His heart missed a beat.

'A gift from God,' breathed Leofwine.

Gyrth came alongside and for a moment the three brothers savoured the scene. Thousands upon thousands of Hardrada's men lay below, resting in the sun.

'Look – those fools are swimming,' said Gyrth, pointing to the river. They were, too, splashing and laughing, in the water, blissfully unaware of the English army above them.

'I wonder where Tostig is,' said Leofwine.

'He's there somewhere,' said Harold. 'We'll get him. Sound the advance. The housecarls will leave all the horses up here and lead the charge; the fyrd can follow as best they can. There's no time to advance in battle-order.'

'We're spotted,' said Gyrth. Harold glanced down; the men on the lookout posts were running towards the river and the small bridge that was the only crossing point.

Harold drew his sword. Around him, the housecarls waited expectantly. One licked his lips, already relishing the revenge for Fulford. Then Harold brought his sword down and the two thousand housecarls moved forward with a roar.

The ragged charge had none of the discipline and co-ordination of the Norman cavalry charge at Dinan, but it served its purpose. The Norwegians fled before them, but the housecarls either cut them down in the long grass or swept them mercilessly into the river.

Harold called a halt close to the bridge. On the east bank, the main host had fled back across the field, leaving their arms and armour in the grass where they had stripped off an hour earlier. One Norseman, still naked from bathing moments ago, lay dead in the reeds, his pale skin gashed red across the stomach, and an expression of horror and surprise etched into his face.

Harold recovered his breath. As yet, his sword – the great sword William had given him, was unbloodied. Others would do the killing. Now was the time to take advantage of the surprise. But the bridge was very narrow. It would give the Norwegians a chance to regroup. 'Gyrth!'

Gyrth came running, his shield on his arm and an axe in his hand.

'Take a hundred housecarls and cross the bridge. Secure the eastern bank.'

Harold watched the fyrd come down the hill and begin the slaughter of those Norwegians now cut off on the west bank. He let them. There could be no quarter after Gate Fulford, and some of the fyrd included survivors of that battle. One Norseman broke free from a group of English men hacking at him and ran for the river. Without hesitation he dived into the rushing waters and disappeared from view. Fully armed and bleeding heavily, he drowned.

Gyrth had his men over the bridge but was encountering fierce opposition from the rearguard of Hardrada's force. In the distance the Landwaster came forward and Harold sensed that the Norwegian troops would advance soon. It was time to form up the fyrd and to stop the slaughter on this side of the bridge.

A great shout came from the other bank. A huge Norwegian, stripped to the waist and armed with a great axe, cut a swathe to the bridge and stood in the middle of it, shouting obscenities.

He was a berserker.

Famed and feared from the coast of Ireland to the markets of Byzantium, the berserkers were unstoppable Viking warriors, worked into such frenzy in battle that they killed anything or anyone – even their own men – within their reach. They had no fear, and were not afraid to die, either: a factor that was worth twenty men.

A man such as this could swing the battle in favour of the shocked and surprised Norwegians. The berserker's comrades defended his back, leaving him free to block the bridge, which was wide enough for only two men to pass at once. Meanwhile Gyrth's escape route was cut off; the Norwegian army – now pushing forward with greater energy – would soon surround and kill him and his men.

'He must be stopped,' said Leofwine, seeing what was happening.

Behind them, the English fyrd had ceased killing the isolated Norwegians and waited silently in line.

'Send a man to fight him.' Harold pointed at the berserker. Leofwine ran off and called for a volunteer. Ten men stepped forward, but there was room enough only for a few at a time.

The first was dispatched before even raising his sword. The axe flashed down and bit deep into his waist. With a contemptuous kick, the Norwegian pushed him into the swirling water, his guts spilling out as he fell.

The second was decapitated after his sword stuck fast in the boards of the bridge. The third managed to get a blow in, but backed off so hastily that he tripped backwards and was sliced like meat on a butcher's slab.

Behind the berserker, Gyrth's fight was becoming desperate. The main Norwegian host was marching in full battle order and with growing confidence. Harald Hardrada was at the head, Tostig by his side. They were cheering at the success of the berserker. 'Come to me, you English bastards,' the Norwegian shouted in English. 'Come on!'

The end came suddenly, and rather ingloriously. Unseen by the Norwegian, a housecarl had found a swill-tub and was paddling up to the bridge.

The English held their breath as the housecarl reached the bridge and crouched in the rushes. Above him, the berserker continued to scream abuse at the English through foam-flecked lips, his great beard and enraged face sprayed with English blood.

'Do it,' whispered Harold. 'Do it now.'

The housecarl in the swill-tub raised a long spear and pulled himself under the bridge. A split second later, the spear reappeared through a gap in the boards and thrust directly into the Norwegian's unprotected groin.

The berserker screamed like a stuck pig and fell writhing to the ground.

With a mighty roar, Harold led the vanguard of the English army across the bridge, trampling the giant Norwegian into the river. Gyrth regrouped his men and the Norwegians, seeing their hero felled, backed off in dismay. Gyrth was wounded. He gave Harold a painful grin. The wound was on his upper arm and the bleeding was profuse but it was worse than it looked.

'Get to the rear,' Harold ordered.

Leofwine formed up the shield-wall with the housecarls at the front. They faced the battered and depleted Norwegian army not twenty yards away in silence, each army studying the other and waiting for what must happen. The Norwegians were aggrieved, the English jubilant and ready to go on. For the first time since the battle began, Harold could hear the gurgling waters of the Derwent and the birds in the small woods beyond the field.

'There's Tostig,' murmured Leofwine.

Harold picked him out. 'Tostig,' he called. Tostig, standing under the Landwaster banner, lowered his shield. 'You've broken your nose.'

Tostig said nothing, his face tense with fear.

'If you join me now, I offer you a free pardon,' Harold said.

There was a grumble of disapproval from the housecarls but Harold ignored it. 'What do you say?'

Harold thought he saw a shadow of a smile on Tostig's face, but whatever it was, it vanished as soon as it had come.

'Never,' said Tostig, his mouth twisting with a hatred that made Harold flinch. 'I'll not join the man who'd bed his own mother to become king of England.' Someone in the Norwegian ranks translated and the Jomsvikings – the Norwegian crack troops – at the front roared with laughter.

Harold gripped his sword tightly. So be it, then.

'If the Hardrada wants my land badly enough, he'll have to fight for it,' he shouted back. 'But if he loses, I'll still offer him land.' Harold looked pointedly up and down at the enormous Norwegian king. 'About seven feet should do it.'

This time it was the turn of the English housecarls to laugh.

Harold raised his arm. All down the line the housecarls shuffled closer, shield joining shield. Opposite them the Jomsvikings did the same. There would be no charge, but rather a slow shuffle into a stalemate of death. And the river was behind them. There was no escape route.

Harold brought his arm down and the housecarls moved forward, shouting: *Out! Out! Out!* working themselves into a killing fury. The Norwegians shouted back: *Thor aid! Thor aid!* They raised their swords, axes and spears, and prepared for the fight.

Tostig shrank back behind the Norwegian shield-wall and swallowed hard. God be thanked he was not directly facing Harry, because he did not want to exchange blows with him. The shock of Harold's sudden arrival was enormous, but the words of defiance Tostig had just uttered did not in any way reflect how he really felt. How in hell had Harry marched so far and so fast? How could Tostig have so underestimated him? And now, this.... a thousand men were dead, three thousand were at the boats and the remainder were here, shocked and barely armed for battle.

Tostig's hands, slippery with sweat, gripped the haft of the axe nervously. At Fulford he'd used a sword; today it would be an axe.

There was no time to think any longer. The Jomsviking in front of him was hacking and stabbing at an Englishman, shouting his anger and fear with all the others. In the second rank Tostig waited his turn, watching for a gap which he would close up.

How long he waited, he didn't know. The lines of fighting men, locked together in grotesque intimacy, moved back, then forwards, then back again. He smelt the sweat, the fear and waited his turn. Men died, others filled their places, but Tostig remained in the second row. To his right, the Hardrada whirled his axe above his head, and somewhere to the right of him was Harold. Tostig wondered whether he was still alive. He must be; if not, the tight ranks of the English would have crumbled and fled by now.

Then the Norwegian in front of him was cut down by a flying spear. Tostig stepped over the body and faced again the ugly hatred of his countrymen opposite him.

*

Eyestein Orre regarded the messenger with disbelief.

'Bullshit,' he said finally.

'It's true,' insisted the messenger. 'I swear on Christ's cross it's true.'

Eyestein shook his head. 'I can't believe that Harold Godwinsson is in the north. It's not possible.'

'I tell you it's true!' roared the messenger. 'I've just come from the battlefield.' His shout woke several of the men who were lying sunning themselves in the boats. There were three thousand men under Eyestein's command: one third of Hardrada's total force, guarding the boats and awaiting the arrival of the hostages from York. But if what this man said was true, then they would be needed at Stamford – God help them, they would be essential.

'It's true,' said the messenger again.

Eyestein stared at the sky for a moment. 'If you're right,' he said, slowly. 'If you're right...'

'I swear on Christ's corpse and all the souls of Valhalla, it's true,' said the messenger.

Eyestein shivered. He turned to the men. 'Get up,' he shouted. 'Move!' His bellow roused those around him. 'Get to your weapons!' he screamed. Harold Godwinsson's army is upon the host at Stamford!'

They looked at him as incredulously as he had done the messenger, but when they saw how serious he was, with growing fear they rose and began to put on armour.

'Move!'

Eyestein watched the soldiers arm and, satisfied they would follow, started to move at a slow run. He hoped to God they would not be too late.

Harold sensed the approaching dusk. Like a thick cloak placed around their shoulders, it enveloped and gradually smothered them, like the exhaustion of battle itself. The Norwegian shield-wall had retreated, their losses at the surprise beginning of the battle now starting to tell.

It became difficult to see where to strike in the increasing darkness; it was a matter of luck if a blow connected, or bad luck if the next man went down with a cry.

'Harold!'

The hoarse voice was familiar, but dimmed amongst all the other exhausted cries. Harold couldn't see who it was. He warded off a blow that materialised out of the dark.

'Harold!'

This time he picked out Tostig, recognised the tight mouth drawn across the pale features, a lock of blond hair protruding from his helmet. It was just light enough to see the glare in his eye. Harold pushed forward and brother faced brother. Neither spoke. Harold raised his sword, wanting to destroy the man who'd broken the unity of the Godwins and brought England to the brink of destruction.

Harold lowered the sword, staring at the mass of jostling men around him. He couldn't strike his own brother.

'Tostig...?'

But Tostig had vanished into the gloom. Perhaps he'd not seen Tostig at all. He was so tired he could sleep forever.

'Hardrada is dead!'

The shout brought him to his senses. Harold searched for the banner, the dreaded Landwaster, but couldn't see it. The Norwegians were moving back fast.

'Hardrada is dead!'

The cry was taken up all along the ragged line and the Englishmen surged forward, confident of victory, scarcely able to believe their ears that the great one, the Hard One, really was dead. The Norwegians turned and ran.

Tostig heard the shout and looked for the banner but couldn't see it. Norwegians around him were running back in terror. He cursed. He could have sworn it was Harold he'd seen minutes before. So sure, he'd shouted his name.

'Stop!' Tostig screamed at the running men. 'Come back, regroup – I am Tostig Godwinsson! Stand with me! To me, I say, to me!'

They ignored him and ran on. It would become a massacre if they didn't run fast enough. So they ran.

Tostig was aghast at the sight of the panicking Norsemen. 'God curse you all then!' he screamed at their departing backs, but as he turned to face the victorious Englishmen, his head met the downward swing of an axe which cut straight through his helmet and into his skull. He didn't even see it and died instantly.

On the edge of the woods, Eyestein Orre surveyed the scene in wordless horror.

He had arrived just in time to lead his men to their certain deaths.

*

Dawn broke with all the promise of a fresh new day. But the air was far from fresh; it was thick with the sweet sickly stench of the dead.

Harold's army camped overnight in the village of Gate Helmsley. He rose from his bed reluctantly when the light crept above the trees. For the first time in years he didn't want to face the world, even after so great a victory.

'We've found him.' Leofwine was at the door to the house. 'He's outside in the cart.'

Harold stumbled wearily into the daylight. With his arm bandaged and crusted black with dried blood, Gyrth stood over the cart weeping unashamedly, blind to Harold's approach.

Tostig's death-wound was to the head. An axe, Harold thought dispassionately; Tostig's blond, matted hair covered most of the wound and beneath it, he looked peaceful – and so young. The lines that had made him ugly with rage had vanished. He was a boy again, scampering across the glade during the hunt. *Good shot Harry! Good shot – you're the best in the family!* And the young man asking for money from his big brother, his laughter echoing across the hall, the girls looking askance at him, hoping for those blue eyes to alight on them for the evening and dance the night away.

Harold bent over the cart, put his hand on Tostig's cold cheek and felt the tears prick his eyes and run down his face, unchecked, unstoppable, uncontrollable. 'Oh Tostig...' he said, and tried to take a breath, but found he couldn't, and sobbed instead, a great, racking sob. 'You fool...you poor, silly fool...'

It was the end of them all; he knew it.

Chapter Fifty-Two
Saint-Valery, Normandy, September 1066

Dawn. Wednesday, 27th September. William rose and pushed back the shutters, as he always did at dawn, and cursed, as he always did afterwards. It was not good to start each and every day with a curse, but if the wind continued to blow from the north, then he would curse until the day he died. He had run out of prayers and was sick of the dawn at Saint-Valery. He wanted to see the dawn in England, see the white cliffs of Dover.

'No change?' Matilda spoke from the darkness.

'No.' He leant over the bed and kissed her lips before she could utter the platitudes of comfort he'd heard day after day in this godforsaken hole called Saint-Valery. Christ knew why the men had remained, though some had deserted. Booty, he supposed. Some had come too far to pack it in and return. And they were being fed; paid for by the foolish duke who had all but emptied his coffers to fund them. If he ever did reach England, and won the throne, the first thing he'd have to do would be to ransack the treasury, loot the churches and bring everything back here, to pay the Norman people who'd surely starve under next year's crippling taxes.

He broke free of her embrace and with a scowl, said: 'I'll go and see whether I have any men left.'

*

He woke his son Robert and together they went in search of breakfast, finding Will FitzOsbern with his personal guard. They all stood up at the duke's arrival and made room for William and his son.

The fourteen-year old Robert bore little resemblance to his father. Where the duke was tall and broad-shouldered, Robert was short and slightly built. He had had the misfortune to inherit his mother's short stature when the age he lived in demanded he appear warrior-like. Robert was aloof and, Will suspected, arrogant. He was nicknamed 'Short-trousers' because of his diminutive height, but behind his back he was, to many, 'short-arse'. Fickle, pompous and weak, he encouraged a following of like-minded young men. William doted on his second son, Richard, who was so much more like him in build and character. But Robert was his mother's favourite, and could do no wrong in her eyes. Will didn't like him, and the dislike was mutual: Robert was jealous of Will's close relationship with his father, and of his position as steward of Normandy, which gave him access to all areas of power. Since the day he'd been invested as duke, as William's heir, Robert had taken to thinking that the duchy was his already.

'I've come to a decision,' said William, once breakfast was finished and the men dismissed. 'This is to be kept secret of course, but I'm giving it one more week.' His voice was as taut as a bow-string. 'Then it's over. If the wind hasn't changed in our favour by then, I'll cancel the invasion.'

'Are you sure?' asked Will.

William nodded. 'The food will last a while longer, but the money is running out fast. I'll not beggar Normandy.'

'But now that we've got this far – and you'll never get such an army together again...' Will faltered, seeing that William's mind was made up. Robert stared at the ground. Will had the sudden, cynical thought that perhaps the boy resented losing his new-found independence so soon, if his father was not, after all, going to England.

'You'll come to mass today, won't you?' asked William, breaking into his thoughts.

'Yes, of course.'

'Good.' William walked on with his son, leaving Will to ponder on how a man he'd known for so long could still baffle him.

The duke had ordered two masses a day to be said in the small church at Saint-Valery. Both were primarily concerned with prayers for a change in the wind and God's aid with the invasion. Will didn't attend the morning mass: trouble had broken out between the Bretons and Angevins. A fight had begun over a woman but escalated rapidly into an excuse to vent frustration at the interminable waiting. He meted out punishment, heard the news of the desertion of twenty more mercenaries from both camps, and ate lunch with his captain.

He managed to attend the second mass, late in the afternoon, and afterwards found his path blocked by William's son, Robert.

'May I speak with you a while, Lord FitzOsbern?'

Will didn't want to spend more time than was necessary with this youth, but he could see that there was something the boy wanted to say, and indicated that he should say his piece.

'I would ask your advice on the matter of my investiture as duke of Normandy. Namely, that if my father is successful in his quest against Harold Godwinsson, and becomes king of England – which God willing he shall – whether I shall then assume full powers as duke of Normandy?'

Will looked hard at the lad's face, thinking it might be a jest, but Robert was serious.

'No,' he said slowly. 'You're only invested with the duchy as William's heir. You are not the duke yet, and nor shall you be until your father is dead. You must understand that.'

Robert shook his head. 'But I am the duke, now...'

'You are not.' Will dropped all pretence of liking the boy, but he didn't care any more. The presumption of the youth was breathtaking. 'William is the duke. And if God favours us, he shall be king of England. King *and* duke; you shall inherit Normandy, at his death, but not before.'

Robert stared back at Will with equal dislike. His lip curled in a sneer of contempt. 'I am old enough. When father was my age –'

'He was a man at your age. More of a man than you will ever be, my boy. He'd seen more and done more than you and your perfumed ponces will do if they live to be a hundred!'

'I hate you,' said Robert. 'You poison father's mind. Mother says –'

'What? What does Matilda say?' Will's hand shot out and grasped the boy's arm, gripping it tightly.

Robert didn't try to free himself but looked steadily back at Will. 'Mother says you are doomed to fail, that it is your fault...'

'Nonsense!' Will refused to believe Matilda could say such things. He'd known her for years, and was well aware of her opposition to this venture. But she'd never say that about him – never. 'You're lying, boy!'

Robert smiled, and in that sly smile, Will saw that the boy was lying and he'd been made a fool of, losing his temper like that.

The shout from the port broke into their thoughts and Will released the boy. Will peered across the village, saw men running, saw the weathervane spinning like a top above the church.

Robert noticed the weathervane too, and for a moment they forgot their differences. 'Look at that,' he said. 'You don't think...?'

The wind had changed. Instead of blowing from the north, it was now coming from a southerly direction. The weathervane ceased turning and settled, pointing triumphantly northwards.

William was in the village when a sailor came running with news.

'What is it?' Matilda came out onto the street to see what the disturbance was.

'The wind has changed at last. My God, we're going to go!' William kissed her. 'Now.'

'No, not now. It is all but dusk...'

'Yes!' William smacked his right fist into his left hand. 'To the boats!' he roared to the soldiers lounging in and around the houses. 'Take up your positions on the boats!'

Will FitzOsbern came hurrying along the street, dodging the running soldiers. 'Are we going now?'

'Yes, damn you,' William grinned. 'We're moving out when we're ready. Tonight. God will change the wind if we tarry.'

'It's divine intervention for sure.' Will smiled back.

'Where's that short-arsed son of mine?' Robert stepped out from behind Will and scowled at his father. William placed his hands on the boy's shoulders. 'There you are, boy. Stop cringing behind people; you're short enough without that, God knows.' Robert's embarrassment was plain to see, but his father hadn't finished. 'I'm relying on you. Do as your mother says and listen to the lords of Avranche and Montgomery. Go back to Falaise now and remain there.'

'God be with you, then, father,' Robert replied in a tone that meant quite the opposite. They embraced briefly but the boy was eager to be away, out of his father's shadow.

'So this is farewell, then,' said Matilda.

William took her hands in his, forcing himself to remain calm. God knows, they'd rehearsed this moment often enough. He glanced at the docks; Odo was standing at the end of the street, hands on hips, laughing at the wind like a mad dog.

Matilda took a silver pendant from her neck and put it around William's. It rested against the chain Richard FitzThurstan had given him so long ago at Falaise when he'd come to claim the duchy.

'It will be next to my heart,' he said. 'I have the holy relics, and will wear those too, when we land.'

'There won't be any room left for your armour at this rate,' said Matilda laughingly.

William smiled back, and saw the tears well up in her eyes.

'I love you,' she whispered, and wrapped her arms around his neck. He lifted her up and put his lips on hers. Behind them, Odo was shouting across to the mass of soldiers and horses rushing to the boats.

'I have to go now.'

'Go on then.' She broke free of him and wiped her eyes. 'God go with you and keep you safe. Send word as soon as you can.'

William nodded, and ran to the docks to where Odo and Robert Montgomery were waiting. He didn't look back.

There was only one way to go now; forward, to England.

To where a dead man had once promised him a throne, and where he would fulfil that promise.

Chapter Fifty-Three
The English Sea, September 1066

It grew dark frighteningly quickly. William's ship was at the fore, the lamps at the stern bobbing insight of the others. It was a clear night and the duke's captain, Reginald of Cabourg, set his course by the stars. William had planned the route long ago: Pevensey would be their destination. The remains of the Roman fort would offer immediate protection of a sort. From there, he would take the cavalry overland to Hastings, where they would meet the infantry in the remainder of the ships. After leaving a guard for the fleet, the whole army would march on London. Spies, guides and his own knowledge accrued over the years had provided the information he needed. There was much that could go wrong. A storm could blow them off course – though the weather was holding now; Harold might have some ships at Pevensey – though most of the fleet had withdrawn to London; and if they couldn't land at Pevensey or Hastings, then they would head for London. It would be the last resort, for the main fleet was in London. But if they couldn't make a safe landing on the south coast, then London it would be.

'Get some sleep, my lord.' Reginald was beside him. 'We are set for the night and the weather will stay calm. There is no more you can do.'

Reginald was right. It was in the hands of the sailors now. William would need all the energy he could muster for the coming weeks.

He slept heavily and deeply for the first time in months. His ship was one of the few which did not have horses aboard.

Reginald's anxious white face was leaning over William as he awoke.

'God is with us this morning, do you agree, Reginald?'

'I wish I could agree, sire.' Reginald said.

'What is it? Are we lost?'

'No, sire. It seems that...the rest of the fleet is lost.'

William got to his feet and scanned the horizon but couldn't see anything in the endless sea. The distant coast of England was just visible but there wasn't another ship in sight. The sky above them was cloudy, with patches of blue, while the sea twinkled its blue-green emptiness mockingly at them.

William spread his arms in despair. 'Where are they?'

Reginald shrugged. 'We're on course for Pevensey. The sea was calm through the night. I cannot understand it.'

Several anxious minutes passed. Then a crew member shouted: 'Ships astern!'

William narrowed his eyes and looked in the direction the look-out was indicating. On the horizon, a ship's mast appeared, then another, and another. A minute later the entire skyline was filled with ships. 'Are they ours?' he asked, cutting short the excited chatter.

'A red cross on a white pennant,' shouted the look-out.

'That's Odo,' William laughed. 'They're ours! We must have sailed faster than the entire fleet put together.'

The relief was tangible. The knights and the crew broke into laughter and William with them. He caught Reginald's eye, aware that a nasty moment had been averted.

William turned to the knights crowded round him. Most of them were half his age, and in awe of the man whose exploits were legendary. He waved a hand and they fell silent. 'It's time to prepare ourselves and pray to God for victory.' He surveyed their youthful faces. 'You will tell your grandchildren of this day.'

There were no English ships in Pevensey. The Norman fleet moved forward into the bay in a great line, each ship twenty yards from the next, unchallenged and unopposed. The flat-bottomed craft would be landed directly onto the wide beach, where the horses could be led onto land.

William was to go ashore first. 'Ready now, sire.' Reginald was beside him, holding his helmet. William took it and pulled it on. He took a deep breath, suddenly giddy at the enormity of the moment. The ship seemed to be rushing across the green water, dipping slightly as they reached the breaking waves. The beaches stretched ahead for miles. 'Don't slip over, will you, sire?'

William smiled. 'That would be a fool thing to do, to drown on reaching England.' But the warning was not to be taken in jest, for the mail hauberk weighed heavily on his shoulders, reaching down to his knees. And as well as that, there was his sword, helmet, and the shield, strapped to his back.

He grasped the side of the ship and climbed over, readying himself for the shock of impact as the boat hit the shallow beach. When it came, he leapt into the water and strode forward, shivering as the cold penetrated his armour. A great cheer went up behind him, a cheer of thousands of men who'd waited for this moment for so many months. A group of screaming gulls swept overhead and he found himself saying, 'England, England. I'm here at last.'

He glanced behind and saw Odo, Will, Robert and scores of knights jumping into the water, cheering, some praying and a few weeping their thanks for the safe crossing. The water was at William's ankles now, the sun rapidly drying his legs. He was almost there. Then a fresh wave broke immediately behind him and whipped the pebbles from under him. He stumbled, cursed, and fell flat on his face onto the beach.

The cheering stopped. Somewhere above, the gulls flew on, screaming loudly. The sound of the sea became a muffled roar. But the hundreds of men were frozen in horrified silence.

William knew what it meant, he knew what all those men were thinking. To fall on his face on reaching the first ground of England was the worst possible omen. The warm water lapped lazily over him, washing around the contours of his body. He resisted the crazy urge to laugh, and grasped two handfuls of the wet sand. He staggered to his feet, saw the water gurgle its way into the imprint his body had made in the sand, and turned to face the gaping expressions of horror on the faces of the men watching him.

'I have taken England without difficulty!' he shouted, holding up the handfuls of sand. Will, Odo, Robert and those nearest him made no move. The sea roared in the distance. 'It is a good omen! God wills that I should seize England with my own two hands!' He let the sand fall slowly through his fingers.'I have taken England for myself!'

Will FitzOsbern stepped forward, to William's side. 'Duke William is the rightful king of England!' he roared. 'King William of the English!'

All the men were cheering, running through the remaining waves and digging up handfuls of sand for themselves and throwing it up in the sky.

William wiped his hands in relief, ridding himself of the slime and seaweed. He expelled a lungful of air through a dry mouth and cursed the fickleness of mankind, to have so many with you one minute and against you in the next.

'A drink, Will. I need a drink.'

Will passed him a flagon of wine and grinned broadly, shaking his head in mock severity. 'You always were a clumsy bastard.'

William chuckled and drank deeply from the flagon. When his face reappeared, it was serious. 'This clumsy bastard's going to be a king,' he said.

*

The horses and knights were all ashore by noon. It was done speedily and thoroughly and when they were ready, the men mounted up. William was taking no chances; reports of the landing would be on their way north and even now, a defending army might appear and force them back into the sea. The main fleet set sail for Hastings under the command of Robert of Mortain. Odo and Will FitzOsbern were to ride with the duke.

'Shall we burn the village?' asked Will when the last of the ships was out of sight.

'No. Not Pevensey.' William looked at the lines of horsemen. Most of them were Norman knights – of good birth and born to fight in the saddle. 'I'll not have the knights sully their hands with such work. We'll send the mercenaries out to earn their bread when we reach Hastings.' Some of the horses had died on the journey, but they had brought extra horses. Each knight had his war-horse and all were ready and waiting. 'The flower of Norman knighthood,' William said softly. 'They'll get their land.'

He raised an arm and the horn blew a long note. They moved off, helmets glinting in the sun, the papal banner and lion of Normandy at their head.

They reached Hastings before dusk, William pushing a hard pace. They passed several villages, where those inhabitants who hadn't taken shelter in the forests stared at the rows of grim, hurrying horsemen, who shouted and laughed in an unfamiliar tongue and swore unfamiliar curses. The people of Northeye, Bexhill and Bulverhythe knew full well who the strange men were, and they cursed the wasted months of guarding the coast when the Normans had come weeks after the fyrd had disbanded. It was God's will, they whispered in the doorways and the fields; God had done this to England to punish her for the sins of the people, even as the old king had said would happen as he lay dying. God had decreed that the king should be in the north when the duke of Normandy came. God had turned His back on the English people. How else could He let such a thing happen?

'The people look sullen and fearful,' said Will, as they rode into Bexhill. An old man carrying a basket of apples dropped them into the gutter and ran off, mouthing prayers at their approach.

'Wouldn't you?' asked William. The thousands of hooves beating into the dusty mud track and the jingle of harness and armour would be menacing enough even to a professional enemy. 'But they're no more sullen and down in the mouth than a Norman peasant. And the countryside differs little from the orchards and fields of Normandy.'

Hastings, a small village huddled at the water's edge, was all but deserted. 'Fear spreads fast,'

William said, searching for the ships. The main fleet was not yet in sight. 'I wonder who will come against us? Hardrada or Godwinsson?'

'They may take weeks to get to us, whoever it is,' said Will.

'We can't afford to wait weeks,' said William. 'I'll give it ten days. Then we march on London and lay waste to the countryside on the way.'

William dismounted, easing his stiff legs to the ground. 'The first supplies to come ashore will be the food for the horses and the timbers for the castle.'

The castle was William's masterpiece. Carpenters and labourers had been employed in cutting down the trees in the forests around Dives, shaping the timbers into the parts needed to construct a fortification which would be put up at Hastings to provide part of the defensive line in case of an enforced retreat. Some two hundred men would be left inside the fort to guard the ships, and to cover any retreat. 'When England is mine,' William had said. 'We shall build hundreds of these castles and control our new country with them.'

Within an hour, the fleet had arrived safely and all the food, arms and armour were quickly unloaded; the months of waiting hadn't been wasted, as William had kept the crews busy practising exactly such manoeuvres.

William didn't get to bed until past midnight. He found a site for the castle and the labourers began work. It wouldn't be complete for several days. Satisfied that the patrols on Telham Hill and the three ships a little way out of the bay guarding the seaward approaches were in position, he went to bed. Most of the infantry would sleep another night on the boats incase the English army came against them by surprise, but morale was higher now than it had ever been.

He said a prayer thanking God for the safe passage He had given them across the sea, and added another for Matilda, remembering her tears at his departure. Guilt struck him hard between times of hectic activity, and it did so now, as he knelt beside the bed. He would see to it that Odo said a mass for all those waiting in Normandy for news of their fate.

He blew out the candle and with that, concluded the business of his first day in England.

Chapter Fifty-Four
Newark, October 1066

Leofwine was used to being summoned by Harold at all hours, especially during these last weeks. After burying Tostig in the Minster at York – Harold swore that their brother would have an honourable funeral – Leofwine had been back and forth between Harold and his scattered army. They were on the march once again, south this time, and would rest up only when London was in sight. A call now, in the middle of the night, was no surprise.

He found Harold in a house in the centre of the small town of Newark, halted for a brief respite with the men – as much as exhausted nerves and aching muscles would allow – with Gyrth at his side and a few trusted housecarl commanders. The younger brother's arm was almost completely healed, but weariness had left a longer-lasting scar. But there was something else, too; the atmosphere in the room was heavy with shock.

'What's the news?' Leofwine glanced round the small room and saw a cup of wine by the fireside. He took it and drank from it. It was sour.

'Read this,' said Harold.

Leofwine took the parchment Harold thrust at him and noticed that it had the great seal of the archbishop of Canterbury attached to it.

William of Normandy has landed on the south coast and is at Hastings assaulting our land and our people. I urge you in the name of God and all that is just to come quickly to defend your homeland and your people. Stigand.

Exhaustion washed over Leofwine as he read the note again. 'I cannot believe it,' he said.

'After everything we've been through in the north,' said Gyrth. 'We must seek peace.' Defeat, as well as anger, registered in his words. Leofwine murmured agreement and some of the houscarls nodded. If they could hold the Norman bastard on the coast, give him a title – earl of Wessex even – or some money like they used to in the days of Ethelred and the Norsemen, then they might be alright.

'No.'

Harold rose from his seat and confronted them all. 'No,' he said again. 'We must push on and take the fight to the Normans. It is the will of God that the wind changed and brought him here, and God's will that we have fought two battles in two weeks after waiting all the summer. I say that we force-march from London to Hastings and push him back into the sea. He'll think we're still in York, fighting the Hardrada.'

'We must stop at London,' said Leofwine. Harold's plan had its merits, but the men were dead tired. And many of the best were just dead. 'It'll allow the fyrd to catch us up. We can gather the troops who stayed in the south – the men from Cornwall and the Welsh borders. Then when we have rested, we'll go to meet him in battle.'

But Harold shook his head. 'We need to move faster than that. If Stigand is right, we could catch the

Norman with his men scattered, pillaging the land. My land,' he added.

'I don't like it,' said Gyrth. 'We won't catch William of Normandy unawares like we did the Hardrada. It's in our interest to do the exact opposite – make him wait until he runs low on food. Then he'll be trapped like the starving mongrel he really is.'

'While he burns and pillages my earldom – father's lands?' Harold said.

Gyrth avoided his gaze. 'If need be: yes.'

'No!' Harold's mouth was tight with rage. 'We must deal with him as soon as possible.'

'You are secure in your kingdom, Harold,' said Leofwine gently. 'North and south support you – more men will come when word gets round of the defeat of Hardrada. Edwin and Morcar will come from York with thousands of good men.'

'We'll wait at London, then,' Harold gave in. 'But not for long. We'll smash him into the sea.'

Leofwine shrugged, seeing that his brother was implacably opposed to waiting over long. Maybe mother would persuade him. 'I don't truly know what is best,' he said slowly, reading Harold's stare. Was it only this morning that they were all thinking that it was all over, and how fortunate they had been. Fortunate! Fortune had truly turned against the Godwins. 'I'm going back to bed,' he said. There was nothing else to do; they needed sleep and rest before they could discuss the matter rationally.

Harold rose from his seat, for once in agreement with Leofwine. 'We'll talk about it in London.'

*

London. 6th October. The streets were lined with people, cheering and weeping at the victorious army, shouting their thanks to God for the safe return of the king and his soldiers. But there were many who kept silent, tempering the news of the victory over the

Hardrada with the knowledge that William the Bastard of Normandy was in England. Harold noticed the looks of pity and fear, and felt their anxiety penetrate his very soul as the long line of housecarls rode slowly through the city to Westminster.

Mother. The dread of telling Gytha and his sister Edith of Tostig's death had enveloped him like smog since leaving York. Burying Tostig in the Minster with all due ceremony had to some extent excised the grief – but not the guilt and the pain – that he felt, and that had put up a barrier between him and his brothers. He must move on to meet William, to seek battle and to cleanse the guilt from his life, with his life, if necessary. But first, mother. How could he tell her? He'd not sent word ahead, not wanting them to learn of it by the impersonal scrawl of ink on parchment. He had decided in York that he would tell them himself.

They dismounted in the yard of the royal palace and Eadgyth ran into his arms, tears falling on his mail coat, her hands running through his matted hair, touching his face, gripping his shoulders tightly. 'You are alive, then,' she cried.

'Of course,' Harold smiled down at her, holding her tight. 'I said I would come back.'

'We heard there was a battle,' said Gytha, taking Harold's arm. Harold turned to his mother. She was tired and strained with anxiety; the waiting had taken its toll on her.

'What of Tostig?' said his sister. Edith stood apart from the brothers, arms folded, clad in a grey habit, hair tied severely into a cloth cap. She looked older, sharper and very like her mother, but without any of the gentleness – and Tostig had been her favourite brother. She had fought for him, had even murdered for him when Edward was king. 'Was Tostig at York?' she demanded.

'We fought a battle,' said Harold slowly. 'Tostig was with the Hardrada.' How could he tell of the last chance he'd offered to Tostig? How could he tell of the hatred that had prevailed, of the confusion and the rage of battle? And how could he tell of the battered body lying in the cart and an honourable, but hurried burial in the Minster? 'I offered him restitution, and would have given it to him, but he refused it.'

Gytha whispered: 'Where is Tostig, then?'

Harold took her hands in his. 'He is dead, mother. Your son is dead.'

'He died in the battle?'

Harold thought of the defenceless, fleeing Norwegians cut down as they ran, and was thankful that Tostig had died in the heat of the battle, fighting rather than running for his life. 'Yes,' he said. 'A wound to the head – he would have died instantly, would have felt no pain...' His voice trailed off, unable to control itself any longer with such meaningless platitudes. Eadgyth slipped her arms around him and wept softly into his chest.

'I thought it would come to this,' said Gytha, touching Harold's face with a trembling hand. 'I knew as soon as you walked through the door. A mother can always tell.'

'Mother, I'm so sorry.' Harold knelt at Gytha's feet, and asked in a cracked voice: 'Do you blame me?'

Gytha shook her head. 'No, I could never do that. Godwin would have been proud of you. There was much of Swegn in Tostig, though he was a better man than Swegn. And now you must fight the Norman.'

'I am not surprised it has come to this,' said Edith harshly. 'Was there nothing at all you could do?'

Leofwine leapt to Harold's defence. 'No, sister, there was not. Tostig fought against his countrymen at Gate Fulford, where his own people from the north died in their thousands. And at Stamford, we gave him a chance to join us. He chose not to take it.'

'It is all Edward Ethelredsson's fault,' said Gytha. 'He should have chosen his heir long before he died and made sure everyone knew of it.'

'I told him,' said Edith. 'I kept telling him all those years ago, but he didn't make a decision. He said it was God's will. God would provide for the English, he said, and so he left it until the end.'

Harold looked over to where Gyrth and Leofwine were standing in sullen silence. 'Now do you see?' he said. 'We shall have to leave soon and fight the final battle.'

*

Tuesday, 11th October. The autumn sunset shimmered above the Thames and cast a golden glow over Harold's bed-chamber. The relief of his safe return had been swamped by the knowledge that he would leave again, soon. News that William of Normandy was burning and wasting the villages on the South Downs in King Harold's own lands could not keep the royal army back for long.

'We leave tomorrow,' Harold said to Eadgyth.

'So soon?' Eadgyth asked quickly.

'You know it must be so. There are more men in the north, but it'll take weeks for Edwin and Morcar to bring them south. I don't know if the men with me will stay. We have about seven thousand with us now, but only a thousand housecarls.' Harold's face darkened. 'Edwin and Morcar's household troops died almost to a man at Gate Fulford and I lost many of my best troops at Stamford. And Tostig took most of his troops with him. The rest are tired, wounded and scattered between here and York, and that bastard from Normandy burns my villages!'

Harold let go her hand and went to the window. Several boats drifted on the Thames, intent on finding a berth for the night. Lamps cast dim shadows on the men working along the quayside; one boatman shouted something, another replied, and laughter followed. Harold wondered whether Edward had stood at this very spot, seen the river and the boatmen at dusk and thought about an heir. Had he really believed that it was God's will, or was that merely the excuse of a weak and vacillating old man? Harold shrugged, and closed the shutters. One thing was certain: England was his now, he was Edward's crowned heir, and no bastard adventurer from over the sea would wrest it from him. England was his, the people wanted him, and would grow to love him as they had old Godwin in Wessex, more than they had ever loved Edward Ethelredsson.

He lit another candle and crossed to the bed. Whatever Edward had or had not done was in the past now. The present was what mattered, and that meant one last night with Eadgyth.

He rose at dawn. Despite a long, deep sleep, he felt that he'd not slept at all, and could lie abed all day, so much had the exhaustion of the past weeks caught up with him. He kissed Eadgyth's bare white shoulder, opened the shutters wide, knelt and whispered a prayer. Below, the courtyard already echoed to the coarse shouts of soldiers and the jingle of harness.

Where was William the Bastard now? Rising for another day on English soil, another dawn of destruction and devastation? Rising with such intent as he had for most of his warring, bloody life? William remembered the evening at Mont St-Michel, the tales of horror and despair that had shaped the duke of Normandy. He had sympathised and pitied the man then: but now that life of blood had turned upon England, and Harold felt no sympathy. The two of them had to finish the game of chess that Edward had started for them, their positions already set, and the ending but a few moves away now.

'Harry...?' Eadgyth sat up in the bed. 'Are you confident of victory?'

Harold hesitated, seeing her bite her lip. She didn't want platitudes of comfort. She wasn't looking for that, and didn't deserve it. She wanted to know – to really know – if he would be back this time. 'William's men are fresh and eager for action,' he said slowly. 'Mine are tired, depleted in number and many are wounded. But if we can catch him unawares and find him scattered across the countryside, I think we shall win.'

'Truly?'

Harold nodded; he wasn't saying it to please her – once his men scented blood, however tired they were – the Norman and his rabble would be hunted like the dogs they were. Off his land, and out of his kingdom. 'And you'll go to Winchester?'

It was what they had decided. Harold was sure that William would head for London. Whatever the outcome of the battle – if there was a battle – London would become a focus of the campaign. Winchester, away to the south, was out of reach. Eadgyth, Gytha and Edith would all seek refuge in that ancient, walled city and wait for news.

'Leave today,' he said. 'Take fifty men as an escort.'

'You'll need those men,' she protested.

'Take them,' Harold insisted. 'I'll give you a few lightly wounded. We'll not miss them that much, God willing.' He stooped and kissed her brow, wiping the tear from her cheek, and felt her hand on his, pulling him closer, willing him not to leave. Her lips sought his, her arms entwined round his neck and a sob was stifled deep in her throat. It was easy for the men, he thought, with a flash of detached consideration, for they have something to do. The women can only wait.

'Go then,' she urged, pushing him away. 'But come back to me. Come back soon.'

'I will.'

When she opened her eyes she saw him standing by the door, a smile on his lips, his long blond hair flecked with grey. He was the image of his father.

'I know you will,' she said.

Harold opened the door, knowing full well that when he closed it behind him, she would soak the pillow with her tears. The waiting this time would be harder than ever before.

'God keep you, my love,' she called softly.

Harold looked into her eyes, remembering the first time he'd seen her at Tofig's wedding, the day Harthacanute died. All those years ago: an age away. 'And you, my love,' he replied.

Then he was gone.

Gytha was waiting in the hall.

'We'll leave via Southwark and camp the night at Greenwich Heath.' He led her into the courtyard, where his sister and brothers were waiting. He took a bite of manchet bread and swallowed some wine Gyrth handed him. 'It'll give the army time to assemble.'

Harold turned to his sister. 'As the dower-queen, you have the keys to the city of Winchester. Take command and close the gates.' He passed her a roll of parchment. 'Here is a writ for the town council. All of you wait there for news of us.'

He stopped and embraced his mother, and whispered in her ear: 'If we should lose, go to

Flanders, where Count Baldwin will grant you asylum for the sake of my father.'

Gytha, dry-eyed and suddenly very old, nodded. 'God go with you, my boy.'

'Look after my sons,' Harold said, embracing her. His three sons, Godwin, Magnus and Edmund, were on their way from Guildford to Winchester with their tutors. At fourteen, Godwin was the eldest, and had begged Harold to let him take up arms and join the troops, but Harold had refused. 'Ensure they do nothing foolish,' he added, thinking of their desire to join him. He'd ordered the tutors to keep a strict watch, in case the boys came to find the army.

Harold mounted his horse and gave a nod to the trumpeter. The gathered crowds cheered, wave upon wave of them, and the cheer became a roar, and when he looked back, Harold could no longer see the palace, his mother, or his sister.

Chapter Fifty-Five
The Sussex Downs, October 1066

On 10th October, news reached William's camp of Harold's return to London and of his victory over the Hardrada. The news swept over the army camped at Hastings like a summer breeze, each soldier reacting in his own way to the word that Harold Godwinsson, so far reviled as a perjurer and usurper, had marched north, defeated the great and legendary Hardrada, and swung south to meet the Norman invader. It was enough to silence many of the men who hitherto had regarded the English king as a fool and a liar. They saw him in a new light: one of awe. It was said that the Hardrada had come to England in over three hundred ships and that the survivors had departed in less than twenty.

William saw the change in the camp and noted it. Harold's achievement, he admitted to himself, had been nothing short of brilliant. The destruction of the entire might of Norway in one day was a remarkable feat of leadership – and one that he could not have equalled. But to the men William did not breathe a word of his admiration for Harold Godwinsson – they were sufficiently struck by the news of the English victory without their duke adding to the praise. William was glad that it was Godwinsson, and not Hardrada, that they would meet in battle. Remembering the quiet courage of the man who had accompanied him on the campaign to Brittany, and his bravery in rescuing one of his knights from the quicksands at Mont St-Michel, William knew that it was fated that he should meet Harold Godwinsson in battle. He suspected that Harold would not wait in London – he would want to keep moving rapidly, and to repeat his success in the north.

After a council of war with Will FitzOsbern, his half-brothers Odo and Robert, Eustace of Boulogne and Brian of Brittany, William summoned the scattered troops who were pillaging the nearby villages, and formed them into marching order. They would advance to London.

By dawn of Saturday 14th October, the Norman army and its French contingents were ready to march on London. The weather was cool, cloudy and dry. The leaves on the trees were just beginning to turn. It was the feast of St Calixtus, and a typical autumn day.

There would be no repeat of Stamford Bridge.

*

Vital shook the last drops from himself and buttoned up his breeches. As one of the duke's scouts, he didn't have to wear the long and uncomfortable mail hauberk, but instead the lighter, leather gambeson with a piece of boiled leather sewn onto the front to serve as a breastplate. His horse was one of the finest and fastest in the army. It was a nervous creature, and temperamental to boot, making much of the crossing. Vital still had memories of that sleepless night on the small boat, sitting up with the terrified animal.

Vital was half-English. At least, he had been told by his Norman mother that he was. His father, so they said, was an English servant who'd seduced his mother in the reign of King Edward. Both had been employed in the English royal court; his father had served the king, his mother had served Ralf of Mantes, earl of Hereford. At the age of seven though, Vital's father had died and Vital had returned to Normandy with his mother. His parents had never married. Vital was called bastard, but he didn't care; the duke was a bastard, so that made him as good as any man. Now, fifteen years later, Vital was in England again. His mother's connection with the ducal court and his fluency in English made him a good choice as a spy; if stopped, he would pretend to be on King Harold's side.

Vital climbed into the saddle and spurred on up the track. God, but he'd needed that piss, spiriting away the ache in his bladder like a witch wishing away a wart. And it was good to be in England, though the countryside so far was much the same as that in Normandy. Behind him lay the hill they called Telham Hill. To the left, the ground climbed slowly to another hill topped by a long ridge. At its base, pools of water and marsh lay in the treacherous undergrowth.

The duke had sent out scouts out in every direction, but Vital's was the main route to London. He was proud to be on it and sure to see the English army before the other scouts did. He spurred on, across the valley bottom and up the slope. It was warm work, and he paused to take a draught of the tepid cider the duke had brought across from the duchy. It was warm and sour, but he drank it down, praising the duke for having thought of everything. There were many who would follow William Bastard to hell and back if he asked them. Vital returned the flask to the saddle bag and thought that they may well have to do just that in the coming days.

Then he saw the English army. A great cloud of dust made the London road indistinguishable from the grey clouds in the sky. Vital swallowed nervously and stared hard down the slope. He had good eyesight – one of the necessities of his job – and knew what to look for. He searched thoroughly and found it. Red banner, white dragon. The dragon of Wessex. Harold of England was there, with his army; this was no advance patrol, but the English fyrd come to do battle.

Vital wrenched at the reins and galloped dangerously fast back along the way he had just travelled.

The two armies were less than five miles apart and closing rapidly.

The duke would be pleased.

Doubts crept in as soon as they had left London. The men were tired – impossibly tired. Marching from London to Stamford was taking its toll. Harold relaxed the marching orders on Saturday. They rose at dawn, and in a line stretching several miles back to London, walked steadily south. Most of the housecarls were now on foot, as their mounts were either dead or too poorly fed to keep up the stumbling, blistered pace of the fyrd.

Harold was everywhere at once, whipping his horse back and forth along the line, shouting encouragement and cracking coarse jokes to keep morale high. But all the while a voice kept whispering to him *you should have stayed in London.*

Pausing in the round of encouragements for a few words with Gyrth and Leofwine at the vanguard of the army, Harold slid to the ground and gratefully accepted the flask Gyrth handed to him. The brackish liquid slipped over his parched tongue and he savoured the luxury of it.

'What news from the scouts?' Leofwine demanded.

Harold swallowed the ale. 'No reports yet.' Local men who knew the district had gone out in all directions, but none had reported back yet. That surely confirmed the fact that William was still with his boats on the coast.

'There is one of the scouts,' said Gyrth.

'Where?' Harold searched the crest of the hill in front of them. Near the summit was an ancient apple tree, withered and knarled with age, solitary in the wide sweep of the Downs. In its shadow was a horse – riderless. Harold handed the reins of his mount to his squire and ran up the slope. The horse looked quizzically at him and continued to graze. The royal scout was lying in the grass beneath the tree.

'Dead?' Leofwine had followed Harold to the summit and stood beside Harold.

'Asleep, damn his soul.' Harold bent over and slapped the man's face hard, twice.

The scout moaned, rubbing his bristled jaw, his eyes flickered open and grewing wide with recognition at the sight of his king. 'Sire,' he gasped, struggling to his feet. 'I had to rest...'

Harold felt a surge of anger, his own utter weariness turning into hot rage at this man's selfishness. 'We're awake,' he said, waving an arm at the creeping, stumbling army in the valley behind them. 'Why aren't you?'

'Lord king,' the scout sobbed, 'I am sorry. I was at the battle of Stamford, my lord, walked from London to York and back...and now this...it's too much, sire, too much...'

'How long have you been asleep, curse you?'

'Not long sire, an hour perhaps ... maybe more.'

Harold looked at the man with contempt. 'I'll have the skin from your back when we halt tonight.' But as he spoke, he knew that it wasn't the man's fault, but his: he had pushed them beyond the limit.

'Harry!'

Gyrth was waving at him from the summit of the ridge like a man possessed.

A cold dread seized Harold then. He ran up the hill to where Gyrth was standing, aware of his heart beating furiously beneath his mail tunic, and his breath coming in short gasps.

'Over there,' Gyrth pointed with a shaking arm towards Telham Hill, across the valley.

In the trees on the ridge were men. Thousands of them, row upon row. Those in the centre were mounted and armed in mail-coats that glinted darkly in the gaps between the trees. They were less than a mile away and in full battle order.

'What do we do now?' gabbled Gyrth. 'The men'll never fight. They're too tired, too exhausted...'

'We should have stayed in London –' said Leofwine, joining them on the ridge.

Harold turned on his brothers. 'God willed it,' he said. An image of Eadgyth lying on his bed, came to his mind. He suppressed it, and saw again the charge of the Norman cavalry at Dinan. The image of Eadgyth reappeared and her words rang in his ears: *Come back to me. Come back soon.* 'God willed it,' he said again. 'God willed it.'

Seeing the pennant of a ducal scout, the marching ranks of Norman foot-soldiers parted to let Vital through. Some shouted obscenities, others asked what he'd seen to make him almost ride into them, but he ignored them all. His news was for the duke alone.

'God be thanked,' said William when Vital finally got to him. 'Was the English army in battle order?'

'No, my lord. They were scattered along the road for some miles and were moving very slowly. I think they are tired, lord.'

William's face broke into his familiar grin. 'He's broken them,' he breathed. 'Godwinsson's broken them.'

The news spread fast. William gathered his leaders around him for a hurried war council.

'Brian, take your Bretons and line them up on the left flank, on the crest of this hill. Robert, you take the men of Beaumont, all the other mounted men of Anjou and Poitou, and go to the right. You go with him, Eustace.' The count of Boulogne grinned, and William noticed the naked satisfaction in that grin, and wondered how many old scores would be settled with Harold Godwinsson this day. 'Will,' he turned to his oldest friend. 'Will, you form up the infantry, archers and crossbowmen in the van, under their captains. Then return to me. We shall lead the knights from Normandy, France and Italy in the centre.' He looked at them all, ready, waiting. He had led them this far, and they had believed in him. Now it would pass out of his hands, and he must have faith in them. 'Go to your posts. Await the trumpet call for the advance.'

William surveyed the valley below him. There was a complete absence of trees and any other vegetation; this would make for easy movement. Then he realised why the ground was devoid of undergrowth – the valley bottom was dotted with marsh and a small lake. He frowned. That could be nasty.

Looking up, he saw Harold. He was standing on the crest of the hill opposite him. To his left was a long plateau. The road from London swept past it and into the marshy bottom. A single, hoary apple-tree stood near where Harold was standing. William studied the area carefully and wondered whether his army could cross the marshes and advance up the slope.

Odo appeared alongside him. 'We're ready,' he said. The plan to march in ready formation had paid dividends. William bent and pulled out from a saddle-bag the bones Harold had sworn over at Bayeux and put them around his neck.

'Shall I conduct a mass?' Odo was fingering a silver cross.

'No time,' William said. The moment had come, and he felt the quickening in his chest as he always did before battle.

'What will he do?' Odo pointed to Harold up on the ridge. The king of England was waving frantically at his troops.

'He'll seize the ridge and form a shield-wall.' William said. 'He'll pack his men in tightly and bar the road to London. We have to push him off the hill.' He signalled to the trumpeter nearby. 'But we'll give him no time to form up. Sound the advance.'

The bugler spat, put his lips to the horn, and blew a long blast.

'Double time,' William ordered.

He took his lance from the squire beside him. The mass of infantry at his feet roared and moved quickly into the valley, sensing victory. They broke into a slow run as the number of Englishmen on the hill gathered ahead of them.

It was nine o'clock.

Harold forced himself to look away from the rows of men and mounted soldiers on the hill. The Norman advance would begin any moment now. There was a mile or so between the two armies and Harold calculated that it would take them a while to cover that distance. Time enough to prepare the defence.

'How in hell do we deal with those horses?' Leofwine demanded.

'Shield-wall,' Harold said. He looked round. Because of the horses, it would have to be a defensive battle, and he'd not bargained for that. How had William got so many horses across the water from Normandy? A flicker of secret admiration for the Bastard's planning was stifled by the memory of the charge at Dinan. The discipline of the knights and the sledge-hammer blow on the target was unforgettable.

'The horses will never charge the shield-wall,' said Gyrth calmly. 'Even Normans cannot make their steeds jump spears and swords.'

Harold stared at his brother. He was right. If they could form a strong enough line, then the cavalry would never get through. They would just have to sit tight and let William throw everything at them.

If they formed up in time.

'Can we fit seven thousand men on that ridge?' asked Leofwine.

Harold nodded. 'Six or seven deep. Housecarls at the front, fyrd at the rear. Do you see the marshes at the bottom of the valley? The horses and men will have to come through those before charging up this slope. The horses will be blown by the time they reach us. If we can hold formation, we'll block the road to London.' Harold paused, and added: 'It's a case of lasting until sunset.'

'It is all we can do,' said Gyrth cautiously.

Harold turned to Leofwine. 'Spread the word that we fight today. Tell them that William Bastard is in our sights and we have to stand here and stop him reaching London. Get the shield-wall into formation, housecarls at the front.'

Leofwine ran down to the tired, hungry troops who had snatched a rest on the hill while their king conferred with his brothers. The men groaned with disbelief, cursing their luck and damning William of Normandy to hell. None of them, though, cursed Harold. They knew that to turn and run would simply invite massacre, but the knowledge that Harold Godwinsson was with them made them remain. He had led them to victory once against the Norsemen, and would do it again. They picked up their spears, swords and cudgels, drawing upon new reserves of energy from the bowels of their exhaustion, fear driving them on. Harold shouted encouragement, and the men cheered at the sight of him. 'You are your father's son, sire!' a toothless peasant shouted, armed only with a staff riddled with iron spikes at one end. 'Would that he were here today!' At the memory of old Godwin, there was a cheer from the men of Kent.

The Norman infantry were deep in the valley bottom, negotiating the marshes slowly, but steadily. Harold watched their approach and, looking back at the confusion to the rear of the English army, which had yet to learn of the coming battle, calculated that the Norman infantry would be upon them before they had completed forming up. The rear of the fyrd were half a mile distant, and could only stand and wonder at the confusion in the van.

'Gyrth!' Harold called to his brother. 'Tell those in the rear to come up quickly.' Gyrth galloped off at a mad pace and Harold turned to inspect the line of men forming up. They knew what to do, and had done it at Stamford. The housecarls were lined up shoulder to shoulder, in groups of twenty; veteran sergeants-at-arms set about marshalling the lesser trained peasant-farmers with perfect drill, heedless of the enemy toiling through the marshes below them a thousand yards away. Harold smiled, satisfied that the army was in capable hands. But so many good men were not with them. They either lay dead or wounded at Fulford and Stamford, or were marching south with Edward and Morcar, but were not here where they were needed. Harold turned to the rear, to where the left flank was still coming up the road.

With the shield-wall on this ridge, they had a chance, and a good one, at that. The hundreds of fyrd flocked behind the housecarls' line, knowing that there lay safety. With luck, many of them wouldn't have to strike a blow: the housecarls' head-chopping axes would do the work.

Gyrth emerged from the road and set his horse into a canter along the line, waving at the cheering troops. The dragon of Wessex – the Godwin emblem of the English royal house – and the fighting man, Harold's own banner, fluttered in the breeze at the core of the tight ranks of housecarls.

Harold stared into the valley and saw the first of the Norman foot-soldiers clear the marsh and stream forward with a roar. A trumpet blasted and they began to run.

Leofwine and Gyrth joined him and for the last time the three brothers stood together.

'Gyrth – you take command of the right wing,' Harold ordered. 'Leofwine, you see to the left. We can't wait any longer.'

Gyrth drew his heavy sword from its scabbard, preferring the long blade to an axe, and said: 'God go with you then, brother.' He leant from the saddle and grasped Harold's outstretched hand. Leofwine placed his gloved hand onto both of them and they held fast for a moment.

'And with you,' said Harold. 'We'll do father proud today.'

They broke apart, and the cheering grew ever louder at Harold's arrival in the centre of the shield-wall. The army shouted his name, Godwin's name, and called upon the Lord God Almighty, Thor and all the souls of Valhalla to give them victory this day. They may have failed to find William resting at Hastings, but William had lost the chance to catch them unawares. Nothing would clear his way to London now.

'Here they come!' someone shouted, and a deathly quiet fell upon the waiting ranks.

The Norman infantry were a hundred yards away now. They paused, gathering breath after the long climb, each army staring in silence at the other. Then Harold waved to the sergeant nearest him and a muffled order rasped out. Stones, sticks, spiked balls and spears were unleashed from the front line and into the Norman foot-soldiers. Men fell, but most pushed on, leaning into the storm. Far into the valley, the Norman cavalry sat waiting and watching.

'Forty yards,' called Harold. 'Prepare arms!'

His shout, echoed by sergeants along the line, was answered by the rasp of hundreds of drawn swords on scabbards and the rattle of axe shafts drummed against shields. Those in the fyrd gripped spears, clubs and pitchforks with sweating hands, aware that their fate depended upon the discipline of those in front of them.

'Stand ready!' Harold roared. The fyrd began the war-cry *Out! Out! Out!* and then the Normans were upon them, engulfing them in a tidal wave sent from the jaws of hell itself.

*

William halted the cavalry in the valley bottom and watched the infantry advance. The weakest point in the English line was to the Norman right, where the road met the hill crest, and where the English were still forming up. Knowing that, he had ordered the full weight of the infantry charge on that flank. But the housecarls appeared to be packed too densely to allow the gap to be exploited. He assumed that the rest of the fyrd was beyond the wall, now firmly encased within a three-sided compact unit.

On the left, the Breton mercenaries were locked in a death-struggle with the housecarls under Gyrth Godwinsson. Dim shouts of '*Out! Out! Out!*' from the hill summit were returned with shouts of '*God aid!*' from the Bretons, and even '*Thor aid!*' from some of the Norman foot.

Then a roar went up as the Bretons and Angevins began to retreat down the hill, pulling the Normans back with them, and the English line echoed with laughter and jeers as the invaders ran away.

'The attack has failed, William,' said a grey-faced Odo from behind William. 'The English line has held.'

'I can see that,' William said. 'Don't tell me the obvious, damn you.' He beckoned to the bugler and ordered: 'Sound the recall. Then sound the advance for the cavalry. The English will never last after our horses have finished with them.'

*

Harold waved for silence amid the jeers that accompanied the Norman infantry's departure. Only on the vulnerable English left flank, where Leofwine was still forming the fyrd, were the enemy still engaged. Elsewhere, they had turned and fled.

'Wait!' he shouted. 'The cavalry charge will come next. You must stand firm and remember that the horses won't charge a man or a spear, but if the line breaks, then they'll be in amongst us!'

At his words, they ceased their noise, their jubilation quelled by the thought of so many feared Norman knights coming at them. None of the English had ever faced such a charge as the one that would come now, and it was left to their imaginations to take over. The sergeants called 'close up' and spears rattled on shields along the hill, then a silence fell. It was gone noon, and the sky was going grey. It didn't look like rain, but if they could hold for long enough...

A blast from a trumpet echoed up the valley and the mass of horses came on towards them, carving a passage through the fleeing Breton infantry. The still October air reverberated to the drumming of hooves, like a roll of thunder, and the men around Harold tensed. He wondered how Gyrth and Leofwine were. Too exhausted to shout, the men stood quietly, some praying, others moving into the front ranks in place of the dead and wounded.

Harold tensed, staring at the mailed men on the horses closing in on them, William's lion of Normandy and the papal banner in the centre, snorting clouds of breath from the savagely spurred animals, the open mouths of the knights – they all seemed so young – the mud-bespattered shields and the long, thin lances couched wickedly at groin level. He thought of Dinan, of the timber walls battered and kicked in and the broken, trampled bodies crushed into the soil. God be thanked most of these men had never seen such a thing, else they would have run by now. *A charge fit to smash the very walls of Byzantium*, someone had said – and today he would be on the receiving end.

The first line of cavalry engulfed the English line like a wave on a rock, and seemed to swallow them whole, then receded, leaving the line miraculously intact. There was no time to act. They could only flinch in terror at the flailing hooves, catch a glimpse of the flared nostrils of the mad beasts above them, and dodge the slashing swords and darting lances aimed at the gaps in the line, ripping remorselessly into unprotected flesh. Behind his shield, Harold gritted his teeth and swore constantly and fluently, screaming his terror back into the wide eyes of the horsemen – they seemed no older than his own sons, now that he saw them closely – and hoped to God that he would remain untouched. Now that the first shock of impact had ended, the cavalry broke into groups, the horses remaining stationary while the riders hacked and stabbed with long swords, casting away their splintered lances. Some yards away Harold recognised Odo, bishop of Bayeux, laying about him with a blood-soaked mace. Near him, the blue banner of St Peter rippled above them, surveying the field. Duke William was nowhere in sight.

A gap appeared in front of Harold then, and a knight made a short charge directly at the banner of the fighting man. The housecarls next to Harold saw him, and a hail of stones and spears ripped into him. A stone took him full in the face, breaking bone and skin, and a spear tore through the neck of his mount, yards from where Harold was standing. Horse and rider went down, meeting death in the same split-second, and in its death-agony the horse careered into the front line, heedless of the shields and spears facing it. Harold raised his shield as the animal ploughed into them, but the hooves caught the wood, splintered it like firewood, and wrenched him to the ground.

The screams of battle dimmed as he hit the ground; he tasted the churned grass and soil, and the blood on his lip where he had chewed his tongue. Warm urine soaked his inside leg, and then strong hands pulled him to his feet, and passed him his sword.

A dismounted Norman knight nearby crawled from under his dead horse and attempted to stand up, but three housecarls kicked him back to the ground while a fourth, ignoring his pleas, swung an axe into his neck. Blood fountained upwards, and Harold watched, fascinated, as the Englishmen around the knight were sprayed by it.

The great charge had failed to break the line, but the dead housecarls were heaped all around him. A price had been paid to halt the Norman assault, and peasants from the fyrd increasingly filled the line. The Norman knights remained in their groups, hacking down at the running, darting foot-soldiers stabbing up at them.

'Kill the horses!' Harold shouted at two farmers who were ineffectually stabbing at a knight with a scythe. One flashed a toothless grin at Harold, and ducked under the horse, dodging a blow. A second later, the beast gave a piteous scream and toppled its rider. The peasant shouted with glee, waved a dagger wet with blood, and was swept away by an unseen knight.

Harold cursed, but then he heard a cry, louder and more urgent than all the shouts around him.

'The duke is dead! Save yourselves! The duke is dead!'

The Norman knights heard the cry and hesitated, looking around them for guidance. One moved back, another followed, and then a entire group wheeled about and made off down the slope. Those remaining paused, while the English fyrd closed up again, and spat curses at them; then they shrugged, and turned back with the others. Harold watched in amazement. Bodies of horses, knights and wounded lay yards away, but the army of William Bastard was back in the valley bottom. The shield-wall held, and the Norman duke was dead.

*

As a boy, William had once seen a hedgehog in a ditch and, being curious, had tried to pick it up. The memory of those hot tears running down his face and blood on his hands was keen, and today he was reminded of it. The wall of spears and spikes facing them at the top of the slope was as impenetrable as the hedgehog had been impossible to pick up. The wall had held, and more than held; the great cavalry charge had been repulsed. English housecarls and the fyrd were dying, but slowly; the knights were at a disadvantage now that the charge had lost its impetus, unable to manoeuvre the large, frightened horses and outnumbered by the mass of foot milling around them. Will FitzOsbern was somewhere to his right, hacking a path through the English lines, but even he was fast becoming an island in the sea of enemy spears, isolated and vulnerable.

William cut his way through to him, twisting his blade upwards as a thegn lunged at him with a cudgel, all but disembowelling the man. 'Will!' he called again, and this time Will heard him. 'Regroup your men!' He signalled to his bugler, waiting yards away, little more than a terrified boy, the younger son of one of the lords of Beléme, given the honour of fighting with his duke this day. 'Sound the retreat,' William told him, and turned to find his squire.

He got no further. A spear materialised somewhere from the rear of the English line and buried itself deep in the chest of his horse. The animal reared, and crashed to the ground.

The years of training served him well; twisting his ankles free of the stirrups, William rolled to the right and sprang to his feet just as the mortally wounded horse thrashed and screamed beside him. Any slower, and William would have been crushed; as it was, he was so quick that he was on his feet, ready and waiting for the three peasants who had scuttled out from the shield-wall anticipating an easy kill, expecting him to be helpless under his mount.

The Englishmen paused, unable to comprehend how this mailed giant had risen before them and was waving a broadsword at them, shouting in a language they did not understand. One turned on his heel and fled; the remaining two moved forward. William flicked his wrist, exposing his chest, and one of the Englishmen lunged forward, scenting blood – but William spun round, and the scythe stuck fast in the shield still strapped to his back. In the same movement he brought his sword down on the other Englishman, slicing open his stomach.

The surviving peasant ran back cursing, leaving the scythe on the ground.

William let him go. With a shock he realised that he was isolated. Will was nowhere to be seen. The tide of battle had moved along, taking him with it like a piece of flotsam cast adrift in the heaving mass of jostling, screaming, hacking humanity. A knight ran past him, both hands severed at the wrist, his life-blood spilling onto the mud-churned grass. An English thegn lay at his feet, a great sword-gash across his mouth giving him a grotesque smile even in death.

William shuddered. Never in all his long experience of war had he seen such slaughter. If he lived, he would never fight another battle such as this.

But where was Will? He couldn't see him, or any of the great lords. Odo, Brian and Robert had vanished with him, along with his squire, who was supposed to remain with at all costs. *At all costs.* Curse the boy, and the bugler. The papal banner and his ducal flag had gone, too. Were they all dead?

A scream nearby brought him to his senses. A knight was down, his horse unharmed. William blundered forward, untouched by the flailing weapons around him, and caught the bridle. He swung into the saddle and dug his spurs into the flank of the horse, looking for Will. It was a relief to be back high above the battle. But all around him men were pulling back; knights were backing their horses, disengaging from the English line which still held.

'No,' he shouted, seeing them retreat. He followed them down the hill, hearing them shout that he was dead: the duke was dead. 'I'm alive!' he screamed at them, but no one heard. '*The duke lives!* He took his helmet off, glad – for an absurd moment – of the rush of cool air on his hair, sticky with sweat. 'I am alive!' he screamed again at the fleeing knights.

Then Will was beside him. 'Are you harmed?' he asked anxiously.

'No,' William gasped, heaving for breath. His head ached and shooting pains danced about his eyes. 'But if the army thinks I am dead, then the battle is lost.' He whipped the horse into a gallop, shouting his name at the running knights, beating the flat of his sword on the rump of one mount. Slowly, they halted, the panic subsiding; it dawned on them that the duke was unharmed, unless this demon shouting hysterically at them was an apparition.

Odo, mace drenched in blood and gore, face white with fatigue, appeared alongside him. 'Thank Christ, but we thought you were dead.'

'Look at the English!' Will pointed up the hill. The entire left flank of the English shield-wall was moving forward, crumbling, breaking into separate groups of men; peasants from the fyrd with billhooks and scythes were running forward after the fleeing Normans.

'Is it a general charge?' said Odo.

If it was, then the Normans were finished. 'No,' said William slowly. 'See – the housecarls are shouting for them to get back. They think we're fleeing the field because I'm dead. *Regroup!*

William was right. Only one section of the fyrd had left the hill-top, streaming down the slope, certain of victory and sensing freedom after so many hours of standing rigidly in line. But within seconds William had gathered his knights around him, only twenty or so, but his charge at the defenceless peasants on the slope cut through them. Seeing their mistake, the English turned back, panicking, but found the shield-wall blocked to them; the housecarls wouldn't jeopardise the main defence by letting them in again. So they ran on, into the valley, and into the marshes, where they were cut down. Many stuck fast in the bogs, skewered like boars caught in a trap by the long lances of the Norman knights eager to avenge their fallen comrades on the hill.

The shield-wall had, on the left flank at least, disintegrated.

Harold and the housecarls in the centre watched the collapse of the flank with wordless horror. The more inexperienced members of the fyrd continued to push through from the rear, thinking that there was a general advance on, ignoring the commands of the sergeants and plunging down into the valley.

A runner bearing Leofwine's colours pushed through to Harold and said, 'Sire, I come from your brother Earl Leofwine. He says the flank still holds firm. All of the army has come up from the road now.'

'Good,' Harold flashed a wan smile of relief. That was one thing, at least. 'Go back and tell him to send a thousand men as reinforcements across to Earl Gyrth, immediately.' The runner stumbled away through the line, but Harold was watching the peasants in the valley, where events had taken a new turn. The Norman knights had regrouped, wheeled about, and were slaughtering the fyrd where they stood. They had no chance. Poorly armed, leaderless and on foot, they were cut down one by one.

Harold closed his eyes. When he reopened them, he saw the last two Englishmen run through by the lances of at least eight knights, and heard a cheer from the horsemen. 'The bloody fools,' he said.

Where was Gyrth? Why hadn't Gyrth stopped them?

Gyrth was dead.

A stray arrow had pierced his leg, catching him exposed and out of line, and a Breton knight had leant from the saddle and dispatched him with a lazy sweep of his right arm. Unable to reach him in time, his loyal housecarls ran after the knight, killing his horse and dragging him back to the ranks where, in their frenzy of grief, they slashed off his genitals, stuffed them in his mouth, and then disembowelled him, leaving him to die on the slope.

But by running down the slope to seize the Breton knight and avenge their lord, the housecarls had broken ranks and led the nervous mass of peasants to believe it was a general advance in the face of the Norman panic. Too late, Gyrth's men shouted the halt, but the levies ran on, seeing only fleeing enemies before them.

*

William drew breath – the first it seemed for minutes, and almost gagged at the reek of blood. All around them, in twisted forms, lay the English dead. He dismounted, feeling no satisfaction at the sight, and wiped his sword amongst the reeds by one of the nearby ponds. He looked away from the heaps of dead, to the hill-top, where Harold was reforming his men. Visibly depleted though it was, the English shield-wall was already regrouping and reinforcing the gaps opened by this latest action. William groaned. Weariness washed over him in a tidal wave of resignation. They might never move the English off that hill of death.

Brian of Brittany splashed through the water up to him with Odo and Will. They had all dismounted, taking the moment to stretch with wary relief. The battle had become a stalemate, and silence reigned over the field, punctuated only by the screams of the wounded.

'Sire, there is a Norman knight from Italy who would speak with you. He says he knows of a way to move the English off the hill. I beg you to give him audience, sire. We have no other chance...'

William stared at the Breton lord. In the position they were in, he'd sell his soul to the devil for a solution. How much longer before the mercenaries and other auxiliaries began to melt away from the field?

'What, then?' he rasped. 'What is it?'

'Listen to this man,' said Brian.

Philippe of Romagny stepped forward.

'I have seen service under Robert the Weasel in southern Italy.' He paused, uncertain of himself in front of so many nobles listening to him by the marsh.

'Get on with it, lad,' Odo rapped out.

Philippe took a deep breath. 'Sire, in Italy we have used the feigned retreat, which worked well against the unruly and ill-disciplined Saracens. We attack, disengage, and pull back with all the appearance of a full retreat, even yelling our panic. On a given signal, we halt, wheel around, and cut down the enemy close on our heels. They believe victory to be in their grasp, but we trick them, sire. It could work here.' The young knight motioned to the piles of English dead.

'Never,' exploded Odo. 'Too risky, too dangerous. Duke William was nearly killed when this happened.'

'Norman knights used it at the battle of Messina, sire, six years ago,' Philippe insisted. 'I was there.'

William stared at Philippe. It might work. It might just work. If not...

'We'll do it,' he said. 'It's our last chance, God help us. If it works, boy, there's an earldom for you. And God help us, it had better succeed.'

They carried Gyrth's body to the van and the grief-stricken housecarls laid him down by the royal standard. Harold couldn't summon the energy to weep, as the men all around him did. His emotions, already blunted by Tostig's death and the glut of killing today, left him cold.

'Tell Leofwine,' he said, in a voice of stone. He looked at Gyrth's body, saw the ugly gash where the Breton's sword had caught him on the neck, and knelt and closed his brother's staring eyes, stroking the unblemished blond hair into place.

Then Leofwine came running, shoving a pathway through the sullen grieving Englishmen, who stood back at the sight of him.

'Not Gyrth. No...' he mouthed, shaking his head.

'Only us, now,' Harold said. There were just two of them left out of the four.

'Sire.' One of the housecarl sergeants-at-arms, Orderic, grasped his arm. 'They're coming again, up the hill.' He was right: the Norman cavalry were coming on again with couched lances.

'Take Gyrth to the rear,' Harold ordered the housecarl. 'Leofwine: get back to the flank.'

Leofwine shook his head. 'I'm too tired to go on.'

'We all are,' said Harold gently. 'Get back to the men. They need you.' Leofwine hesitated. 'Do it for father and mother.'

Leofwine swallowed his fear and embraced his brother. 'God keep you, Harry,' he whispered.

*

William led the first charge, letting the thrill run through him, relishing the risk of the ploy. There was nothing to lose by attempting it, and the sky above told them all that he didn't have much time before Harold Godwinsson could creep away in the darkness and fight another day.

They met the English line with a weary crash, and again it held. He saw Harold standing head and shoulders above everyone else, cleaving Norman flesh with a great axe. William tried to cut his way through to him, but the retinue of veteran housecarls around the English king were too numerous. Then, at his signal, the bugler sounded the retreat, and he pulled back with the other jostling horses, shouting feigned panic and waving as he galloped down the hill. Will and Odo were close by, Odo's face a mask of real fear at the risk they were taking. Near the foot of the hill, William glanced back and bit his lip with shock.

The English fyrd were following in their hundreds, streaming down the hill after them, confident of their victory.

William waited.

When they were almost close enough to overwhelm the retreating Normans, William gave the signal. The knights around him wheeled as one in their small groups and crashed in among the poorly armed levies. The Breton infantry moved up from the marshes and cut off any chance of retreat.

They did it twice more, until the English line on the ridge was reduced to a core of housecarls near the king who were too well trained to leave the ridge. But down in the valley, thousands of the fyrd had come off the shield-wall, only to be slaughtered in the killing ground that was Hastings Fight.

Helpless to do anything about it, Harold and his men could only watch and despair. He had no means of preventing the ill-disciplined fyrd from venting their despair on the fleeing Normans. Those nearest the centre remained, sensing shelter amongst the solid experience of the housecarls, but both the right and left flanks had gone, destroyed so quickly after holding out for so long. Leofwine had regrouped his household troops and joined Harold at the centre.

'Nightfall will save us,' he said, looking up at the sky.

Harold nodded. The shield-wall was so depleted that only a thousand or so remained. But the Normans had blown their horses, and the English forces on the ridge wouldn't be tricked into leaving. The only hope now was the night. Above them, the autumn sky was darkening rapidly now, the red ball of the setting sun smearing the clouds like a ghastly wound. It was at once beautiful and awful; and it was their salvation. Harold tightened his belt, grimly reflecting on how it had seemed only minutes ago that the army was intact, strong enough for anything – and now they were praying for darkness, so that they could run away like whipped curs into the night.

'Sire,' said Orderic. 'Why don't you flee now? There are horses enough for you and Lord Leofwine. We will cover your retreat, and there are men in London who can swallow up these bastard Normans whole in another battle.'

'Never,' Harold said. 'I'll not leave you now. I am your crowned king, and I will fight with you to the death.' He had led these men here to fight and die and he could not, however many men were waiting in London, turn tail and leave them.

Harold addressed the men around him in a strident voice, his last effort to rally them: 'God has brought us to fight the invader, and God shall see it to the end. Remember the *Song of Maldon*: Brihtwold shouts to his men: "Thoughts must be braver, hearts more valiant, courage the greater, as our strength grows less!"'

They cheered, as he knew they would, inspired by this heroic story, and then someone shouted: 'They come again, sire!' and with a renewed vigour they set about defending the blood-soaked earth they'd stood on all day.

William stared at the determined huddle of housecarls on the ridge.

'He's waiting until nightfall,' said Will.

William knew that the feigned retreats had been devastatingly successful, but in doing so had finished his horses and lost more men. And those English left numbered too many to defeat with ease, because they were the core of royal housecarls.

'We'll lose too many men if we keep on,' said Odo.

Something had to be done before it became too dark. It was today or never.

'Order the archers to shoot high into the sky,' William said. The archers had been left in reserve after their failure at the opening of the battle and had sat in the woods on Telham Hill. 'The English won't see the shafts in this light.' He turned to the bugler. 'We'll send the infantry in when the archers loose their arrows, then we'll follow. Those without mounts can come on foot. Will, see that the men understand the orders.'

Will rode off to the detail archers in their task. William looked at Odo, but could see only utter defeat written on his half-brother's face. Night, with its cloak of invisibility, was fast closing in on them.

This would be the last assault on the English.

Harold sensed a lull. There were no jeers or cheers as the Normans retreated again. The English were shattered but they stood defiant, preparing for the next onslaught.

'Please God, let them come no more,' prayed Leofwine, looking hard at the sky. The fading sun, bereft of its glorious final burst of colour, had sunk into the horizon; an eerie beacon of light flickered over the grey valley and behind the English, the pale moon shone its own silvery light down onto them.

Then: *'Arrows!'*

Though the dusk, hissing shafts plummeted into the diminished ranks of defenders. There was no time to dodge them, or seek cover. The slim, deadly weapons pierced many of the exposed heads, necks and shoulders of the housecarls before they could raise their great shields.

'Jesus God,' Harold muttered, unharmed beneath his shield. 'Leofwine – are you hit?' Leofwine shook his head, dazed, but all around them men were screaming in agony at the hellish, searing jolts of pain that had burned into their flesh from out of the sky.

'Infantry!' warned one of the thegns.

Out of the gloom the Breton mercenaries were, in much depleted numbers, swarming up the slope, greatly heartened by the screams of the English on the summit.

'Breton hirelings!' Harold shouted. 'Kill the scum!'

The two forces met with a half-hearted crash, and the housecarls fell back.

'Stand!' Harold called, but it was no use. They could hold out no longer. Sobbing with despair, Harold screamed his weariness into the faceless invaders; Orderic went down, spitted by a spear; others fell with him, but Leofwine was still standing, and the brothers fought on, back to back.

Then the Bretons broke off the fight and pulled away.

'What is it?' Harold gasped, looking into the dusk. 'Have they given in?'

The arrows came down again, pouring into the small group with appalling accuracy. Harold cringed instinctively, and felt for his shield, but couldn't find it this time. He was thrown backwards by a tremendous blow to his eye.

'Harry!' Leofwine was above him.

Harold swallowed and rolled sideways. He couldn't stand up. There was an arrow shaft protruding from his left eye.

'Harry,' Leofwine was calling to him. *'Harry!'*

Then the Norman cavalry were upon them, and Leofwine went down, swept aside by the great hooves.

Harold managed to get to his feet, unaware of any pain in his eye, just tremendous shock and a numbing sensation. He stumbled over Leofwine's body and staggered to his knees.

Everyone around him was either dead, or dying.

He heard King Edward say to him: *To you, Harold Godwinsson, my brother, I commit this kingdom and this people,* and he saw Eadgyth, the love of his life, waiting in the bed, smiling at him.

Then a Norman knight rode up and drove his sword into his chest, but Harold was already dead.

*

William dismounted. The ground was wet with blood. The twisted bodies of the English, Breton and Norman warriors were joined in the close intimacy of death.

'Christ on the cross,' William whispered, as the extent of the slaughter grew apparent in the light of the moon. The dragon of Wessex banner, the flag of the royal house of England, still fluttered in the breeze, untouched, unconquered. William recognised the body of young Philippe de Romagny, twisted horribly beneath a horse. He would never have his earldom now. Such a long way to come to die.

'They died like men.' Will FitzOsbern was at his side.

'Our losses are almost as great as theirs,' said William. 'Truly our victory was given by God, so terrible has this fight been.'

'Will you let me say my mass, now, brother?' Odo joined him.

William nodded. 'Say a mass for the dead, and have a Te Deum sung – for them all,' he added. He turned to Will. 'We'll camp here tonight, on the hill we fought so hard to take. And here on this hill I will build a church, so help me God, to thank the Lord Almighty for our victory.' He laid a shaking hand on Will's shoulder. 'Find Harold's body for me...bring it to me now.'

It took Will an hour to do as William asked, so tightly packed were the corpses around the royal banner. First Will sent the duke the fighting man, Harold's own battle standard, crumpled and bloodied, still gripped by the severed hand of a housecarl. Then Harold's body was carried to William's tent soon afterwards.

William surveyed the defeated king by the light of flaming torches. The shaft of the arrow had snapped off, leaving a stump protruding from a crusted, bloody hole. Harold's chest and legs were scored with numerous sword cuts. In his hand was his sword.

'I think that belongs to me.' William stooped and prised his weapon gently from Harold's unresisting hand. Remembering Harold's bravery at the sands of Mont St-Michel, where he'd rescued foolish Bevin from the quicksands on the causeway, he said: 'He was a brave man. Never let it be said otherwise. He's to be buried on the cliffs.'

Will FitzOsbern, Odo, Robert and Brian had all joined him in the tent. The flaming torch flickered across their faces as they stared down at Harold, and they nodded in agreement.

'He fought for what he saw was right,' said William. 'But that was not God's right, or God's will. He lost, and God has provided for the kingdom of the English.'

Chapter Fifty-Six
Winchester, October 1066

Eadgyth looked to see if Gytha was asleep, saw that she was, and blew out the last candle. Carrying her own candle, she made her way along the dark passage and into the hall where Magnus, Edmund and Edith were seated around the fire.

'How is she?' Edith spoke from the corner. She was pale and wan, her voice husky.

'Asleep,' replied Eadgyth, taking a chair closer to the fire and absent-mindedly stroking one of Harold's dogs.

'Too exhausted to stay awake, I imagine,' said Edmund.

It was five days since a sobbing and incoherent messenger from Stigand had broken the peace in the royal palace in Winchester. Five days since he'd told them of a great battle on the South Downs near Hastings, and that the king and both his brothers had been killed. Thousands and thousands had died on both sides, but the duke of Normandy had survived to claim the day – by the grace of God alone.

Icy shock had melted into raw, frenzied grief, rage and finally exhaustion after the hours of weeping. Guilt and recrimination followed the anger; guilt at allowing the army to leave London when they did, guilt at not talking them into seeing that the men were too tired, and that it would be wiser to wait for Edwin and Morcar to come south with the many men from the north. Five days of knowing that the clock couldn't be turned back, and that they could never wait for those men now.

The news spread rapidly throughout the shires. In the town of Winchester the people boarded up the windows, wore black and grieved in the silent, sullen way that was particular to the people of Wessex – and no more than in the heart of the Godwin earldom. In London, the people unanimously declared their grief for their king by barring the gates to the approaching Norman army and by putting forward Prince Edgar as Harold's successor.

But in Winchester they feared also for Gytha. She was frail, and had seen all four of her sons die in the past month. She was resilient, and had suffered much grief before, but privately many people believed this was the end for her. The people turned their grief into seething hatred and frustration as the days passed; they turned to God to answer their questions but He gave them no word. Why had the wind changed and allowed the duke to land unopposed when the king was in the north fighting the Hardrada? Why had God seen fit to favour the bastard of Normandy when the old king had named Harold as his heir? After much praying and fraught discussion, the people could only shake their heads and attribute it to the mysterious ways of God. The church said that the people of England were being punished for their sins, even as the dying King Edward had foreseen in his vision.

'The archbishop of Canterbury writes that London will hold,' said Magnus. 'Edwin and Morcar will stand by Prince Edgar.'

'Yes,' said Eadgyth. She bit her lip to prevent it trembling, and looked at her sons. They must all be brave, she told herself repeatedly, for Harry's sake, for Leofwine and Gyrth, for all those who had died.

'They say the duke of Normandy is grievous sick at Canterbury and may die of the bloody flux,' said Edmund.

'God strike him dead, then,' spat Magnus. He turned to his mother, his long blond hair shining in the light of the fire. 'Is it true, mother, that it took all the duke's efforts to defeat father's army, and that every last housecarl stood with father until the end?'

Eadgyth nodded, unable to trust her voice as the tears welled up again. 'Yes,' she managed to whisper. 'They all stood by him to the last. They were few in number, but brave in the extreme.'

'It was trickery that won them the battle,' said Edmund. 'God strike the Frenchmen down. People say that the horsemen pretended to flee, and tricked the fyrd from the hill. Father would still be here now if they had fought with honour...' The boy's voice dissolved into tears, huge sobs of grief racking his body.

'Hush,' said Magnus. 'It was the devil's work that won them the battle. It must have been - an English king hasn't died in battle since since the Norsemen came two hundred years ago. William of Normandy had the devil on his side.'

Edmund wiped his eyes. 'We must avenge father. We must lead the next army against the bastard of Normandy.' He looked at his mother and aunt, and saw only fear in their faces.

'That is what we shall do,' agreed Magnus.

*

With the backing of Edwin, Morcar and Stigand, Prince Edgar claimed the throne of England as was his by right of blood through King Edward, King Alfred and Odin. London held firm, forcing the duke of Normandy to lead his beleaguered army westwards, burning and pillaging a path of terror and destruction across Kent, Sussex and Hampshire. So fearsome was his march, that Edith, who held the keys to the city of Winchester, eventually surrendered them to him on his formal request, and the ancient capital of Wessex was spared any damage.

With south-eastern England under his command, William wheeled north and proceeded to isolate London by crossing the Thames at Wallingford and encircling the capital in a brutal march that ended at Berkhamsted. In November, Stigand submitted to the duke, and was followed by Edwin, Morcar, Prince Edgar and Archbishop Ealdred of York. Resistance was futile - so many fighting men lay dead at Fulford, Stamford and Hastings, and there was nobody left with hope in them to fight again. The leading men gave hostages, accepted William as their liege lord, and allowed the duke into London, his prize after so long.

The people let him through with ill-grace, and he was crowned king of England on Christmas Day in Westminster Abbey, confirming the claim he had won in blood at Hastings Fight. But it was Ealdred, archbishop of York, who officiated at the ceremony, not Stigand. Stigand was declared schismatic and unworthy. The man who had begun as a humble clerk from Norwich and risen to the highest ecclesiastical office in the land, now knew that what he had feared for years had finally come to pass. His days in office were numbered.

Chapter Fifty-Seven
St Omer, Flanders, April 1068

Gytha turned from the window and listened again to her grandsons arguing about Exeter. She sighed, having heard it all before, time and time again.

King William had survived the first real test of his powers. The south-west of England had broken into revolt, starting at the city of Exeter. Gytha had gone with Eadgyth to Exeter, and soon afterwards her grandsons landed at Bristol. There, they called men to the standard of Godwin.

The end came quickly. Moving fast, William subdued Gloucester. Hearing of his approach, the citizens of Bristol repelled the sons of Harold Godwinsson, who then marched into Somerset. William moved on to Exeter, where the city held out for eighteen days. The fear of the king's wrath and a last-minute promise by William to confirm the ancient privileges of the city were enough to break the rebels' will. The town surrendered and Gytha and Eadgyth fled with her sons, Godwin, Edmund and Magnus. The five of them took ship to St Omer, where they were granted asylum by the new count of Flanders, Baldwin VI.

'We should have joined Prince Edgar,' Magnus was saying. 'I told you then that we should. With him on our side, we could have had a claim to put to the people of the south – an alternative to the bastard of Normandy. We could have marched from Exeter to Bristol and Gloucester, then Winchester...' He paused, and threw his grandmother a quick glance.

'What are you saying?' Gytha asked.

Magnus looked at his grandmother and said in a defiant tone: 'I was wondering whether Aunt Edith should have yielded the keys to the city as readily as she gave them to William. *King* William, as we must call him.'

'She had no choice,' said Edmund.

'She did,' said Godwin bitterly. 'Of course she did. But she didn't want to do the right thing. She couldn't surrender the town fast enough to the Normans.'

They fell silent, remembering the moment when Edith had calmly announced to the whole family that she was going to pass the town – hers by right of Edward's will and Harold's confirmation – to the duke, and barely a month after Hastings.

'She never did want father to be king,' said Magnus in a voice full of sudden hatred. 'Uncle Tostig was her favourite, and she wanted him to be king and follow Edward. She betrayed father, the bitch.'

'That isn't true!' Edmund raised a fist.

'Enough!' Eadgyth had entered the room and was between her sons, pushing them apart. 'Enough, I say. Heaven knows the fight between your father and Tostig killed them all, without you beginning it all over again...'

They were all shamed into silence. 'What were we thinking of?' said Magnus, ashen-faced. The brothers shrugged, looking at the floor, sullen and repentant.

'We must all stand together.'

Gytha's strident voice cut across the room. The old widow of Godwin, bereft of husband and sons, had recovered from the shock at Winchester and had proved to be of great strength to them all. 'We can't repeat the mistakes of the past,' she said. 'What is done, is done. Nothing can change that. There is a future, and we must build for it today.'

*

'Where will you go?'

Gytha studied Eadgyth carefully, deciding that she would tell her now. Over the years, the two women had grown close, and since Hastings, even closer. But Gytha had made up her mind, and would stick by that decision.

'To Denmark,' she said gently. The younger woman said nothing, though she couldn't hide the dismay in her hazel-brown eyes.

The Godwinsson exiles had to leave St Omer. The young count had finally bowed to the pressure exerted on him by the new king of England, who had discovered that he was harbouring the Godwin family in Flanders. Not wanting to upset William, now the undisputed leader of northern Europe, Baldwin politely but firmly informed Gytha that they would have to go. It was time, Gytha realised with a heavy heart, for the parting of the ways.

'Denmark?' Eadgyth asked slowly. 'Why?'

Gytha placed a frail hand on Eadgyth's arm. The touch was feather-light, but insistent. 'There's no place for me in England now. William will never countenance my return, and remember – I am Danish. It is time for me to go back, after all these years.' Gytha smiled, seeing again the icy-blue seas, the snow-capped mountains and great fjords of Norway where Ulf and Canute had taken her, and where she'd met Godwin, a penniless thegn who'd taken her away from everything she knew, to build a new life in England. And what a life! And now it was almost over, and she would return home for the first time in fifty years. 'My nephew King Svein will make me more than welcome,' she said. How peaceful Denmark would be now that the Hardrada was dead. For years Svein had waged war unsuccessfully against the mighty Norwegian warrior, losing battle after battle. And in the end it had been her son, her Harry, who had dispatched the Norwegian to his Valhalla.

This last thought rushed her back to the present and the grief, still raw, was too close to think of with a clear head. It would be good never to have to return to England, to those many memories of another life. Denmark would have her back, and she could live her last days in peace there.

'And you, love, will you come with me to make another life in the north?'

Eadgyth shook her head, smiling weakly. 'You know that I cannot,' she said. 'It is a second home to you, a return to the old ways.'

Gytha nodded sadly, knowing in her heart that it was true; Eadgyth didn't belong in Denmark. 'Where, then? England?'

'Yes, to England. William has no quarrel with me – that I am sure of. And Harold left me some money hidden in the garth at Midhurst. I will live quietly there at peace.'

Eadgyth knew that Gytha appreciated what her going to England meant: her sons would never be able to join her. King William had issued an edict proclaiming the sons of Harold Godwinsson wolf's head. He would execute them, or anyone sheltering them, if they were found on English soil.

'The boys say they will go north and join Prince Edgar in Scotland,' Gytha said, reading Eadgyth's thoughts. 'They could come to me, in Denmark. Svein will take them into his household troops, I know that for sure...'

'I know my boys have a future,' Eadgyth smiled at Gytha. 'There is a whole world out there,' she said. 'They need not think of England – or of me.' She passed Gytha a roll of parchment. 'It's from Harold. He wrote it when he was in York, quelling the disquiet after the rebellion in Tostig's earldom, the Easter after his coronation.' Seeing Gytha hesitate, she added, 'Go on, read it.'

With shaking hands, Gytha unrolled the creased and worn letter, which began,

My dearest Eadgyth,

My marriage to Gisla must come as a great shock to you, but I assure you my love, that I am only doing my duty to secure the future of the realm. You must never forget that it is you that I love, and always will, and that no other can come between us...

Gytha thrust the parchment back to Eadgyth. 'I cannot read this – it is between you and Harry.' She felt the tears well up faster than she could blink them back. To read Harold's words, to hear his thoughts like this was too hard - impossibly hard - to bear, even though two winters had passed.

Eadgyth pushed the letter gently back into her hand. 'Not that,' she said softly. 'Read on, to here.' She waved a finger at the bottom of the sheet. 'Read it. It's a passage from the works of King Alfred. Harold was always reading from Alfred's own works and translations.'

As Gytha began to read, she could hear Harold's voice reading to her:

No man need care for power or strive for it. If you be wise and good, it will follow you, though you may not desire it. You shall not obtain power free from sorrow from other nations, not yet from your own people and kindred. Never without fear, difficulties and sorrows, has a king wealth and power. To be without them, and yet have those things, were happy. But I know that cannot be.

The words had been penned two centuries before, but the words sent an ache of anguish through Gytha. The words written by Alfred, another king of the English beset by invasion and devastation, applied with soul-wrenching familiarity to Harold and his own short reign. Gytha passed the letter back to Eadgyth, who took it and folded it carefully. Then Gytha embraced Eadgyth tightly, and Eadgyth whispered into her ear: 'He stood no chance. The odds were against him from the start.'

'I know,' said Gytha. 'I know.'

They clung together until the fire had all but died, and then wept a little until they were too exhausted. Gytha had thought she had no more tears left in her, but it was not so, and Eadgyth...

'They are saying that Harry seized the crown and that Edward didn't promise it to him after all,' said the younger woman. 'And when Harry was sent across the sea to Normandy before Edward died, they say he swore an oath to uphold William's claims to the throne, not Prince Edgar's, and then he broke the oath on becoming king. They say that he was a perjurer and a usurper in Normandy, and people are beginning to think it so in England.'

'The people of Wessex will never have it so,' said Gytha sternly. 'You must know that they loved him and Godwin. The northern army died in their thousands for him at Gate Fulford when he wasn't even with them.'

'But it's so unfair that these things should be said.'

Gytha sighed. 'It's always thus with conquering armies. I mind how Canute put about that Ethelred was a useless ruler, poorly advised and cruel. Don't forget that Ethelred ruled England for over thirty years, despite the manner in which his reign ended.'

'And his son for twenty-three years,' added Eadgyth.

They fell silent, thinking of Edward, of his exile and return, and the longevity and relative peace his reign had brought – though his failure to choose a successor had brought them all to this. 'He had the last laugh on us Godwins,' said Gytha with a sudden bitterness that surprised both women. 'Edward Ethelredsson must be laughing in his tomb now.'

This time it was Eadgyth's hand that reached out and gently squeezed Gytha's. 'That may be so,' she said firmly. 'But in England we shall always remember that Harold Godwinsson was the last English king of all the English.'

Epilogue
Saint-Gervais, Rouen, September 1087

All the court came to see the king die.

In July William had led a mighty army into the Vexin to recover lands from his enemy, King Philippe of France. At Mantes, only thirty miles from Paris, his horse had trodden on a burning coal following the sack of the town, and had thrown him with such force against the high pommel of the saddle that his spleen was ruptured. In agony he had returned from the Vexin to Rouen, hoping that the pain would abate, but in the summer heat and noise of the city, it had grown worse.

In August, William gave orders that he should be carried to the Priory of Saint-Gervais on a hill in the western suburbs of the town. There, Gilbert Maminot, bishop of Lisieux and Gontard, abbot of Jumièges, confirmed that the king was dying.

Messengers were sent across the duchy and within weeks a large company had gathered by his bedside. His brother, Robert of Mortain, William Bonne-Anne, archbishop of Rouen, Gerald the Chancellor and two of his sons, William and Henry, were present. His first-born son, and heir to the duchy, Robert, was in Paris, in open revolt with the king of France against his father. And Odo, his other brother, was incarcerated in a dungeon in Rouen for treason against his brother. Will FitzOsbern, his life-long friend and ally, was long dead, and so was his beloved Matilda.

On Tuesday, 6th September, William made his confession and received absolution. He commanded a lavish distribution of alms, making the clerks record the names of those who were to benefit from his gifts. In particular, he asked that a special distribution be made to the clergy of Mantes, to restore what he had burnt. He exhorted those present to have a care after his death for the maintenance of justice and the preservation of the faith.

Too exhausted to say more, he slept, and Tuesday slipped slowly into Wednesday. Early on Wednesday morning he announced that today he would dispose of his realm as he saw fit.

*

The stench hit Robert of Mortain as soon as he entered the passageway. It was beyond doubt the most nauseating, gagging smell he had known. The reek of death was in the air, and an agonisingly slow death at that. For all the things William had done – the killings, plunder and often wholesale destruction – he didn't deserve to die like this, delirious with pain, his innards irreparable and the physicians helpless.

The passageway was lined with people. Robert knew some of them, others were strangers. The great, the good the cruel, the unknown – all were there, waiting in silent prayer outside the chamber to hear the last will and testament of their king-duke. Sycophants most of them, likely praying for a speedier end to their lord so that they could flee back to own lands and look to their own.

Robert pushed past them, nodding at a few, ignoring most. The stink was becoming unbearable now and he gritted his teeth and defied the instinct to retch. The door to the bedchamber opened before him, and Gilbert Maminot rushed into the passageway, arms hugging a bowl of colourless vomit. 'Not long, now,' he gasped, scuttling to the privy.

Robert grimaced and walked into the chamber. Though it was mid-morning, the shutters were closed tightly, and the room was in semi-darkness. This only added to the fetid stench. Several candles flickered around the bed, illuminating the watchful servants of the court, their yellow faces peering anxiously forward. William's face was not even white, but rather a ghastly grey. Streaked with sweat, his iron-grey hair fell in lank locks onto the pillow. His breathing came in shallow bursts, each rise and fall of the chest emitting a grunt of agony with it.

'Richard,' he was saying as Robert reached his bedside. 'Where is my son, my boy Richard?'

Nobody answered. Nobody dared remind the king that his favourite son was dead, along with his mother.

William spoke again, this time more lucidly, and to Robert. 'Robert. You came.'

'Of course, William.' Robert forced a smile and laid a hand on his brother's arm. 'I am here.'

'You always were the faithful brother,' William muttered. 'Odo was too ambitious, too clever for his own damned good. He'd have sold his soul to advance himself in this world.'

'But there is something you can do for him, William.' Robert leant forward. 'Release him. As one of your last, most magnanimous acts, set Odo free. He is your brother.'

'No.' William shook his head. 'No, I cannot do that.'

'You can,' Robert insisted. 'He has done no wrong, not in truth.' Lowering his voice, Robert added: 'Do it for mother's sake, for our Herleve.'

At the mention of the legendary Herleve who had borne the bastard who became king of England, each man in the chamber held his breath and watched for the reaction, for the vitriolic rebuke to be spat back at the count of Mortain for daring to evoke his mother's name over such an issue.

But it didn't come. Instead, William nodded weakly, and said: 'Yes, damn you to hell. I'm too tired to argue. Release the bishop of Bayeux.'

An audible gasp followed this announcement.

Robert snapped his fingers and two household guards marched out with the order to release Odo from his captors.

'Now, to my last will and testament.' William struggled up in the bed, waving back Gilbert and Gontard. The room became silent again, each man aware that the moment had come. The king of England and duke of Normandy was to dispose of his worldly goods and make his peace with God. 'I am much disappointed with my first-born,' William began. 'Robert has disobeyed me, he is disloyal and treacherous, inconsistent and above all, weak. I despise weakness. Even now, he is with the king of France, Philippe, that whoreson offspring of Henri Capet, who betrayed me and Normandy all those years ago.' William paused, breathing slowly. Sweat ran freely down his face, and there wasn't a man in the chamber who did not know what it cost him to utter these words. 'But Robert, curse him, is my first-born, and to keep the peace I decree, against my instinct, that he should have Normandy.'

A great sigh of relief went up. The duke had, at the last, followed convention and agreed with the unwritten Norman law that the first-born should inherit the patrimony. Against his will, the duke had kept the peace. There would be no further bloodshed.

'Now, to England.' The crowd hushed again. England was more problematic than Normandy; there was no precedent for her next ruler. 'I conquered England and acquired my royalty not by hereditary right, but by judgement on the field of battle,' William rasped. 'And this only after thousands of good men, English and Norman, lay dead. My kingdom was won by God and I dare not leave England to anyone but God.' He paused to allow Gilbert Maminot to wipe his brow. Many in the room cast quick, sidelong glances at the king's second surviving son, William Rufus, who sat crouched by his father's head. It was he, the young man with the short beard glowing golden in the candle-light, who above all hoped to have England.

'God curse the English,' William pushed Gilbert away. 'God curse them, for they have given me nothing but twenty years of war, and death, and constant treachery.' His voice grew louder, its bitterness filling the room and echoing into the passageway. 'It was the devil's inheritance I had from Edward Ethelredsson, and nothing less. By wrong I conquered England. By wrong I seized the throne to which I had no right. The English say that Harold Godwinsson was the boldest man in England and that he was the best knight, both of old and new times. It is true. For all the good the wretched island people did me, I should have let Harold keep his kingdom. They were his people and his was the right, not mine. But we met under ill-fated stars, and each of us has been the loser.'

The duke-king lay back in the great bed, his gasps the only sound in the stunned silence that followed his announcement. It was the first time that the king had admitted in public that he had had no right to the throne of England, and that he had won it by blood, in blood, and kept it by blood. And that he regretted it bitterly.

'Father.' William Rufus tugged gently at the king's arm. 'Father, the kingdom of England is yours by right of acquisition and yours to dispose of as you see fit. To whom do you leave it?'

William eyed his son. 'I would leave it to God, as it came from God. But I hope that God would grant it to you, William, my son. To you I give my sceptre, my sword and my crown. Go now, and may God help you with that race of people.'

It was the answer his son wanted. William bent hastily, kissed his father's damp hand and stumbled from the room, shouting for his knights.

'And me, father – what do you leave me?'

This was Henry, the last of the sons. Tall, thoughtful and scholarly, he stood to gain very little as the youngest.

William smiled a mocking smile. 'Ah, Henry, there is nothing for you. Robert has Normandy and William has England – both of them undeserving. I leave you money. Five thousand pounds in my treasury at Rouen. Get to it before Robert does. I'll wager both your brothers will not spare you the time of day when I am dead.'

Five thousand pounds was a fortune – but in a world where land was power, it didn't mean a lot. The disappointment was plain to see on the young man's face.

'Wait –' his dying father muttered. '– I would say more.' He grasped Henry's cloak, pulling him closer. 'England is a land that has cursed me, and it will destroy William and Robert. See that you benefit from their destruction.' William's voice faltered, tears mingling with the sweat on his cheeks. 'See that you try to remedy the damage I have done. Try to bring peace, boy, to those unhappy people after what I did to them. Say...say that you are sorry to Harold, to all of them...'

The dying man's fingers slipped from Henry's cloak and the youngest son of the Conqueror rose from the bedside hesitantly, unable to comprehend the true meaning of those words.

'Go then,' William ordered. 'Go now, claim your money. And God keep you.'

Henry kissed William's hand and walked swiftly from the room. Behind him, William gave a great sigh, and closed his eyes.

Seeing that it was over, Robert waved the courtiers from the room. 'Leave now,' he ordered. 'Retire to Rouen. The king must rest. He must receive the sacrament. Go.'

They left, shuffling silently from the chamber, digesting the words they had heard spoken. The words of remorse, the regrets, and the mysterious reference to the young Henry one day reigning over a united and peaceful people after his brothers, gave them much to think over. But one thing was certain:

England belonged to God, and the dying duke wished with all his heart that he'd left it to God all those years ago, instead of claiming it for himself.

*

William died very early on the morning of Thursday, 9th September 1087. He passed Wednesday night in tranquility and the last sound he heard was the great bell of St Mary's, in the cathedral of Rouen.

The reign of an indomitable man risen from bastard minor to king of England, who believed the promise of a weak and vacillating old man, who rode roughshod over established rights and a chosen heir, and who fulfilled an ancient prophecy, was at an end. The Conqueror was dead. He had changed the course of history, and with his passing went an England never to be recalled.

the end

Historical note

The Devil's Inheritance is based on the contemporary accounts which include the *Anglo-Saxon Chronicles*, a series of annals written at Canterbury, York and Worcester; the *Life of Edward the Confessor*, probably written before 1075; the Bayeux Tapestry, an astonishing pictorial history of the Norman Conquest, and the *Deeds of Duke William*, by William of Poitiers, a chaplain in the duke's service, from which the details of William's minority and the Battle of Hastings come. These are all standard texts for the period and their authenticity is generally accepted.

The kingship of England fifty years before the Norman Conquest was complicated. Canute's invasion ousted the Old English monarchy who returned in 1043, but the confusion over Edward's succession reopened all the old wounds and laid the kingdom open to another, final conquest. Both English and Norman sources acknowledge that the dying Edward the Confessor nominated Harold Godwinsson as his heir to the throne of England in January 1066. The problem was that in by-passing Prince Edgar, Edward's great-nephew, Harold would establish a new dynasty, something Duke William – Edward's second cousin – couldn't afford to permit, especially as Harald Hardrada of Norway was going to invade. The Norman claim that Edward promised William the throne during Godwin's exile in 1052 matches the English reference to William's visit to Edward's court that year, but Harold Godwinsson's visit to Normandy in 1064/5 is purely from the Norman sources, and what he swore at the oath remains a matter of conjecture.

All the leading characters in the novel are based on real people and events from the sources. They were a remarkable bunch, from Earl Godwin, an obscure thegn who rose to be the greatest power in the land, to Queen Emma, wife of both Ethelred and Canute, who rejected her English sons but whose marriage to Ethelred in 1002 set in train the Anglo-Norman alliance that would have its consequences in 1066. William the Conqueror's childhood was indeed mired in treachery and assassination, but by sheer force of personality he and his close companions took power in Normandy, dominated the neighbouring regions and launched the audacious invasion of England in a winning gamble that changed Britain's entire social, cultural and political landscape. The Godwin family dominated England for thirty years, the last four brothers all killed at Stamford Bridge and Hastings. Harold was one of only two English kings killed in battle in the whole of English history (the other being Richard III, whose body has recently been discovered in Leicester). The Normans employed archers, cavalry and the famous feigned retreats at Hastings, but their victory was by no means assured. Harold's task was to hold the ridge and wait for reinforcements. William had the sea to his back, limited supplies and no reinforcements; Harold's mistake, understandable in the heat of the moment, was to rush south and confront William. His victory against the most feared warrior of the age, Harald Hardrada, at Stamford Bridge was one of the most stunning victories of the Middle Ages, but is often overshadowed by the defeat at Hastings weeks later.

As for the last English prince, Edgar the Aethling, his life was long and eventful. His niece married Henry I, William the Conqueror's third son, who did indeed rule both England and Normandy, and from that union the Old English line continued into the new Anglo-Norman dynasty from which Queen Elizabeth II is descended.

The best biographies remain Frank Barlow's *Edward the Confessor* and David C Douglas' *William the Conqueror*, along with David Bates' *William the Conqueror*, Jim Bradbury's *The Battle of Hastings* and most recently Marc Morris' *The Norman Conquest*, but there is a wealth of books on the period too numerous to list here. The BBC History website is a useful starting point for further research (www.bbc.co.uk/history) and for the original documents, see the Fordham University website (www.fordham.edu).

Acknowledgements

Huge thanks to a wonderful collaboration of talents in the production of this book, with superb original artwork by William John Jones – including the cover photo of the Suffolk marshes at dawn, and the drawings; the brilliant cover design by Diane Wheel and relentlessly thorough copy-editing by Jane Anson, which saved me from many errors and oddities – any remaining mistakes are my own. The map of England and Normandy is from D. C. Douglas' *William the Conqueror* (Methuen, 1964, p.456). The original hand-written manuscript was rescued and formatted by Martin and Chris Halls. The inspiration to publish at this time came from Kurt Shead, a former student of mine and literary star in his own right (see his novel *Able*). Having a wonderful family home and place to work is of inestimable value, thanks to Chrissie and Martin, and it is my wife Cerys who has never stopped believing in me and ultimately has enabled this novel to emerge from the shadows where it has lain for many years.

About the Author

Toby Purser grew up in the Welsh border counties of Shropshire and Herefordshire. He read History at Oxford University (Mansfield College) where he was a scholar, and after a Master's degree at Oxford, completed a PhD from the University of Southampton. Toby has taught history in a range of schools and colleges across the UK and has published four history textbooks for GCSE and A level. His teaching and research has taken him to Prague, Vienna, Budapest, Berlin, Istanbul, Normandy, Israel, Jordan and the battlefields of France, Belgium and Gallipoli.

Toby is married to mezzo-soprano Cerys Jones. They have three young boys, to whom this novel is dedicated, and they live in the Cotswolds.

If you enjoyed *The Devil's Inheritance* please spread the word by writing a review on Amazon. More information about Toby and his novels can be found at www.tobypurser.org.uk and on his Facebook page at Toby Purser Author where you can post comments and share the page.

Read Toby's next novel, due out in paperback on 31st October 2013, available online and in all good bookshops...

THE ZAHAROFF CONSPIRACY

A Septimus Oates Mystery

A secret marriage, a lost memoir, a terrible injustice.
And a 150-year-old tale of revenge.

Christ's College, Oxford, June 1914

If Septimus Oates had known he was to witness a murder that Friday afternoon, he would have thought twice about answering the tentative knock at the door...

When Oxford historian Septimus Oates is handed a bundle of documents including a certificate of a secret marriage dated to 1759 between the Prince of Wales, later King George III, and Hannah Lightfoot, a Quaker's daughter, he discovers that the documents reveal the existence of a son, George Rex, the rightful heir to the throne, whose story is told in a lost memoir.

Witness to a brutal killing that June afternoon, Septimus flees Oxford only to find himself enmeshed in a web of deception, at the heart of which lies a burning desire for revenge by George Rex's descendants. Drawn further into the dark secrets and betrayals of eighteenth-century England, Septimus discovers the horrifying truth which threatens to bring the legacy of George Rex's vengeance to a dreadful conclusion in the summer of 1914.

From the quadrangles of Oxford to the mountains of Austria and Bohemia and the streets of Prague, Vienna and Sarajevo, accompanied by his schoolmaster colleague Peddle, and shadowy forces of the fledgling British Secret Intelligence Service, Septimus uncovers plans for an imminent assassination that could bring Europe – and the world – to the brink of total war.

Made in the USA
Charleston, SC
18 November 2013